B L U E

l e n a n o t t i n g h a m

ISBN 978-1519785183

To those of you who have been reading from the beginning. I hope this book and these characters can become an escape for you, if that's what you need.

Thank you for making me feel so loved.

➸

table of contents

CHAPTER 1

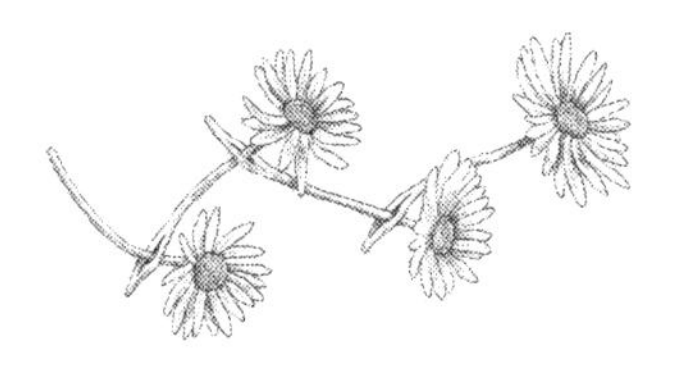

Paisley skipped outside, feeling the hot summer sun beat down on her skin. She spotted a glimmer of blonde hair and happily ran towards the woman in the garden, letting her dress flow freely behind her.

"Boo!"

The woman jumped, causing Paisley to giggle and plop down to the ground beside her.

"Hey, goofball, you scared the crap outta me," her aunt laughed, ruffling Paisley's hair. "What's up?"

"Uncle Tommy told me to get outta' his hair, so I came out here," Paisley shrugged, leaning over to watch what her aunt was doing. "Are those roses?"

"Tulips," her aunt corrected her, continuing to use the small shovel to dig small holes in the garden. "Don't listen to him. He's just grumpy," she added, giving Paisley a soft smile.

"I know," Paisley smiled widely. "I just try to be nice to him, cause if you're nice to people, then they have nothing to hold against you. Right?"

"Right," the blonde woman nodded, crinkling her nose. "How'd you get so smart, kiddo?"

"You," Paisley laughed, crawling forwards and helping her pat down the dirt around the tulips she'd just planted. "And my parents, when they were alive, at least."

"You talk about them a lot, yeah?" Aunt Susie paused her motions and looked over at Paisley. Confused, the smaller girl just nodded.

"Is that a bad thing?" Paisley asked, tilting her head to the side. She liked talking about her parents. The more she talked about them, the easier it was for her to remember them. The last thing she wanted was to just forget them.

"Of course not," her aunt laughed softly. "I'm just surprised."

"I like talking about them," Paisley shrugged and studied the flowers intently. "They were good people. They deserve to be talked about. I don't think they would want to be forgotten, would they?"

"You're too smart for your own good, kiddo," the blonde woman smiled softly and squeezed Paisley's shoulder. "I'm so proud of the person you're becoming, did you know that?"

Paisley giggled shyly and looked down, shaking her head. "You are?" she asked, looking up once more.

"Of course I am," the woman laughed, turning her attention away from the garden. "You're not the type of girl to just sit back and blindly accept what people tell her. You question things. You see things, and you interpret them on your own. You're pretty extraordinary, Paisley."

The smaller girl smiled bashfully and clasped her hands together. "I'm glad I get to stay with you guys," she said softly.

"You're not 'staying' with us, Paisley. You're just... with us. This isn't a temporary thing. We're a family now, okay?"

"Okay," Paisley nodded softly, crawling over and wrapping her arms around her aunt. "Thank you."

"No need to thank me," the older woman laughed softly, ruffling Paisley's hair. "Now go on inside and grab your script, okay? We'll practice one more time for the play before

dinner is ready. I expect you to be the best Tree #2 your school has ever seen!"

Giggling, Paisley nodded. She scrambled up to her feet and ran back into the house, finding her script and smiling widely. Maybe this whole 'family' thing could really work.

Exactly sixteen hours later, Susan Maverick was pronounced dead due to natural causes. Paisley found herself in the hospital bathroom, tracing her fingers across the red blotch on her cheek. How could her uncle do something like that to her?

Hot tears stung at her eyes and she squeezed them shut. She was supposed to have a family. This was supposed to work. Everything was falling apart, once again.

The small girl shook her head, moving away from the mirror and leaning against the bathroom door. Her heart was beating rapidly as she was suddenly faced with the flashes of a memory she wished had never happened.

Bringing her hands up to her face, Paisley willed herself not to cry. If she did, Shiloh would hear her. If Shiloh heard her, she would ask her what was wrong. And if Shiloh asked her what was wrong, Paisley would have to tell her.

Paisley didn't want to tell her. She didn't want to tell Shiloh about the bad things. Because then she would get in trouble. She didn't want to be hurt, and she didn't want to hurt anyone.

She struggled to understand why that memory had just appeared. It had been so… intense. Squeezing her eyes shut, Paisley buried her head in her knees and began taking deep breaths, just as her therapist had taught her to do.

After a few minutes of sitting in silence, Paisley jumped when she heard someone calling her name from downstairs. Shiloh. She'd recognize that voice from anywhere.

"I am coming!" she called, standing up quickly and wiping her eyes on the sleeves of her hoodie. A small smile spread across her face when she realized Shiloh was finally home from school.

"There you are," Shiloh laughed softly when Paisley appeared at the bottom of the stairs. She smiled at the sight of her girlfriend in one of her hoodies, but when Paisley moved closer, she instantly knew something was wrong.

"Lolo," Paisley smiled softly, quickly pulling Shiloh into a hug. When the hug pulled away, Shiloh studied the smaller girl up close.

"What's wrong?" Shiloh asked, biting her lip. Paisley panicked, looking down at the ground and shrugging softly. She couldn't tell Shiloh the truth. The truth was bad.

"Did you have another nightmare?" Shiloh guessed, noticing how distraught Paisley appeared.

Thankful that Shiloh had practically given her a way out, Paisley nodded softly and looked up. Lying was bad, she knew. But she thought that the truth was even worse.

"Pais," Shiloh sighed, tossing her backpack aside and pulling Paisley into another hug. "You know the bad things aren't real. They're just dreams. Remember?"

Paisley nodded softly. Another lie. Because the bad things were real. She had seen them so vividly, even more realistically than her dreams.

"Are you gonna be okay for the party?" Shiloh asked, placing her hands on Paisley's shoulders and looking the smaller girl in the eyes. Paisley grew confused.

"Ryland and Vanessa's new year's party," Shiloh explained.

"Parties are new," Paisley bit her lip and thought about her words for a moment. "I have never had one."

"It'll be fun," Shiloh smiled, even though she wasn't so sure. She knew her entire night would be chasing after Paisley and making sure she didn't get herself into trouble.

When Ryland had informed her that the party would take place in their apartment, Shiloh was hesitant. But the girls assured her that it would only be a small group of people. Things wouldn't get out of hand. Boy was she wrong.

A few hours later, people began casually strolling into the apartment. Ryland and Vanessa were passing around drinks, and Leah was deep in conversation with an attractive guy from Ryland's hip hop class.

"Be careful," Shiloh jumped forwards, taking the soda bottle from Paisley's hands. "You're going to spill it."

"I was not," Paisley shook her head and pulled her cup away just as Shiloh was about to pour her drink. "I want to do it," she said quietly, reaching to take the bottle away from Shiloh.

"I just don't want you to spill it," Shiloh sighed, trying to take the cup away from Paisley. The smaller girl shook her head and held her ground.

"Stop," she whined, moving away from Shiloh. "I can do it," she set her cup down and grabbed another bottle of soda, not caring what it was. She just wanted to prove to Shiloh that she could do it on her own.

After successfully pouring herself a cup, she held it up proudly. She had expected Shiloh to be happy with her, but instead the green eyed girl just nodded once and moved down the table, grabbing two paper plates.

"C'mon," Shiloh said, handing Paisley a plate. Furrowing her eyebrows, Paisley followed Shiloh over to the boxes of pizza that were stacked on the table.

"I want this one," Paisley pointed to an open box of pepperoni.

"That's spicy," Shiloh shook her head and opened a box of plain cheese pizza. "You always have cheese."

"I know," Paisley nodded, grabbing a piece of pepperoni and plopping it onto her plate. "I want this one."

"You won't like it," Shiloh sighed, taking Paisley's plate out of her hand. Paisley whined, moving forwards and trying to grab it back.

"I can do it," Paisley shook her head. "I want to do it."

"Paisley, you *always* get cheese," Shiloh tried to reason with the girl. "I'm just trying to help you."

"I do not need your help!" Paisley huffed, crossing her arms and glaring at Shiloh. She was already in a bad mood from the events prior, and this wasn't helping.

A look of hurt flashed across Shiloh's features but was quickly replaced by one of annoyance. "Fine," Shiloh said coldly, handing Paisley back her paper plate. "I'll be... over there somewhere," she pointed off in the distance and before Paisley could argue, she was swallowed up by the crowd.

"Lolo?" Paisley mumbled, looking down at her plate and biting her lip. She was quickly distracted though, when Ryland grabbed her arm and brought her over to introduce the smaller girl to some of her friends.

A while later, Paisley had finished her pizza. She hated to admit, but she should've gotten cheese. She would never tell Shiloh, though. She didn't want to hurt her.

"Everyone give it up for DJ Bradley!" a voice rang out from the crowd. Paisley looked up, walking forwards slightly to see what was going on. One of the college students climbed on top of one of the tables and clapped his hands together.

"Now the real party is starting," she heard someone say from beside her. Paisley nervously looked down at her hands, unsure of what was going on.

Before she could ask, a deafening noise filled the room. Paisley's drink fell out of her hand and she quickly covered her ears with her hands. Suddenly, everyone was moving around, and she was practically bounced around the room like a pinball machine.

They were… dancing. Paisley realized. Her heart sped up as the music continued to pound into her ears. It was painfully loud. She felt a knot form in her chest and she willed herself not to cry. Not here, not in front of everyone.

She pushed her way back out of the crowd and stood on her tiptoes to try and find Shiloh. She called her name, but no one could hear her over the music.

Finally, the flashing lights coming from the front of the room sent her over the edge. She'd have to find Shiloh later. Just as the tears broke free of her waterline, she scrambled up the stairs and down the hallway.

She burst into Shiloh's bedroom, hoping for some privacy to try and calm herself down. Which is why she nearly screamed when she saw someone on the bed. Shiloh.

"Babe?" Shiloh quickly sat up, throwing her phone aside and jogging over to the distraught girl. "What's wrong? What's going on?"

Paisley just shook her head, squeezing her eyes shut and keeping her hands over her ears. Everything felt so overwhelming, as if the walls were closing in on her.

"Pais, Paisley, look at me," Shiloh squeezed Paisley's shoulders and tried to get the girl to open her eyes. "Is it the music?"

Paisley nodded furiously, leaning forwards and practically forcing Shiloh to wrap her into a hug. The green eyed girl felt her heart breaking at the sight of Paisley so panicked, and knew what she had to do.

"C'mere," she whispered, leading Paisley over to the bed and sitting her down. She grabbed her phone, plugging in her headphones.

Paisley allowed Shiloh to slip her hands away from her ears, replacing them with her headphones. The smaller girl tilted her head to the side, biting her lip. But she couldn't help the small smile that spread across her face when Shiloh tapped the screen and her favorite Coldplay song filled her ears.

"I'll be right back, okay? You're safe," Shiloh nodded once and quickly slipped out of the room.

She jogged downstairs, resisting the urge to cover her own ears. The music *was* loud. She could only imagine how terrifying the whole situation must be for Paisley.

Without a second thought, she yanked the cord to the speakers. Suddenly, the room fell quiet, and all eyes were on her.

"What the hell?"

Shiloh bit her lip when someone's voice broke the silence. Vanessa and Ryland pushed through the crowd, sending her glares of confusion.

"Shy, what are you doing?" Vanessa half-whispered, nodding towards the crowd of people. Shiloh took a deep breath and shook her head.

"Party's over!" she yelled, dropping the cord to the ground and crossing her arms. "Go find somewhere else to celebrate new years."

"What the hell?" Ryland hissed, moving forwards and grabbing the cord from the floor. Shiloh shook her head quickly.

"Paisley can't handle it," she said between gritted teeth, looking at Ryland pleadingly. "I'm sorry… but she—,"

"You heard her!" Vanessa yelled, turning around and facing the crowd. "Party's over."

Grunts and groans of disapproval echoed from the crowd, but luckily people began to gather their things and leave. Shiloh sighed in relief, biting her lip and turning back to her roommates.

"I'm sorry," she shook her head. "She just... loud noises and stuff freak her out. I didn't realize."

"It's fine," Ryland said half-heartedly, waving her hand and dismissing Shiloh. The green eyed girl could tell she was annoyed.

Deciding against pushing an apology, Shiloh simply nodded and slipped back upstairs. When Paisley saw the older girl re-enter the room, she carefully took out her headphones and was relieved when she could no longer hear the music blasting from downstairs.

"It's taken care of," Shiloh sighed, sitting down on the end of the bed.

Paisley set the headphones down and crawled next to Shiloh, studying her composure carefully. She looked... annoyed.

"I ruined it," Paisley mumbled, shaking her head and crawling back to the other end of the bed. She knew that if Shiloh was mad with her, she wouldn't want to be close to her.

"Stupid," Paisley whispered to herself, attempting to tug the blankets over her but huffing in frustration when she couldn't move them from beneath Shiloh.

"Hey," Shiloh grabbed the blankets to keep Paisley from moving them. "You're not stupid."

"I was the only one," Paisley let her hands fall to her sides and she slumped down against the headboard. "No one there was scared. Only me."

"No one there *is* you, Paisley," Shiloh sighed, scooting up the bed and leaning against the headboard beside the small girl. She gently pulled Paisley into her side, to which the girl quickly snuggled up next to her.

"I do not like… being me," Paisley admitted, shaking her head.

Shiloh bit her lip, feeling overwhelmingly guilty. "Why?" she asked, curious as to what Paisley would say.

"I am different," Paisley sighed.

"And what's so wrong with that?" Shiloh turned to face her, cupping her cheek and running her thumb across her smooth skin. "You're using that word as if it's a bad thing."

"It is bad," the smaller girl furrowed her eyebrows.

"No it isn't," Shiloh shook her head. "I like you cause' you're different. That's what makes you, *you*. And you're pretty extraordinary, Paisley."

Paisley's eyes widened, remembering when her aunt had said those same words to her. She balled her fists to try and hide her anxiety, but Shiloh had already noticed.

"Did I say something wrong?" the green eyed girl quickly drew her hand away from Paisley's face. The smaller girl shook her head quickly and reached out to grab Shiloh's hands.

"No," she bit her lip and thought for a moment. "I am just tired." Another lie. She took a deep breath and tugged on the blankets once more.

"But what about the countdown?" Shiloh bit her lip, glancing at the clock. 11:43.

"I do not care," Paisley muttered, giving up and yanking the blankets overtop of them. "I want to sleep."

The smaller girl bit her lip when she felt Shiloh sigh heavily. The older girl gave in, lying down on the bed and rolling onto her back. Paisley squeezed her eyes shut. All she wanted to do was sleep. When Shiloh didn't make a move, Paisley gave in and turned over, curling up against the older girl.

"Goodnight, Lolo," Paisley whispered, lifting her head and studying Shiloh's face. "Happy New Year."

Shiloh nodded softly, kissing Paisley's forehead. "Night," she said quietly, taking a deep breath. She could have sworn she heard Paisley whimper.

Would things ever be normal between them? Shiloh was scared. What if things only got worse with Paisley? What would happen then? She stole a glance at the smaller girl next to her, biting her lip nervously.

Paisley needed to get better. Shiloh realized this. But she was also scared of giving the girl her independence. She'd tried earlier that night, and Paisley had only come running back to her. What was she supposed to do?

She sighed, laying her head back down and trying to rid her mind of those thoughts. Tomorrow, she decided, she'd start trying to help Paisley gain independence.

CHAPTER 2

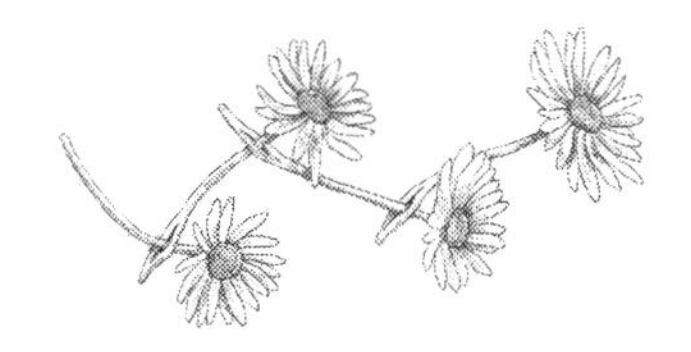

"C'mon," Shiloh laughed softly, watching Paisley hop around the room on one foot, attempting to get her shoes on. The smaller girl giggled and fell back on the bed, finally tugging on the second shoe.

"Where are we going?" Paisley asked, tilting her head to the side. She stared questioningly at her shoelaces before looking up at Shiloh.

"The mall," Shiloh informed her, bending down and knotting Paisley's shoelaces. "You need new shoes. And clothes."

"I do?" Paisley furrowed her eyebrows, looking down at her shoes. They seemed perfectly fine to her.

"You've practically worn holes into these shoes," Shiloh laughed, standing up and motioning for Paisley to follow her. "Plus, you need an actual winter coat. Even though it's January, winter doesn't look like it's gonna end anytime soon."

"Oh," Paisley nodded once and studied Shiloh's face. "You are mad at me."

Now it was Shiloh's turn to be confused. "Mad?" she raised an eyebrow. "What makes you think I'm mad at you?"

"I was bad," Paisley shook her head and followed Shiloh across the parking lot. Once they reached the car, the smaller girl sighed softly and buckled herself into the passenger seat.

"Are you talking about last night?" Shiloh asked as they pulled out of the parking lot. Paisley nodded hesitantly.

"I ruined it," Paisley crinkled her nose. "Why am I like this?"

"Because you're you," Shiloh shrugged and reached over to lace their fingers together. She wasn't going to deny that Paisley was different. The girl already knew that. Shiloh just wanted to make sure that Paisley didn't owe anyone an apology for the way she was.

"And I am stupid," Paisley muttered, shaking her head and looking down.

"Pais..." Shiloh sighed. "You're not stupid." This conversation had become a recurring one lately.

"But I do not..." Paisley groaned and pulled her hand out of Shiloh's. "I do not want to talk right now," she mumbled, shaking her head and pressing her forehead against the window.

Sighing, Shiloh retracted her hand back to the steering wheel. She wasn't sure anything she said would make Paisley believe her.

The rest of the car ride was practically silent. Paisley didn't understand the tension between them. Was Shiloh mad at her? The girl had been annoyed with her the night before.

Paisley squeezed her eyes shut. Everyone must be annoyed with her. They didn't understand. She took a deep breath, like she'd been taught to do when she was feeling anxious.

"We're here," Shiloh said softly, pulling into an open parking spot. Paisley lifted her head and studied the large building in front of them. She suddenly felt increasingly nervous.

The minute she got out of the car, she scurried over to Shiloh's side and held onto her forearm. The last thing she wanted was to be separated from the other girl. Shiloh was her security, her safety. Without her, everything was ten times scarier.

Shiloh looked over at Paisley, biting her lip as she led the smaller girl into the mall. "I'm not going anywhere, Pais," she laughed softly. Paisley looked up at her, and Shiloh could see the nervousness in her features.

"C'mon, it's less crowded in here," Shiloh pulled them both into the first clothing store she could find. Paisley relaxed slightly, following behind Shiloh when she began to search through the racks of clothes.

"For you," Paisley giggled, pulling a pair of cat ears off of one of the displays and holding them out for Shiloh to see.

Shiloh crinkled her nose and shook her head, taking the cat ears and putting them back where Paisley found them. "We're not shopping for me, anyway. We're trying to find clothes for you."

Paisley pouted playfully, retrieving the cat ears once more and attempting to put them on. Shiloh didn't take it as a joke, though. She snatched them away from Paisley and tossed them up onto a higher shelf so the smaller girl couldn't reach them.

Confusion instantly washed over Paisley's features. She'd only been joking around. Why had Shiloh gotten so mad at her? Paisley bit her lip, realizing she must be an annoyance to everyone around her.

"Sorry," Paisley mumbled under her breath, turning around and scanning the store for anything interesting. A flash of yellow in the corner caught her eye and she glanced back at Shiloh before wandering over to investigate it.

Her lips curved up into a wide smile when she pulled the yellow beanie off of the mannequin and studied it. She ran her hands over the soft material and instantly decided that she wanted it. Hurrying back over to Shiloh, she tugged on the older girl's sleeve and held up the yellow cap.

"Can we get this?" she asked hopefully, nodding down to the beanie in her hands. Shiloh tilted her head to the side and thought for a moment before nodding.

"Thank you! You're welcome," Paisley smiled widely, hugging the beanie tight to her chest. She paused when Shiloh held out a collection of bills in front of her. Paisley tilted her head to the side.

"Go pay for it," Shiloh urged her to take the money and nodded towards the cash register. Paisley instantly took a step back and bit her lip. Shiloh had always done this for her.

"But…" Paisley shook her head and glanced anxiously at the cash register. Shiloh was supposed to do these things for her. What if Paisley messed up? What if she dropped the money? Or forgot what she was supposed to say? What if the cashier thought she was weird?

"It's not a big deal, Pais," Shiloh laughed softly, nudging Paisley in the direction of the checkout. "Just give them the beanie and the money."

"I-I can not," Paisley shook her head and shoved the money back in Shiloh's hands, looking at her pleadingly. "You do it? Please?"

"Yes you can, Paisley," Shiloh sighed and shook her head. "I'm not doing it. If you want it, you can buy it on your own. You need to learn how to do these things."

"Why are you being like this?" Paisley looked down at the beanie in her hands and felt her chest tighten. Just the thought of doing something like that on her own made her hands shake in fear. "Please?"

"No, Paisley," Shiloh shook her head, trying to be firm in her decision. "I'm trying to help you get better."

"I am better," Paisley mumbled, letting her head hang down. "Please, Lolo?" she asked, holding the beanie up hopefully. When Shiloh shook her head, Paisley huffed and threw the beanie down to the ground.

"This is not funny," Paisley mumbled, slipping past Shiloh and out the front of the store. Shiloh rolled her eyes in frustration. This was going to take some getting used to. She forced herself to ignore Paisley's meltdown and continue shopping as normal.

Bending down to pick up the beanie, Shiloh set it back on the shelf and huffed. When she glanced behind her, she saw Paisley peering in the front of the store anxiously, waiting for her. The second they made eye contact, Paisley ducked out of her view.

Shiloh sighed, walking over to the checkout counter and waiting impatiently as the cashier bagged her things. She left the store without another word, walking straight past Paisley and down the corridor.

Paisley's eyes widened when Shiloh walked past her and she quickly scrambled to catch up with the girl. She was still upset with her, but that didn't mean she wanted to lose her.

Shiloh was aware Paisley was following closely behind her. When she looked back, Paisley's face lit up, but the smaller girl quickly forced herself to look away from Shiloh. She was still confused about what Shiloh had done earlier.

This carried on for the rest of their time at the mall. Paisley would wait anxiously at the front of the store while Shiloh shopped, retrieved her bags, and then left. The green eyed girl was forcing herself to be tough with Paisley.

Paisley was the first to break the silence once they made it back to the car.

"I am sorry," she mumbled, even though she wasn't sure what she was apologizing for. She just wanted Shiloh's forgiveness.

"You don't have to apologize," Shiloh sighed, shaking her head. "Just forget about it."

Paisley furrowed her eyebrows and glared at Shiloh. "That is not funny," she muttered, shaking her head and turning away from the green eyed girl in her seat. Shiloh grew confused.

"What?" Shiloh glanced over at Paisley. "It wasn't supposed to be funny."

"You were making fun of me," Paisley shook her head. "You told me to forget. That is not funny."

Oh. Guilt instantly washed over Shiloh. She reached over and placed a hand on her girlfriend's thigh.

"That's not what I meant, Paisley," she said softly. "You know I'd never make fun of you."

"Then what did you mean? I do not understand," Paisley turned back around and tilted her head to the side.

"It's just a saying," Shiloh shrugged. "It just means to move on, I guess."

"Oh," Paisley looked down at her hands in her lap. "I thought you were making f—,"

"I know," Shiloh interrupted her, laughing softly. "It's fine."

Paisley bit her lip and nodded. She still felt like she was annoying the other girl. She couldn't help how she felt. Sighing, she pulled her legs up to her chest and stared out the window longingly.

Once they arrived back at the apartment, Paisley stood hesitantly at the back of the kitchen while Shiloh began cooking dinner.

"What are you making?" Paisley asked quietly, taking a few steps forward and leaning over Shiloh's shoulder as the older girl pulled a carton of eggs out of their refrigerator.

"Omelets. We have leftover ham from Christmas and we need to use it before it goes bad," Shiloh explained, pulling another plastic container out of the fridge.

"Those are good, I remember," Paisley smiled softly, following Shiloh over to the stove where she'd already set out a pan. She watched as Shiloh cracked an egg into a bowl and widened her eyes.

"Can I try?" she asked, tilting her head to the side.

"I don't know if that's a good i—,"

"Please?" Paisley looked up at Shiloh pleadingly. She wanted to prove to the older girl that she could help.

Sighing, Shiloh gave in and handed Paisley an egg. "Crack it into that bowl. Carefully," she warned. Paisley nodded and scooted forwards.

Taking a deep breath, Paisley attempted to crack the egg against the side of the bowl. She didn't know her own strength, though, because when she brought the egg down, it cracked against the side of the bowl and broke all over the counter. Paisley winced, afraid to see Shiloh's reaction.

"Go wash your hands," Shiloh sighed, nudging Paisley towards the sink and grabbing a handful of paper towels. Paisley hung her head down, trudging over to the sink and running her hands under the warm water.

"I am sorry," Paisley looked up, turning off the sink and looking at Shiloh hopefully. If there was one thing she hated, it was disappointing people. Especially Shiloh. She was still getting used to the fact that she was allowed to make mistakes, and she wouldn't get hurt if she messed up.

"It's fine," Shiloh shrugged and poured the egg mixture into the pan. Paisley jumped slightly when a loud sizzling noise filled the room.

She turned around when the apartment door opened, revealing their three other roommates. Smiling excitedly, Paisley hurried over to them and clapped her hands together.

"How was school?" she asked, eager to learn what they'd done today. Her face dropped when they practically ignored her, tossing their bags aside and hurrying into the kitchen to see what Shiloh was cooking.

Brushing it off, Paisley followed them into the kitchen. "Ryland?" she tilted her head to the side, walking over to the light haired girl. "How was school?"

"Good," Ryland shrugged. She grabbed a water bottle from the refrigerator. Paisley hopped forward to grab one for herself, but flinched when it shut before she could. Ryland hadn't noticed.

Paisley let her hands drop to her side. Giving up on trying to start a conversation with them, she slumped down on the couch in the living room and reached for the remote. The minute she turned on the TV, she heard Shiloh calling them all into the kitchen for dinner.

Sighing in frustration, Paisley trudged into the kitchen. She met Shiloh's eyes and smiled softly, but the girl had already looked away from her. Feeling defeated, Paisley took her plate from Vanessa and hurried back into the living room.

"Are we really watching another episode of *Friends*?" Ryland groaned from her spot on the couch. Paisley looked down at the remote in her hand and then back at the light haired girl.

"It is good, right?" she asked, confused by what she meant. All of her roommates just shrugged.

"This is a funny one," Paisley pointed to the screen with the remote. "Is something wrong?"

"It's just we watch this show *every night*, I'm a little t—,"

"It's fine," Leah shoved Ryland's arm, trying to get her to be quiet. Paisley just nodded softly and pressed play, forgetting all about dinner. She didn't understand what she was doing, but apparently she was getting on everyone's nerves.

She turned around and gave her roommates a hopeful smile, but they were all too fixated on their phones. She glanced at Shiloh pleadingly, but the girl didn't notice.

Giving up, Paisley scooted closer to the TV and focused her attention on the characters on the screen. She didn't like feeling so left out.

Near the end of the episode, Shiloh set her plate down on the table and stood up.

"I've got homework to work on," she nodded towards the stairs. Ryland gave her a thumbs up, not looking up from her phone. Shiloh giggled and glanced at Paisley, who seemed too be completely lost in the television. She slipped upstairs without another word.

When the episode ended, Paisley giggled happily and got up to bring her plate to the sink. When Shiloh wasn't in the kitchen doing the dishes, she grew concerned. She hurried back out into the living room, but Shiloh wasn't there either.

"Lolo?" she called, looking around the room. When she didn't get a response, she ran over to the front door and gazed out in the hallway.

"She went upstairs," Ryland informed Paisley from her spot on the couch. The smaller girl instantly breathed a sigh of relief and padded up the spiral staircase.

"Knock knock," she hummed, tapping on the closed door. Her eyebrows furrowed together when there was no response. "Lolo?"

She slowly opened the door, smiling widely when she caught sight of Shiloh in the corner of the room. She was working intently on something on her easel, the one her parents had gotten her for Christmas.

"Lolo?" Paisley took a few steps forwards and studied Shiloh's painting. It appeared to be a broken piano. It was quiet sad-looking to Paisley.

"Pretty," she chimed, moving to the side. When Shiloh didn't acknowledge her presence, she noticed the headphones in her ears. Giggling to herself, she tapped Shiloh's shoulder. The older girl jumped, nearly dropping her paintbrush.

"What?" Shiloh pulled one of the earbuds out of her ears and raised an eyebrow at Paisley.

"It is pretty," Paisley pointed to the painting. Shiloh just nodded and turned back to the canvas, putting her headphones back in.

"Thanks," the older girl said softly, bringing her brush to the canvas once more and filling in the background. Paisley scooted closer, leaning in to watch what she was doing.

A few moments later, Shiloh turned to wash off her brush, but practically elbowed Paisley in the stomach. The smaller girl was leaning over her shoulder.

Paisley simply giggled, but Shiloh's eyebrows furrowed and she tugged her headphones out of her ears.

"Can't you see I'm trying to concentrate?!" she snapped, glaring at the smaller girl. Paisley flinched, bringing her hands up in front of her face and backing away.

"Please," she shook her head. She hadn't meant to upset Shiloh. She only wanted to watch. Paisley enjoyed seeing Shiloh concentrating so hard over something. But if Shiloh wanted to concentrate without her, she would let her.

"Sorry," Paisley sighed. Shiloh merely nodded before turning back to her painting and shoving her headphones back into her ears. Paisley stayed frozen for a few moments, looking down at her hands and wondering what had changed.

She tiptoed over to the bed, trying to be as quiet as possible. She didn't want to bother Shiloh. Paisley was scared. Scared, because this was the same thing that had happened before her uncle started hurting her. She had annoyed him.

That was the last thing she wanted to happen, so she quietly slipped under the blankets on the bed. She grew confused when she felt tears brimming her eyes, and she quickly wiped them away with the sleeve of her sweater. She couldn't cry. Crying was bad.

A while later, Shiloh set her paintbrush down and wiped her eyes. She stood up, taking her headphones out and stepping backwards to admire the finished painting. It wasn't her best work.

Just as she was about to sit back down, she heard a sniffling noise from behind her. Her mind instantly brought her back to when she'd snapped at Paisley earlier that night, and guilt washed over her.

Slowly, she walked over to the bed and placed a gentle hand on Paisley's shoulder. The smaller girl jumped, turning around to see who had touched her. She relaxed when she came face to face with Shiloh.

"Mind if I join you?" Shiloh asked softly, motioning to the bed. Paisley looked shocked, but the smaller girl simply nodded and rolled over.

Shiloh lay back on the bed next to Paisley and glanced over at the smaller girl, who had her back turned. She furrowed her eyebrows and tapped Paisley's shoulder.

"Don't you wanna cuddle?"

Paisley lifted her head slightly and studied Shiloh's face. Was she joking? When she saw sincerity on Shiloh's features, she nodded quietly.

"Well then get over here," Shiloh laughed, motioning for Paisley to come closer. The smaller girl rolled over, scooting next to Shiloh and giving her a nervous smile.

"You're mad at me, aren't you?" Shiloh sighed, reaching out and pulling Paisley into her side.

"You are mad at *me*," Paisley lifted her head. "I am annoying."

Shiloh's eyes widened while her heart dropped into her chest. She shook her head and turned on her side so she was facing Paisley.

"You're anything but annoying," Shiloh reached out and tucked a loose strand of hair behind the smaller girl's ear. "I'm sorry if I scared you," she added, biting her lip.

"It is not your fault," Paisley shook her head. "I was annoying. It made you mad."

"I shouldn't have been like that in the first place, Pais. It's not your fault," Shiloh tried to reassure her. Paisley just nodded, images of her uncle apologizing flashing through her head.

"I want to sleep," Paisley said softly. Her eyes met Shiloh's pleadingly. She didn't want to talk about this anymore.

"M'kay," Shiloh gave her a soft smile, trying to show her that it was okay. Paisley sighed contently and allowed Shiloh to pull the blankets over them.

"Lolo?" Paisley lifted her head slightly. "Can you sing? Please?"

"Of course," Shiloh giggled, kissing Paisley's forehead. "Only for you."

Shiloh smiled when Paisley sighed contently, realizing the smaller girl had fallen asleep once she finished singing. She placed a soft kiss on the smaller girl's forehead before closing her eyes and inviting sleep to overtake them both.

CHAPTER 3

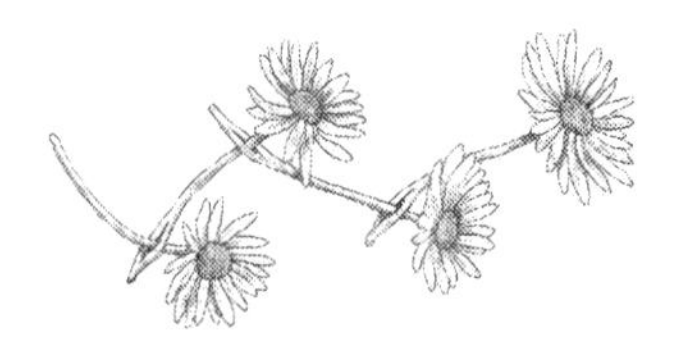

Paisley crinkled her nose, rolling over to try and avoid the blinding light streaming through the windows. A few moments later, her mind caught up with her and she sat up quickly. Her eyes scanned the room and a state of panic set in.

"Lolo?" she said anxiously, looking over to the empty spot beside her where Shiloh had been. She rolled off of the bed and bit her lip nervously. Where had Shiloh gone? Paisley was always the first to wake up.

"Hello?" Paisley raised her voice, beginning to pull the blankets off of the bed and look for any hints to where Shiloh might be. "Lolo?"

She jumped when the door to the bedroom flew open and Ryland appeared, raising an eyebrow at the smaller girl.

"She's at class, Paisley, you know that," Ryland wiped her eyes.

"She did not say goodbye," Paisley shook her head and slumped down on the bed. "She is mad at me."

"Or maybe she was just running late," Ryland sighed and walked over to Paisley, sitting down next to her. "She'll be back before dinner. She always is."

"I know," Paisley crawled back up on the bed and pulled the blankets up, completely covering her body. Ryland looked at her questioningly.

"What are you doing, Paisley?" Ryland laughed, nudging the figure under the blanket. Paisley scooted away and shook her head.

"I am sleeping. Please go away," Paisley curled the blanket around her fists and took a deep breath. She didn't want Ryland knowing how much it bothered her that Shiloh hadn't said goodbye.

Goodbyes scared Paisley. But at the same time, they comforted her. She'd had way too many goodbyes in her life. What if Shiloh never came back? She wouldn't even remember the last words that they exchanged.

Ryland sighed, deciding against trying to get Paisley to move. She left the room without another word, causing the smaller girl to flinch when the door shut behind her.

Paisley lifted her head carefully and bit her lip. She slowly untangled herself from the blankets and padded down the hallway. Music was blasting from Ryland's bedroom, and she assumed Vanessa was still asleep. Leah and Shiloh both had class.

Quietly, Paisley sat down on the floor by the door and pulled on her worn converse. She wasn't quite sure what to do with the laces, so she just allowed them to hang freely. Scrambling back up to her feet, she checked to make sure no one had seen her before slipping out of the apartment door.

The park was just across the street, she remembered. A soft smile graced her features when she recalled the flowers Shiloh had planted there. They'd been so busy with the holidays that they hadn't been back to visit them in a while. Paisley figured it was time she gave them some attention.

She shivered when she made it outside, watching the cars buzz by in the busy street. Cars were bad. Unless you were inside them. If you weren't inside a car, walking around them wasn't too safe. Shiloh had taught her that.

Shiloh had also taught her how to cross the street so she wouldn't get hurt by the cars. Paisley looked up at the sky and smiled, happy to be outside. It was cold, but she wasn't too bothered.

She stood patiently on the edge of the sidewalk, watching the light across the street that signaled to her when it was time to walk. Only a few moments later, the traffic slowed down and the light changed colors. Paisley giggled excitedly and jogged across the street.

She quickly followed the path into the park, picking up the pace as she neared the familiar corner where her flowery friends resided. They reminded her of Shiloh. Pretty and colorful. But Shiloh was annoyed with her, so her flowers were the next best thing.

Her expression quickly changed, though, when she rounded the corner and was met with something completely different than what she'd expected.

The once colorful flowers all lay dead on the ground, coated in a thin layer of frost. Paisley immediately ran over to them, dropping to her knees and gently patting the tops of the flowers.

"Someone killed you," she whispered, feeling guilt wash over her. She hadn't been there to protect them. She had let the flowers die. This was all her fault.

Paisley blinked a few times, growing confused when she felt something warm on her face. She slowly brought her hand up to her cheek and realized she was crying. Growing frustrated with herself, Paisley wiped the tears from her eyes and continued trying to get the flowers to stand back up.

"You have to stand up," Paisley mumbled to the plants, sitting cross legged and trying to use sticks to create some sort of splint for their stems. No matter what she did, the flowers would always fall back over.

"I am so sorry," the smaller girl wiped her eyes once more. Shiloh wasn't going to be happy with her either, Paisley thought. She rose slowly to her feet and let her eyes trace over the patch of dead flowers. She'd let the pretty things die.

Unsure of what else to do, Paisley slowly padded over to the bench and sat down. She curled her legs up and hugged them to her chest. This gave her a clear view of the dead flowers. She deserved to be sad over them. She had killed them.

Two hours later, Shiloh was busy packing up her art supplies. Her advanced art class had definitely proved to be a challenge, and she'd just spend the last few hours attempting to add the finishing touches to one of her projects. Every time her teacher would walk by, though, he'd grimace. Shiloh grew frustrated with herself for not being able to produce something worthy of his approval.

She slipped out of the classroom as soon as she was finished packing up. It was freezing cold outside, and she wrapped her jacket tight around her shoulders.

To be quite honest, she felt guilty for leaving without waking Paisley that morning. Something was off between them. She didn't want to disturb the younger girl. She looked forward to having Paisley waiting for her when she got home.

Paisley wasn't waiting for her.

The second Shiloh opened the door and came face to face with an empty apartment, she knew something was up. Looking down, her suspicions were confirmed. Paisley's converse were gone. Shit.

Shiloh tossed her bag aside and ran upstairs, hoping Ryland or Vanessa knew where she was. She let herself into Ryland's room without knocking.

Ryland's head shot up from her laptop. She raised an eyebrow at Shiloh's worried expression.

"What's up?" she asked, tugging her headphones out of her ears. Shiloh brought her hands up to her hair and shook her head.

"Paisley's gone," Shiloh stared at Ryland, hoping she knew where the smaller girl was. "Her shoes are gone. She's mad at me."

"She was upset when you didn't say goodbye to her this morning," Ryland noted, remembering her conversation with Paisley earlier. "She's really not in your bedroom? That's where she's been all day."

"Are you sure?" Shiloh asked, running out of the room and across the hallway before Ryland could answer. The light haired girl quickly followed her and watched as Shiloh tore the blankets off of an empty bed.

"At least… she *was* in there," Ryland added, running a hand through her hair.

"Shit," Shiloh shook her head and kicked the doorframe out of frustration. "I'm always doing this! What if she's hurt? This is all my fault." She clenched her fists.

"Hey, hey, okay," Ryland grabbed Shiloh's shoulders to calm her down. "Let's not make assumptions. Now, if you were Paisley, where would you go if you were bored?"

Shiloh took a deep breath and thought for a moment. *The park.*

"Thank you," she sighed, pushing past Ryland and back down the staircase. "I'll be back. Call me if she comes back or anything!" Shiloh called, running out of the apartment.

She sprinted across the street, shivering in the cold winter air. Shiloh wasn't one to believe in superstitions, but she found herself crossing her fingers and praying that Paisley was alright.

She skidded to a stop when she rounded the corner and saw a figure on the bench. Leaning over to catch her breath, she wiped her eyes and looked back up. She let out a sigh of relief when she saw Paisley, curled up on the bench and staring blankly into the distance.

Unsure of how to approach this, Shiloh slowly walked over and sat down on the bench beside the girl.

"Aren't you cold?" she asked, raising an eyebrow at the smaller girl in only a t-shirt. Paisley slowly lifted her head and smiled widely when she saw Shiloh. But she quickly wiped the smile off her face when she realized why they were there.

Shiloh's smile faltered when she saw the expression on Paisley's face. She swallowed her pride, shedding herself of her jacket and slowly laying it across Paisley's shoulders. The smaller girl didn't argue, due to the fact that she truly was freezing.

"I'm sorry I left without saying goodbye," Shiloh began, looking down at her hands in her lap and sighing. "I was already running l—,"

"I killed them."

Shiloh paused. "What?"

Paisley squirmed slightly and shook her head, burying her face in her knees. Shiloh was going to be mad at her. She didn't want to annoy her any more than she already was.

"Paisley, what?" Shiloh scooted closer to Paisley and placed a hand on her arm. "You did what?"

"I killed them," Paisley lifted her head slowly. Shiloh's mind instantly went to the worst case scenario, remembering what had happened with her uncle.

"You killed *who*?" Shiloh asked hesitantly, becoming increasingly worried by the second. Paisley just squeezed her eyes shut and pointed forwards.

"Huh?" Shiloh turned her head, her eyes landing on the flowers across from them. "*Oh,*" Shiloh whispered. She breathed a sigh of relief.

"You didn't do that, Paisley," she ran her hand down the smaller girl's arm and laced their fingers together.

"Yes I did," Paisley snapped her head up and furrowed her eyebrows. "I let them die. I did not come visit them." She wiped her eyes with the back of her hand.

"Pais," Shiloh laughed softly, shaking her head and reaching out to wipe the tears from Paisley's cheeks. "You didn't kill them. It's what happens every winter."

"I kill them *every winter*?" Paisley's eyes widened.

"No," the green eyed girl quickly shook her head. "That's not what I meant."

"I do not understand," Paisley furrowed her eyebrows.

"Flowers always wilt at this time of year," Shiloh scooted closer to Paisley and draped an arm across her shoulders. "They can't live when it gets so cold out."

"So they *always* die?" the smaller girl whispered in shock, looking across at the flowers. "Why would the sun let that happen? They do not deserve to die."

"I wish I knew, Pais," Shiloh turned to look at Paisley and gave her a soft smile. "It's *okay*, Paisley. There will be more flowers in the spring."

"But *these* ones are dead," Paisley pointed to the flowers across from them. "I let them die."

"You couldn't have done anything," Shiloh leaned forward and kissed Paisley's temple. "It's just how nature works."

"You are not mad at me?" Paisley's cheeks blushed pink when she felt Shiloh kiss her.

"Why would I be?" Shiloh asked, tilting her head to the side. "I thought you would be mad at me for leaving without saying goodbye."

"I was not mad," Paisley said softly, looking down at her hands. "I was only sad."

Shiloh felt increasingly guilty. "I'm sorry," she whispered. "I didn't mean to make you sad."

Paisley just shrugged and gave Shiloh a soft smile. "It is okay. I forgive you. You're welcome."

"I'm welcome?" Shiloh giggled, raising an eyebrow. Paisley nodded proudly.

"Thank you, you're welcome," she smiled happily.

"You're a dork," Shiloh laughed, nudging Paisley's shoulder. "C'mon, let's get you inside. It's freezing." She stood up and held out her hand for Paisley to take.

The smaller girl giggled and crinkled her nose. She was instantly comforted by the fact that Shiloh wasn't mad at her.

"Am I annoying?" Paisley asked timidly as they walked back up to the apartment. Shiloh immediately stopped walking and gazed at Paisley in shock.

"Are you annoying?" she asked, making sure she had heard her correctly. Paisley nodded softly and Shiloh shook her head. "What makes you think that you're annoying?"

"No one wants to talk to me," Paisley remembered how ignored she had felt the other day. "I am annoying."

"I want to talk to you," Shiloh squeezed Paisley's hand. "If I had to pick only one person to talk to for the rest of my life, it would be you. I like hearing you talk."

"I am an idiot," Paisley shook her head. She brought one of her hands up to her face, wiping her eyes.

"Don't say that, Paisley," Shiloh said firmly, grabbing both of Paisley's hands and looking her straight in the eyes. "You are not an idiot, okay? You are Paisley. And Paisley is pretty awesome just the way she is."

Paisley tried to hide her smile, but failed. She looked down shyly and shrugged, shuffling her feet on the cold ground. "Lolo is awesome, too."

"I know," Shiloh teased, tilting her chin in the air to feign cockiness. Paisley giggled.

Once they made it back to the apartment, Paisley followed Shiloh into the kitchen as the green eyed girl began searching the pantry to find something to make for dinner.

"Ryland was supposed to go grocery shopping," Shiloh sighed, crossing her arms and scanning the nearly empty shelves. Paisley padded over and did the same.

"Noodles," Paisley observed, grabbing a box off of the bottom shelf and holding it up. "We can make pash.... psh...."

"Pasta?" Shiloh tilted her head to the side, trying to complete Paisley's sentence. The smaller girl shook her head and furrowed her eyebrows in thought.

"Pa... psh'getti!" She clapped her hands together, finally finding the right word. Shiloh giggled and took the box from her.

"You mean *spaghetti*?" Shiloh raised an eyebrow.

"That is what I said," Paisley nodded once and grabbed a jar of spaghetti sauce from the cabinet. "Psh'getti."

"Psh'getti," Shiloh imitated her, filling up a pot with water and placing it on the stove to boil. When she turned back around, she noticed how Paisley was hugging her hands around her torso.

"Go get changed if you're cold, silly," she laughed, walking over and placing her hands on Paisley's shoulders. "I'll be right down here."

"M'kay," Paisley hummed, kissing Shiloh on the cheek before shuffling over to the staircase and disappearing up the stairs.

As Shiloh poured the pasta into the pan, she heard a set of footsteps behind her.

"Where was she?" Ryland asked, hopping up and sitting on the island.

"Park," Shiloh shrugged and stirred the noodles. She glanced back at Ryland and raised an eyebrow. "Where's Nessa?"

"On a date," Ryland smirked, glancing at the door. "She met this guy the other day. He's in a frat."

"A frat?" Shiloh laughed, setting the wooden spoon down and turning around to face Ryland.

"Yup," Ryland pulled her phone out of her pocket, going into Instagram and handing her phone to Shiloh. "That's him. Tall one on the right."

"Oh," Shiloh nodded, setting the phone back on the counter. "Good thing I'm gay," she teased, earning a playful shove from Ryland.

"He's having a party tomorrow night," Ryland added. "He told us to invite all the couples we know." Shiloh glanced up, assuming Ryland would extend her an invitation.

"All the *normal* couples, I mean," Ryland laughed, hopping off the counter and ruffling Shiloh's hair. "I knew Paisley would never go to a party in a million years."

Shiloh just crinkled her nose and turned her attention back to the pasta, unaware of a quiet Paisley standing at the bottom of the stairs, going over everything she had just heard in her head.

CHAPTER 4

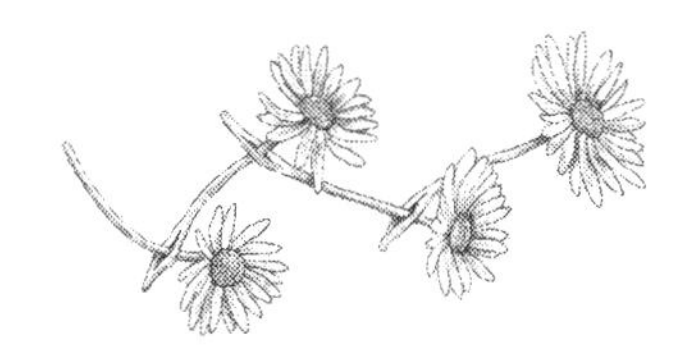

Paisley furrowed her eyebrows. This didn't look right. She twirled around in front of the mirror and huffed.

"You are not pretty," she stated, pulling the navy dress over her head and tossing it aside. Her eyes landed on the pastel yellow dress hanging in the closet, but she forced herself to look away. It was bright. That wasn't normal. Shiloh wanted her to be normal.

After Shiloh had left the next morning, Paisley immediately locked herself in the bedroom and began practicing. Practicing for being normal.

Ryland had said the 'normal' couples went to the party. So Paisley had to be normal. That's what Shiloh would want.

The smaller girl padded back over to the closet. She didn't want to wear a dress, she decided. That was okay. Normal people could wear skirts, too.

Paisley retrieved her favorite purple skirt from the closet and slipped it on. She smiled happily at herself in the mirror, pleased with her reflection. After finding a ruffled white top to wear as well, Paisley studied herself in the mirror. She looked normal.

Luckily, she had watched Shiloh do her hair enough times to catch on to what she needed to do. She shuffled across the hallway and found the pink spray bottle that the older girl always used. Paisley turned it around in her hands, furrowing her eyebrows when she realized she wasn't sure how to use it.

A few seconds later, she was coughing and spitting out the foul tasting substance into the sink. Well, at least she found out how to use it.

After wiping her face on a towel, Paisley sprayed the product in her hair a few times and set the bottle down. She studied her reflection intently while she ran her fingers through her hair.

All that was left was makeup. This was the part she was unsure of. She remembered Shiloh using a black bag in the cabinets. Paisley knelt down, retrieving the makeup bag and dumping its contents onto the counter.

The smaller girl immediately grabbed a colorful container, struggling to pop the lid off. She didn't know her own strength, though, because once she finally got the lid off, bobby pins went flying across the tile floor.

"Shhh," Paisley whispered, bending down and beginning to pick all the small pieces up. When she stood up with her handfuls of bobby pins, she nearly fell back down as she came face to face with Vanessa.

"What're you doing?" the taller girl asked, raising an eyebrow at Paisley's outfit.

"I..." Paisley shook her head, spilling the bobby pins back into the small container. "I am getting ready."

"For what?" Vanessa asked. Paisley motioned to her outfit and smiled.

"The party," she hummed, turning back to the sink and studying the makeup products she'd placed on the counter. "Me and Lolo are going."

"Does Shiloh know this?" Vanessa laughed softly, slipping past Paisley and sitting on the edge of the bathtub. Paisley furrowed her eyebrows and shrugged.

"She will when she gets back," Paisley giggled and held up a makeup brush. Tilting her head to the side, the smaller girl grew confused.

"I do not know what I am doing," Paisley confessed, turning to Vanessa and holding up the brush. The other girl laughed, standing up and shaking her head.

"You don't use that first," she took the brush from Paisley and placed it back down on the counter. "You don't need a lot of make up."

"But I have to be pretty," Paisley raised her eyebrows pleadingly.

"You already are, doofus," Vanessa laughed and grabbed a circular container of blush, opening it and turning to Paisley. "Is it okay if I help you?"

Paisley nodded, smiling excitedly. Vanessa laughed and gently turned Paisley so she was facing her. She began brushing the blush on Paisley's cheeks, which caused the smaller girl to giggle.

"That tickles," Paisley whispered, trying to keep her face as still as possible. Vanessa laughed and nodded in agreement. She set the blush brush down and grabbed the lip gloss, dabbing a small amount on her finger and dotting it across Paisley's lips.

"Smack your lips," Vanessa instructed, turning back to the counter and beginning to look for an eyeshadow brush. She immediately looked back up when she heard a loud clapping noise.

"Ouch," Paisley mumbled, bringing her hand away from her face and rubbing her lips.

"No, I didn't mean *smack* your lips," Vanessa laughed and quickly wiped the excess lip gloss off of Paisley's hands. "I meant rub them together. Like this." She demonstrated with her own lips.

"Oh," Paisley giggled, imitating Vanessa and then looking at the older girl hopefully.

"Good job," Vanessa gave her a thumbs up and grabbed a palette of eyeshadow, opening it and holding it between them. "Pick a color."

"This one is..." Paisley furrowed her eyebrows and pointed to the color that caught her attention. "It is pink... but it is... it is... glowing?"

"Sparkly," Vanessa laughed, swiping the brush across the color Paisley was pointing to. "Sparkly, shimmery, shiny – all those words work."

"Shimmery," Paisley whispered, liking the new word she'd discovered. It tickled her lips when she said it. "Shim... shimmery," she giggled.

"Exactly," Vanessa crinkled her nose and tapped the space between Paisley's eyes. "Close your eyes, and keep 'em closed until I tell you to open them again. Okay?"

Paisley nodded and squeezed her eyes shut. She felt Vanessa's fingers holding her head in place and she giggled when the brush swept across her eyelids.

"You can open them now," Vanessa set the brush down on the counter and watched as Paisley turned to look at herself in the mirror. She closed one eye, trying to get a glimpse of the eyeshadow.

"Shimmery," she noted, smiling at herself in the mirror. She turned back to Vanessa and giggled softly. "Is there more?"

Vanessa held up the cylinder of mascara and debated whether or not to use it. Paisley furrowed her eyebrows and studied the colorful container.

"What is that?" she asked, tapping the mascara. Vanessa unscrewed the lid and showed it to the smaller girl.

"It's mascara. It goes on your eyelashes," Vanessa explained. Paisley nodded and bit her lip.

"You don't have to do it if you don't want to," the older girl began to screw the cap back on, but Paisley reached out to stop her. The smaller girl shook her head and smiled nervously. She needed to be normal.

After a few minutes of Paisley struggling to keep her eyes open, Vanessa finally was able to get a decent amount of mascara on the smaller girl's eyelashes. Paisley sniffed, wiping the tears from her eyes and turning to look at herself in the mirror.

"Do I look pretty?" she asked, tilting her head to the side.

"Of course," Vanessa laughed and piled all of the makeup back into the small bag. "Is that what you're wearing?"

Paisley nodded and fluffed out her skirt slightly, with a soft smile on her face. "Yes. Will Lolo be happy?"

Vanessa just shrugged and leaned against the doorframe. "I thought you didn't like parties?" she asked, genuinely curious about Paisley's sudden interest in the going out.

"I want to," Paisley shrugged. "I want to, for Lolo."

"You're sure?" Vanessa raised an eyebrow. Paisley just smiled and nodded.

"Yes. I am sure," she crossed the hallway and sat down on Shiloh's bed, bending down and tugging her white converse onto her feet. They were the only shoes she liked to wear. It seemed that every other pair she tried on had something wrong with them. They were either too itchy, or too loose, or way too small. So she stuck with what she knew.

Before Vanessa could respond, both girls heard the front door of the apartment slam shut. Paisley's face lit up and she hopped up from the bed.

"Lolo!" she called, practically falling down the stairs. She grabbed the banister at the bottom to steady herself and smiled widely at Shiloh. "Hi," she giggled.

"Careful there, Pais," Shiloh laughed, tossing her bag aside and giving the smaller girl a once over. "What are you…?"

"I am dressed," Paisley twirled in a circle and smiled proudly. "For the party."

"Party?" Shiloh raised an eyebrow.

"Yes, party?" Paisley tilted her head to the side and approached Shiloh. "Remember? You were talking about it yesterday."

"Oh, right," Shiloh nodded, remembering her conversation with Ryland. "I didn't realize you would want to go."

Paisley bit her lip. Truth is, she was scared of going to this party. But her desire to be normal and please Shiloh was greater. "I want to go, can we?" she asked hopefully, studying Shiloh's face.

"Well since you're already dressed…" Shiloh laughed softly and twirled a piece of Paisley's hair around her finger. "I guess I should go get ready?"

"Yes!" Paisley smiled excitedly and practically tackled Shiloh into a hug. She could prove to the older girl that she was normal. "Thank you, you're welcome."

Paisley waited patiently in the living room, watching an episode of *Friends* while Shiloh got dressed. She was so entranced by the characters on the screen that she didn't hear the soft footsteps coming down the stairs.

"Is this okay?" a soft voice came from behind her. Paisley turned around, her eyes widening when she saw Shiloh. The older girl was wearing black jeans with a burgundy top underneath her signature leather jacket. Paisley struggled to find her words.

"Pretty," she said after a few moments, scrambling to her feet and hurrying over to Shiloh. She ran her fingers over the smooth material of the girl's jacket. "You are so pretty."

Shiloh blushed and hid her face, which only made Paisley giggle. "We're riding with Ryland and her date, so whenever he gets here we're gonna leave," Shiloh explained, reaching out and placing her hands on Paisley's waist. The smaller girl shivered.

"Are you sure you wanna do this, Pais?" Shiloh asked, pressing her forehead against Paisley's and feeling the smaller girl's warm breath against her skin. "If you don't feel comfortable, we don't have to go."

"I want to," Paisley furrowed her eyebrows. She didn't like Shiloh trying to get her to admit that she was scared. She had to be normal. "I want to," she repeated, finality in her voice. Shiloh sensed this and decided not to push the topic any further.

"Hey, it's okay," Shiloh laughed softly, still slightly concerned. "I was just making sure."

"Oh," Paisley mumbled, shaking her head and looking down at the ground. "Do I look weird?" she asked, taking a step back and smoothing out her shirt. She was growing increasingly nervous.

"You look beautiful," Shiloh gave her a soft smile. "But what's new?" she raised an eyebrow.

Paisley blushed, looking down at the ground. "I think you are so beautiful, Lolo. I am glad I get to tell you." She reached up and ran her thumb across Shiloh's bottom lip, studying her face intently.

Shiloh's face turned red and she shivered. Paisley slowly moved her hands up to Shiloh's shoulders and stood on her tiptoes, bringing their lips together softly.

Paisley felt the all-too-familiar feeling of butterflies in her stomach. It wasn't something she ever wanted to forget. No one else made her feel like this. Only Shiloh.

"Hey losers, our ride's here!" Ryland called, jogging down the stairs and interrupting the two girls. Shiloh jumped, turning around and quickly trying to hide her frustration. Paisley whimpered at the loss of contact.

"Y'ready?" Shiloh asked, turning to Paisley. She bit her lip, looking down at the ground. She wasn't sure about this, but she had to prove to Shiloh that she could be normal. Paisley didn't want to lose her. So she nodded softly.

"Let's go," Shiloh grabbed Paisley's hand, leading her towards the door. The small gesture gave Paisley a burst of confidence, and she skipped happily behind the older girl. She quickly realized that skipping wasn't normal, though, and slowed her pace to a simple walk.

Within the fifteen minutes it took to get to the party, the sun disappeared behind the horizon. Paisley squeezed her eyes shut in the back of the car. She didn't like the dark. There were bad things in the dark. Anything unknown was bad.

"Pais," Shiloh nudged the smaller girl's arm, bringing her out of her trance. "We're here." Paisley nodded quickly, crawling out of the car behind Shiloh. She was instantly met with the loud pounding of the bass coming from the house.

Shiloh glanced at the smaller girl, concerned. "Are you sure about this?"

"Yes," Paisley nodded firmly. "I told you already."

Shiloh took a deep breath, squeezing Paisley's hand and slowly walking towards the house. To be honest, Shiloh didn't quite like parties either. But Paisley had been so serious about wanting to come. Shiloh didn't want to take the opportunity away from her.

Paisley followed timidly behind Shiloh. The loud music was physically painful in her ears, but she forced herself to endure it. For Shiloh.

She jumped when a drink was shoved in her hand the moment they set foot in the house. Paisley tilted her head to the side, sniffing the liquid and then bringing the cup to her lips. Before she could take a sip, though, Shiloh practically snatched it out of her hands.

"Don't drink that, it's bad," she warned, shaking her head and placing the cup down on a random table. Paisley furrowed her eyebrows, picking the cup up again and studying it. It smelled all too familiar.

A nauseating feeling washed over her and she quickly set the cup back down, shaking her head and backing up into Shiloh. "Bad," she whispered, clenching her fists.

"Hey, hey, it's okay," Shiloh grabbed Paisley's hand and led her into the kitchen. She had to speak loudly to be heard over the music. "What do you want to do?"

"What… what is there to do?" Paisley scanned the room. A couple was pressed up against the wall, practically eating each others faces. Paisley grimaced.

"I'm not sure, honestly," Shiloh shrugged. "This is Ryland and Nessa's turf, not mine. They can barely get me to come to one of th—," she stopped speaking when she realized Paisley wasn't paying attention to her.

Instead, the smaller girl had her eyes fixed on a group of teenagers in the living room. A crowd had formed around two college aged boys, staring each other down. Suddenly, a punch was thrown, and Paisley flinched.

"Shit," Shiloh cursed under her breath, grabbing Paisley's hand and pulling her out of the room before the smaller girl had to witness anything else. She located the back door and quickly led them both out into the backyard.

"Why were they fighting?" Paisley asked shyly, glancing back in the direction of the house. She followed Shiloh over to a circle of chairs on the patio.

"Alcohol makes people do crazy things sometimes," Shiloh shrugged, biting her lip when she heard a crash coming from inside the house. She cursed herself for allowing Paisley to come with them.

"I do not like alcohol," Paisley shook her head and looked down.

"Neither do I," Shiloh admitted, reaching out to take Paisley's hand. At the same time, though, the smaller girl remembered that she was supposed to be normal. Paisley jumped to her feet and glanced towards the door.

"I want to go back inside," she said nervously, walking towards the door. Truth is, everything about this place was terrifying her. The loud music, the people, the flashing lights – everything. She hated it. But she wanted to spend time with Shiloh.

She shuffled towards the door and pulled it open slowly. Just as Shiloh caught up behind her, two guys stumbled through the door and practically slammed into Paisley. She scrambled backwards, bringing her hands up just as she fell to the ground.

"Please," she shook her head, feeling her hands begin to shake. They were too drunk to notice her, they just walked straight past the smaller girl on the ground. Paisley whimpered.

Shiloh balled her fists and glared at the two men before quickly running to Paisley's side.

"C'mon," she said softly, giving up on allowing Paisley to try and stick out the party. She knew it was bothering the girl. "How about we get out of here?"

Paisley wiped her eyes, looking up at Shiloh and feeling a lump form in her throat. This wasn't normal. Shiloh wanted her to be normal. She shook her head slowly.

"Well too bad," Shiloh grabbed Paisley's hand and pulled her up to her feet. "I don't want to be here either, Paisley."

"Really?" Paisley tilted her head to the side. Shiloh nodded quietly, leading Paisley around the front of the house.

"But parties are normal," Paisley whispered. Shiloh laced their fingers together and looked at the smaller girl questioningly.

"What?"

"I am not normal," Paisley shook her head and brought her hands up to wipe her eyes. "I need to be normal. Normal is good."

"You're crazy," Shiloh kept a firm grip on Paisley's hand. "What's wrong with not being normal? Who wants normal?"

"You," Paisley pointed to the older girl. "Ryland too."

Shiloh suddenly remembered the conversation Paisley had happened to overhear and was instantly washed over with guilt.

"I don't want normal, Pais," she stopped walking once they reached the front of the house. "I want you. I don't need normal."

"But..." Paisley looked down at the ground and sighed. "I am annoying. I am not normal. No one will like me unless I am normal."

"Hey, don't you dare say that," Shiloh cupped Paisley's face and stared her straight in the eyes. "I like you. Ryland likes you. Leah likes you. Vanessa likes you. So many people like you. You don't have to be normal. Normal is overrated."

"I am sorry," Paisley whispered. Shiloh shook her head.

"You have nothing to be sorry for, babe," she kissed Paisley's forehead and pulled the smaller girl into a hug. "To be honest, I probably hate parties just as much as you do."

"You do?" Paisley giggled softly, pulling away from the hug.

"I do," Shiloh reiterated what she had said. She gave Paisley a goofy smile and cupped the smaller girl's cheek. "I hear there's a really good frozen yogurt place just a few blocks away. I think we should go check it out."

Paisley's face lit up and she nodded quickly. "I like froyo, much better than parties." Shiloh laughed and rolled her eyes playfully.

"Me too, Pais," she led the smaller girl down the sidewalk, kicking a pebble as they walked. Maybe Paisley was right, this wasn't normal. But hell, this was exactly what she wanted.

CHAPTER 5

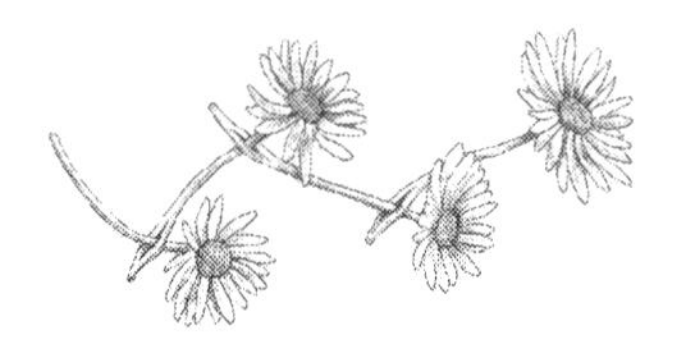

Paisley kicked at a pebble as they walked, occasionally looking over at Shiloh with an idiotic smile on her face. She was relieved that the older girl wasn't unhappy with her.

"What's gotten into you?" Shiloh raised an eyebrow when she caught Paisley staring at her. The smaller girl's face grew red and she giggled nervously.

"I am happy, that is all," Paisley shrugged.

"You're about to be even happier," Shiloh smirked, tugging on Paisley's hand and leading her across the street. "Cause' we're here," she turned the corner and pointed to the frozen yogurt shop. Paisley's face lit up and she practically dragged Shiloh through the large front doors.

Paisley shivered as soon as they set foot in the store. Noticing this, Shiloh slipped her leather jacket off and laid it across Paisley's shoulders. The smaller girl looked up at her in shock.

"But this is yours, Lolo," she said softly, trying to shrug the jacket back off her shoulders. Shiloh simply laughed and shook her head.

"I want you to wear it," Shiloh helped Paisley slip her arms into the jacket, feeling butterflies in her stomach from seeing the smaller girl in her clothing.

"Banana," Paisley smiled widely, spotting the banana flavored yogurt machine and grabbing a cup. Shiloh did the same, keeping a close eye on Paisley as she dispensed a large amount of frozen yogurt into the small bowl.

"What are you getting?" Paisley asked, shuffling back over to Shiloh with her bowl in both hands.

"I dunno," Shiloh shrugged and handed her cup to Paisley. "Surprise me."

"Okay!" Paisley hummed, switching her bowl with Shiloh's and slowly scanning the row of machines. For her, this was a big deal. Shiloh had entrusted her with this mission, and Paisley was determined to pick the perfect ice cream flavor.

Her eyes landed on the picture of a strawberry above one of the machines and she smiled. She liked strawberries. Leah had let her try a chocolate covered strawberry once, and then the smaller girl had to hide the remains from Paisley because she kept begging for more.

That was it! Chocolate covered strawberry. Paisley internally fist bumped herself for her amazing discovery.

First, she hopped to the strawberry machine, filling up half of the cup with strawberry flavored frozen yogurt. Then, she took a few steps to the side and topped it off with chocolate yogurt. Adorning a wide smile, she turned around and skipped back over to Shiloh.

"Chocolate covered strawberry," Paisley chimed, handing Shiloh her cup and taking back her own. Shiloh looked down and giggled.

"You're too smart for your own good," she teased. Paisley crinkled her nose, heading over to the topping bar. Shiloh followed and watched as Paisley added a stack of banana slices to the top of her cup.

"I love bananas," Paisley laughed softly and held her cup up to show Shiloh. "Are you getting anything?"

"Nah," Shiloh shook her head and nudged the other girl towards the counter. "I think what I've got is good."

"That is boring," Paisley shook her head and turned back around, plucking a gummy bear from the toppings bar and placing it on top of Shiloh's ice cream. "Mr. Bear," she nodded once.

Before Shiloh could reply, Paisley quickly gasped and turned to grab another gummy bear. She placed it next to Mr. Bear, and sighed in relief.

"What?" Shiloh laughed, raising an eyebrow.

"Mr. Bear was lonely. So I got him another Mr. Bear," Paisley nodded once, pointing to the gummy bears.

"What about Mrs. Bear?" Shiloh asked, tilting her head to the side. Paisley just giggled and shook her head.

"Mr. Bear is not into that," she laughed quietly to herself and padded over to the counter. Shiloh quickly caught up with her, placing her chocolate covered strawberry and gay bear frozen yogurt on the scale. After paying for their food, Paisley led her over to one of the circular booths in the back of the store.

They sat in comfortable silence for a while, Paisley happily devouring her ice cream, while Shiloh took small bites and watched Paisley adoringly. Mr. Bear and his partner sat happily on a napkin between them. Shiloh didn't have the heart to eat them.

"Talk about a throwback," Shiloh broke the silence, listening to the old song that was playing softly throughout the store. Paisley furrowed her eyebrows and listened for a moment.

Suddenly, she was met with an overwhelming rush of familiarity.

Paisley shuffled her white cheer shoes against the pavement. Wiping her eyes, she glanced back at the group of girls behind her. She quickly slowed her pace, not wanting to appear too excited about going out for frozen yogurt.

"My hair was a mess today," Harper rolled her eyes. "Coach made me use way too much hairspray for the game." Paisley bit her lip, moving her hands up to comb her fingers through her hair. Did her hair look okay? She hadn't even thought about it. She had been too excited to perform.

"Scott was practically making heart eyes at you from the stands, Paisley," another one of the girls, Caitlyn, spoke up. Paisley internally grimaced. She didn't want to think about Scott at the moment. Or ever, really.

"I think we did well," Paisley said softly, trying to turn the conversation in another direction. She pushed through the doors and into the frozen yogurt shop, smiling softly.

After grabbing her cup, Paisley grew confused. Upon turning around, she realized all of the girls had already sat down without getting anything. Paisley furrowed her eyebrows and walked over to them.

"What are you guys doing?" she asked, tilting her head to the side and holding up her cup. "Aren't we getting froyo?" Practically all of the girls crinkled their noses and shook their heads.

"Not during cheer season," Sydney explained. Paisley raised an eyebrow.

"Well then why did we come here?" she asked.

"For that," Harper smirked, nodding towards the door, where the entire basketball team was filing into the store. Sydney grabbed Paisley's arm and tugged her down into the booth. The girls quickly scooted over to make room for her. Paisley sighed softly and placed her empty cup on the table in front of them.

"We're wasting our time just to watch boys?" Paisley asked in disbelief. Hell, she'd much rather watch girls. One girl in particular. But she wouldn't say that aloud. Ever.

"Not just any boys," Harper scoffed, shaking her head. "Only the most angelic faces to ever grace Miami," she swooned, earning nods of agreement from the other girls.

Paisley crinkled her nose in jealously as she watched the basketball team all pile their cups full of the sugary substance.

"Oh my god, Paisley, is that a hickey?" one of the girls practically squealed. Paisley whipped her head around and looked at the blonde in confusion.

"What are you talking about?" she asked, quickly bringing her hands up to cover her neck. She couldn't possibly have a hickey. Her and Scott barely kissed.

"Not there," Harper shook her head and leaned across the table, pulling down the shoulder of Paisley's unzipped jacket and pointing to the mark on her shoulder. "There."

Paisley's eyes instantly widened and she snatched the material out of the girl's hand, quickly covering up the bruise. She scanned the faces at the table, meeting eyes with Sydney pleadingly.

"Who the hell gives someone a hickey on their shoulder?" Sydney directed her question at Harper. Paisley sighed when the other girls laughed, silently thanking Sydney for diverting the attention away from her.

"I dunno, maybe Paisley's into kinky stuff," Harper shrugged and drummed her fingers on the table. Paisley grimaced and pulled her jacket further over her shoulders. Sydney kicked her foot under the table, waving her hand and signaling to her that it was okay. No one had caught onto anything.

Paisley still felt the need to cover her tracks, though. "I fell the other day during practice," Paisley shrugged and looked down at her feet. "That's probably what it's from."

"Did coach see?" Bethany looked up from her phone for the first time that night. "You know, if you keep goofing off in the gym, you're never going to get center flyer next year." The jealously radiating off of the girl was palpable.

Paisley simply shrugged. She honestly didn't mind what position she held on the team, as long as she got to cheer. It wasn't even her favorite thing, but it gave her a place to be other than her house. She needed that.

"Look who it is, Paisley," Harper smirked and nudged the smaller girl's arm. Paisley gave her a look of confusion, turning around and looking at the door. Her hands balled into fists when she saw Scott enter the store.

"Hey babe," he smirked, spotting Paisley and the other cheerleaders in the back of the room. Paisley bit her lip nervously, but stood up when he walked over to them.

"Hey, what are y—?" Paisley began, but was cut off by Scott pushing her against the wall and practically shoving his tongue down her throat. She shivered. Public displays of affection weren't generally her thing.

"Scott," she warned, pushing her boyfriend off of her and quickly wiping the back of her mouth with her hand. His actions earned an array of hoots and hollers from the girls at the table, which caused Paisley's face to turn bright red. She felt overwhelmingly uncomfortable with everyone's eyes on her.

"Loosen up, Paisley," he chuckled, ruffling Paisley's hair. She scoffed and took a step away from him, shaking her head.

"I've got to go home," she lied, pretending to check the time. "My uncle's expecting me back by 9."

"Nine?" Scott laughed. "You're such a liar, Paisley. Tom doesn't give a fuck what you do." His words hit her harder than they should've and Paisley looked down at her shoes embarrassingly.

Everyone envied her for having such a lenient guardian. But what Paisley really wanted was someone who cared. Not Tom. He didn't care. Not Scott, either. No, she wanted someone who craved to be around her. Someone who was actually interested in what she had to say. She felt tears well up in her eyes when she realized how alone she truly was.

Sighing in defeat, she sat down slowly. Scott slid into the bench next to her, pulling her into his side. Paisley tried to hide her discomfort. She would just have to get used to this.

"Pais," Shiloh snapped her fingers in front of the smaller girl's face, making Paisley jump and widen her eyes.

"You zoned out," Shiloh laughed softly. Paisley, on the other hand, took a deep breath and blinked a few times. It took her a moment to realize where she was. Everything slowly fizzled back into reality, and she bit her lip anxiously.

"Is something wrong?" Shiloh grew worried, grabbing Paisley's hand and running her thumb over the back of the girl's palm. Paisley met Shiloh's eyes and debated what she should do for a moment.

"I am just cold," Paisley lied, tugging the leather jacket over her torso and shivering for effect. Luckily, Shiloh bought it. The green eyed girl glanced down at their nearly empty froyo cups and stacked them on top of each other.

"Good thing we get to go home and cuddle now," Shiloh laughed softly and stood, holding out her hand for Paisley's. The smaller girl nodded and took her hand, allowing Shiloh to lead her as she threw away their trash and then exited the small shop.

Shiloh fished around in her pocket, making sure she had enough money before hailing a taxi. The car ride was fairly silent. As they neared the house, Shiloh heard Paisley gasp.

"Lolo," Paisley quickly turned and tugged on Shiloh's sleeve, tapping the window with her other hand. Shiloh raised an eyebrow, studying as Paisley began tracing downward lines on the window.

"What are you doing?" Shiloh asked, unbuckling her seatbelt and scooting over. Paisley tapped on the window once more. It was then that Shiloh saw the small white flakes drifting down from the sky.

"It is snowing," Paisley smiled widely and turned to face Shiloh. "The sky gave us a present."

Shiloh giggled, pulling Paisley into her side and kissing the small girl's forehead. "Y'know, I used to hate snow," she confessed. Paisley practically gasped.

"But why?" the smaller girl raised her eyebrows.

"It was just a nuisance," Shiloh shrugged and absentmindedly traced circles in Paisley's palm. "But then you came along, and I guess you've sorta helped me see that everything is beautiful."

"Duh," Paisley crinkled her nose. Shiloh feigned disbelief and nudged the smaller girl playfully.

"Look, Lolo," Paisley ignored her actions and quickly turned back to the window. "The snow is... shimmery!" she clapped her hands, proud of herself for using the new word she had learned. The events of the hours prior were completely forgotten.

"Woah," Shiloh whispered, scooting closer to the window and watching as the snow at the bottom of the hill reflected the moonlight. Paisley was right, it was shimmery.

"It's beautiful," Shiloh said softly.

"No," Paisley shook her head and turned to Shiloh, studying her face for a few moments. "It is pretty. *You* are beautiful." Shiloh's cheeks grew bright red and she was thankful that it was already dark out.

"We're here," Paisley noted, pointing to the building. Shiloh paid the driver as they rolled to a stop, and by the time she looked up, Paisley was already standing outside the car. Both girls hurried inside the warm building.

Paisley pushed open the door to the apartment, gasping when she saw the window in the back of the room. It was snowing even more now. She practically sprinted across the apartment and pressed her hands against the cool glass, staring intently at the scene before her.

Shiloh sighed contently, turning one of the dim lights in the living room. The apartment lit up just enough so that she could see. Paisley turned around and smiled widely.

"Come look, Lo," she said softly. Shiloh joined her at the back of the apartment. Paisley immediately found Shiloh's hand and laced their fingers together.

After a few minutes of silence, Shiloh turned to Paisley and squeezed her hand. "Can we go upstairs? I wanna talk to you about something."

"Is it bad?" Paisley asked worriedly after turning to face the taller girl. Shiloh shook her head, and tugged on Paisley's hand. She led her upstairs without another word, as Paisley grew worried.

Shiloh closed the bedroom door behind them. Paisley bit her lip, shuffling over to the bed and hugging a pillow to her chest once she sat down.

"You look nervous," Shiloh laughed softly and sat down on the edge of the bed. Paisley remained silent and Shiloh furrowed her eyebrows. "Hey, don't be nervous," she scooted next to Paisley and patted the space beside her.

"Did I do something bad?" Paisley asked, timidly crawling next to Shiloh and lacing their fingers together. "I did not mean to."

Shiloh quickly shook her head and tugged one of her blankets over their feet. "Just because I want to talk about something doesn't automatically mean you're in trouble," she said quietly. "It just means I wanna talk about something when we're both not distracted by other things."

"Oh," Paisley hummed softly and began picking at a loose strand of string on the blanket. "What is it, then?"

"Well..." Shiloh took a deep breath. "Remember when we were in the store and you wanted me to buy the beanie for you?" Paisley nodded softly, looking down. She was ashamed of how she'd acted earlier.

"Hey, no, it was my fault," Shiloh grabbed her hand and cradled it in her own. "I shouldn't have put you on the spot like that. It would've been a better idea for me to talk to you about it first."

"About what?" Paisley asked, shivering when Shiloh ran her thumb over the back of her palm.

"I wanna help you… be a better person," Shiloh tried to string her words together so she wouldn't confuse Paisley. "I want you to be able to do things like that on your own."

"You want to fix…" Paisley continued her sentence by bringing her hands up and knocking on her forehead. "My brain."

"No," Shiloh quickly shook her head and reached out to bring Paisley's hands away from her face. "You don't need to be fixed. You aren't broken."

"But…" Paisley sighed and looked down. "Why did you get mad?"

"I wasn't mad," the green eyed girl looked down at their hands anxiously. "I just… I want you to learn how to do those things. So you can take care of yourself."

"But why?" Paisley tilted her head to the side and studied Shiloh's face.

"What happens if I'm not around and you don't have anyone to help you?" Shiloh looked up. Paisley's eyes widened and she quickly shook her head, moving forwards and burying her head in Shiloh's shoulder.

"I want you to stay around," Paisley's small voice squeaked out, and Shiloh physically felt her heart breaking. She wrapped her arms around the small girl and rested her chin on Paisley's head.

"I know, baby," Shiloh whispered. Paisley lifted her head slowly and wiped her eyes.

"I'm gonna stay around. For as long as I can," Shiloh quickly interlocked their pinkies and kissed Paisley's hand. "But I want to be around to see you do these things. I want you to learn how to be independent. There's no better feeling than being able to do things for yourself."

"But you w—" Paisley stopped speaking abruptly when a small noise escaped her lips. She quickly cupped her hands over her mouth and widened her eyes in fear.

"You will s—" Paisley slapped her hands back over her mouth when her chest spammed again, making her bounce slightly on the bed. Terror flickered in her eyes and she quickly curled up into a ball.

"I am breaking," Paisley whispered, shaking her head. She covered her face with her hands just as her body jolted for a third time. A small whimper escaped her mouth.

Shiloh had to bite her lip to sustain her laughter. She quickly shook her head and tried to pull Paisley's hands away from her face.

"You're not breaking, babe," she giggled. "You just have the hiccups."

"The wh—," Paisley cupped her hands over her mouth when another hiccup escaped her lips. "The what?" she asked quickly this time to beat the next hiccup.

"The *hiccups*, Pais, it happens to everyone," Shiloh laughed softly. Paisley furrowed her eyebrows.

"It is not—*hiccup*—funny," Paisley pouted, jutting out her bottom lip and crossing her arms. Seconds later, she hiccuped again and hugged her knees to her chest.

"Pais," Shiloh bit her lip to hide a smile and she pulled Paisley closer to her. "It's fine. Everyone gets the hiccups, it's not big deal."

"I don't like them," Paisley mumbled, shaking her head. The bed bounced slightly when she hiccuped once more. Shiloh couldn't help but giggle.

"Here," Shiloh crawled across the bed and snatched a water bottle off of her nightstand, handing it to Paisley. "Drink something. It'll make the hiccups go away."

Paisley eagerly brought the cup to her lips, throwing her head back and downing practically half the bottle in three gulps. She stopped drinking when she hiccuped once more, causing water to dribble down her chin and onto her shirt.

"Now they will be gone?" she asked as Shiloh reached out to wipe the water off of her chin.

"Probably," Shiloh shrugged. She wasn't used to having to explain something as trivial as the hiccups to someone. Poor Paisley had been terrified.

"That was easy," Paisley laughed softly, but was met with another hiccup mid-laugh. She huffed, letting her hands fall to her sides. "You—*hiccup*—lied," she muttered, cupping her hands over her mouth.

"Sometimes they've just got to go away on their own," Shiloh bit her lip and opened her arms, motioning for Paisley to scoot closer. The smaller girl practically crawled into Shiloh's lap, wrapping her arms around her shoulders and burying her head in Shiloh's neck just as another hiccup made the bed jostle slightly.

"There's other ways to get rid of the hiccups, y'know," Shiloh said softly after a few moments of silence. Only Paisley could manage to make Shiloh feel bad for her when she had the hiccups.

"How?" Paisley mumbled against Shiloh's hoodie, trying to hold in another hiccup but failing.

"You could hold your breath, or do a handstand, or scare them away," Shiloh said, beginning to list tricks she'd learned on getting rid of the hiccups.

"Scare them—*hiccup*—away?" Paisley asked, keeping her head buried in the crook of Shiloh's neck.

"Yeah, like you get someone to g—" Shiloh began, but was cut off by her bedroom door being burst open. Paisley screamed, snapping her head up and colliding the top of her head with Shiloh's chin.

"I'm *not* drunk!" Ryland slurred, practically tripping over her own two feet and into the middle of the bedroom. "Don't trust anything that Vanessa s—"

"Ryland, I swear," Vanessa groaned, appearing in the doorway. She grabbed Ryland's arm, dragging her out into the hallway and passing her off to Leah, who was waiting by Ryland's bedroom door.

"I'm sorry about her," Vanessa laughed softly, looking at the two girls on the bed. Shiloh had her hands cupped over her chin, and Paisley had her eyebrows furrowed, rubbing the top of her head. "What did I just walk in on?"

"I have the hiccups," Paisley muttered, turning to Shiloh and observing the girl's expression. "Did I hurt you?" she asked quietly, suddenly becoming concerned. The brown eyed girl gently cupped Shiloh's face in her hands and tilted her chin upwards.

"I should be asking you the same thing," Shiloh laughed, tapping the top of Paisley's head lightly. She took Paisley's hands in her own and turned back to face Vanessa, who raised an eyebrow at them.

"Where'd you guys even disappear off to?" Vanessa asked, placing a hand on her hip suggestively. Shiloh's face grew red, but Paisley beat her to an answer. She crawled off of the bed and smiled excitedly.

"We got yogurt," she explained. "The frozen kind. With Mr. Bear. And then we came back here and… we talked. And then I hiccuped. It was the best day ever."

"The best day ever?" Vanessa laughed softly, Paisley nodded. After a few moments, though, she shook her head to take back her answer.

"Tomorrow is always the best day ever," Paisley glanced back at Shiloh, smiling like an idiot.

"Why tomorrow?" Vanessa and Shiloh both asked at the same time. Paisley giggled, as if the answer was obvious.

"Because tomorrow is always a promise for another day with her," Paisley turned around and pointed to the green eyed girl on the bed, blushing slightly.

Shiloh's face instantly turned red, and no matter how hard she tried, she couldn't hide the smile that spread across her face. She realized then that tomorrow was her favorite day, too. If it meant having another day with Paisley.

"Y'all are gross," Vanessa teased, nudging Paisley's shoulder playfully. "I'll leave you to it, then," she smirked and winked at Shiloh, who sent her a warning glare. Vanessa ignored her, laughing and slipping out of the bedroom.

Paisley giggled quietly and hopped back onto the bed. Shiloh raised an eyebrow.

"Looks like Ryland really scared those hiccups outta' you," Shiloh smirked. Paisley paused for a moment, her face lighting up a few seconds later.

"It is a Christmas miracle!" Paisley exclaimed, throwing her hands in the air and falling back on the bed. Shiloh raised an eyebrow.

"It isn't Christmas, goofball," Shiloh laughed, lying back on the bed so her head rested on her pillow. Paisley frowned and crawled to the space next to her girlfriend.

"It is a... just a miracle," Paisley giggled. She curled up in Shiloh's side and sighed contently.

"We never finished talking..." Shiloh said softly. Paisley lifted her head and thought for a few moments. She slowly reached up and traced her fingers over Shiloh's jawline.

"You can help me..." she whispered, thinking for a second before continuing. "You can help me. But, you have to promise to still sing to me every night."

"Of course I promise," Shiloh laughed and kissed Paisley's forehead. "Only for you."

Shiloh's voice quieted to a whisper once she finished the song. Paisley hummed contently and snaked her arms up the sleeves of Shiloh's hoodie, seeking warmth in the chilly apartment.

"Goodnight, Lo," Paisley whispered. Shiloh shivered at the feeling of Paisley's soft breath against her neck.

"Night, princess," Shiloh smiled, pressing a kiss to the top of Paisley's head. She pulled the blankets over them, closing her eyes and appreciating their little world of bliss while the snow blanketed the streets around them.

CHAPTER 6

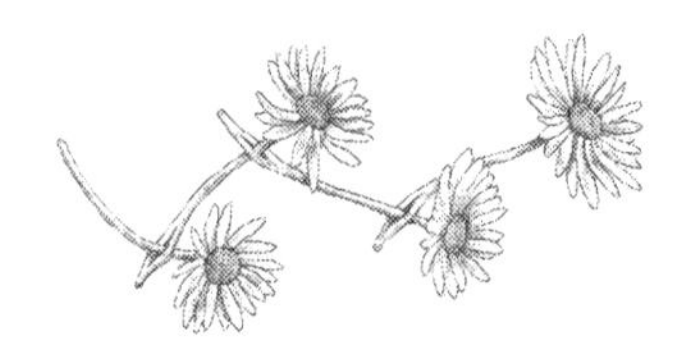

"She's not gonna wake up, Ryland, I already tried," Shiloh whispered, glancing at the small girl on the bed. Ryland dismissed her claim and smirked.

"Pizza's here!" she yelled, clapping her hands together.

Paisley's eyes fluttered open and a few moments later, her head shot up in confusion. "Pizza?" she mumbled, blowing a loose strand of hair out of her face and looking at the two girls that stood in front of her.

"Holy shit," Shiloh laughed under her breath, raising an eyebrow at Ryland. Paisley groaned and buried her face in the pillow.

"That is not funny," Paisley's muffled voice rang out from against the pillow. Shiloh laughed and scooted closer to the bed, finding Paisley's hand under the blanket and squeezing it.

"Hey, c'mon, you get to come to class with me today," Shiloh said softly, biting her lip and hoping Paisley wouldn't react negatively. The small brown eyed girl immediately looked up in confusion.

"Leah's schedule got turned around and so now you're gonna have to tag along with me on Tuesdays and Thursdays," Shiloh subtly motioned to Ryland that she could handle it from there. The light haired girl got the message and slipped out of the room.

It wasn't that Shiloh didn't trust Paisley home alone, because she did. It was just that she'd rather not spend the day worrying about the other girl. She would much rather have Paisley by her side.

To be frank, she *did* panic when she realized Leah wouldn't be home with Paisley. She was slightly worried about what having Paisley with her would do. But she was also comforted by the fact that her teacher had already met Paisley, and seemed to be accepting of her. She just hoped he wouldn't mind having an extra student in his class.

"What?" Paisley pushed herself into a sitting position, wiping her eyes and looking around the room tiredly. Shiloh couldn't help but smile at the small girl's sleepy confusion. Paisley yawned softly and gave Shiloh a tired smile.

"You get to come to class and watch me draw, is that cool?" Shiloh asked, sitting down next to Paisley and smoothing out her tousled hair. Paisley's face lit up and she nodded.

"You know how to act in a classroom, right?" Shiloh tilted her head to the side. Paisley giggled.

"Duh," she raised her hand up in the air. "You raise your hand when you have to go to the bathroom."

Shiloh bit her lip nervously. "Actually—,"

"I was joking," Paisley laughed. Shiloh sighed in relief. Paisley had been cracking believable jokes more often, and Shiloh still wasn't used to it.

"I will be good, do not be annoying," Paisley teased and stood up from the bed. She opened the closet and scanned it slowly, before looking back at Shiloh. "What do I wear?"

"Whatever you want," Shiloh walked up behind the small girl, wrapping her arms around her waist and planting a kiss on her cheek. "Just make sure it's warm, cause' the studio is freezing."

Paisley giggled, watching as Shiloh reached over her shoulders and grabbed a pair of jeans out of the dresser. Once she found what she wanted to wear, she slipped into the bathroom while Shiloh got changed in the bedroom.

Shiloh paused for a moment when she heard a sound of frustration coming from the bathroom. Raising an eyebrow, Shiloh tiptoed across the hallway.

"You okay in there?" Shiloh knocked on the door twice. When she didn't receive an answer, she opened the door slowly and peered into the small bathroom. Paisley was leaning over the sink, trying to apply mascara to her eyelashes with a shaky hand.

"What're you doing?" Shiloh laughed softly. Paisley huffed and looked up, clenching her fist around the makeup brush. She had small dots of mascara streaked around her eyes.

"I cannot do it," Paisley mumbled, turning back to the mirror and holding her eye open with one hand. Shiloh grabbed her wrist before she could bring the mascara back up to her eye.

"Hey, you don't need makeup," Shiloh said softly, gently taking the mascara from Paisley's hand and setting it on the counter. "There's no point. I wanna see you just the way you are." She held Paisley's chin with one hand and grabbed a makeup wipe with the other, carefully dabbing the spots around her eyes.

"But I am not pretty," Paisley whispered, standing still while Shiloh continued to wipe the smeared makeup off of her face. Shiloh shook her head, furrowing her eyebrows and leaning in closer to get the corners of Paisley's eyes.

"Yes you are," she pulled back and ran her thumb over Paisley's cheek. "I think you're the prettiest girl in the world. Not that it matters, though. There are so many other things about you that are way better than just the way you look."

She took step back and studied the outfit Paisley had chosen. Black jeans, a red pea coat, and a white scarf.

Complete with her white converse, of course. Shiloh was endeared.

"And I think your sense of style is adorable, too," Shiloh giggled and kissed Paisley's forehead. The smaller girl looked down shyly, hiding the blush that had spread across her cheeks.

Paisley studied Shiloh's outfit. She would never choose the dark jeans and black band t-shirt for herself, but it's what she adored about Shiloh. Furrowing her eyebrows, Paisley watched as Shiloh grabbed her makeup bag from the counter.

"No," Paisley shook her head and slid forward. "I do not want you to. You are pretty without it."

Shiloh bit her lip, looking down at the products in her hands. She didn't like going out without makeup. It was like her mask. But she realized she had just told Paisley the same exact thing. She would be contradicting herself if she didn't oblige.

"You're too smart for your own good," Shiloh teased, giving Paisley a soft smile and pushing the makeup bag aside. Once they brushed their teeth, she combed her fingers through her own hair and glanced in the mirror once last time before turning to Paisley. "Looks like we're ready, then."

Paisley smiled and followed Shiloh into the bedroom, waiting as the older girl zipped up her combat boots and tugged a beanie onto her head. Her eyes widened.

"I want one," Paisley hopped forwards and pointed to Shiloh's beanie. Shiloh raised an eyebrow. The beanie she currently had on was the only one she owned. That was, until, she remembered something. She held up a finger to signal for Paisley to wait.

Digging around in the back of her closet, Shiloh smiled when she finally found what she was looking for. She stood up and held the baby blue beanie out in Paisley's direction.

"I forgot I even owned this," Shiloh laughed softly, watching as Paisley's face lit up and she gently took the beanie from Shiloh's hands. "I used to wear it all the time in high school."

Paisley studied the beanie in her hands before tugging it on. She was met with an overwhelming sense of familiarity as Shiloh stepped forward and adjusted the material on her head.

"I love it," Paisley smiled, reaching up to pat the top of her head.

"Y'look cute," Shiloh laughed softly before turning around and grabbing her backpack. Paisley clapped her hands together.

"I want one," Paisley pointed to Shiloh's backpack. The green eyed girl couldn't help but laugh.

Without another word, Shiloh dug around under her bed until she found one of her old backpacks from high school. Paisley's eyes widened.

"You like blue," she noted, pointing to the color of the backpack. Shiloh nodded and walked over to her desk, tossing a few colored pencils and a pad of paper into the bag.

"It's my favorite color," Shiloh said as she handed the bag to Paisley. She watched as the smaller girl carefully adjusted the straps over her shoulders.

"It is?" Paisley tiled her head to the side and looked up at Shiloh. "I thought it was yellow."

"That's *your* favorite color, doofus," Shiloh teased, opening the door for Paisley as they exited her bedroom. "Mine has been blue since I was little."

"Oh," Paisley looked down at her shoes as she shuffled them towards the front door. "Because of the sky, right? Because it makes you think of the sky, even when you are inside."

Shiloh raised her eyebrows. "Y'know, I never thought about it that way," she laughed as they entered the elevator. Paisley pushed the button for the ground floor proudly, adjusting her beanie in the mirror and smiling at her reflection.

As Shiloh drove them to the school, she noticed Paisley growing more and more anxious. It was prominent in the girl's features. Her eyebrows would furrow together in concern, and she bounced her leg softly.

"Hey," Shiloh reached over and laced their fingers together. "What's up?"

"What if they do not like me?" Paisley looked over at Shiloh and then down at their hands.

"They will," Shiloh squeezed her hand just at they pulled into the back of the parking lot. "Everyone likes you. Including me. Don't worry your pretty little mind."

Paisley crinkled her nose, slowly exiting the car once Shiloh opened her door. "I am still nervous," she confessed, following quickly behind Shiloh as they walked towards the large building. Shiloh stopped walking, holding her hand out and waiting for Paisley to take it. Once she did, Shiloh kissed her cheek gently.

"You won't even have to look at anyone if you don't want to. It's a workshop day today anyway," she shrugged and continued walking. "All I'm doing is working on a painting. You can help me out, if you want."

"I will mess up," Paisley shook her head, planting her feet in the ground just outside the front door and looking at Shiloh pleadingly.

"Pais," Shiloh stepped forwards and pulled the door open. "You've got my lucky blue beanie on, you can do anything."

"Anything?" Paisley giggled, tilting her head to the side.

"Anything," Shiloh confirmed. She squeezed Paisley's hand, leading them into the building. When they reached her classroom, she adjusted her backpack on her shoulder and gently held the door open.

Paisley followed her shyly into the classroom, looking around slowly. All the other students were too busy in their work to notice the extra member.

"Ah, Shiloh!" Mr. Robertson waved her over, noticing Paisley. "I finally got your forms for the showcase next Tuesday," he handed a stack of papers to Shiloh and then glanced at Paisley. "And who may this be?"

Before Shiloh could answer, Paisley smiled softly and waved. "My name is Paisley," she said gently. She had Shiloh's beanie on, she could do anything. Shiloh smiled proudly.

"My girlfriend," Shiloh added, turning to slip the papers into her backpack. "Is it okay… if she just sorta… sits with me while I work? There was a schedule mishap—,"

"That's fine," he shrugged it off. Shiloh breathed a sigh of relief.

"Wait a minute, Paisley, could you help me with something?" he bent down and opened a drawer in his desk, digging around for a moment before emerging with a stack of papers.

"I teach my daughter's art class, and I was supposed to grade these, but I completely forgot. Can you just put a sticker on each one?" he asked, looking down at the childish crayon drawings. Paisley looked to Shiloh for approval before nodding softly.

"Thank you," he chuckled, handing Paisley the papers and a pad of colorful stickers. Shiloh had to stifle a laugh when Paisley's face lit up.

"Thanks, Mr. Robertson," Shiloh added, grabbing Paisley's hand and leading her over to an empty table in the back. As the two girls sat down, Paisley suddenly became aware of a few wandering eyes on them. She looked down shyly, not wanting to make any eye contact.

"Where are you going?" she panicked when Shiloh stood up.

"Just over there to grab an easel, I'll be right back," Shiloh assured her. Paisley bit her lip as Shiloh disappeared in the back of the classroom. She looked around slowly, making eye contact with a boy a few tables over and quickly looking away. She felt judged.

Shortly after, Shiloh returned with an easel and what appeared to be a half-finished painting. Paisley leaned over the table to watch as Shiloh began adding lighter blues to the ocean in the picture.

"Pretty," Paisley observed, sitting back down and turning her attention to the stack of papers in front of her. She had to do this perfectly. She'd been trusted with an important job from an important person, and she couldn't mess this up.

She pulled the first drawing off of the pile, admiring the picture of what appeared to be a dog. Carefully, she peeled a purple sticker off of the pad and smoothed it into the top corner of the paper. Once she was finished, she held it up proudly before setting it aside.

She watched Shiloh paint for a few moments before moving onto the next picture. She became so distracted by choosing the perfect sticker for each picture that by the time she was on the last paper, she didn't notice the other students filing out of the classroom.

"Pais," Shiloh giggled, snapping her fingers in front of Paisley's face to get her attention. The smaller girl jumped and looked up.

"Class is over," Shiloh laughed, holding her finished painting carefully. "I'm gonna go put this in the back to dry, did you finish those?" Paisley nodded.

"Can you go give them back to him? Or do you want me to do it?" Shiloh asked, glancing at the teacher in the front of the classroom. Paisley shook her head and held the papers against her chest. She could do it herself.

"I can do it," she said softly, standing up. Shiloh laughed and nodded.

"I'll be right back," she leaned in and kissed Paisley's cheek before jogging to the back of the classroom. Paisley took a deep breath. She could do this. She reached up and patted the beanie on her head before slowly padding to the front of the classroom.

"Hi," Paisley said softly, placing the papers on the teacher's desk. Mr. Robertson turned around from the whiteboard and smiled when he saw Paisley had finished.

"Awesome," he took the papers, studying them for a moment before nodding in approval. "Thank you, Paisley."

"Thank you, you're welcome," Paisley smiled proudly. The professor simply chuckled before placing the papers carefully in the top drawer of his desk.

Shiloh jogged to the front of the room and twirled a piece of Paisley's hair around her finger, making the smaller girl jump. Paisley turned around and giggled when she came face to face with Shiloh.

"You ready to go?" Shiloh asked, tossing her backpack over her shoulder. Paisley nodded softly and tugged her beanie further on her head.

Shiloh mouthed a 'thank you' to her professor as Paisley pulled her out of the classroom. He just nodded in understanding.

"That was fun," Paisley chimed as they made their way back to Shiloh's car. She swung their hands back and forth, looking up and studying the clouds in the sky.

Two days passed, and Shiloh found herself waking up to Paisley nudging her shoulder gently. Her eyes fluttered open and she gazed confusingly up at the smaller girl, who was already dressed.

"Today is Thursday," Paisley said softly. She sat down on the edge of the bed and began to comb her fingers through Shiloh's hair aimlessly. "You have class, right?"

"Mhm," Shiloh sighed, wiping her eyes and gazing up at Paisley. "You really like that beanie, don't you?" she giggled, pointing to the baby blue material on Paisley's head. The smaller girl had practically never taken it off.

"Yes," Paisley nodded. "It is your favorite color."

"My favorite color on my favorite girl," Shiloh whispered, propping herself up on her elbow and pulling Paisley down to kiss the top of her head. The smaller girl giggled shyly.

Shiloh crinkled her nose, rolling out of bed and trudging over to her dresser to get a change of clothes. Paisley sat down on the bed, crossing her legs and tracing patterns in the bed sheets.

Once Shiloh was dressed in her usual leggings and sweatshirt, both girls headed downstairs. Paisley crawled on top of the island and sat quietly while Shiloh poured them two bowls of cereal.

"Why do you like to draw?" Paisley asked as Shiloh hopped up on the counter beside her. Shiloh shrugged and took a bite of her cereal.

"Cause it's fun. You get to make things that may not exist in real life," Shiloh finished chewing her food and crinkled her nose.

"Oh," Paisley thought about it for a moment before taking a bite of her food and looking over at Shiloh with a cheesy smile on her face. "You are very good at it."

"Hush," Shiloh said bashfully, continuing to eat her cereal. Once both girls were finished, they headed upstairs and brushed their teeth. Shiloh braided Paisley's hair while the smaller girl made a tower out of bobby pins on her counter.

"Ready?" Shiloh asked, handing Paisley the same blue backpack she had used on Tuesday. Paisley nodded, slinging the bag over her shoulder and following Shiloh down the hallway. Once they reached the car, Paisley hummed softly along with the radio.

As soon as Shiloh parked the car, Paisley adjusted her beanie and skipped across the parking lot to the front of the school. Shiloh practically had to sprint to catch up with her.

"Someone's not nervous today," Shiloh teased, grabbing Paisley's hand as they walked into the school. The smaller girl laughed softly, knowing that she had been caught.

Paisley was given another stack of crayon drawings to "grade" with stickers while Shiloh set a blank canvas on her easel and studied it quietly. After ten minutes had passed and the canvas remained untouched, Paisley looked up slowly.

"Paint a butterfly," Paisley whispered, leaning over and tapping on Shiloh's shoulder. The green eyed girl turned around and raised an eyebrow.

"A butterfly," Paisley pointed to the canvas, further explaining herself. "Like the ones in the park," she pointed to the window.

"Only for you," Shiloh laughed, grabbing a paintbrush out of her backpack. Paisley smiled softly, feeling butterflies of her own erupt in her stomach. Something about having Shiloh all to herself made her feel invincible.

Shortly after, Paisley ran out of drawings to grade and sat quietly. She watched Shiloh for a while, but found the rhythmic brushstrokes putting her to sleep. After scanning the classroom for a few moments, something caught her eye.

She craned her neck slightly to try and see what the boy a few tables behind them was doing. Narrowing her eyes, she could barely make out a few shapes. Eventually, her curiosity took over and she slowly padded across the room.

Paisley stopped walking when she was a few steps behind him, standing on her tiptoes to get a better view. She realized he was making something out of clay.

"Do you wanna see?"

Paisley jumped when the boy turned around to address her. She was about to flee back to her seat, but she paused for a moment to study his face. He didn't appear to be angry with her.

"It's a sculpture of the Greek goddess Selene," he explained. When Paisley didn't reply, he motioned for her to take a step forwards. Paisley shyly moved to the edge of the table and let her eyes scan the clay figure.

"She was the goddess of the moon," the other girl at the table spoke up, causing Paisley to jump. "Don't let him fool you. He found it all online."

Paisley smiled shyly and looked over at the other girl. She had a small easel set on the table, working on something in black and white paint. When she saw Paisley eyeing the canvas, she turned the easel slightly so the smaller girl could see.

"What is that?" Paisley asked softly, becoming less shy when she realized these strangers didn't mean any harm. She took a few steps closer to the girl and leaned down to study the painting.

"It's gonna be Saturn, the planet, but I'm nowhere close to being done," the girl laughed, looking over at Paisley. "I'm Maia, by the way," she held out her hand for Paisley to shake. "And that's my boyfriend Toby." The boy on the other side of the table was focused intently on his sculpture.

Paisley stared down at the extended hand. Unsure of what else to do, she held out her fist and looked at Maia hopefully. The other girl just laughed and bumped Paisley's fist. Toby added the exploding noise from across the table, which caused both girls to laugh even more.

"I am Paisley," the brown eyed girl said softly. She leaned in as Maia began adding streaks of black around the edges of her canvas. "You are good at that."

"Thanks," Maia laughed softly and turned to dip her brush in the palette. Paisley moved her hand at the same time, though, and the brush ended up leaving a dot of black on the back of her palm.

"Sorry," Paisley mumbled, shaking her head and taking a step backwards. Maia simply shrugged it off, grabbing Paisley's hand before she could leave.

"No big deal," she laughed softly. "Here, I'll fix it," she set Paisley's hand down on the table and began running the brush over her skin. Paisley watched in awe as the black dot of paint was turned into a small flower.

"There," Maia laughed, wiping her brush off and setting it down. "Just be lucky it didn't get on your clothes," she added in a whisper, pointing to Toby's shirt, which was covered in the gray excess from his clay. Paisley giggled.

"Thank you," Paisley smiled, looking down at the flower on her hand. She had to show it to Shiloh. Now she could match her tattoo. That was, until it washed off.

"No problem," Maia grabbed her brush and turned her attention back to her painting. Paisley gave her a soft smile before shuffling back over to Shiloh.

"Lo," Paisley whispered, tapping on the girl's shoulder. Shiloh jumped, looking over at Paisley and setting her paintbrush down. "Look," Paisley held out her hand proudly.

"How'd you do that?" Shiloh laughed softly and gently took Paisley's hand in her own, studying the flower.

"I did not," Paisley pointed across the room to the table where she had just been. "Maia did."

Shiloh raised an eyebrow, looking across the room. She didn't know Maia very well, but she'd had a few conversations with the girl and her boyfriend before. They seemed like nice people.

"Yeah?" Shiloh smiled.

"Yeah," Paisley nodded once and sat down on the chair next to Shiloh's. "She was nice. She did not make fun of me."

"I don't think anyone could ever make fun of you, doofus," Shiloh laughed and turned back to her painting. "Is this a good butterfly?"

Paisley scooted closer and laid her head on Shiloh's shoulder, studying the colorful painting. She was constantly amazed by what Shiloh could do with a paintbrush.

"Duh," Paisley giggled. "You made it." She tugged on her light blue beanie, looking down at the flower on her hand. She felt happy. Maybe this was progress.

CHAPTER 7

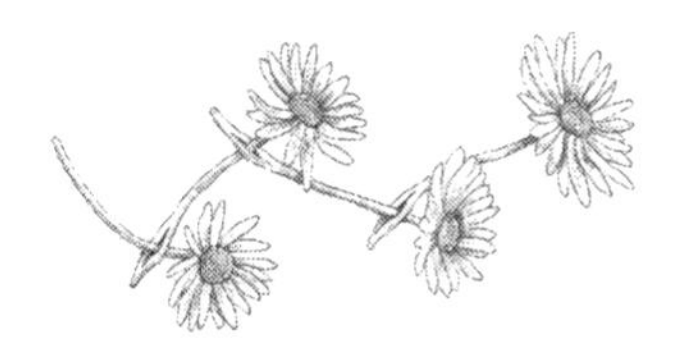

"Y'ready, Paisley?" Vanessa knocked softly on the bedroom door. Paisley tugged her beanie onto her head and padded over to the door, opening it slowly and smiling when she saw the taller girl on the other side.

"Ready," Paisley nodded once. "Will Shiloh be here when we get back?"

"She gets back from class in an hour," Vanessa pushed the door open wider and motioned for Paisley to follow her. Paisley had her weekly therapy appointment that day.

"I do not like going," Paisley confessed as she followed Vanessa out to the car. The dark skinned girl raised an eyebrow, making sure Paisley buckled her seatbelt before they pulled out onto the road.

"Why not?" Vanessa asked. Paisley sighed and shook her head.

"I do not know her," Paisley pulled her legs up to her chest and stared out the window. "She does not know me. Strangers are not friends."

"I get what you mean," Vanessa said honestly. "But she's a doctor, you've got to at least try to let her help you."

"Why do I need help?" Paisley lifted her head and looked over at the older girl. She didn't understand why she needed to go.

"I'm not sure," Vanessa drummed her fingers against the steering wheel. "There's just some things you've got to work on, that's all. Everyone needs to work on some things. You just need a little extra help."

"But not everyone has to go and talk to a stranger," Paisley sighed. This made her feel different. It made her feel stupid. Why was she the only person who needed help?

"That's a lie," Vanessa shrugged. "I have to go after class and get help from my teacher sometimes. It's practically the same thing. It's just I need help with dancing in heels, and you need help with your emotions. It's nothing to be ashamed of."

Paisley nodded slowly. What Vanessa was saying was starting to make sense. But she still couldn't let go of that fact that she felt different. Not the good kind of different, either. The kind of different that made people stare at you when you went out in public.

Once they reached the doctors office, Paisley was led back into the small room. She sat down in the same red chair she had sat in multiple times before. There were a few different chairs in the room, but she chose the red one because it was the furthest away from the therapist's desk.

"How've things been at home, Paisley?" the dark haired woman looked up from her desk. Paisley hung her head down and played with her hands nervously.

"Good," she shrugged and tugged at the beanie on her head. Shiloh had given it to her, she remembered. It was the girl's lucky beanie. As long as Paisley was wearing it, she could do anything.

"What have you been up to since we last met?" the woman tapped her pencil against her desk. The noise made Paisley's anxiety heighten.

"I went to class with Lolo," Paisley remembered, feeling a small smile form on her face.

"Don't you mean Shiloh?" the woman asked. Paisley nodded.

"That is what I said," the smaller girl grew nervous. "Her name is Lolo. Only I can call her that. She is my Lolo."

"Oh," the therapist jotted something down. Paisley didn't like her facial expressions. They worried her.

"I made a friend, too," Paisley blurted out. She knew whenever the woman wrote something down that she had said something wrong. "Two of them."

"You did?" the woman looked up. "Tell me about them."

"They are in Lolo's class. There is a girl named Maia. And her boyfriend is named Toby. He makes things with clay," Paisley looked down at her arm, where Maia had painted the flower. It had washed off in the shower, but there was still a slight shadow where the black paint had been.

"Did you talk to them?"

"Duh," Paisley crinkled her nose and looked up. "I got bored. And I watched them, and they talked to me. They were very nice."

"Do you like having friends besides the ones you live with?" the woman wrote something down quickly.

Paisley thought about this for a moment before shrugging. "I like having friends. It does not matter where they come from."

Her therapist pursed her lips, nodding and scanning the papers in front of her. "Has anything else been happening lately? Anything I should know about?"

Paisley's mind instantly went to the images that had been flashing across her memory for the past week or so. They scared her. But she couldn't say a word about them. She didn't know how people would react.

"I made psh'getti," she giggled to herself, looking up at the woman, who had a stern look on her face. Paisley swallowed the lump in her throat, forcing herself to keep the bad images to herself.

Meanwhile, Shiloh was putting the finishing touches on her butterfly painting. It made her smile each time she looked at it. Paisley had been the one who gave her the idea. She may or may not have added a little bit more yellow to the flowers than she would have normally.

She quickly got up to place her canvas in the back of the room. Most of the students had already left the classroom, class had been dismissed five minutes earlier. A few had stayed behind to catch up on their projects.

"Shiloh, right?"

The green eyed girl jumped when a quiet voice appeared next to her. She quickly regained her composure and looked over at the other girl, tilting her head to the side.

"You wouldn't mind putting this up there for me? I'm short," Maia laughed softly and held up the small canvas in her hands.

"Oh, sure," Shiloh laughed, carefully taking the wet painting out of the girl's hands and placing it on the top shelf of the drying rack. "Maia, right?" she turned back to the girl.

"That's me," the girl wiped her hands on her pants and looked back up. "You're Paisley's girlfriend."

Shiloh nodded with a soft smile. "Yeah," she thought for a moment. "Thanks for being so nice to her the other day. She needed it." A look of soft confusion spread across Maia's face.

"I only talked to her for a few minutes," she chuckled, moving across the room and beginning to wash her brushes in the sink. Shiloh followed and began to do the same.

"Well, yeah. But she's... Paisley. She doesn't make friends easily," Shiloh bit her lip and turned on the faucet of the sink besides Maia's, watching as the bright colors were washed down the drain.

"Why?" Maia inquired. "Is she shy?"

"Hell no," Shiloh laughed and shook her head. "You know what I mean."

"I really don't," Maia looked over and furrowed her eyebrows together. "What *do* you mean?"

"You really can't tell?" Shiloh was surprised. Maia retained her look of confusion and Shiloh bit her lip. "She's actually at the doctor right now. She was in… an accident. There was a lot of brain damage." It made Shiloh's blood boil just thinking about it.

"Her past is horrible," Shiloh shook her head. "So she's pretty… insecure about being around people, I guess. She's afraid they won't like her."

"I couldn't tell," Maia shrugged. "I just figured she was one of those free spirited, artsy types. You get a lot of those in classes like these," she chuckled. "She's cool. I see why you two get along."

"You really couldn't tell?" Shiloh raised an eyebrow. She suddenly felt a wave of guilt wash over her. She'd been defining Paisley by her insecurities this whole time, when Maia couldn't even tell she was any different. What had Shiloh been missing out on?

"I mean, I see it now that you mention it," Maia simply shrugged. "I'm not one to judge," she laughed, motioning to the array of colorful paint stains on her jeans. "We've all got something that makes us different."

"You're sure smarter than I am," Shiloh mumbled and laid her brushes out on a paper towel to dry. "Thanks for making her feel normal."

"No problem," Maia gave Shiloh a soft smile. "Tell her I say hi," she added, slinging her backpack over her shoulder.

"I will," Shiloh nodded once. The girls said their goodbyes. As Shiloh silently packed up her bag, she realized how horribly she'd been viewing Paisley. She'd been letting the girl's weaknesses define her, rather than her strengths. There was so much more to Paisley than just her past.

As she drove home, Shiloh hummed softly to herself. She was always excited to get home and see Paisley, but today felt different. It was like she was going home with a completely different view on the smaller girl. It was refreshing.

The second Shiloh's keys entered the doorknob, the door flew open and Paisley practically tackled Shiloh into a hug. The green eyed girl couldn't help but laugh softly.

"Hey, how was the doctor's?" Shiloh asked, smoothing out Paisley's hair and studying the smaller girl's expression.

"She looks at me weird," Paisley mumbled. "She does not like me." Shiloh's expression softened and she shook her head.

"She's probably so intimidated by you that she doesn't know how to act, that's all," Shiloh shrugged and kissed Paisley's forehead. The smaller girl just sighed and shook her head.

"It was really that bad?" Shiloh asked, noticing Paisley's hesitation. The smaller girl simply nodded, and Shiloh bit her lip. "Why don't you run upstairs and get dressed into something warm, and we'll walk down to the park?" she asked, trying to distract Paisley.

It worked. The smaller girl's face lit up and she nodded excitedly. "I will be right back," she smiled, kissing Shiloh's cheeks before hurrying upstairs. Paisley's excitement made Shiloh laugh.

The green eyed girl laid her backpack down beside the door and headed into the kitchen. She grabbed a water bottle from the refrigerator and jumped when she turned around and nearly ran into Vanessa.

"Shy, can I ask you something?" the other girl said quietly, trying to keep her voice down. Shiloh immediately grew concerned.

"Yeah, what's up?" Shiloh set her water bottle down and leaned against the counter.

"How're things with Paisley?" Vanessa bit her lip, watching as Shiloh grew confused. "I mean, you guys really… haven't *progressed* or anything. Not that it's a bad thing, I was just wondering what you're thinking."

At the same time, Paisley had padded softly down the stairs to grab her shoes from the front door. When she heard her name, she paused and listened quietly behind the wall.

"It's… okay," Shiloh shrugged. Vanessa gazed at her, knowing that Shiloh had more to say.

"I don't want to force anything," Shiloh sighed, admitting what she'd been keeping to herself for a while. "I've just sorta been letting her initiate everything."

"Have you said that you love each other yet?" Vanessa asked, watching as Shiloh's face dropped slightly. The green eyed girl shook her head and shrugged.

"Not yet," she admitted. Meanwhile, Paisley furrowed her eyebrows from her hiding spot, thinking intensely about everything she'd just overheard. Quietly, she hurried back upstairs.

"Why not?" Vanessa leaned against the counter, trying to be careful about how many questions she asked. Shiloh shrugged.

"I don't wanna say it and not have her say it back," Shiloh said softly, running a hand through her hair. She'd been trying to avoid thinking about this.

"You…" Vanessa raised an eyebrow. "You love her?"

"Of course," Shiloh shrugged, looking down at her feet. "She makes it impossible for me not to."

"Then tell her!" Vanessa reached out and squeezed Shiloh's shoulder. "What've you got to lose?"

"Her," Shiloh shook her head. "I'm fine with the way things are. As long as I get to be close to her." She looked up and bit her lip. Vanessa thought about this for a moment before nodding softly.

"I understand where you're coming from," the other girl admitted honestly. "But just... don't cause yourself any harm by keeping your mouth shut, okay?"

Shiloh nodded softly. She grabbed her water bottle from the counter and nudged Vanessa softly. "It'll be fine, don't worry," she reassured the other girl, even though she wasn't quite sure herself.

Vanessa gave Shiloh a soft smile before the other girl jogged upstairs. Shiloh took a sip from her water bottle, pushing the door open with her hip. The second she entered the room, she was practically knocked over by a small blur.

"I love you," Paisley grabbed Shiloh's hands and looked into her eyes hopefully. She wanted those words to make Shiloh happy.

The green eyed girl's eyes widened and she stumbled backwards, nearly running into the wall. She studied Paisley's face for a few moments before she realized what the smaller girl had overheard.

"I..." Shiloh quickly shook her head and pulled them both into the room, closing the door behind them. "You don't have to say it if you don't mean it. I know you don't mean it."

Paisley's face dropped and she looked away from Shiloh, tugging frantically at the beanie on her head. She mumbled something to herself that Shiloh couldn't understand, and before the green eyed girl could say anything else, Paisley turned around and hurried over to the bookshelf in the corner of the room.

Shiloh stood frozen as Paisley began pulling books off of the shelves, opening them and paging through them. She huffed in frustration, obviously not finding what she needed.

"Pais," Shiloh stepped forward, finally regaining her voice. "Paisley." She grabbed the small girl's arm to stop her from trashing the entire bookshelf. Paisley's eyes shot up and met Shiloh's and she quickly shook her head.

"What are you doing?" Shiloh asked worriedly. Paisley mumbled something quietly once again, slithering out of Shiloh's grip and grabbing another book off the bookshelf.

"Paisley," Shiloh grabbed the smaller girl's shoulders and pulled her away. "You're making a mess, what's going on?" Paisley whimpered and looked down at the pile of books by their feet.

"I need a word book," Paisley said quietly, avoiding eye contact with Shiloh. "I need to find one."

"A what?" Shiloh scanned the books on her shelf and slowly realized what Paisley was looking for. "Why do you need a dictionary?"

"I need to learn about love," Paisley took a step backwards, ashamed of her words. She fiddled with her thumbs nervously, anxious to get back to the bookshelf and find a dictionary. But Shiloh had moved in front of the wall to block her.

"You can't learn about that kind of stuff from a dictionary," Shiloh shook her head, taking a step towards Paisley. The smaller girl held her breath.

"You can not?" Paisley asked hesitantly. Shiloh shook her head.

"Everyone knows what love is," the green eyed girl shrugged. "Even you."

"I do?" Paisley whispered. She didn't. At least, she didn't think she did. "I do?" she repeated, looking up at Shiloh pleadingly.

A sudden realization washed over Shiloh and her eyes widened. "Do you, Paisley?" she asked quietly, bringing her hand up to toy with her bottom lip.

"No one has taught me," Paisley mumbled, tugging on her beanie. "I have not…" she shook her head and walked over to the bed. "I have not seen it. I do not know… I do not know."

Shiloh felt her heart physically shatter, for more than one reason. She took a step forwards, watching as Paisley crawled onto the bed and hugged a pillow to her chest.

"Love can't be taught, Paisley," Shiloh sighed, shaking her head and looking down at the ground. "It's just... *there*. You just know."

"Oh," Paisley whispered, deep in thought. She looked up at Shiloh, just as the dark haired girl walked towards the door.

"I... I need to go help Nessa with dinner," Shiloh said softly, tugging on the door handle. "I'll call you down when it's ready." She bit her lip, fleeing the room before Paisley could protest. Before Paisley could see the tears fall.

Paisley flinched when the door shut. She shook her head, squeezing her eyes shut.

"Stupid," she mumbled, shaking her head. She should know what love is. Shiloh wanted her to know, she could tell. She was stupid for not knowing. She buried herself under the covers and tried to take a deep breath.

"You should know," she whispered, curling up in a ball and burying her head in her legs. Everyone knew. Everyone but her. She didn't want to disappoint Shiloh. But even more importantly, she wanted to know. She craved to know what this foreign feeling was.

She reached up, tugging at the blue beanie on her head. And then suddenly, she was met with an overwhelming sense of familiarity. In flashes of black and white, a flood of memories hit her like a train.

CHAPTER 8

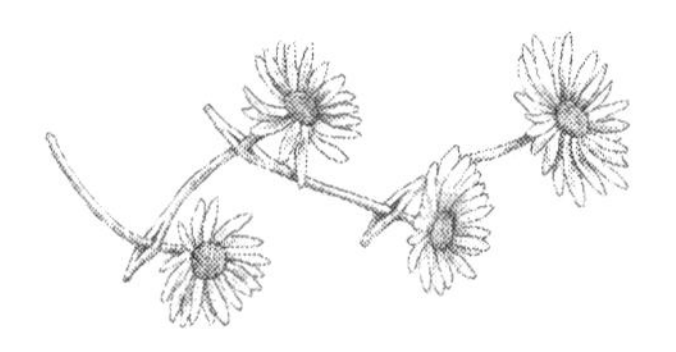

"It's cold, mija!" the woman called after her. Paisley turned around, looking down at the snow underneath her boots and crinkling her nose.

"But I wanna go sledding!" the smaller girl protested, turning around and looking up at the sky. She caught a snowflake on her tongue and smiled happily to herself.

"Is it that obvious that she's never seen snow before?" her mother laughed and turned to her father, who was tugging on his own boots. Paisley's parents stood on the front porch of their cabin at the ski lodge. Paisley was knee deep in snow a feet few away from them.

"You need a jacket, silly," her mother laughed, motioning to Paisley to join them on the porch. Huffing, the smaller girl trudged back through the snow and hopped onto the wooden steps.

"But it's not cold," Paisley protested, just as a swift breeze caused her to shiver. Her mother simply laughed and ushered the younger girl into the front room of the cabin.

"You'll be cold, trust me," the dark haired woman chuckled. She grabbed the pastel yellow coat from the hanger by the door. Paisley allowed her to help her slip into the jacket, wiggling her arms when she realized the sleeves were slightly too long.

"Where does snow come from?" Paisley asked, sitting down on the small bench by the door and gazing longingly out the window.

"It's just really cold rain," her mother laughed and knelt down in front of the small girl, smoothing out her hair and gently slipping a yellow beanie onto her head. Paisley smiled, tugging the material down and turning to look at her reflection in the window.

"At least we know we won't lose you," her father laughed, appearing in the doorway. Paisley looked up and giggled, clasping her hands together.

"Can we go sledding now?" she asked pleadingly, pressing her palms against the cold glass.

"Whatever you want, kiddo," her father laughed and ruffled her hair. Paisley gasped playfully, bringing her hands up to her head to fix her beanie. Both of her parents laughed.

"Can we bring some snow home?" the smaller girl asked, hopping down the front steps of the cabin and stomping her boots in the snow. She was fascinated by the white flakes slowly drifting down from the sky.

"It'll all melt in the Florida heat," her mother laughed. Paisley pouted and hopped into a snow bank, giggling when she practically sunk knee-deep in the snow.

"I'm stuck!" she cried dramatically, falling backwards and gazing up at the sky. She narrowed her eyes, suddenly growing distracted by the flakes falling from the sky.

"Look!" Paisley pointed upwards. "Look at the snow!"

"What about it, mija?"

"It's just so... beautiful," the child breathed out, in awe by the image above her. "Mommy, come lay down and look up." Moments later, she was joined by both of her parents, lying back in the snow next to her and gazing up at the sky.

"You're right," her mother laughed, reaching over and wiping the snow off of her daughter's face.

"This is so much better than rain," Paisley giggled, bringing her hands above her head and trying to catch snowflakes on her mittens. "This is the best day ever."

"Ever?" her father raised an eyebrow. Paisley giggled and copied him, tilting her head to the side.

"Yeah, ever," she confirmed. She stuck her tongue out and caught a snowflake before resting her head back on the snow and sighing softly. "Thank you."

"For what, mija?"

"For being the coolest parents ever," Paisley giggled. She sat up and tugged her beanie back onto her head.

"Thanks for being the coolest daughter ever," her mother laughed and helped Paisley fix the material on her head. "We love you very much, Paisley."

"I know," Paisley laughed, rolling her eyes playfully. "You tell me all the time."

"We just wanna make sure you don't forget, that's all," the woman laughed and smoothed out her daughter's hair.

"I love you more," Paisley looked back and forth between her parents. "More than... more than mac and cheese." Both of her parents gasped in fake shock, causing Paisley to giggle incessantly.

"I never wanna grow up," Paisley sighed, looking up at the sky. Little did she know, she'd be forced to grow up drastically in the next few days.

Paisley frantically wiped her eyes, trying to understand the images that she'd just seen. That was her. It was real. She quickly scrambled out from under the blankets and hurried over to the mirror. This was her.

And suddenly, she realized what Shiloh had been saying all along. She couldn't be taught what love was. She already knew. She remembered.

Shiloh.

Paisley balled her hands into fists and looked at her reflection. She loved Shiloh. She knew she did. Except it was different. A good kind of different. She loved Shiloh in a completely different way than she loved her parents.

She needed to tell her.

Paisley quickly scrambled to open the door, running down the hallway and practically falling down the stairs into the living room. Vanessa looked up quickly from her place on the couch.

"Where is Lolo?" Paisley looked around frantically. She had to tell her. She was scared she would forget again.

"She said she was going for a drive," Vanessa raised an eyebrow. "Why? What's going on?"

Paisley was already out the door by the time Vanessa finished her sentence. The older girl hopped to her feet to follow her, but Paisley was nowhere to be seen.

Meanwhile, Shiloh had finally calmed herself down enough to start the car. Just as she was about to pull out of her parking spot, there was a frantic knocking at her window. Shiloh jumped, whipping her head to the side and biting her lip when she saw Paisley tapping on the window repeatedly.

Hesitantly, Shiloh rolled down the window after wiping her eyes. "What?" she asked softly, scared of what was about to happen. Paisley shook her head and reached inside the car window, running her fingers across the older girl's jawline.

"I remember," Paisley looked into Shiloh's eyes hopefully, retracting her hand and tugging on her beanie anxiously. "I remember love. I know it."

"I—," Shiloh opened her mouth to speak but Paisley jumped forwards and cupped her hand over the older girl's mouth.

"I know what it is," Paisley continued pleadingly. "I know what I love. I love flowers, and friends, and the sky, and the stars, and music, and warm blankets, and the sky when it turns pink, and yellow, and..."

Shiloh bit her lip and looked down at her hands, trying to hide her disappointment. She hadn't meant to get her hopes up. But she was hoping to have been at the top of Paisley's list.

"But you are my favorite."

Shiloh lifted her head slowly at Paisley's next words, growing confused. Paisley reached out and ran her thumb over Shiloh's bottom lip.

"My favorite love, Lolo," she said quietly. "I love you the most, I know."

Shiloh's breath got caught in her throat and she struggled to find her words. Just as she opened her mouth to respond, there was an ear piercing screech from behind them and then the sound of metal clashing against metal. Both girls whipped their heads around.

Shiloh's eyes widened when she saw the two cars collide in the street behind them. She sat frozen for a moment, watching the smoke clear around the two vehicles. By the time she turned her head back around, Paisley was gone.

She saw a glimpse of the smaller girl's figure disappear behind the back of the apartment building. Without any hesitation, she sprinted out of her car and after the smaller girl.

She rounded the back of the building. When she caught sight of Paisley, she picked up her speed and grabbed the smaller girl by the wrist. Paisley panicked, trying to pull away, but Shiloh kept a firm grip on her. The green eyed girl grabbed Paisley's shoulders and pushed her back against the wall, trying to calm her down.

"Paisley," Shiloh brought her hands up to the smaller girl's face and cupped her cheeks. "Paisley, look at me," she tilted the smaller girl's head. Paisley had her eyes squeezed shut and tried to bring her hands up to cover her face.

The smaller girl opened her eyes hesitantly. The moment brown eyes met green, Paisley burst into tears and practically fell into Shiloh's arms.

"Th-that could have been y-you," Paisley managed between sobs. Shiloh felt her heart drop in her chest and she quickly shook her head.

"But it wasn't," the green eyed girl wrapped her arms around Paisley and held the younger girl close to her chest. "I'm right here."

Paisley just continued to cry into Shiloh's shoulder, balling her hands into the back of the older girl's shirt and clinging onto her for dear life. Shiloh felt her heart physically shatter into a million pieces.

"You're okay, Paisley, I've got you," Shiloh whispered, running her hands through Paisley's hair in an attempt to soothe the smaller girl. Paisley took a deep breath, but tensed when she heard the sound of police sirens in the distance.

"Okay, c'mon," Shiloh kept her arms around Paisley, starting to lead them towards the back entrance of the apartment. Paisley kept her hands tight in Shiloh's shirt, not wanting to let her go.

Slowly but surely, they made their way back up to their apartment. Shiloh led the smaller girl into the front room. Paisley glanced around nervously the entire time. Shiloh couldn't remember ever seeing her this terrified.

Vanessa and Ryland both jumped up from the couch, looks of concern washing over both of their faces. The sudden movement made Paisley reel backwards, tightening her grip on Shiloh.

'Don't' Shiloh mouthed, shaking her head at the other girls. They got the message, but they couldn't help but be confused at the sudden change in Paisley. They stepped out of the way as Shiloh led the smaller girl upstairs and into her bedroom.

She sat Paisley down on the bed, kneeling down in front of the girl and taking both of her hands in her own.

"Pais, breathe," Shiloh whispered. Paisley took a deep breath in, but gasped when she heard the sirens directly outside the apartment. Shiloh shot up, pulling the curtains shut and looking around the room quickly.

She quickly headed over to her iHome, plugging in her phone and putting her music on shuffle. *'Pressure'* by The 1975 quickly filled the room and Shiloh turned it up slightly, so the sirens could barely be heard.

"C'mere," she whispered, hurrying back over to the bed and sitting down next to Paisley, pulling her into her lap. Paisley practically collapsed into her arms, wrapping her arms around her neck and trying to take deep breaths to calm herself down.

Shiloh couldn't stand seeing Paisley this scared. She glanced around the room, her eyes landing on the blankets on the bed.

"We're safe under here," Shiloh said softly, pulling Paisley back on the bed and pulling the covers over them. Laying on her back, she bit her lip as Paisley practically climbed on top of her and snaked her arms up the sleeves of her hoodie.

"You're here, Paisley," Shiloh said softly, running her fingers up and down the girl's arm. "You're safe. You're alive. You're breathing. I've got you."

"Promise?" Paisley's shaky voice finally filled the room. Shiloh nodded and found Paisley's hand in the dark, locking their pinkies together.

Shiloh sang softly along with the song, feeling Paisley's breathing begin to slow down. She reached up and ran her fingers through the girl's hair, humming the last few lines of the song quietly.

"Are you okay?" Shiloh asked softly after a few moments of silence. Paisley shivered, lifting her head and studying Shiloh's face. The green eyed girl reached out to wipe the tears from under Paisley's eyes, allowing her thumbs to linger against Paisley's smooth skin.

"I love you," Paisley whispered, reaching up and placing her hand on top of Shiloh's. "You make it easy."

"I... what?" Shiloh nearly choked on thin air. Paisley sniffed and rolled over, curling up against Shiloh's side and nodding.

"I do," the smaller girl said softly. "I love you."

Shiloh's heart fluttered. Something about the way Paisley said this was different. A good kind of different. She took a deep breath and tried to hold onto the happiness she felt in that moment.

"I love you, too," the green eyed girl turned slightly so she could see Paisley's face under the blankets. The smaller girl's eyes widened, as if she hadn't been expecting that response.

"You... you do?" Paisley lifted her head and looked at Shiloh in confusion. The green eyed girl raised an eyebrow.

"Of course I do," she whispered, growing confused at the smaller girl's confusion. "I figured it was pretty obvious."

"I..." Paisley looked down at her hands. She wasn't sure how to receive this. She didn't understand the floating feeling in her stomach, or the blush that slowly spread across her cheeks. This wasn't something she was used to.

"I love your sleepy smile when you wake up in the morning, even though I'm the furthest thing from a morning person," Shiloh continued, pulling Paisley even closer to her and running her fingers through her hair.

"I love your compassion for everyone and everything around you. I love the way your voice gets all raspy when you're sleepy. I love your affection for all things yellow," she giggled, kissing Paisley's temple. "I love all the things that make you, you. But most importantly, I love you. Just you."

Silence fell over them for a few moments before Paisley turned slightly to get a better view of Shiloh.

"Thank you," the younger girl whispered. She reached out and traced her fingers across Shiloh's jawline.

"You don't have to thank me for loving you," Shiloh laughed softly. Paisley shook her head, trying to correct her.

"No," Paisley retracted her hand, only to find Shiloh's and lace their fingers together. "Thank you for showing it to me."

Shiloh's breath caught in her throat. For someone who wasn't expected to have normal speech patterns, Paisley sure had a way with words. Maybe it was her blatant innocence. She felt tears well up in her eyes.

Paisley instantly grew concerned when Shiloh pulled her hand away to wipe her eyes. "Why are you crying?" Paisley sat up slightly. "Did I do something bad?"

"No," Shiloh quickly shook her head. "No, Pais, of course not." She swallowed hard, trying to think of a way to explain her feelings to the smaller girl. "I just…" she paused to take a deep breath.

"I've never been in love with someone. I never expected to fall in love with anyone, really. I just didn't think that's what the universe had planned for me," she confessed, feeling Paisley's small hand find hers under the blankets.

"But then you showed up at our door one day and changed everything for me," Shiloh smiled softly, using her free hand to wipe the tears that had fallen from her eyes. "And I didn't even realize it at the time, but every little thing you did made me fall more and more in love with you."

Paisley's lips slowly curved into a smile and she wrapped her arms around Shiloh, nuzzling her head into the crook of her neck. "I love you, Lo," she whispered. "I do not have the words to tell you why. I just do." When Shiloh didn't reply, Paisley lifted her head.

"I do, Lolo, I do. I mean it," she said quickly, hoping Shiloh didn't think she was lying. Shiloh raised an eyebrow.

"I believe you," the green eyed girl whispered, pulling Paisley back down against her. "I'm just... I didn't realize how amazing it would feel to hear you say that."

"You get the butterflies too?" Paisley reached up and twirled a piece of Shiloh's hair around her finger. Shiloh laughed quietly.

"All the time," she whispered, sighing contently. She hadn't realized the relief that came with knowing that Paisley loved her. She loved Paisley, Paisley loved her. Simple as that.

Shiloh giggled when the brown eyed girl next to her yawned softly. She raised an eyebrow and smiled at Paisley. "Do you want me to sing?" she asked, watching as Paisley's lips curved into a smile.

"Only for me?" the smaller girl asked innocently. Shiloh nodded.

"Only for you," she whispered.

Paisley looked up slowly when Shiloh's voice softened and eventually disappeared completely. She was confused at first, but quickly realized the green eyed girl had fallen asleep. Smiling widely, Paisley wiggled out of her grip and sat up slightly, studying Shiloh's peaceful form.

"I love you, Lo," Paisley whispered, being careful not to wake the girl. She kissed the tips of her fingers, pressing them gently against Shiloh's lips. After a few moments of silence, Paisley leaned down and planted a kiss on Shiloh's forehead.

She smiled softly, not wanting to take her eyes off of the older girl that she was so infatuated with. She really did love her, she realized. It was a new, exciting feeling. Yet it already felt so comfortable.

She wiggled out from under the blankets, carefully adjusting them over both of their bodies. Making sure Shiloh was warm enough, Paisley sang softly while she straightened out the blankets around them.

Paisley quietly sung the words she'd heard Shiloh sing before. She continued singing the same line, the only one she could remember well.

Her singing soon turned to soft humming once she had tucked them both in to her liking. She curled up in Shiloh's side and snaked her hands up the sleeves of the green eyed girl's hoodie, making sure she could hold onto her all night.

"I really do love you," Paisley mumbled, nuzzling her head into the crook of the older girl's neck. "Very much." She closed her eyes slowly, feeling waves of exhaustion wash over her. The small girl feel asleep quickly in the comfort of Shiloh's arms.

CHAPTER 9

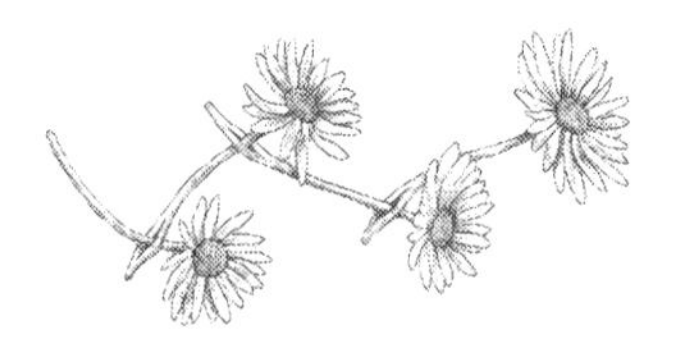

Shiloh woke up to a beam of sun streaming across the bedsheets, practically blinding her. She groaned, rolling over and reaching out for the smaller girl next to her. When all her hand found was a clump of blankets, she grew confused.

The green eyed girl groggily sat up, wiping her eyes and looking around the room. There was no sign of Paisley. Her mind instantly thought back to the night before, to what they'd confessed to one another. Shiloh's heart stopped.

Was it too much for Paisley? Had she gotten up and left in the middle of the night? Anxiety boiled in Shiloh's veins and she quickly threw the blankets off of her legs, hurrying down the hallway to confirm her greatest fear.

She let out a sigh of relief when she found Paisley's white converse in the same spot they had been the night before, at the bottom of the stairs. Just as she was about to call out for the girl, she heard a groan of frustration echoing from the kitchen.

Shiloh moved forward slowly, listening for a moment.

"Now add one forth of a cup of oil and—,"

"No!" Paisley huffed, tapping on the iPad and rewinding the video. Shiloh peered out from behind the wall, watching the small girl in her pajamas studying the iPad intensely.

"Add one tablespoon of salt," the voice rang out from the iPad. Paisley groaned, pausing the video and looking around the kitchen slowly. Her eyebrows furrowed together in annoyance.

"There is no spoon on the table, I told you!" she mumbled, shaking her head and pressing her palms on the counter. She picked up the empty bowl, holding it up and eyeing it suspiciously. This wasn't turning out the way she thought it would.

She started the video over, watching as the woman added a cup of flour into the bowl. A cup. One cup. That sounded familiar. Paisley walked over to the cabinets, finding the yellow cup she usually drank out of and padding back over to the counter.

Before she could scoop it into the container of flour, though, Shiloh quickly scooted out from behind the wall and caught her attention.

"That's not the kind of cup they're talking about," Shiloh laughed softly, walking over to Paisley and opening one of the drawers. She pulled out a measuring cup and handed it to the smaller girl.

Paisley's shoulders dropped when Shiloh appeared. This was supposed to be a surprise. And now she'd ruined it, because she couldn't follow the simple instructions in the video. Shiloh noticed this.

"Hey, hey it's okay, cooking is never easy," Shiloh ran her hand down Paisley's arm and squeezed her hand. "Following a video is pretty hard too. You can never keep up with them."

Paisley shook her head and took a step backwards. "I was trying to make you a surprise," she admitted, sighing heavily. The smaller girl turned back to the iPad, slamming her hands down on the island.

"You lied about the tablespoons!" she shook the iPad, groaning in frustration. Shiloh bit her lip, grabbing Paisley's hand before she broke something valuable.

"Pais, it's fine," Shiloh laughed softly and shook her head. "It's no big deal. I appreciate the effort, though." She gave Paisley a comforting smile.

"No," Paisley pulled away from Shiloh and began pacing back and forth. "I am broken, this is not normal. I am bad. I can not do this. I should be able to do this."

Shiloh opened her mouth to speak but Paisley continued pacing in circles around the island, mumbling to herself. Growing frustrated, Shiloh slammed her hands down on the counter.

"You don't need to be fixed, Paisley! You aren't broken!"

The smaller girl jumped backwards, staring at Shiloh with wide eyes. The older girl's outburst was unexpected. She took a few steps away from Shiloh and brought her hands up in front of her face.

"Pl—,"

"No," Shiloh cut her off quickly, immediately regretting her actions. "No, no, I'm sorry," she shook her head, crossing the room quickly and grabbing Paisley's hands. "I didn't mean to scare you, it's okay. I'm sorry," she pulled Paisley into a hug gently.

"I am sorry," Paisley shook her head, feeling Shiloh's hand rubbing soothing circles in her back. "I made a mess," she added quietly, pulling away and pointing to the counter.

Shiloh refused to look where Paisley was looking. Instead, she stepped to the side to block her line of sight and placed both hands on the smaller girl's shoulders.

"It doesn't matter," she shook her head and took a deep breath. "I just get… frustrated sometimes. I want you to see yourself the way that I see you."

"No," Paisley shook her head and quickly dodged around Shiloh, running over to the cabinets and grabbing a plate in each hand. She started making her way back to the counter, but Shiloh moved to try and block her.

Paisley attempted to move out of the way, but ended up tripping backwards. One of the plates slipped out of her hand and fell to the floor, shattering into pieces. She gasped, instantly sliding down to her knees and trying to piece the porcelain back together.

"Paisley."

The smaller girl ignored Shiloh, wiping her eyes and using her shaky hands to try and line up the broken pieces.

"Pais."

Shiloh bit her lip as she watched Paisley struggle to stay calm. The smaller girl's knuckles were growing white due to her strong grip on the sharp pieces. Shiloh took a deep breath.

"You're killing the flowers, Paisley."

That caught her attention. Paisley whipped her head up, glancing at Shiloh in confusion. "I am… what?" she tilted her head to the side like a confused puppy.

"You're killing the flowers," Shiloh repeated, bending down slowly and kneeling next to Paisley. She reached up and slowly cupped the side of Paisley's face, running her thumb across her forehead.

"There's flowers in your brain," she explained, using her free hand to lace their fingers together. "You hurt them when you're mean to yourself."

"I do?" Paisley whispered, looking down at her hands and then back up at Shiloh.

"You've got beautiful flowers in your mind, Paisley," Shiloh said softly. She used her free hand to push the broken plate out of the way and sat cross legged, tugging on Paisley's hand until the smaller girl did the same.

"They're pretty flowers, too. In all different colors," she squeezed Paisley's hand. "Even yellow."

"And blue?" Paisley tilted her head to the side.

"And blue," Shiloh confirmed with a soft laugh. "Just like me and you." Paisley nodded quietly, looking down at her hands.

"When you're nice to yourself, you give the flowers water and sunshine. They can grow big and tall and soak up all the sun they need. And people will see just how beautiful they are," Shiloh continued, running her thumb over the back of Paisley's hand absentmindedly. "But when you're hard on yourself, and say mean things about yourself, which are untrue — you're stepping on the flowers and hurting them."

Paisley's face dropped slightly and she reached up to place her hand on Shiloh's forehead. "Do you have them too?"

"Of course," Shiloh nodded, placing her hand on top of Paisley's and moving both of their hands to press against Paisley's forehead. "We all do. There's an endless garden of thoughts and feelings in our bodies, and we have to make sure we treat them nicely."

"Oh," Paisley nodded softly. She was slowly beginning to understand what Shiloh was trying to convey to her. "Are you nice to your flowers?"

"I try to be," Shiloh admitted, squeezing Paisley's hand. "Sometimes it's really hard, though. Cause they don't grow as fast as I want them to. But wanna know a secret?" Paisley thought for a moment before nodding.

"What do you do in a day, Paisley?" Shiloh asked, scooting forward slightly so their knees were touching. A look of confusion spread across Paisley's face, but she looked down at the ground and thought intently.

"I wake up. And I get dressed. And spend time with you. Sometimes I watch *Friends*," Paisley said quietly. "Why?"

"That doesn't seem like much to you, does it?" Shiloh continued, choosing to ignore Paisley's question at the moment. Furrowing her eyebrows, the smaller girl nodded slowly.

"But now, think about what you can do in a week," Shiloh glanced over at the door. "Remember when you used to always struggle with unlocking the door, and you'd get mad at yourself because you couldn't get the key to fit?"

Paisley crinkled her nose at the memory, remembering how bad she had felt. She nodded.

"But every day, I still made you try to unlock it. And little by little, it got easier for you. And now, you don't even have to think about it, do you?" Shiloh smiled softly when she saw a look of realization cross Paisley's face.

"But it took time. You don't see the progress you make in a day, even though you do make progress. Little by little. And then you look back, and you realize why everything happened the way it did. You just don't know it at the time," Shiloh laughed softly to herself. "It can be kind of annoying sometimes, because everyone wants change right away. But it's always worth the wait."

"Like Leah and the laundry," Paisley giggled softly at her memory. Shiloh grew confused.

"Me and Leah did the laundry. And she could not reach the orange… spray stuff," Paisley explained, pretending to spray the bottle with her fingers. "So next time, she used a stool. So she could be tall."

Shiloh laughed softly and nodded. "Exactly. We all adapt eventually. But wanna know another secret?" Paisley nodded excitedly.

"Flowers grow better in groups," the green eyed girl reached out and tucked a loose strand of hair behind Paisley's ear. "When flowers grow together, they can hold each other up."

"There's nothing wrong with asking for help, Paisley," Shiloh said softly, running her thumb over the brown eyed girl's cheek. "No one expects you to do anything but try."

A few moments of silence passed between them as Paisley looked down and thought over Shiloh's words. Everything slowly came together and she looked up shyly.

"Can you help me?" the brown eyed girl studied Shiloh's face, glancing at the broken plate beside them.

"It would be an honor," Shiloh giggled, kissing Paisley's forehead. "I'm very proud of you, by the way," she whispered, before pulling back and pushing herself up to her feet. She offered Paisley her hand, helping the smaller girl up.

"Let's clean this up first," Shiloh said, bending down and pulling a trash bag out of the bottom drawers. "What were you trying to make?" she asked.

"Waffles," Paisley said softly, pointing to the iPad. "I can not do it," she sighed, hanging her head down. She felt Shiloh's eyes on her and looked up slowly.

"I mean… I can do it," she whispered, shaking her head. "With help." She couldn't help but smile when Shiloh did the same.

"There we go," Shiloh laughed, kissing Paisley's cheek. "I'll show you how to make them, so maybe next time you can try more on your own. Sound good?"

"Yes, thank you," Paisley smiled. "You're welcome."

"Hold this open for me," Shiloh instructed, handing Paisley the trash bag and kneeling down. She carefully picked up the shards of the plate and tossed them into the bag one by one.

"You can water other people's flowers too," Paisley said abruptly, interrupting the comfortable silence between them. Shiloh stood up, wiping her hands on her pajama pants and tilting her head to the side.

"If you are nice to people, you can help their flowers," Paisley continued as Shiloh took the bag from her and tied it off. "You have helped my flowers before."

Shiloh giggled, feeling butterflies in her stomach. "You've helped mine, too. You bring the sunshine," she smiled when Paisley crinkled her nose playfully.

"But you have to remember that at the end of the day, only you are in charge of taking care of yourself. No one else can do it all for you," Shiloh said softly. "But they can hold you up until you learn to do it on your own."

"I can learn?" Paisley asked quietly. "And you will stay?"

"You can learn," Shiloh reiterated her words. "And I will stay. Always."

"You and me," Paisley smiled, hopping forwards and kissing Shiloh's cheek.

"Me and you," Shiloh laughed and wrapped an arm around Paisley's waist, leading her over to the island.

"The first step to making waffles is to turn on the waffle iron and let it heat up," the older girl explained, studying Paisley's response.

"I know where that is," Paisley smiled proudly, padding over to the cabinet and returning with the circular device. She placed it on the island and looked at Shiloh for approval before plugging it in.

"See? You already know what you're doing," Shiloh laughed, retrieving the box of mix from the pantry and setting it on the island. She turned the box of waffle mix over, scanning the instructions.

"It calls for one cup of the mix," Shiloh said before sliding it over to Paisley. The smaller girl furrowed her eyebrows and gazed at the box.

"Aunt Je-nine-ma," Paisley mumbled, holding the box closer to her face. "John Ja'myma," she shook her head and giggled. "That is not it," she bit her lip, looking up at Shiloh.

"Aunt Jemima," Shiloh corrected her, surprised that Paisley wasn't getting frustrated with herself.

"Yes, that," Paisley smiled softly and tore open the top of the box, pulling out the bag of mix and looking at Shiloh. "Now what?"

Shiloh handed Paisley the measuring cup and pointed to the bag. "That's one cup. Measure it out and dump it…" she placed the bowl in front of Paisley. "In there."

Paisley nodded, struggling to open the clear bag. Shiloh took a step forward to help her, but Paisley held out a hand to stop her. She set the bag down and retrieved a pair of scissors from the drawer beside her. The smaller girl smiled proudly when she opened the seal, scooping out a cup of flour and dumping it into the bowl.

They carried on like this for the next few minutes, until all that was left was two eggs. Paisley knew. She bit her lip nervously and watched as Shiloh retrieved the yellow foam carton from the refrigerator.

"It's easy once you get the hang of it," Shiloh said, sensing Paisley's anxiousness. She handed the girl one of the eggs and gave her a supportive smile. "Go ahead."

Turning the egg around in her hands, Paisley took a deep breath and attempted to crack the egg against the side of the bowl. The shell cracked, but she had such a tight grip on the egg that it completely crumpled in her fist. She whimpered and quickly brought her other hand to cup the gross substance that had dripped on the counter.

"Hey, hey, it's okay," Shiloh quickly said, grabbing a paper towel and stepping forwards. She led a quiet Paisley over to the sink, turning on the faucet and bringing her hands under the stream of water.

"I messed up," Paisley sighed as Shiloh dried their hands off with a paper towel. Surprisingly, Shiloh just shrugged and pulled her back over to the island.

"Just be gentle this time," she handed Paisley another egg. The brown eyed girl looked at her in shock.

"Again?" Paisley asked, holding up the egg. Shiloh nodded almost immediately.

"Practice makes perfect," the green eyed girl smiled. "Once it has a little crack, use your thumbs to split it over the bowl." She moved behind Paisley, placing her hands on top of the smaller girl's to guide her fingers.

"All you have to do is tap it..." she whispered, moving their hands and gently tapping the shell against the side of the bowl. "Until it cracks."

"It cracked," Paisley said softly, moving her finger slightly to motion to the jagged line on the front of the egg.

"See?" Shiloh smiled, pushing Paisley's thumbs towards the center. "Now just press down until it cracks more, and pull them apart."

Paisley nodded. Taking a deep breath, she pressed her fingers down slowly. As soon as the crack grew, she carefully pulled the two halves of the egg apart, allowing the inside of the egg to fall into the bowl.

"There you go," Shiloh smiled, grabbing a paper towel and giving it to Paisley. "Told you that you could do it."

"I did it," Paisley whispered, smiling widely.

"One more," Shiloh grabbed another egg, moving her hands to guide Paisley's once more. Surprisingly, Paisley stopped her, taking the egg out of her hands.

"I can do it," Paisley smiled shyly. She was somewhat afraid that Shiloh would react poorly, but surprisingly Shiloh took a step back and leaned against the counter.

"Well then let's see you do it," the green eyed girl smiled. Paisley took a deep breath before tapping the egg against the side of the bowl. Another deep breath. Moments later, she was holding an empty eggshell in her hands.

"I did it!" she smiled widely, carefully turning to throw the shell away. "I did it, Lo."

"You did," Shiloh laughed softly and kissed her forehead. "I told you so."

They carried on like this until Paisley was holding up a plate next to Shiloh, watching as the green eyed girl pried each waffle out of the iron with a fork. She plopped them onto the plate in Paisley's hand until the iron was empty.

"And there you have it," Shiloh imitated the woman's voice in the video Paisley had been watching. "That concludes cooking class with Ms. Everest."

Paisley giggled and set the plate down. "You are crazy," she teased, moving forwards and standing on her tiptoes so she could plant a kiss on Shiloh's lips.

"Morning, lovebirds."

Both girls jumped when Ryland appeared in the kitchen. They watched as the light haired girl's eyes widened when she looked at the counter next to them.

"Ooh, waffles!" Ryland clapped her hands. "Just what I needed." Before either girl could argue, the plate was snatched from the counter and Ryland was already adding syrup on top of her breakfast.

The dark haired girlfriends turned to look at each other, erupting into laugher moments later.

"I guess this calls for a second batch," Shiloh laughed, running a hand through her messy morning hair. Paisley nodded quickly.

"I can do the eggs!" she exclaimed, padding back over to the counter and smiling widely.

C H A P T E R 1 0

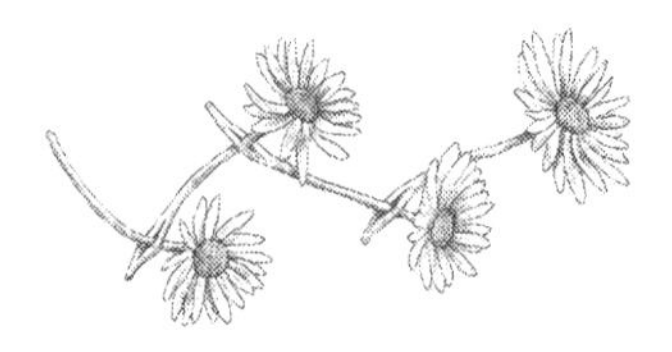

"Do you think Maia will be there today?" Paisley asked, hurrying to catch up with Shiloh as they made their way towards the front of the school building. It was now the first week of February, and things had been running pretty smoothly for them.

With the exception of Paisley and Maia's growing friendship.

"She's always there," Shiloh shrugged. She couldn't help but be jealous. Shiloh was well aware that she couldn't have Paisley *all* to herself. But she was also scared that Paisley could easily replace her.

"Oh," Paisley giggled, finding Shiloh's hand and kicking a pebble as they walked. "I like her. She is funny."

"I know. You told me already," Shiloh mumbled, pushing through the large doors of the building. Paisley grew confused at her abrupt change in mood, but quickly scrambled to follow her into the classroom.

"Hey, Paisley!" one of the boys waved to her. Paisley smiled and padded over to him, bumping her fist and making an exploding noise. In the classes she had been present in, she'd somehow managed to make friends with almost every student in the room. Shiloh watched bitterly for a few moments.

In some ways, the green eyed girl was proud of the fact that Paisley was branching out. And granted, she should be happy that Paisley was making progress. But with her progress came Shiloh's worry. She wished it was easier for her to protect Paisley. But now, the smaller girl needed her freedom.

Paisley greeted a group of students before quickly scanning the room and hurrying back to Shiloh's side.

"What are you painting?" Paisley asked, pulling a stool up next to Shiloh. The green eyed girl was staring absentmindedly at a blank canvas.

"I don't know yet," Shiloh shrugged, looking down at the palette of paints in her hand. "What should I paint?"

"Hmm," Paisley leaned forward and rested her chin on Shiloh's shoulder so she could study the canvas up close. "Paint a tiger."

"A tiger?" Shiloh raised an eyebrow. "I don't know how..."

"You can do it," Paisley smiled and kissed Shiloh's cheek. Shiloh sighed and shook her head.

"Only for you," she whispered softly, knowing she couldn't resist the smaller girl. Paisley clasped her hands together and smiled widely.

"I love you," she hummed, leaning in and kissing Shiloh's cheek before disappearing across the room. Shiloh bit her lip, looking down at her paints and then up at the canvas.

Meanwhile, Paisley smiled happily as she made her way over to Maia's table. The girl seemed focused on something, so Paisley quietly pulled up a stool next to her. She watched for a minute or two, tugging at the signature beanie on her head.

"Paisley, look," Toby took a large lump of clay, holding it above his head and letting it fall down to the table. It landed with a *plop*, flattening out slightly. Paisley jumped, but laughed once she realized it wasn't harmful.

"Wanna try?" Toby tore off a small chunk of clay. Paisley nodded as he rolled the material across the table, but Maia reached out to stop him before Paisley could get her hands on it.

"Let's not make a huge mess. You already make enough for all of us," she laughed, setting down her paintbrush and motioning to the excess clay covering his clothing. Paisley furrowed her eyebrows.

"But I want to try," she said quietly, pointing to the clay and then looking at Maia hopefully. The other girl thought for a moment before standing up, signaling for Paisley to wait before disappearing in the back of the room.

"I do not understand," Paisley turned back to Toby, who chuckled to himself.

"Neither do I," he laughed, rolling the clay between his hands and shaping it with some sort of wooden tool. "She's crazy."

Paisley giggled and leaned over so she could study what Maia had been painting. It was something in black and white, but she couldn't quite make out what it was yet. She quickly looked up when she heard footsteps approaching.

Moments later, a medium sized white canvas was placed in front of her on a tabletop easel. Paisley raised an eyebrow and looked at Maia, utterly confused.

"Here," the other girl laughed and handed Paisley a paintbrush. "Paint something. You can use my paints." She slid her palette between them.

Paisley glanced back at where Shiloh was sitting before looking down at the collection of paints next to her. "I need colors," she said softly, pointing to the black and white colors Maia had been using.

Maia laughed and fished around in her backpack. Soon, a set of watercolor paints were placed in front of Paisley. The small girl smiled when she saw the colorful options she had.

"Thank you, you're welcome," she smiled, picking up the paintbrush and dipping it in the small cup of water. She studied the paints closely, trying to figure out which color to use first. After glancing at Shiloh from across the room, she chose blue.

Shiloh watched subtly from the other side of the room, watching Paisley lick her lips in concentration and lean in closer to the canvas Maia had given her. The green eyed girl couldn't see what Paisley was painting, and it frustrated her.

It was her job to help Paisley, not Maia's. Why had Paisley gone over there in the first place? Had she not been enough? Shiloh forced herself to look away from Paisley and continued adding the small shadows of orange on her own painting.

Her grip on her paintbrush would tighten every time she heard Paisley giggle from across the room at something someone else had said. She couldn't help but feel annoyed that Paisley hadn't chosen to spend any time with her. Every time she would look up, Paisley would be focused only on the canvas in front of her.

Finally, five minutes before class ended, Shiloh "accidentally" spilled paint on her table. She quickly got up and crossed the room to grab a handful of paper towels. As she passed Paisley's table, she craned her neck to see what the small girl was painting. Paisley noticed this right away, though, and quickly turned the easel away from Shiloh.

This only confused Shiloh even more. What was Paisley's problem? The green eyed girl tried to think back to that morning, wondering if she had done anything to make Paisley mad. Shiloh took a deep breath and trudged back over to her table to clean up the paint.

Once class was dismissed, Shiloh watched as Paisley tugged Maia over to see what she had painted. Maia seemed surprised. The other girl helped Paisley clean off her hands before taking both of their canvases in the back to dry. Shiloh looked down at her phone and rolled her eyes.

"Did you paint the tiger?"

The green eyed girl jumped when Paisley's soft voice appeared next to her. She shrugged and looked down at her phone. "Some of it."

"Where is it?" Paisley smiled, sitting down on the stool next to Shiloh's and looking around. "Can I see it?"

"I already put it away," Shiloh locked her phone and tossed it into her bag. "C'mon, let's go home."

Furrowing her eyebrows, Paisley decided not to question the sudden change in Shiloh's attitude. She grabbed her backpack and ran to keep up with the older girl, who was already halfway down the hallway by the time Paisley caught up with her.

"Maia has a cat," Paisley blurted out, trying to think of something to fill the silence between them. Shiloh just nodded in recognition. Paisley raised an eyebrow.

"Her name is Vega," Paisley continued, shuffling her shoes on the sidewalk. She hopped down from the sidewalk onto the parking lot asphalt, but tripped and ended up grabbing on Shiloh's arm to steady herself. The smaller girl grew worried when she saw Shiloh flash her a look of annoyance.

"Sorry," Paisley whispered, hurrying over to the passenger side of the car. She didn't want to get annoying again. That was the last thing she wanted.

For the next week, Paisley seemed to be attached to Maia's side as soon as they would set foot in the classroom. Shiloh tried her best to contain her jealously, but sometimes she grew distant from the smaller girl without even realizing it.

It was now the day before Valentine's Day, and Shiloh was adding the finishing touches to her painting. Paisley had wanted a tiger, so Shiloh had painted a tiger — despite the comments about being whipped from her other three roommates.

She would glance up at Paisley occasionally, who was still painting on the same canvas Maia had given her the week before. Every time Shiloh would try to sneak a peek at it, Paisley would practically knock over everything in her way to make sure Shiloh couldn't see.

Class had just been dismissed but no one seemed to care. This always happened on Fridays. People would stay a little longer to finish their projects before the deadline. Luckily, Shiloh had just set down her paintbrush and deemed her painting finished.

She caught sight of Paisley out of the corner of her eye. The smaller girl looked worried, and was talking animatedly with Maia. Just as Shiloh was about to go see what was wrong, Paisley turned on her heel and hurried over to the green eyed girl.

"Can I go to Maia's house?" Paisley asked pleadingly, glancing back at the girl's table. "I can come home later, right?"

Shiloh clenched her jaw slightly and looked over at Maia. She couldn't help but feel like that girl posed a threat. But glancing back at Paisley, she saw the hopeful look on the girl's face and felt all her resistance deteriorate.

"Fine," Shiloh sighed, turning back to her table and beginning to clean up her brushes. She felt Paisley's presence still behind her and took a deep breath. Grabbing a scrap piece of paper, she jotted down her number.

"Here," she folded the paper in half and handed it to Paisley. "Give this to Maia. Call me if you need anything, or whatever." Without another word, the green eyed girl swung her backpack over her shoulder and trudged out of the classroom.

Just as Paisley was about to run after her to say a proper goodbye, she felt a hand on her shoulder. "Ready to go?" Maia asked, raising an eyebrow at the other girl. Paisley looked down at the paper in her hands before nodding softly.

"Do you really think she will like it?" Paisley asked, holding the drying canvas carefully out in front of her as she followed Maia and Toby to his car.

"Of course she will," Maia laughed, helping Paisley place her things in the trunk of the car so they wouldn't be ruined on the drive. "She loves you, doesn't she?"

Paisley blushed and nodded softly. "Yes," she followed their lead and slid into the backseat of the car. "I love her, too."

"Well then she'll love anything you give her," Maia laughed softly and turned on the radio as Toby pulled out of the parking lot. Paisley couldn't help but smile.

"Why is there not a Va...." Paisley furrowed her eyebrows. "Valen... Valentimes?" She shook her head, thinking for a moment before speaking again. "Valentines. Why is it not every day?" she asked, biting her lip.

"Cause that would be way too expensive," Toby spoke up from the driver's seat, earning himself a shove from Maia. Paisley giggled at their playfulness. She could tell they loved each other.

"It's just a gimmick to make people waste tons of money on candy," Maia shrugged and turned slightly in her seat so she could see Paisley. "But I think it's nice, especially when you make homemade gifts. It's always good to surprise one another every once in a while."

"Surprises are fun," Paisley nodded in agreement from the backseat. Comfortable silence fell over the trio as they drove back to Maia's house. Paisley was in awe when they pulled up in front of a rather large, two story building.

"You live here?" Paisley asked in shock. Maia just laughed and nodded, hopping out of the car and motioning for Paisley to do the same. The small girl immediately retrieved her canvas from the trunk of the car.

"My dad is the CEO of a big computer company," Maia explained as they walked up the long gravel driveway. "It sucks."

"Why is it bad?" Paisley asked in confusion.

"Because his daughter is a free spirit," Toby spoke up, appearing behind them after locking his car. "And he's only concerned with numbers and calculations."

"Precisely," Maia shook her head. "Going to school for art wasn't exactly what he had in mind for me."

"Does it make you happy?" Paisley asked, waiting as Maia moved her backpack to her other shoulder and retrieved her key from her pocket.

"Of course," Maia laughed, pushing open the front door and allowing both Paisley and Toby to step inside. Paisley was in awe by the size of the house. It scared her somewhat, though. So much empty space. She would much rather have the small apartment she shared with her roommates.

"If you are happy, then everything is okay," Paisley shrugged. She followed the other two students upstairs and into Maia's bedroom. It was quite different in contrast to the rest of the house. The walls were painted dark purple, and there were all types of artwork posted around the room. Paisley looked around, taking in all the colors.

Within a few minutes, Paisley was sitting on the floor with a small easel in front of her, continuing to work on her painting. Maia sat on the bed, flipping through songs on her iTunes. Toby was working on some sort of paper for his art history class, and would groan in frustration every few minutes. Paisley giggled every time.

A few hours later, Shiloh lay in bed staring up at the ceiling. It was nowhere close to bedtime, but she didn't know what else to do, so she resolved for blasting music through her headphones and shutting out the world.

Meanwhile, Paisley slowly opened the door to the apartment and glanced back at Maia, biting her lip. She made sure no one was downstairs before motioning for the girl to follow.

"We need a good hiding spot," Maia said quietly, holding Paisley's finished painting in her hands. They had wrapped it in tissue paper to keep it safe. Paisley looked around the room before her eyes landed on the entertainment center.

"Over here," Paisley pointed and took the painting from Maia, hurrying over and sliding it between the piece of furniture and the wall. She took a step back to make sure it was well hidden.

"Perfect," Maia laughed and gave Paisley a high five. "She'll love it, I know she will."

"I hope so," Paisley laughed softly and pulled Maia into a hug. "Thank you for helping me."

"No problem," Maia ran a hand through her hair and glanced at the door. "I better get going before I ruin the surprise, though. I'll see you in class."

"Bye," Paisley waved softly as Maia slipped out into the hallway. Once the door closed quietly behind the girl, Paisley eagerly made her way upstairs.

"Knock knock," she tapped on Shiloh's door. Moments later Shiloh's voice rang out from the other side.

"It's open."

Paisley's shoulders fell, but she kept her mouth shut and opened the door slowly. Her eyes landed on Shiloh's figure on the bed and she happily hurried over to the girl, crawling on the bed and kissing her forehead.

"Hi," she giggled, sitting on the edge of the bed and looking at Shiloh. "I love you."

Shiloh simply forced a smile and kept her eyes locked on her phone. Paisley grew worried, and leaned in closer to the older girl. "Is something wrong?" she asked timidly, biting her lip.

"I'm fine," Shiloh shook her head, trying to dismiss Paisley. The smaller girl knew better than to believe her, though. She reached out and moved Shiloh's phone away from her face. Bad idea.

"What do you want, Paisley?!" Shiloh snapped, sitting up and glaring at the younger girl. Paisley quickly reeled back, moving off the bed and shaking her head quickly.

Before she could say anything, everything started to come back in flashes of black and white.

CHAPTER 11

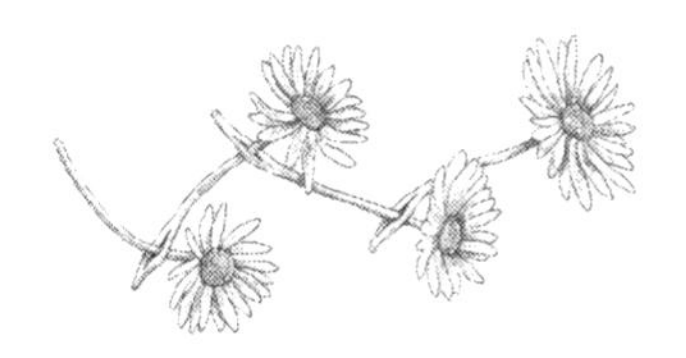

"What the hell do you want, Paisley?"

The brown eyed girl took a deep breath and stood still as the green eyed girl stared at her. She deserved this.

After outing Shiloh, Paisley had received a lot of soul eating glares from the other girl's group of friends. But never from Shiloh. Shiloh had always resolved to keeping her head down and avoiding the girl. But apparently things could change, too.

She had just gotten into the library during their free period, disappointed to see that she didn't recognize anyone in the small room. Wandering aimlessly over to the line of couches against the wall, her eyes landed on the familiar dark haired girl. Shiloh.

Before she had time to stop herself, Paisley hurried over to the couch, tossing her backpack down and sitting down on the opposite end from Shiloh. She just craved to be close to the girl. But she knew she couldn't blame Shiloh for hating her.

Obviously, her abrupt intrusion had caught Shiloh's attention. And now, here they were.

"I don't want anything," Paisley said quickly, shaking her head. "I was just trying to study..." she held up her backpack and took a deep breath. This had been a bad idea.

"There's plenty of couches," Shiloh spat, standing up and motioning around the room. "I bet you wouldn't want to be caught sitting next to a dyke," she said, laughing bitterly.

"I-I didn't—" Paisley swallowed hard and quickly stood up so her height matched Shiloh's. The older girl saw this as a threat, though, and took a step forwards. Paisley held her breath.

"I don't care, Paisley," Shiloh shook her head. "You're a pretty fucked up person, did you know that?"

Paisley just stood still. She knew Shiloh was physically more powerful than her, and if the older girl did attempt to beat her up, it would be successful.

As much as she wanted to hate Shiloh for saying these things to her, she knew it was an appropriate reaction to what she had done to her. She'd practically outed Shiloh in front of the whole school. Not that it had been her choice, but Shiloh wasn't aware of that.

"Shy?"

Paisley jumped when another voice appeared from behind Shiloh. Ryland jogged up next to her friend and sent Paisley a questioning glare.

"I really didn't—," Paisley started, wanting to prove her point. She wasn't exactly sure what she was going to say, but she didn't have the time to think, either. The moment she stepped forwards, Ryland moved inbetween the two girls and collided her fist with Paisley's nose.

"Don't you dare go near her again," Ryland growled.

Inhaling sharply, Paisley quickly fell to her knees and cupped her nose as Ryland and Shiloh disappeared out of the room. When the initial pain subsided, she slowly drew her hand away from her face and grimaced when she felt the dark red liquid running from her nose.

She looked around the room for help with pleading eyes, but everyone simply ignored her. She deserved this. Paisley squeezed her eyes shut and held back tears before slowly staggering to her feet and disappearing into the bathroom.

Paisley's eyes shot open and she inhaled sharply, stumbling backwards off the bed. She brought her hands up to her nose, swearing that she could still feel the throbbing from her memory.

In a state of confusion, she wiped her eyes and looked around the room. It took her a few moments to come back to reality, realizing where she was.

"What's wrong?" Shiloh shot up from her spot on the bed, noticing the immediate change in Paisley's disposition. She moved forward to grab Paisley's hand, but grew confused when the smaller girl practically flew backwards out of her reach.

A rush of adrenaline shot through Paisley's veins when she saw the girl in front of her. Suddenly, she wasn't sure what to believe. The girl in her memory and the girl she was facing right now were so different, yet so similar. A wave of fear washed over her.

"Paisley..." Shiloh took a step forwards. Paisley immediately searched the room, finding the door and sprinting towards it without hesitation. She practically ran straight into Ryland as she hurried down the hallway.

"Paisley?" Ryland raised an eyebrow at the panicked girl. Paisley's eyes shot wide open when she recognized the girl. More importantly, what the girl had done to her. Her hands involuntarily moved up to cup her nose and she searched the hallway in a panic. She needed an escape.

Paisley burst through the first open door she could find and slammed it shut behind her, breathing heavily. This was all too real.

"What the...?"

Paisley jumped when there was a voice from behind her. She turned around quickly, only to grow confused when she saw Vanessa sitting on her bed, a laptop next to her.

Furrowing her eyebrows, Paisley thought for a few moments. Vanessa was nice. Vanessa hadn't hurt her. At least she didn't think so. She could trust her.

The minute Paisley made the connection that she had someone who was her friend, she burst into tears and padded over to the bed, burying her head in her hands.

"Oh my god," Vanessa quickly jumped to her feet and placed her hands on Paisley's shoulders. "What's going on?"

Paisley just shook her head and practically threw herself into Vanessa's arms, crying into the older girl's shoulders. She was so… confused. She didn't understand why all these memories were coming back to so suddenly.

"Do you want me to get Shiloh?" Vanessa pulled back and studied the younger girl in her arms. The minute theosewords left her mouth, Paisley's eyes shot up and she shook her head furiously.

"No," she whimpered, another sob escaping her lips. Vanessa didn't have time to react before Paisley had burrowed under the blankets in her bed and curled up into a ball.

Utterly confused as to what was going on, Vanessa slipped out into the hallway, only to be met with a confused Ryland and distraught Shiloh.

"Where is she?" Shiloh stepped forwards, biting her lip. Vanessa nodded towards her door.

"Crying in my bed…" she ran a hand through her hair. "Care to explain what the hell is going on?" Vanessa looked back and forth from Ryland to Shiloh.

"I don't even know," Shiloh sighed in a mix of worry and frustration. "I kind of snapped at her… but then… I don't know," she shook her head. "She wouldn't even let me touch her… she was terrified."

"Of you?"

"Both of us," Ryland spoke up, squeezing Shiloh's shoulder to try and comfort her. "She booked it out of here as soon as she saw me."

"Then why would she come to me?" Vanessa asked. The other two girls were clearly as lost as she was. Ryland shrugged and Shiloh looked down at her feet guiltily.

"I should go in there," Shiloh blurted out, moving forwards. Ryland and Vanessa both made eye contact, silently aware that it wasn't a good idea right away. Vanessa moved to block the door and Ryland laid a hand on Shiloh's shoulder.

"You should wait," Vanessa bit her lip. "I asked if she wanted me to get you and she sorta… panicked. I don't think it's a good idea right away."

Shiloh's face dropped and she nodded slowly, feeling drained. Ryland sighed.

"It's getting late," Vanessa said softly, checking her phone. "Let's just… go to bed. If she calms down she'll come back to your room."

"What if she doesn't?" Shiloh looked up innocently.

"Then we'll figure this out in the morning," Vanessa glanced at her door. "I really don't know what else to tell you."

Shiloh wasn't sure what to feel. She just *had* to snap at Paisley and screw everything up once more. She simply nodded and disappeared back into her bedroom before her roommates could see the tears fall.

Sleep didn't come easy for Shiloh. She tossed and turned practically all night, painfully aware of the empty space in the bed beside her.

After countless hours of staring at the ceiling, Shiloh gave up on getting any sleep that night. With a heavy sigh, she pushed herself out of bed and trudged out into the hallway. She listened quietly as she passed Vanessa's door, but she figured both girls had already fallen asleep.

Once she made it downstairs, Shiloh grabbed a drink from the kitchen and fell back on the couch. The older girl furrowed her eyebrows when she attempted to turn the TV on, but was met with the same black screen instead of Netflix.

Her frustration was evident, now, and she frustratingly made her way over to the piece of furniture across the room to check if the television was plugged in. She squinted, moving the entertainment center slightly to see behind it. Something shifted and caught her attention.

Growing confused, Shiloh reached forwards and grabbed the odd material. When she pulled it out from the crack in the furniture, she took a step back to observe her findings. She casually removed the tissue paper from around the rectangle and nearly gasped when she realized what she was holding.

Shiloh quickly moved back over to the couch, not peeling her eyes off of the painting she held in her hands. Right away she had known it was by Paisley. Paisley had painted her.

Paisley had painted her.

Shiloh took a deep breath and studied the canvas. It was better than what she would have expected from Paisley, but she could still tell it wasn't the work of a professional artist. She didn't realize how much attention to detail the smaller girl had. It was endearing. It was perfect.

Shiloh had to set the canvas down to wipe the tears from her eyes. This is what she had been doing with Maia. God, Shiloh had been such an idiot for suspecting anything.

She wasn't sure how long she stared at the painting for. All she knew was that she only moved from her spot on the couch when she heard two pairs of footsteps behind her.

The second Shiloh turned around, Paisley stopped in her tracks. She hadn't seen the older girl on the couch. As soon as their eyes locked, Shiloh grabbed the painting and jumped to her feet.

"Pais…" Shiloh hurried over to the smaller girl and held up the painting. Vanessa watched in confusion. "I'm sorry. I didn't mean to snap at you. I should've asked… I—," She was cut off when Paisley quickly moved away and hid behind Vanessa.

"Paisley," Shiloh held up the painting and shook her head. "I said I was sorry," she met the smaller girl's eyes pleadingly. Paisley just moved further behind Vanessa. Shiloh felt her heart breaking.

She met Vanessa's eyes pleadingly, even though she was aware there was nothing her friend could do. With a sigh, Shiloh let her shoulders drop.

"I'll be upstairs if you need me," she mumbled, leaving the painting on the couch and disappearing up the spiral staircase. Paisley followed her with her eyes, waiting until she heard the bedroom door shut to move out from behind Vanessa and walk over to inspect the canvas on the couch.

Three days passed of complete silence between the two girls. No matter how many times Shiloh would try to apologize to Paisley, or even simply sit next to her, Paisley would run to Vanessa or Leah. For some reason, she would avoid Ryland as well.

Part of Shiloh was concerned that Paisley's avoidance wasn't just because of her outburst. Paisley seemed genuinely terrified whenever she was around Shiloh. The thought made Shiloh feel sick to her stomach.

It was now Tuesday morning, and Shiloh had made a point to leave the house before anyone else woke up. She didn't want to have to deal with the pain that came with seeing Paisley go out of her way to stay away from her. She'd rather just disappear before they could notice she was gone.

She knew Paisley wouldn't want to come to class with her. Instead, she drove to school alone, blasting the radio to try and keep her mind off of things. The thing that scared her the most was the thought that maybe this was it for them. Maybe Paisley had just decided that she was done.

She smiled sadly at Maia as she made her way over to the desk, knowing the other girl was wondering where Paisley was. Shiloh avoided talking to any of her classmates and pulled out her sketchbook. She didn't feel like starting another painting. She had nothing to paint.

Class passed by painfully slow. About fifteen minutes into the class, she heard quick footsteps down the hallway and then the door of the classroom was burst open. Everyone turned their heads as a small girl in a blue beanie quietly entered the room. Shiloh grew confused, craning her neck to try and get a better view.

She raised an eyebrow when Leah poked her head into the room and searched the desks. When her eyes found Shiloh, she held up her phone and pointed to it, signaling for Shiloh to do the same. Before Shiloh could respond, the older girl was gone. Paisley had already made her way over to Maia's table.

Shiloh pulled her phone out of her pocket. Seconds later, a message appeared on her screen.

`[Leah – 10:38] She woke me up saying she was ready for class. She wouldn't take no for an answer.`

Shiloh just sighed and put her phone away, forcing herself to keep her eyes off of Paisley. This was going to be a long day.

Meanwhile, Paisley set her backpack on the ground and sat down in one of the stools at Maia's table. She watched for a few moments before the other girl broke the silence.

"How'd Shiloh like her present?" Maia smiled, turning to wipe off her paintbrush and giving Paisley her attention. Paisley hung her head down, realizing that Valentines Day had come and gone without a word exchanged between them.

"Is something wrong?" Maia turned slightly in her chair, sensing the change in Paisley's personality.

"There are bad things," Paisley mumbled, shaking her head and looking up at Maia. "I can not tell you." Immediately, Maia glanced over at Shiloh.

"Have you told anyone?"

Paisley shook her head. Confused, Maia made an abrupt decision. She subtly unlocked her phone, opening the audio app and pressing record. She was sure Shiloh might need to know anything that came out of their conversation. Hiding her phone behind her backpack, she gave Paisley a comforting smile.

"What kind of bad things?" Maia asked carefully, watching as Paisley's face distorted into one of fear.

"Bad things," Paisley thought for a few moments. "From a long time ago."

"Like what?" Maia glanced back over at Shiloh, who seemed to be falling asleep while sitting up.

"I… They are scary," Paisley tugged at the beanie on her head. "It is like having a dream, but it is real." She swallowed the lump in her throat. "Very real."

Before Maia could say anything else, Paisley stood up and shook her head. "I have to go to the bathroom," she mumbled, padding out of the classroom before the other girl could stop her. Maia glanced over at Shiloh, who seemed to have had the same idea she had. Both girls locked eyes and when Shiloh looked away, Maia grabbed her phone and headed over to her table.

"You should hear this," Maia said softly, pulling up a stool next to Shiloh and holding out her phone. Shiloh raised an eyebrow, but quietly took the device from the other girl and held it up to her ear before pressing the play button. Paisley's voice appeared.

"Bad things... They are scary... It is like having a dream, but it is real. Very real,"

Shiloh's face slowly dropped as she gained a basic idea of what was going on. She sat in frozen confusion for a few moments before Maia spoke up.

"She's in the bathroom," the other girl mentioned, pointing to the door. Shiloh stood up slowly and debated her options for a moment. She couldn't just sit and wait for Paisley to come back to her anymore. After quietly thanking Maia, she excused herself from class and hurried down the hallway.

Paisley sat in the bathroom, watching the light above her flicker on and off slightly. The smaller girl had closed the toilet seat and curled up on top of it, keeping her feet off of the floor. She tugged on her beanie just as she heard the door of the bathroom open.

There were a few quiet footsteps and Paisley held her breath when the noise stopped. Suddenly, she was met with a sense of déjà vu when Shiloh's voice filled the room.

"Hello?"

The younger girl felt the same rushing feeling she'd experienced before, as everything slowly flashed before her eyes.

CHAPTER 12

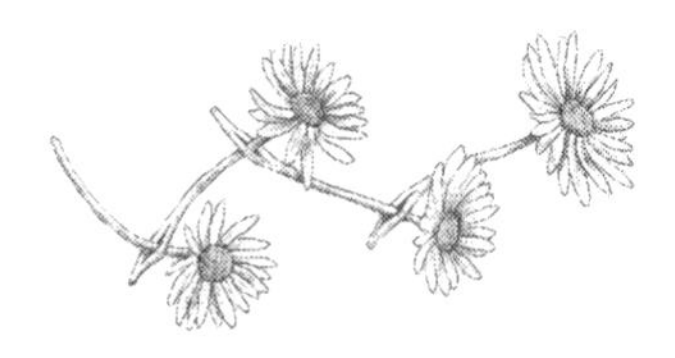

The steady drip of the bathroom faucet was the only thing Paisley could hear as her shaky hands dug around in her backpack. It was early. Earlier than most people arrived at school. But Paisley had things to take care of.

She took a deep breath as she retrieved her small makeup bag from her backpack, zipping it open and wincing when she moved her shoulder too quickly. Her torso throbbed in pain and she had to steady herself against the bathroom wall. No matter how badly she just wanted to break down and sob, she knew it would only cause her more pain.

Sniffing, she lifted her shirt above her head and used her small handheld mirror to inspect the bruises. Paisley dabbed a small amount of her foundation onto the markings, gently blending it in to try and cover up the discoloration. This had basically become a morning routine for her.

As her thoughts began to wander, she thought back to life before her parent's death. Bad idea. She quickly brought her hand up to her mouth to stop herself from bursting into tears. She set down her makeup bag and carefully tried to wipe her eyes to keep her mascara from running.

The small girl jumped when she heard the familiar creak of the bathroom door. She froze. Holding her breath, she listened as light footsteps entered the bathroom.

Shiloh tossed her backpack on the floor next to the sink, taking a step back and fixing her hair in the mirror. This was supposed to be a quick bathroom visit, but she paused when she heard a small sniffle from one of the stalls.

"Hello?"

Paisley froze when she heard the raspy voice filling the room. Shiloh. As much as she wanted to answer, she knew better than to bother the girl. She held her breath and tried to stay as still as possible.

Shiloh lowered her head slightly, not recognizing who the white converse under the stall belonged to. Whoever it was obviously didn't want company. Shiloh bit her lip and glanced over at her backpack. Quietly, she opened the bag and dug around for a few moments.

Paisley jumped when something was slid under the stall. She squinted her eyes, realizing it was a small granola bar and a pack of gum. She grew confused.

"Be nice to yourself," Shiloh's soft voice filled the room. Paisley felt her heart drop in her chest. "Summer's almost here."

The dark haired girl stood up just as Paisley quietly bent down to pick up the wrapper. She listened as Shiloh's footsteps moved towards the bathroom door. Then the room grew silent.

"They want all seniors in the gym, by the way," Shiloh spoke once again. "I don't know if you're graduating today... but if you are... I figured you'd wanna know," the green eyed girl cleared her throat. "Uh, yeah. I hope you feel better," she stammered, cursing herself for being so awkward.

Paisley couldn't help but smile. The girl was just so adorable. If only she had known who was inside the stall. She definitely wouldn't have been that nice.

Once the bathroom door closed, the smaller girl slowly opened the granola bar and took a bite as she pulled her cap and gown out of her backpack.

She studied and blue and yellow material, turning it over in her hands and sighing softly. Today she graduated. Today, everything changed.

Paisley pressed her hands against the bathroom stall as she was practically thrown back into reality. So many conflicting feelings were running through her head.

Shiloh was just about to leave the bathroom when she heard two feet hit the floor. She paused as the stall door opened slowly and Paisley took a small step forwards.

"Paisley, I—," Shiloh started to try and apologize, but was interrupted when she was nearly tackled to the ground by the small girl. It took Shiloh a few seconds to realize what was going on, but when she felt the girl's tears soaking through her shirt her mind suddenly caught up with her body.

Shiloh quickly wrapped her arms around the brown eyed girl and held her close. Comforting Paisley was practically instinct to her. After basically not having any contact with the girl for the past few days, Shiloh was relieved that she finally had Paisley in her arms again. But something was wrong.

"What's going on?" Shiloh asked quietly. Paisley pulled away when she heard Shiloh's voice, studying the older girl's face and feeling tears fill her eyes once more.

"I need help," the smaller girl's voice came out as merely a whisper. Shiloh felt her heart breaking.

"Help?" Shiloh reached out and laced their fingers together, trying to calm Paisley as much as possible. "What's going on?"

"There are bad things," Paisley shook her head. The small girl squeezed her eyes shut and Shiloh quickly pulled her back into her arms. She was suddenly reminded of the conversation Maia had shown her.

"Okay," Shiloh whispered. "We're gonna go home and we're gonna figure this out, okay?"

"You and me?" Paisley asked shyly, looking up at Shiloh. She was scared the older girl would be mad at her for avoiding her for the past few days. To her surprise, Shiloh just nodded and kissed her forehead.

"Me and you."

Shiloh texted Maia to let her know they were leaving class early. The girl met them at the front of their classroom with their backpacks so they wouldn't have to disturb the class. After thanking Maia, Shiloh led Paisley out to the car.

The drive was quiet. Paisley just looked down at the floor, feeling guilty. Shiloh kept her fingers intertwined with Paisley's the entire drive, tracing circles in the back of her palm with her thumb.

Once they reached the apartment, Shiloh sat them both down on the couch. Noticing Paisley was shivering, she pulled a blanket over the small girl.

"What's going on, Pais?" she asked carefully. Paisley met Shiloh's eyes for a few moments before scooting into her side and curling up beside her. Shiloh automatically wrapped an arm around her girlfriend.

"There… there are bad things," Paisley looked down at the floor. "I do not know how to explain them."

"Try," Shiloh squeezed Paisley's hand. "Just try."

Paisley took a deep breath and thought for a few moments before closing her eyes and trying to relive what she had seen. Shiloh watched, hoping this wasn't pushing the smaller girl too far.

"I see… dreams," Paisley opened her eyes. "I saw you. In the school bathroom. You gave me a granola bar."

This time, Shiloh was the one being hit with a rush of memories. The girl in the stall had been Paisley? She shivered and nodded for Paisley to continue.

"I did not… know this… before," Paisley shook her head. "You were there, Lo," she reached up and cupped Shiloh's cheek, studying the girl's face. "But…"

"But…?" Shiloh urged her to go on.

"One time you were mean. You yelled. And Ryland hit me," she swallowed the lump in her throat and drew her hand back. "That is why I hid from you. I was… scared."

"Oh my god," Shiloh whispered under her breath, feeling increasingly guilty. If she had any clue what Paisley was going through at the time, she would have never let any of that happen.

"I'm so sorry," Shiloh reached out and laced their fingers together. "I… I'm *so* sorry."

"No," Paisley shook her head. "I was bad. You did not do anything wrong. I know."

"I still didn't have any right—"

"I saw my parents," Paisley blurted out. "I saw them. I saw a lot of things. I…" she shook her head as she felt tears well in her eyes once more. "I do not understand," she managed to whisper before she buried her head in Shiloh's shoulder.

Shiloh was met with so much information. Paisley was remembering small pieces of her past. The doctor had warned them about this. She stared at the wall on the other side of the apartment as she held Paisley close. What was she supposed to do about this?

"I… Paisley?" Shiloh asked softly after a few moments of silence had passed. "Let's go upstairs. You should lay down… and I need to call your doctor."

"Doctor?" Paisley eyes widened and she looked up quickly. "Why?"

"It's not bad," Shiloh quickly shook her head. "You said you wanted help. And I need his help to help you."

"Oh," Paisley whispered, but didn't protest. She stood up slowly and waited to Shiloh to follow her. The moment they set foot in the bedroom, Paisley burrowed herself under the covers. Shiloh felt physically sick seeing Paisley this drained.

"I'll just be right out in the hallway, okay? I won't be long," Shiloh promised, kissing Paisley's hand before slipping back out of the bedroom. She sat down against the wall as she dialed the phone.

"Hello?"

Shiloh took a deep breath. "Mr. Conlon? It's Shiloh... Paisley's roommate. You told me to call you if anything happened?"

"Of course," the man on the other line replied. Shiloh sighed in relief, glad that he knew what he was doing. "What's going on?"

"She's remembering things," Shiloh bit her lip before continuing. "I don't really know much... she can't explain them very well. She's just... they're really bothering her."

"Ah," she heard the man move slightly in his chair. "These... flashbacks, are they good ones? Or bad?"

"Both," Shiloh nodded softly. The pieces were slowly coming back together in her mind. "I don't know what to do... I just... what do I tell her? She doesn't understand..."

"The process of regaining some of her memory is going to be a confusing one," he admitted honestly. "I mean, it would be for anyone. She suddenly is met with all this new information that she doesn't know what to do with. It's hard for her to separate the past from the present."

"What do I do?" Shiloh leaned her head back against the wall and stared up at the ceiling.

"We'll make an emergency appointment for her to meet with someone tomorrow," Shiloh heard the rustling of papers on the other line. "But from what I can tell, she doesn't really like opening up to people she doesn't know very well."

"Yeah…" Shiloh mumbled.

"This is going to happen no matter what, we can't stop her from remembering. You've just got to be there for her. Let her open up to you. We can go over a safety plan tomorrow," he replied. Shiloh looked down at her shoes.

"That's all? There's no… I don't know, medicine or something?"

"Nope. No medicine," the doctor replied with a sigh. "I wish there was. You've just got to guide her through it. Not all memories are bad, though."

"Most of hers are," Shiloh mumbled, scuffing her shoes against the floor.

"And that's why she needs you," he answered. "She's got the best team of people supporting her right now. We can figure everything else out tomorrow."

"Okay," Shiloh paused for a moment and sighed. "Thank you."

"No problem, Shiloh. Paisley's a strong girl, she'll get through this," he chuckled softly. "I'll email you the appointment information."

After the call ended, Shiloh entered the bedroom once more, finding Paisley in the same spot as she had been when she left. Slowly, the green eyed girl sat down on the edge of the bed.

Feeling the mattress move slightly, Paisley poked her head out from underneath the blankets and gave Shiloh a sad smile. The green eyed girl reached out and wiped the tears from Paisley's cheeks.

"Y'know, Paisley," Shiloh started, moving to sit cross legged on the bed. "If you keep remembering things… some of them may not be things you think you would want to remember."

Paisley tilted her head to the side slightly, but moved out from underneath the blankets and sat up so she was facing Shiloh. She could sense the girl's sincerity.

"They might be scary, I don't really know," Shiloh admitted, taking Paisley's hands in hers. "But one thing is not gonna change, okay?"

Paisley nodded softly.

"I'm always gonna be here. No matter what," Shiloh reached out and cupped Paisley's cheek. "You're stuck with me, Pais," she laughed softly.

"I like that," Paisley smiled sadly and placed her hand overtop of Shiloh's. She looked down quietly. "Even though there are bad things?"

"Even though there are bad things," Shiloh confirmed. "You're so strong, Paisley. Stronger than anyone I know," she gave the girl a soft smile. "You've got this, Paisley. You can make it through anything."

"Promise?" Paisley asked, holding up her pinkie. Shiloh couldn't help but smile.

"Promise." The green eyed girl locked their fingers together and kissed the back of Paisley's hand. "Me and you?" she directed the question back to the other girl.

"You and me," Paisley giggled and kissed Shiloh's hand in return. "Thank you."

"You're welcome," Shiloh smiled softly. "And about... what you remembered about me..." she shook her head. "That was before I got to know you. The *real* you. And if I had known the real Paisley then, I would have been a lot better of a friend to you."

"I love you," Paisley leaned forwards and kissed Shiloh's cheek. "It does not matter. We are here now. I am happy with you."

"I…" Shiloh couldn't help the blush that spread across her cheeks. No matter how much time passed between them, she still got the same flying feeling whenever they shared these moments. "I love you too."

"I love saying that," Paisley laughed softly, wiping the tears from her eyes. Shiloh crinkled her nose playfully, reaching out and removing Paisley's beanie from her head so she could smooth out the smaller girl's hair.

"Me too," Shiloh giggled, gently pulling the beanie back onto Paisley's head and kissing her forehead. "Let's lay down for a bit and try to get some rest. Sound good?"

Paisley nodded softly, looking at Shiloh mischievously before leaping forwards and tackling her back onto the bed. Shiloh laughed once she realized what the smaller girl was doing.

"Make a fort," Paisley whispered, pointing to the blankets. Shiloh pulled the covers over them as she felt Paisley curl up into her side, tangling their legs together under the sheets.

"Sing?" Paisley looked up at Shiloh with a hopeful look on her face.

"Greedy today, aren't we?" Shiloh joked and pulled Paisley closer to her, placing a kiss on her forehead. "Only for you."

"I love you, Lo," Paisley mumbled against Shiloh's shoulder once she finished singing, allowing her arms to wrap around the girl's waist and pull her even closer. "I love you, and your ocean eyes. Thank you for being here."

"Thank *you* for being you," Shiloh laughed softly, kissing the top of her girlfriend's head.

"Thank you, you're welcome," Paisley whispered with a soft laugh, feeling Shiloh lay her head down on the pillow. With a soft sigh, both of the girls allowed sleep to overtake them.

CHAPTER 13

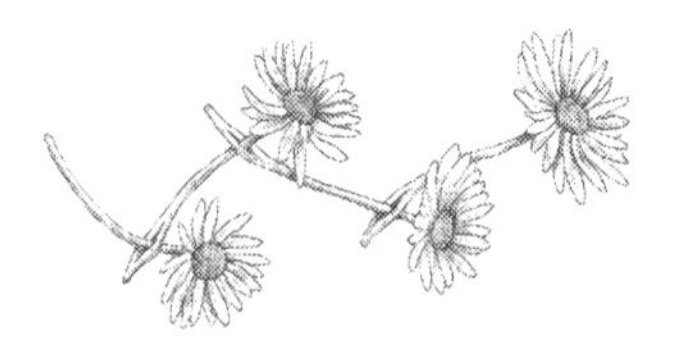

Shiloh was awoken when a weight was suddenly lifted from the bed. Before she could figure out what was going on, she heard rushed footsteps disappear out of the room.

"Wha...?" Shiloh sat up groggily, rubbing her eyes and looking around the room. Paisley wasn't there. Inhaling sharply, Shiloh quickly wiped her eyes and pulled the blankets off of her legs. She glanced at the clock. *12:15*. They had barely been asleep for an hour.

"Paisley?" Shiloh raised her voice, trying to shake off her exhaustion and walking over to the door. "Paisley?!" she called louder when there wasn't an answer. Just as she was about to exit the bedroom, she heard quick footsteps coming up the stairs.

Paisley appeared at the top of the stairs, holding the medium sized canvas and hurrying towards Shiloh. As the small girl got closer, Shiloh realized there were tears streaming down her face.

"What's wrong?" Shiloh asked quickly, stepping forwards just as Paisley shoved the painting into Shiloh's hands.

"I forgot," Paisley shook her head and took a step back. "I am stupid. I am sorry," she looked down at the ground, frantically wiping her eyes with the sleeve of her sweater.

"You what?" Shiloh asked, looking down at the painting she had found a few days ago. It still gave her goosebumps.

"It was a present," Paisley stepped forwards and pointed to the painting. "For you. But it is too late," she sighed and buried her face in her hands. She didn't want Shiloh to see that she was crying.

"Why is it too late?" Shiloh grew confused, using her free hand to reach out and pull Paisley's hands away from her face. "Why are you crying? This is beautiful, Paisley," she looked down at the canvas in her hands.

"It was for Valentine's Day," Paisley bit her lip and allowed Shiloh to reach up and wipe her eyes. "But I... It is too late."

"Oh, babe," Shiloh shook her head and led Paisley into the bedroom. "No it isn't..." she sighed and propped the painting up on her desk so it could be seen from the bed. "I didn't..."

Paisley followed Shiloh over to the bed and sat down slowly. The dark haired girl thought for a moment before speaking once more.

"I didn't give you anything either..." Shiloh shook her head. "I mean, I obviously got you something... but when you didn't talk to me I... I just didn't think you really cared."

"I do care," Paisley scooted closer to Shiloh and grabbed her hand. "I do, Lo. I do. I was scared."

"I know," Shiloh cupped Paisley's hand between her own. "But Valentine's Day is just a day, right? I mean, who says we can't have out own day right now?"

"Right now?" Paisley tilted her head to the side.

"Yeah," Shiloh nodded and stood up, moving over to her desk and rummaging around in the drawer for a moment. "Right now," she sat back down on the bed and set a small box in Paisley's lap. "Happy... Happy *Us* Day," she smiled softly, kissing Paisley's cheek.

"For me?" Paisley whispered softly, holding up the box and turning it around in her hands.

"Only for you," Shiloh laughed softly and crossed her legs underneath her. "Open it."

Paisley's small fingers gently tore at the wrapping paper, revealing a small cardboard box. She lifted the lid, furrowing her eyebrows at what was inside.

"A string?" the smaller girl looked over at Shiloh in confusion.

Laughing, the dark haired girl gently lifted the material out of the box and unrolled it. "Close," she smiled. "It's shoelaces. For your shoes," she motioned to the tattered white converse in by the door.

"I know you won't let me buy you new shoes, but I figured this was the next best thing," Shiloh smiled softly.

"It is yellow," Paisley giggled, her lips parting into a wide smile. "I love it," she wrapped her arms around Shiloh and pulled the older girl into a hug. "Thank you, you're welcome."

"That's not all," Shiloh smirked, holding up a finger to signal for Paisley to wait. She reached under the bed and pulled out a shoebox, placing it on Paisley's lap. The smaller girl looked up at Shiloh for approval before slowly removing the lid.

"It's a yellow beanie," Shiloh explained, pulling the cap out of the box and showing it to Paisley. "Now you have your own." She gave the girl a soft smile before reaching to remove the blue beanie from Paisley's head. Surprisingly, Paisley reached up to stop her.

"But… But I like this one," Paisley said hesitantly, holding onto her beanie. "It is blue. Your favorite."

"Oh," Shiloh looked down at the beanie in her hands and then back up to Paisley. "I just figured s—,"

"I am sorry," Paisley shook her head, feeling guilty. But for her, there was just something special about wearing Shiloh's blue beanie.

"It's fine, Pais," Shiloh laughed softly and shook her head. When Paisley didn't look up at her, Shiloh smoothed out the beanie and tugged it onto her own head. Typically, she wouldn't wear yellow. But she'd do anything for Paisley. "There," she reached out and squeezed Paisley's hand. "I'll wear it."

Paisley looked up slowly, giggling when she saw how crooked the beanie was on Shiloh's head. Gently, she reached up and moved the older girl's hair out of her face, tugging on the beanie until it was properly positioned on her head. Her lips curved into a small smile when she remembered something.

"My favorite girl in my favorite color," Paisley hummed happily, moving her hand down to cup Shiloh's cheek.

Shiloh felt butterflies erupt in her stomach and it took her a few seconds to find her words again. She smiled softly and placed her hand on top of Paisley's.

"I could say the same for you," she laughed and pointed to Paisley's beanie. The smaller girl's face lit up, as if she hadn't considered this before.

"It is perfect!" Paisley clapped her hands together. "This is perfect," she said softer, crawling forwards and cupping Shiloh's face. She brought their lips together in a kiss that lasted longer than usual. When she pulled away, she smiled widely and kissed Shiloh's forehead before sitting back down. "I love you."

Shiloh had to shake her head slightly to bring herself out of her trance. Paisley was just full of surprises. "I love you too," she whispered, squeezing Paisley's hand.

"Duh," Paisley teased, looking around the room for a moment. Her eyes landed on the painting and she bit her lip. "Do you like it?"

"Like what?" Shiloh followed Paisley's line of sight, realizing what she was referring to. Reaching over, she grabbed the canvas off of her desk and held it in her lap. "You painted this?"

"I did," Paisley smiled shyly. "It is you, see? And the ocean is behind you, because it is reflecting off of your eyes."

"I love it," Shiloh smiled and kissed Paisley's cheek. "It's the best present I've ever gotten."

"Really?" Paisley nearly gasped in disbelief. "But it is messy, see? I messed up right there," she pointed to a small smudge in the corner of the painting.

"I didn't even notice," Shiloh shrugged. "I was too distracted by all the wonderful things about this painting. No one's ever done something like this for me…" She paused for a moment. "It means a lot."

"Well I love you," Paisley smiled shyly. "And I wanted to make you happy. I wanted you to see my Lolo," she pointed to the painting. "I wanted you to see you the way I do."

Shiloh felt butterflies in her stomach for the millionth time that day, and she couldn't hide her smile. "You're pretty amazing, Paisley," she whispered, bringing Paisley's hand up to her lips and pressing a kiss to the back of her palm.

Paisley blushed softly, glancing at the door before gaining an idea. "Can we make cookies? For our day?" She looked at Shiloh hopefully.

"Cookies?" Shiloh tilted her head to the side in confusion.

"Yes," Paisley nodded, clasping her hands together. "Maia and Toby made cookies for Valentine's Day… can we do it today?"

Shiloh laughed when she realized what Paisley meant. "Duh," she giggled, imitating the smaller girl. "Sugar or chocolate ch—?" she began, but didn't have time to finish.

Paisley was already halfway down the hallway. Shiloh hopped to her feet to follow her.

"What do we need?" Paisley turned around when she heard Shiloh enter the kitchen. Before Shiloh could answer, Paisley was already grabbing a container of eggs from the refrigerator and setting them on the counter.

"Butter, flour, suga—," Shiloh began listing ingredients, but was interrupted.

"Flour! I know where that is!" Paisley smiled widely and hurried over to the pantry, grabbing the bag of flour and hugging it to her chest. She hurried to place it on the counter, but misjudged where she was setting it down. The bag slipped out of her hands and smashed to the floor, exploding open and creating a large white cloud around her.

Shiloh was shocked initially, but as the white dust settled and Paisley was visible once more, she couldn't help but laugh softly. The small girl was covered in the white powder.

"Stupid," Paisley mumbled, shaking her head and coughing slightly when she breathed in. Shiloh quickly stifled a laugh and moved across the kitchen to the other girl.

"Hey, hey, it's okay," Shiloh said softly, biting her lip to hide her smile. Paisley looked adorably pitiful covered in flour. "It's only flour, it's no big deal."

"I broke it," Paisley sighed, letting her shoulders drop. "Why can I not do anything right?" she asked, her voice cracking on the last word as she felt tears threaten to fall.

"Babe, no," Shiloh shook her head and reached out, wiping the flour from Paisley's eyelids. She tried to stifle a laugh when she smoothed out Paisley's hair and a small amount of flour puffed out.

"You are laughing," Paisley lifted her head, wiping her eyes quickly. "I am sorry," she shook her head, causing more flour to fall to the ground.

"Paisley," Shiloh laughed softly and shook her head. "You don't have to apologize. It's just… you kinda look like a ghost," she bit her lip. Paisley furrowed her eyebrows.

Sensing Paisley's frustration, Shiloh bent down and cupped a large amount of flour in her own hands. Without hesitating, she threw it on herself, creating another cloud of the white powder and covering herself in it, as well.

Paisley gasped and backed away in confusion. Coughing, Shiloh wiped the flour from her eyes and laughed softly.

"See? No big deal," the older girl shrugged and blew a puff of the excess flour off of her hand in Paisley's direction. The smaller girl bit her lip to hide a smile.

"You kinda do look like a ghost…" Paisley mumbled softly, wiping her eyes and looking up at Shiloh.

"Oh, do I?" Shiloh giggled, bending down and grabbing another handful of flour. "You should see yourself," she smirked, taking a step forwards and raising an eyebrow.

"Lolo!" Paisley squealed, ducking down as Shiloh tossed the flour in Paisley's direction and added even more of the white powder on the smaller girl's sweater. "It is messy!"

"Who cares?" Shiloh shrugged. "Everything's washable."

"But…" Paisley bit her lip and looked down at the ripped bag on the floor.

"Exactly," Shiloh laughed. She took a step backwards, spreading out her arms. "C'mon. It's your turn to get me."

Paisley's eyes widened and she stood still. "I… I can not."

"Yes you can," Shiloh bent down and scooped up a large amount of flour, placing it in Paisley's hands. "You know you want to." She giggled when Paisley failed to hide her smile. "C'mon, you've got a free throw."

"If you say so…" Paisley giggled, tossing the flour forwards and enveloping Shiloh in a giant cloud of the substance. The smaller girl giggled wildly when Shiloh's face reappeared, covered in flour.

"See?" Shiloh coughed, shaking the flour out of her hair. "It's fun," she held out her hands and blew a cloud of flour in Paisley's direction. "There's no need to take everything so seriously. You've gotta laugh at yourself sometimes."

Paisley giggled, waving the flour of the air. "So do you," she smirked, bending down and cupping more flour in her hands. When she stood back up, Shiloh had already taken off across the apartment.

"That is no fair!" Paisley yelled after girl, laughing as she chased after the older girl. She liked this. This was fun. They could worry about the mess later.

When she reached the top of the stairs, she listened carefully for any signs of Shiloh. Just as she turned to walk down the hallway, Shiloh jumped out from behind one of the doors.

"Boo!" the green eyed girl clapped her hands together. Paisley jumped, whipping around and tossing flour all over both of them. Shiloh burst into laughter when she realized her plan had backfired.

"I should've thought that one though," Shiloh admitted, wiping the flour from around her eyes and blowing her hair out of her face. She giggled when Paisley brought her hands up to ruffle the flour out of her hair.

"I love you," Paisley laughed softly, moving forwards and using her fingers to wipe the flour off of Shiloh's cheek so she could press a kiss against the girl's smooth skin. "Even if you are a ghost."

"Hey!" Shiloh nudged the smaller girl playfully and crinkled her nose. "You're forgetting one very important detail," she raised an eyebrow and placed her hands on Paisley's hips, pulling the smaller girl closer to her.

"What is it?" Paisley bit her lip to try and contain her smile. Shiloh pressed their foreheads together and met Paisley's eyes.

"You're a ghost too," Shiloh whispered, pulling back and wiping the flour from her hands onto the top of Paisley's head. The smaller girl laughed softly and crinkled her nose.

"*Very funny*," Paisley mumbled sarcastically, shaking her head. Shiloh raised an eyebrow.

"You've been hanging around Ryland too long, haven't you?" Shiloh teased, kissing Paisley's forehead and pulling the smaller girl into her side.

Paisley held her breath. *Ryland.* Her shoulders dropped and she looked down at her feet. Shiloh noticed this.

"What's wrong?" Shiloh asked quickly, pulling away so she could face Paisley. "Did I say something?"

Paisley just bit her lip and looked up. "Ryland..." she whispered, hoping Shiloh would understand what she meant.

"Oh," Shiloh nodded in understanding. "You remembered."

"She punched me," Paisley said quietly, bringing her hand up to her nose. She could practically still feel the throbbing that she had felt in her flashback.

"She was just... trying to protect me, I guess," Shiloh reached out and adjusted Paisley's beanie, which was also covered in flour. "That doesn't make physical violence right... but she's always been protective of her friends. Even you. You're one of them now."

"I am?" Paisley bit her lip.

"Of course you are, Pais," Shiloh laughed softly and shook her head. "She loves you. And friends forgive friends."

"But..." Paisley looked down at her hands. "I have to tell her?"

"It's up to you," Shiloh said honestly. "They won't judge you. It's nothing bad," she took a step forward and laced their fingers together. "You can tell her as much as you want, or as little as you want. But I think it'd be good for them to know what's going on."

"Can you help me?" Paisley asked softly. "I want to tell them. But… I am not sure how."

"We have a doctor's appointment tomorrow," Shiloh remembered. "We can talk to them after that, okay? Don't worry."

"There is something else," Paisley looked down to hide her smirk. Shiloh tilted her head to the side.

"What?" the dark haired girl grew concerned. Paisley giggled, lifting her hands and blowing flour in Shiloh's face. The older girl gasped and nearly fell backwards, making Paisley laugh even more.

"I had to," Paisley giggled, looking up at Shiloh innocently. She crinkled her nose when she breathed in a cloud of the white powder, coughing slightly.

"Payback," Shiloh laughed, reaching out to wipe more of the flour from Paisley's face. "C'mon, let's go get you cleaned up," she smiled softly, kissing Paisley's cheek and leading her towards the bathroom.

CHAPTER 14

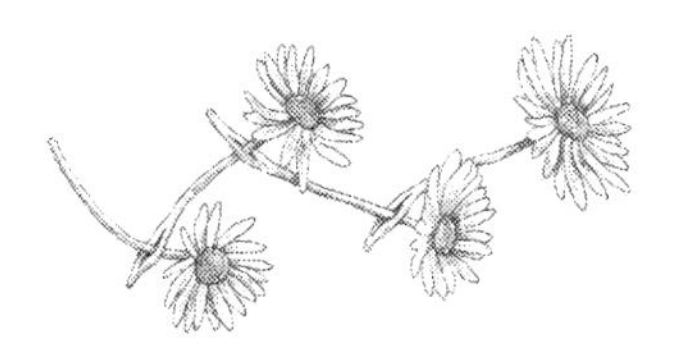

"Come, Lo," Paisley whined, holding out her hand and trying to pull Shiloh into the bathroom. The dark haired girl just bit her lip and stood her ground.

"You need to shower," Shiloh pulled her hand back and shook her head. "I'll be across the hall when you're done."

Paisley stuck out her bottom lip and shook her head, which caused small tufts of flour to fall to the floor around her feet. Shiloh looked down at her own hands, which were practically ghost white from the white powder.

"You are messy too," Paisley said softly, reaching out and grabbing Shiloh's hand once more. "Please?" she looked up hopefully, meeting Shiloh's eyes.

"Paisley, I—," Shiloh began, but lost her words when Paisley stepped forwards and tugged at the hem of her shirt.

"It is just a shower," Paisley shook her head and curled the ends of Shiloh's shirt around her fingers. "You need to be clean," she said quietly. Looking up at the older girl for approval, Paisley slowly began to lift Shiloh's shirt upwards. "I love you. Do not be scared."

Feeling her breath catch in her throat, Shiloh found herself growing nervous. Nervous? Nervous for what? She internally cursed herself. It was Paisley. She shouldn't be this scared to be so… exposed.

With a deep breath, she took a sidestep into the bathroom and closed the door behind them. Paisley took this as a sign to continue, and she lifted up Shiloh's shirt. The dark haired girl brought her arms above her head and allowed Paisley to remove the material from her torso.

It was silent for a few moments as Paisley traced her eyes over Shiloh's figure, familiarizing herself with the newly exposed skin. Shiloh held her breath.

"Pretty," Paisley mumbled, giving Shiloh a shy smile before reaching up to run her fingers through the girl's hair.

Shiloh exhaled slowly, beginning to calm down. This was Paisley. She had already exposed herself to the girl emotionally. This was just the next step, as innocent as it could get.

"Here," Shiloh whispered, gently rolling up the bottom of Paisley's hoodie. "Is this okay?" she asked nervously before biting her lip. Looking up at the smaller girl, she tugged gently on the material.

"Yes," Paisley giggled softly, sensing Shiloh's anxiety. She lifted her arms as Shiloh pulled the heavy material over her head and let it fall to the floor. Once her torso was exposed, Paisley turned to the mirror and ran her hands over her collarbone.

"I am clean," Paisley said softly, studying herself in the mirror. She trailed her fingers over her own shoulder, almost as if she were in awe by her own skin. Shiloh grew confused.

"I thought the point of taking a shower was to *get* clean," Shiloh laughed nervously, unsure of what Paisley meant. The smaller girl just shook her head, grabbing Shiloh's hand and placing it where her shoulder met her collarbone.

"Not like that," Paisley shook her head softly. "My skin. There are no bruises. I am not hurt," she slowly moved Shiloh's hand over to her shoulder.

The green eyed girl studied Paisley's skin for a moment before nodding softly. She was filled with a mix of adoration and anger. Anger that someone would have ever hurt Paisley in the first place.

"And I intend on making sure you stay this way," Shiloh said softly after a few minutes of silence. She brought both of her hands up and ran them down Paisley's arms, lacing their fingers together. "You're safe now. No one's gonna lay a hand on you."

Paisley's lips pursed together slowly, as if she were deep in thought. Shiloh ran her thumb over the back of the smaller girl's hand in an attempt to comfort her.

"There were bad things," Paisley said softly, taking a step away from Shiloh and bringing her hands to the waistband of her own pants. "But they are gone now. They are only dreams," she mumbled, shedding herself of her jeans and kicking them aside.

Shiloh had to stop herself from staring. Everything about the smaller girl was just… perfect. She wished Paisley could realize that.

"I'm so fucking proud of you," Shiloh laughed softly and moved forwards, kissing Paisley's forehead. "You don't even know how amazing you really are."

Paisley blushed, looking up at Shiloh and smiling softly. "I love you," she whispered, standing on her tiptoes and kissing Shiloh's cheek. "I do."

"I love *you*," Shiloh laughed quietly, glancing over Paisley's shoulder and at the shower. "C'mon," she whispered, taking a step backwards and removing her own jeans. Paisley watched, unashamed.

Shiloh turned on the shower, allowing the water to warm up before shedding the rest of her clothes. After the initial uncomfortableness, she found herself completely at ease allowing Paisley to see her like this. She'd never felt this way around anyone else. It was a freeing feeling.

"Help," Paisley mumbled, awkwardly fumbling with the clasp on the back of her bra, which was the only piece of clothing she had left on besides her beanie. She huffed and let her hands fall to her sides in frustration.

"Hey," Shiloh shook her head. "Don't worry, these things are hard to work," she scooted behind Paisley and messed with the clasp for a few moments, laughing softly at her own struggle.

"There," she sighed once she finally got the clasp undone. Paisley shrugged the material off of her shoulders and turned around. Shiloh's breath caught in her throat when she suddenly realized that they were both completely uncovered.

It wasn't even in a sexual way. She was just completely in awe that Paisley was comfortable enough to do something like this around her. When they had first met, the smaller girl would practically lock herself in the bathroom just to change her socks. It warmed Shiloh's heart knowing that Paisley had grown to be this comfortable with her.

"C'mon," the older girl whispered, gently removing Paisley's beanie and placing it on the counter. Taking Paisley's hand, Shiloh led the brown eyed girl over to the shower. She pulled the curtain aside, stepping into the bathtub and away from the stream of water.

Paisley suddenly grew nervous. She wasn't even sure why. This was just... different. She had never been this intimate with someone before. It was new, and she wasn't sure how she should take it. Shiloh grew concerned when she smaller girl stood hesitantly in front of the bathtub.

"It's just a shower, Pais," Shiloh ran her thumb over the back of Paisley's palm, repeating the words that Paisley had said to her earlier. The smaller girl took a shy step forwards, meeting Shiloh's eyes.

"It's me, Paisley," Shiloh whispered, grabbing Paisley's other hand and lacing their fingers together. "It's okay. I've got you," she gently pulled the smaller girl forwards.

Paisley nodded softly and stepped into the bathtub, suddenly only inches away from Shiloh. She subtly studied the older girl's figure, biting her lip. She decided she liked being in love. It was a good feeling.

"You're still covered in flour," Shiloh giggled, placing her hands on Paisley's shoulders. She turned them around so the smaller girl could back up into the stream of water.

"Is it warm enough?" Shiloh asked, bringing her hands up to smooth Paisley's hair out of her face. The smaller girl nodded, leaning her head back slightly to keep the water out of her eyes.

"Here," Shiloh whispered, pouring a small amount of shampoo into her hand before moving behind Paisley. "Is this okay?" she asked quietly, bringing her hands up and slowly massaging the substance into Paisley's scalp.

"It tickles," Paisley giggled, leaning her head back to make things easier for Shiloh. The older girl rolled her eyes playfully, working the shampoo throughout her hair.

"You know something, Lo?" Paisley asked, allowing Shiloh to move her back slightly so she could rinse the shampoo out of her hair.

"What?" Shiloh laughed softly as she worked her hands through Paisley's curls. Even though she couldn't see Paisley's face, she could tell the smaller girl was deep in thought.

"You are…" Paisley bit her lip. "You are… eth… ethereal," she clasped her hands together once she found the right word.

Shiloh raised an eyebrow, feeling butterflies erupt in her stomach. "That's a new word," she managed to say, still in shock by Paisley's sudden comment.

"I know," Paisley hummed. Shiloh reached over the small girl and grabbed the conditioner, squeezing a generous amount into her palms and beginning to work it through Paisley's hair.

"Where'd you learn that?" Shiloh asked, curling the ends of Paisley's hair around her fingers and waiting curiously for an answer. The smaller girl tilted her head to the side slightly.

"Maia," Paisley nodded once. Shiloh furrowed her eyebrows. "I asked her. I needed a word. Because pretty is not enough, Lo. Do you know that?" The smaller girl turned around to face Shiloh, studying her features.

"So we used a word book. And I liked that word. So I made sure to remember it," Paisley smiled softly. She looked up at her girlfriend hopefully.

"Wow…" Shiloh breathed out, biting her lip. "No one's ever told me something like that before," she admitted, reaching up and moving a loose strand of wet hair from Paisley's face.

"Well they should more often," Paisley shrugged, turning back around and moving back under the water to rinse the rest of the conditioner out of her scalp. "Because it is true."

"You know what you are, Paisley?" Shiloh asked, a small smile creeping across her lips. Paisley paused her motions for a moment to look at Shiloh over her shoulder.

"You…" Shiloh began, moving forwards and wrapping her arms around Paisley's waist. "You are captivating," she whispered against the small girl's ear before placing a soft kiss against her neck. "Always have been."

Paisley laughed softly and tilted her head to the side, resting it against Shiloh's. "I did not know that," she admitted. Shiloh's eyes widened and she pulled her head back.

"You didn't?" the green eyed girl asked, moving in front of Paisley and studying her eyes. Paisley shook her head slowly, slightly confused by Shiloh's sudden change in disposition.

"I need you to know," Shiloh said firmly, placing her hands on Paisley's shoulders and pressing her forehead against the smaller girl's. "You are beautiful, Paisley," she whispered, ghosting her fingers down Paisley's shoulder blades. "No one can take that away from you."

Paisley's eyes moved down to Shiloh's lips and then back up to the girl's green eyes, studying her closely. "Thank you," she said quietly. "You make me feel beautiful."

"Then I'll continue telling you that until the day we die," Shiloh nodded softly. A soft smile curved across Paisley's lips and she closed the gap between them, bringing their lips together for a soft yet deep kiss. And for someone who had little experience, Paisley sure was a good kisser.

Shiloh practically had to catch her breath when their lips parted. Her heart was racing a million miles per hour, and she blinked a few times to clear her clouded vision.

"Wow," Paisley mumbled, bringing her hand up to roll her bottom lip between her fingers. "I like kissing you."

Shiloh couldn't help but laugh. Even in the most intimate of moments, Paisley somehow managed to maintain her innocence. She reached out and cupped Paisley's cheek, pressing a kiss to the smaller girl's forehead. "Me too," she whispered against the soft skin. Paisley shivered under her touch.

"Your turn," Paisley laughed softly, reaching for the shampoo and using her free hand to spin Shiloh around so now she was under the stream of warm water.

Shiloh inhaled slowly when she felt Paisley's fingers work their way through her hair, massaging the shampoo into her scalp and down her long waves. It was as if every little thing Paisley did made her fall more and more in love with the smaller girl.

Paisley grew confused when Shiloh let out a soft laugh. She pulled her hands away and tilted her head to the side. "What is funny?" the smaller girl asked.

"I just..." Shiloh shook her head and glanced back at Paisley. "I was just thinking how far we've come."

"What do you mean?" Paisley asked, pulling Shiloh backwards so she could rinse the shampoo out of her hair.

Shiloh leaned her head back, staring at the ceiling and thinking for a moment.

"Not even as a couple," Shiloh said, closing her eyes and thinking. "Just… when you first came here, all you could talk about was how you needed a bed before it got dark. And now…" she turned around, smiling softly. "Look at you. You've grown so much."

"Is that bad?" Paisley pursed her lips. Shiloh quickly shook her head.

"Of course not," she smoothed out Paisley's hair and gathered it over her shoulder. "And I mean… look at how far we've come," she laughed quietly. "You completely turned my opinion of you around. And yes, that's a good thing. A very good thing."

Paisley smiled shyly, biting her lip. "Stop," she mumbled, nudging Shiloh's shoulder.

"Stop what?" the older girl raised an eyebrow.

"Stop making me love you more," Paisley laughed and hid her face with her hands. Shiloh couldn't help the smile that tugged at her lips, and she pulled Paisley's hands away from her face to lace their fingers together.

"I don't think I can do that," she laughed. "I'm only stating the truth."

The older girl planted a kiss on Paisley's cheek before grabbing the bottle of conditioner. Paisley helped her work it through her hair, taking her time as she combed through the dark locks with her fingers. Everything about Shiloh amazed her. Before Shiloh, she never knew that humans could be works of art.

"C'mon," Shiloh whispered, turning off the water and reaching out of the shower to grab a towel. She stepped out of the shower, drying herself off and wrapping the towel around her torso before grabbing another towel and helping Paisley out of the bathtub.

"There," she laughed after Paisley secured the towel around her chest. "All clean." Paisley smiled softly, standing in front of the mirror and studying her reflection.

And then suddenly, something clicked. Something felt familiar. Too familiar. She was hit with a rush of memories, inhaling sharply just as flashes of the past invaded the darkness.

C H A P T E R 1 5

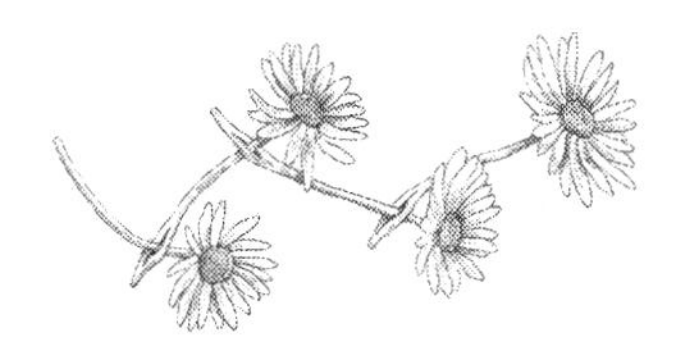

Paisley stood in front of the mirror, wiping carelessly at the makeup on her face. She hadn't even wanted to go to the stupid party, but the girls on the cheer team had convinced her to go. As soon as they had gotten there, though, she'd been completely abandoned. Having no one to talk to, Paisley walked home. In the rain.

She huffed, curling her small fingers around the edges of the counter and hanging her head down to take a deep breath. As if her day couldn't get any worse, she heard heavy footsteps coming up the stairs.

Frantically, Paisley flipped the light switch off and pressed her back against the bathroom door. As the footsteps got closer, she could practically hear her heart pounding against her chest. Not now. Not tonight.

The footsteps paused outside the door, and moments later her uncle's loud voice appeared inches away from her ear.

"Where have you been?"

Paisley winced, squeezing her eyes shut. Just stay quiet. He would eventually give up and go downstairs. Unfortunately, she couldn't stop herself from gasping when he slammed his hand against the door.

"Paisley, where have you been?" his voice was low and intimidating. "Get out here. Now."

Paisley shivered. Clenching her jaw, she slowly turned around and pulled the door open. Right away, she smelled the alcohol on the older man's breath. It made her sick to her stomach.

"I was just—"

"Don't," he cut her off, taking a step forwards. Paisley took a step backwards in return, biting her lip when her back pressed up against the wall. Her eyes darted around the empty hallway, desperate for some kind of escape.

"You've been sneaking out again?" he sneered, tilting his head to the side and leaning forwards. Paisley just remained silent. Silence was better than anything she could say. "I thought you learned your lesson last time," he growled.

"Speak up, girl," he jabbed her shoulder with his index finger. The small girl took a deep breath and bit her lip, avoiding his eyes. The air reeked of alcohol and it stung her eyes, aiding the tears that were already threatening to fall.

"The cheer team wanted me to go to this party..." Paisley said softly, hanging her head down. She closed her eyes, wishing that she could click her heels and magically make all of this disappear. But this wasn't a movie. This was real life. Too real, in her opinion.

"Bullshit," he spat. Paisley inhaled sharply when he grabbed her chin with his hand, pulling her forwards and forcing her to meet his eyes.

After a few seconds of tensed silence, Paisley glanced over at the small table in the hallway. Her eyes landed on a picture of her Aunt Susie and her, at one of her birthday parties. For some odd reason, a small smile formed on her face.

It quickly diminished, though. The second her uncle saw what she was looking at, he shoved her back and sent the frame flying across the hallway. It collided with the wall, sending glass flying in all directions.

Without thinking, Paisley gasped and ran forwards, sliding down to her knees and grabbing the photo from underneath the broken glass. She yelped when a hand grabbed the back of her sweatshirt, practically throwing her up to her feet. Paisley met her uncle's eyes pleadingly.

"Give me that," he spat, tearing the picture out of the smaller girl's hands. Paisley whimpered, forcing herself to stay still instead of fighting him for it. It would just end badly.

He turned the picture around in his hands, letting go of Paisley's shirt. She quickly took a step backwards, feeling glass crunch under her worn tennis shoes.

"You don't deserve to be associated with her," he laughed bitterly. Paisley fought back tears as she watched him tear the picture in two, tossing the paper behind him and taking a step towards her.

"It should've been you," he practically growled. Paisley felt the first tear escape her waterline. Shit. If he caught her crying, it would only prolong the inevitable. In a panic, she quickly tried to escape past him and to her bedroom. Bad idea.

The smaller girl winced when strong fingers curled around her wrist, yanking her backwards and slamming her against the banister. She gasped, looking behind her at the long drop down the stairs. Her free hand immediately clenched the railing, trying to keep her feet planted firmly in the ground.

"I'm sorry," Paisley whispered, feeling her voice crack on her words. She couldn't control the tears, and she used a shaky hand to try and wipe her eyes before he caught on. Unfortunately, moments later she was met with his raised hand connecting with her face. She flinched, feeling the sting of his hand throbbing against her cheek.

"No you're not," he laughed bitterly. "You killed her. Don't you think you've avoided death one too many times?"

Paisley just stood still, focusing her eyes on the wall behind his head. Her breaths were unsteady, and she was still haunted by the sudden drop directly behind her. If he wanted to, he could send her flying over the banister with just one push.

His hands were brought up to her shoulders, digging his thumbs into the space beneath her collarbones. She whimpered, trying to shake him off. He only tightened his grip on her, moving impossibly closer to her face.

"We should have never taken you in," his voice was a low rumble, in an octave that Paisley could only associate with pure hatred. She squeezed her eyes shut, trying to erase the scent of alcohol from her memory.

"You're like a fucking bad luck charm," he continued, digging his nails into her back. It took everything in her not to scream. If she did, it would only make things worse.

"First your parents, then Susan, who's next? Me?" he chuckled, letting go of Paisley with a small shove that nearly sent the girl tumbling backwards. She quickly grabbed onto the banister, wincing when she felt the small cuts in her shoulders.

"I could tell someone, you know," Paisley blurted out. She didn't know what inside of her had driven her to open her mouth, but she regretted it the second she did. The large man whipped his head around, glaring at her.

"What was that?" he stared her down, making Paisley's heart race. "And what exactly would you tell someone?"

Paisley swallowed hard, clenching her fists. "About this," she motioned to him. "About you."

"But you wouldn't," he laughed bitterly. Paisley inhaled slowly, knowing her was right. He was the only family she had left. And family was family, no matter how fucked up they seemed to be.

Knowing he'd won, he chuckled to himself and disappeared down the hallway. The second Paisley heard his bedroom door slam shut, she hurried back into the bathroom. She didn't have time for tears.

When this had first started, she would spend hours crying. But now, she'd grown used to it. Paisley figured there was no point in feeling sorry for herself. This was just how her life was supposed to be. Some people were meant to be politicians, some garbage men, and Paisley was just meant to be at the receiving end of someone's abuse. That must have just been how the universe settled things for her.

She locked the door behind her, leaving it unlocked was a fatal mistake she had made before. Her hand found the light switch and she toyed with it for a few moments. Biting her lip, she kept the light off. She'd rather be in the darkness than be faced with her reflection. It would only make things more real for her.

The small girl peeled off her shirt, tossing it aside and running her fingers across the newly opened wounds in her back. It was almost as if digging his nails into her shoulders was a signature mark of his. As if he wanted to make sure it scarred over, leaving her with a permanent reminder of the pain he had inflicted.

When she pulled her hands away and felt blood, Paisley sighed softly. The nightlight in the bathroom gave her just enough light to make her way around. Quietly, she dampened a paper towel and dabbed her shoulders, ridding her skin of the red substance.

Once she had cleaned herself up, she splashed cold water on her face to try and keep the tears away. With a deep, shaky breath, she slipped out of the bathroom and tiptoed down to the opposite end of the hall.

She flicked the light on once she reached her bedroom, surrounded by the blinding yellow color of her walls. The small girl changed into her pajamas, collapsing onto the end of her bed with a heavy sigh.

A movement from the corner of her eye caught her attention. Paisley sat up slowly, scooting closer to her window. The house next to her had a window across from hers, and she could make out two silhouettes from behind the curtain.

One was a little girl. She knew that, she'd seen the young family outside on occasion. She watched as the smaller girl jumped into the figure's arms, wrapping her small arms around the person's neck. Paisley sighed. In a burst of frustration, she yanked her curtain shut and kicked the edge of her nightstand. It wasn't fair.

Why did it have to be her?

Paisley turned off the lights, having no interest in being awake for any longer. She would gladly take any kind of escape that sleep had to offer her. Gently, she crawled under her blankets and curled her hands up in the covers.

When she was a little girl, Paisley always believed that her covers could keep the bad things away. No matter what, it was as if the imaginary monsters couldn't get her as long as she was under the blankets. But now, that wasn't true. Because here she was, under her blankets, and she could still feel the stinging sensation on her cheek from where her uncle had hit her.

If the covers didn't keep the bad things away, then what did?

"Paisley?"

The smaller girl jumped when Shiloh's voice invaded her visions. Suddenly, she was swept back into reality. Everything began to fizzle in her vision until eventually she could see clearly. The smaller girl shivered, turning around and putting on a brave face in front of the green eyed girl.

"Did it just…?" Shiloh pointed to Paisley and then back to herself. "Did you just…?" She struggled to find the right words.

The second Paisley looked up at her with glassy eyes, Shiloh stepped forwards and cupped the smaller girl's cheeks. "Hey, hey, look at me," she said softly, keeping her voice low in an attempt not to scare the girl.

Paisley blinked a few times, looking up at Shiloh pleadingly. The green eyed girl could practically feel the pain radiating off of the smaller girl.

"Paisley, look at me," Shiloh repeated herself. "This..." she motioned around the room. "This is real. This is right now."

"And that..." she reached up and tapped her index finger against Paisley's temple. "That's not real. It's in the past. It's gone... it's over."

All the smaller girl could offer was a slow nod before she brought her hands up to hide her face, feeling the first tear roll down her cheek. Shiloh took a deep breath and pulled Paisley into her arms.

"Let's go lay down, okay?" Shiloh held up her towel with one hand and led Paisley down the hallway with her other hand. She was thankful their roommates didn't get home for a few hours, otherwise she'd have a lot of explaining to do.

Once they got into the bedroom, Paisley sniffed softly and padded over to the dresser. Shiloh did the same, changing into a loose tank top and leggings. Paisley opted for a pair of boy shorts and one of Shiloh's oversized band shirts. Paisley watched anxiously as Shiloh finished changing.

Without any words, Shiloh crawled onto the bed. She patted the space beside her, which Paisley quickly filled. Laying back, Shiloh pulled Paisley into her side. The smaller girl rested her head on Shiloh's shoulder, trying to take deep breaths and will the remnants of her memory away.

"Tell me about it," Shiloh whispered after a few moments of silence. Paisley looked up in confusion, her glazed eyes meeting Shiloh's.

"Try and tell me what you saw," Shiloh explained, reaching over and smoothing out Paisley's hair. "You've got so much locked up there," she whispered, running her thumb across Paisley's forehead. "That's a lot to handle for someone so small. Maybe telling someone will help take the weight off."

"He hit me," Paisley whispered, looking away from Shiloh in shame. The black ink near the girl's collarbone caught her attention and she slowly reached out, running her fingers over the exposed skin of her tattoo. Shiloh shivered.

"Keep going," the older girl whispered, even though she would rather not hear these memories. Paisley didn't deserve everything that had happened to her. And now, she had to practically live them all over again. But Shiloh would do anything to ease her pain.

Paisley's fingers continued to trace the outline of Shiloh's tattoo, moving with the shape of the daisy petals. She bit her lip and glanced up at Shiloh.

"It was night," she continued, remembering more details. "And I came back from a party… and he was mad. And he hit me. And…" Suddenly remembering something, Paisley sat up quickly.

Shiloh grew confused when Paisley quickly lifted her shirt over her head. The small girl turned her head as far as she could, trying to see the back of her shoulders.

"What are you doing?" Shiloh sat up beside the girl, placing a hand on Paisley's shoulders. Moments later, the smaller girl couldn't stop herself from bursting into tears.

"What's wrong?" Shiloh quickly pulled Paisley into her lap, and the smaller girl buried her head in the older girl's neck. Shiloh's eyes traveled down to Paisley's exposed shoulders, realization flooding over her when she saw the small scars on either side.

"Did he do this?" Shiloh asked softly, running her fingers over the raised white ridges. Paisley flinched at first, but eased into her touch. The smaller girl simply nodded, ashamed that she had let this happen to her.

"Here," Shiloh whispered, reaching over to her nightstand and grabbing a black marker. Paisley grew confused when Shiloh uncapped the pen and began drawing something on her back.

"What are you doing?" Paisley sniffed, lifting her head slightly and trying to crane her neck back.

"Giving you the stars," Shiloh bit her lip in concentration before setting the pen down. Before Paisley could ask any other questions, Shiloh eased them both off of the bed and spun Paisley around so her back was facing the mirror on her wall.

"Turn your head a little," Shiloh instructed, gently pushing Paisley's chin to the side so she could see her reflection in the mirror. The smaller girl's eyes widened when she saw small, black stars doodled where her scars had been.

"You're a galaxy, Pais," the older girl whispered, trailing her fingers down Paisley's spine. "There's an endless amount of thoughts and feelings and emotions all stored in you."

"And just because some bitter black hole tries to steal you away, nothing can control you," Shiloh continued, meeting Paisley's eyes in the mirror. "In the end, you win just by continuing to exist."

"And yeah, maybe you've got a few scars to show for it," Shiloh shrugged and kissed Paisley's cheek. "But there's so much more to you than just your body. He can't damage what really matters." She turned Paisley around and pressed her hand just above her heart.

"It doesn't matter how we fall, or what scars we have to show for it," Shiloh ran her thumb over the smooth skin of Paisley's cheek, catching the tears that had fallen. "All that matters is that you get back up."

A moment of silence passed between them as Paisley's glassy eyes studied Shiloh's. She abruptly moved forwards, practically tackling the older girl into a hug. Her hands clung to the back of Shiloh's shirt and she buried her head into the crook of her neck.

"Thank you," Paisley mumbled against Shiloh's skin, making the other girl shiver. "You help me so much. I do not know what I would do without you."

"I may say a bunch of fancy words, but at the end of the day you're the one that's pretty amazing, Paisley," Shiloh squeezed the smaller girl's hand and gently led her back over to the bed. Paisley immediately crawled under the covers, looking at Shiloh hopefully.

Once Shiloh laid back down, Paisley resumed tracing the outline of her tattoo. "He broke a picture," the smaller girl began to continue.

"You don't have to…" Shiloh whispered, lifting her head when she realized Paisley was still trying to explain what she had seen. The brown eyed girl shook her head.

"I want to," she bit her lip. "I need to."

"If you feel like you can," Shiloh gave the girl a soft smile. Paisley just nodded and directed her attention back to Shiloh's tattoo, giggling softly when she saw she had given the girl goosebumps.

"The picture was of me. And Aunt… Aunt Susie," Paisley swallowed the lump in her throat. "He broke it… and he… he hit me," she took a deep breath and looked up at Shiloh to study her reaction.

"Do you wanna stop?" Shiloh asked, noticing Paisley's anxious features. The small girl just sighed and nodded, resting her head on Shiloh's shoulder.

"Sing?" Paisley whispered, glancing up at the green eyed girl. Shiloh laughed quietly and smoothed out Paisley's hair.

"Only for you," she kissed Paisley's forehead and stared up at the ceiling as she began to sing. As her voice began to fade out, Paisley rolled over on her side and gave the girl a soft smile.

"More?" Paisley giggled, looking up at Shiloh hopefully. The older girl just laughed softly and combed her fingers through Paisley's hair.

"Only for you."

CHAPTER 16

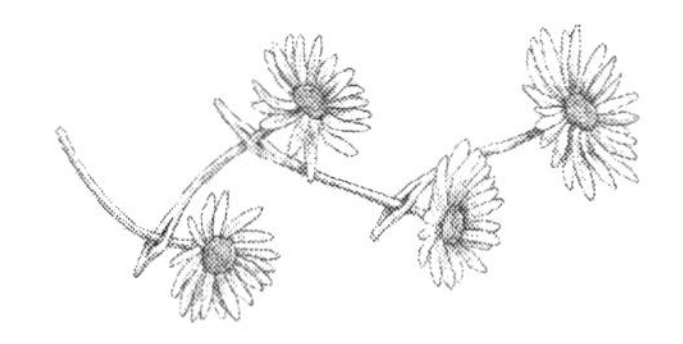

Shiloh had nearly fallen asleep when she heard the apartment door slam shut and the jingle of keys, signifying that someone was home. Before she could open her mouth, Paisley was already scrambling off of the bed and running down the hallway.

Confused, Shiloh wiped her eyes and got up to follow the small girl. When she reached the top of the stairs, she paused.

"Ryland?" Paisley's small voice echoed through the large apartment. Realizing what her girlfriend was doing, Shiloh took a step backwards and quietly slipped back into the bedroom.

To say the light haired girl was surprised when she heard Paisley call her name was an understatement. She jumped, turning around and looking at the smaller girl who had practically been avoiding her for the past few days.

"Yeah?" Ryland wasn't sure what reaction Paisley would be expecting from her, but she tried to act as normal as she could.

"I…" Paisley looked down at her shoes and then over at the couch. "I need to talk to you," she looked over at Vanessa, who was scanning the refrigerator intently. "Alone," the smaller girl added.

Vanessa turned around, looking from Paisley to Ryland. Her and Leah had practically been Paisley's shield from Shiloh and Ryland for the past few days. So to say she was in shock that Paisley was suddenly reaching out to Ryland would be an understatement.

"Is everything okay?" Vanessa asked quietly. She glanced at Ryland, who appeared to be just as confused as she was. Paisley nodded quickly.

"Yes," she looked up from the ground and send Vanessa a hopeful look. Not wanting to interrupt anything, Vanessa simply grabbed a water bottle and made her way upstairs.

"Can we..?" Paisley motioned over to the couch. Ryland just nodded and followed Paisley into the living room, plopping down on their signature blue couch.

"What's up?" Ryland asked, brushing her hair out of her face and giving Paisley her full attention. She noticed how the smaller girl squirmed in her seat awkwardly.

"I am sorry," Paisley spoke hesitantly, looking up at Ryland and biting her lip. She wasn't sure what kind of reaction she was expecting. "Shiloh called the doctor."

"What?" Ryland grew confused. "Why?"

"You punched me," Paisley mumbled, looking down at her shoes.

"I punched you and Shiloh had to call the doctor?" Ryland didn't have a clue what was going on. "We haven't even talked for the past week?"

"Exactly!" Paisley jumped to her feet and shook her head, beginning to pace back and forth in an attempt to collect her thoughts.

"I remembered," Paisley abruptly stopped walking and turned to face Ryland. "I remembered you. At school… and you…" she involuntarily brought her hands up to cup her nose. Ryland realized what she was referring to almost instantly.

"Fuck," the light haired girl cursed under her breath and shook her head. "I—,"

"I know," Paisley cut her off, stepping forwards in a burst of courage. "Do not say sorry. Do not." The smaller girl shook her head and held up a finger to signal for Ryland to wait.

"I am remembering," Paisley continued after taking a deep breath. "But… I do not understand much," the small girl bit her lip and looked down. "But I am trying."

"As long as you get better," Ryland shrugged. Paisley looked up in confusion.

"You can ignore me for as long as you want if it means you get better, Paisley," Ryland chuckled. "I just want you to get better. I think we all do."

"I do not want to ignore you," Paisley furrowed her eyebrows. "I did not mean to… I was scared." She sighed heavily and sat back down on the couch. "I am sorry."

"You know I'd never do that to you again, right?" Ryland raised an eyebrow. Paisley nodded softly.

"I know," she gave the girl a shy smile. "You were protecting Lo. That is a good thing."

"Come here, you dork," Ryland laughed, opening her arms and standing up. Paisley's face lit up when she realized Ryland wasn't mad at her, and she practically jumped into the girl's arms.

"Thank you," Paisley giggled when Ryland nearly picked her up off the ground. "You're welcome."

"You really thought I'd be mad?" Ryland raised an eyebrow when they pulled away from the hug. Paisley simply shrugged.

"Just don't hurt Shiloh," Ryland teased, holding up a fist and making Paisley giggle.

"I will not," she shook her head furiously. "Ever. Promise."

"Bump it, dork," Ryland laughed, holding out her fist. Paisley giggled and bumped it, making an exploding noise and crinkling her nose. Both girls jumped when they heard Leah's voice appear out of nowhere.

"Oh my god!" the smaller girl gasped when she saw the kitchen. "There's flour everywhere!"

Paisley's face grew red and she could've sworn she heard Shiloh laughing from upstairs.

Nearly two weeks had passed since Valentine's Day. Everything seemed to be going smoothly. Paisley and Shiloh were as close as ever, and the couple had even grown closer to Maia and Toby.

Currently, Paisley was wildly digging through the dresser. She huffed in frustration, unable to find what she wanted.

"Looking for something?"

Paisley turned around when she heard Shiloh's voice fill the empty room. The dark haired girl had her hands behind her back, smirking as she took a step forward.

"I can not find my b—," Paisley was cut off when Shiloh pulled the light blue beanie out from behind her back and tugged it onto Paisley's head with a small smile.

"It was in the bathroom, doofus," she laughed, winking at the smaller girl.

"Oh," Paisley giggled and fixed the cap on her head, walking over to the mirror to make sure it looked okay. Shiloh followed her, wrapping her arms around the younger girl's waist and lying her head on her shoulder.

"You look cute today," the green eyed girl whispered, meeting Paisley's eyes in their reflection. The smaller girl blushed, looking down at the ground shyly.

"Look at yourself," Shiloh laughed softly and tilted Paisley's chin back up so she could look at herself in the mirror. "Not many people could pull of a red coat and a blue beanie," she kissed Paisley's temple. "You're so gorgeous."

"Stop," Paisley giggled bashfully, bringing her hands up to cover her face. Laughing, Shiloh spun the smaller girl around and placed her hands on her waist.

"Do you know what today is, Pais?" the dark haired girl asked softly. Paisley furrowed her eyebrows for a moment before shaking her head. Shiloh bit her lip and nodded.

"Friday," Shiloh crinkled her nose. "I think I should get a celebratory kiss."

Paisley giggled, seeing no point in arguing. She wrapped her arms around Shiloh's neck and stood on her tiptoes so she could bring their lips together.

"You're good at that," Shiloh teased once they pulled away. Paisley just giggled bashfully and grabbed Shiloh's hand, tugging her down the hallway and into the living room.

"Class?" Ryland asked, looking up from her spot on the couch. Shiloh nodded, giving Ryland a knowing look. The light haired girl stood up to hug her.

"You sure you've got everything?" Shiloh whispered against Ryland's ear.

"Have some faith, loser," Ryland chuckled, nudging Shiloh's shoulder when she pulled away. "Leah and Nessa are out getting some stuff now."

Shiloh gave her a soft nod before turning back to Paisley, who had wandered over to the window to watch the cars on the street below.

"C'mon," Shiloh laughed, lacing their fingers together and nodding towards the door.

Once they made it to the school, Paisley eagerly ran ahead of Shiloh to the classroom. She spotted Maia and Toby at their usual table in the back, and practically dragged Shiloh over.

"Happy Friday," Shiloh groaned dramatically, making Paisley laugh from beside her. She tossed her bag onto the ground and sat down on the wooden stool, grabbing Paisley's hand once she did the same.

"What're your guys' plans for the weekend?" Toby asked, looking up from his sculpture for a moment. Shiloh bit her lip and glanced at Paisley.

"Go grab us a canvas, Pais," she nudged her girlfriend. Paisley tilted her head to the side.

"Do you wanna work on something together?" Shiloh asked, giving Paisley a soft smile. That was all it took for Paisley to smile widely and hurry off to the back of the classroom. Shiloh immediately leaned in closer to her other two classmates.

"It's Paisley's birthday today," she whispered, glancing back in the smaller girl's direction.

"It is?" Maia's eyes widened and she took her attention off of her sketchbook. "Does she know?"

"I think we'd be hearing about it from her if she knew," Toby spoke up. Maia shoved him playfully, nearly knocking him out of his chair. He scoffed and turned back to his sculpture.

"I think she will," Shiloh smirked. Before Maia could ask more, Paisley appeared back at Shiloh's side with a small canvas, presenting it to the older girl proudly.

"What do you wanna paint?" Shiloh asked, giving Maia a knowing wink and turning back to Paisley. Over the past weeks Paisley had accompanied her to art class, she had found it was a much more rewarding experience to paint what Paisley suggested. That way, she had someone to please. It encouraged her to work harder, and to go out of her comfort zone.

"Hmmm," Paisley hummed and sat down. Shiloh dug her brushes out of her backpack while Paisley thought.

"A castle," Paisley's eyes widened when she finally came up with an idea.

"A castle?" Shiloh raised an eyebrow at the smaller girl, who simply nodded.

"Yes," Paisley pointed to the canvas. "A big gray castle. With moss and vines on the walls," she traced the shape on the white material. "And a big tower right here," she tapped the upper corner. Shiloh laughed softly.

"Well if you're so sure on what you want, why don't you start?" Shiloh handed Paisley one of her paintbrushes. The smaller girl's eyes widened in shock and she turned the brush around in her hands.

"Me?" Paisley looked up at Shiloh in confusion.

"Yes, you," Shiloh laughed. She saw worry spread across Paisley's features and quickly squeezed her hand. "I told you we would work on this one together."

"But…" Paisley looked down at the brush and bit her lip. "What if I mess up?"

"Then we fix it," Shiloh shrugged. "Together."

"Together," Paisley whispered softly, looking at the palette of paints in from of them. She looked up at Shiloh for approval before moving to dip her brush in the gray paint.

"Wait," Shiloh reached out and grabbed Paisley's hand gently. "It's easier if you start by painting the background first, and then you move on to the closer things."

"Oh," Paisley moved her paintbrush and pointed to the blue paint. "The sky?"

Shiloh nodded, watching as Paisley carefully dipped the brush in the paint and brought it to the canvas. Pausing for a few moments, the small girl began to blend in the sky in small strokes.

"Good job," Shiloh smiled, scooting her stool closer to Paisley so she could have a better view. Maia looked up from her painting and smirked at the two girls.

They worked on their painting for the rest of the class, and Shiloh practically had to pry the paintbrush out of Paisley's hands when it was time to leave.

"Have fun," Maia laughed softly, giving Shiloh a hug as they said their goodbyes.

Laughing, Shiloh rolled her eyes playfully. "Do you want to meet us for dinner?" she asked, glancing back at Paisley to make sure she wasn't listening. "We're going to Lorienzo's for pizza."

"Toby," Maia nudged her boyfriend, who was nearly falling asleep at the table. He whipped his head up in confusion, making both girls laugh. Maia leaned down and whispered something in his ear, which earned a soft nod from the boy.

"We'll be there," Maia laughed. Shiloh thanked her before retrieving Paisley from a group of students on the other side of the room. Once they made it out to the car, Paisley clapped her hands together.

"Today is good," she sighed contently, bringing her knees up to her chest and resting her chins on her knees. Shiloh laughed softly and leaned over to kiss Paisley's cheek before she started the car.

When they reached the apartment, Shiloh quickly sent Ryland a text to let them know they were there before running after Paisley, who was already waiting in the elevator.

"What's the rush?" Shiloh laughed nervously, reaching out and fixing Paisley's beanie. The smaller girl just shrugged. Shiloh's phone buzzed and she quickly checked her messages.

[4:23 – Ryland] Not ready yet!! Stall!!

Shiloh cursed under her breath, quickly trying to think of a way to keep Paisley occupied. Without thinking, she reached out and pressed a handful of buttons on the elevator console. Paisley furrowed her eyebrows.

"What was that for?" Paisley asked, growing confused when the elevator started going downwards once more. Shiloh bit her lip and shrugged, looking back down at her phone.

[4:24 – Shiloh] Hurry.

When Shiloh looked back up from her phone, Paisley was watching the screen above the doors in confusion. The numbers changed randomly as the elevator moved from floor to floor.

"Sorry," Shiloh mumbled, biting her lip.

"I do not understand," Paisley turned to the older girl. Before Shiloh could answer, though, the elevator finally dinged. The large silver doors rolled open. Shiloh didn't have a chance to protest before Paisley was skipping happily down the hallway to their apartment.

"Paisley, wai—!" Shiloh cut herself off when Paisley pushed the door wide open. The dark haired girl quickly ran up behind her.

"SURPRISE!"

Paisley stumbled a few steps backwards, scared of the loud noise. She practically ran into Shiloh, who had just skidded to a stop in front of the door. The second Shiloh saw the look of terror on Paisley's face, she instantly regretted what she had done.

"Surprise!"

Paisley gasped, running into the living room and falling onto her knees next to the large dollhouse. She glanced up at her parents with a look of sheer joy on her face.

"This is for me?" she asked, running her fingers over the colorful walls of the wooden dollhouse. Her father chuckled and sat down on the floor beside her. Her mother followed suit.

"Yes ma'am," her mother reached over and smoothed out the smaller girl's hair. "Your father made it himself."

"You made this?!" Paisley gasped, leaning in to inspect the dollhouse once more. She decided this was the best birthday present she had ever gotten.

"I know you were expecting a lot, but we just didn't have the money, mija," her father sighed and ran a hand through his hair. "I figured this w—,"

"It's perfect!" Paisley squealed, crawling over and tackling her father in a hug. "It's even better because you made it," she giggled.

"Thank you, thank you, thank you!" she smiled widely and hopped over to give her mother a hug, as well. "This is the best birthday ever!"

Her parents exchanged surprised glances. They had expected her to be disappointed with the lack of presents after her father lost his job. But instead, Paisley had been grateful for whatever she got.

"We definitely lucked out with you, kiddo," her mother smiled softly, pulling her daughter into her lap and kissing her forehead. "You're gonna do great things one day."

"Yeah, but I have to play with my dollhouse first!" Paisley smiled widely and wiggled out of her mother's lap so she could go retrieve her dolls from her room.

Paisley's tiny footsteps disappeared down the hallway, leaving her parents in the living room. Her mother wiped away a few tears.

"God, I love that kid," the woman laughed, glancing back to the hallway where Paisley had disappeared down.

"She's got something special, that's for sure," her father laughed as Paisley came scrambling back into the room with a handful of small toy dolls.

Shiloh was surprised when as soon as Paisley's eyes were brought out of their distant state and focused back on her, the smaller girl burst into tears and threw herself into Shiloh's arms.

"What's going on?" Ryland and the two other roommates jogged out into the hallway. Shiloh gave them a look of confusion, holding the crying girl tightly against her chest.

"I'm sorry, Paisley, I didn't mean to s—,"

"I m-m-miss them," Paisley managed to whisper between sobs. Shiloh's eyes widened and without another word, she scooped the smaller girl up into her arms and carried her into the apartment.

Silently, the other three roommates closed the door and followed after Shiloh, who sat down on the couch and pulled Paisley into her lap. The girl had her head buried in Shiloh's shoulder.

'I'm so stupid' Shiloh mouthed to her other three roommates. They all stayed quiet, sitting down around the girl and exchanging glances.

"Pais," Shiloh whispered, moving Paisley's hair out of her face. "What did you see?"

Paisley looked up slowly, holding her breath to try and stop her tears. For the first time in a long time, Shiloh didn't recognize the look on the smaller girl's face.

"My…" Paisley choked back a sob and shook her head. "My parents," she whispered, burying her head back in Shiloh's shirt. The older girl felt her heart drop, instantly realizing what the expression on Paisley's face had been.

Remorse.

Shiloh opened her mouth, but couldn't find any words. She'd never been in this situation with Paisley before.

"Paisley," Vanessa spoke up, shooting Shiloh a comforting look before scooting over on the couch and placing a hand on the smaller girl's shoulder. "They're still with you."

Paisley and Shiloh both looked at the other girl in confusion, but Vanessa continued to talk.

"Every part of them is in every part of you," Vanessa continued. "They're still there, they're just up here," she pointed to Paisley's head. The smaller girl furrowed her eyebrows.

"You keep people alive by remembering them," Leah spoke up from the other side of the couch. "It's okay to miss them. It's okay to feel sad about it. But you've got to remember they're never truly gone."

Paisley looked up slowly. Shiloh reached out to wipe the tears from the small girl's cheeks.

"But what if I don't remember?" Paisley asked shakily, bringing her arms up and wrapping them around Shiloh's neck.

"You just remembered, didn't you?" Shiloh asked. Paisley turned to look at the green eyed girl, deep in thought.

"If they made someone as extraordinary as you, I doubt it'll be easy to forget them," Shiloh reassured her, continuing to wipe the tears from Paisley's cheeks. "You're still carrying on their legacy."

"I love you," Paisley whispered, burying her head in the crook of Shiloh's neck and earning various coos from the girls around them. For the first time since they got back to the apartment, Shiloh heard Paisley giggle.

CHAPTER 17

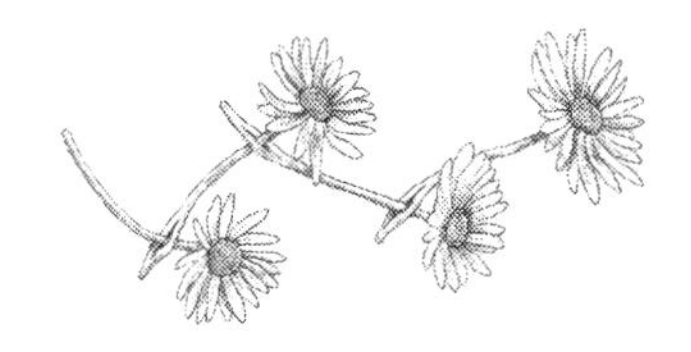

"It is my birthday?" Paisley asked quietly from the backseat of Leah's car. After they had calmed Paisley down, the smaller girl had been ecstatic that they were going out for pizza.

Shiloh had explained to her that it was her birthday, but Paisley still couldn't quite believe it. The brown eyed girl assumed she would automatically remember when it was her birthday. She felt out of place.

"It's March 3rd, Pais, that's your birthday," Shiloh laughed softly, placing her hand on Paisley's knee and absentmindedly tracing circles in her jeans.

"Are you sure?" Paisley tilted her head to the side.

"Yes, goofball," Shiloh laughed and shook her head. "Why would we be lying about that?"

"I did not remember," Paisley looked down at the ground and sighed. "I did not know my birthday."

"Well now you do," Leah spoke up from the driver's seat. "You were born on March 3rd. Which is today. Which makes today your birthday."

"Oh," Paisley whispered. Shiloh reached out and took her girlfriend's hand, pressing a kiss to the back of her palm.

"It's no big deal," Shiloh said softly. "You know now, that's all that matters. Now we just get to celebrate."

"With pizza," Paisley mumbled, a small smile creeping onto her face. Shiloh couldn't help but laugh.

"Speaking of pizza," Vanessa pointed out the window as Leah pulled into the parking lot of the brick restaurant. Paisley's face lit up, and Shiloh had to grab her hand to stop her from hopping out of the moving car.

"Someone else is having dinner with us, too," Shiloh smiled, noticing Toby's black truck in the corner of the parking lot. Paisley paused, giving her girlfriend a look of confusion.

"Who?" she asked. All the girls unbuckled their seatbelts and exited the car once Leah parked. Shiloh pointed in the direction of Toby's truck, where Maia was just exiting the passenger side.

"Be careful!" Shiloh called after Paisley, who had already taken off across the parking lot. Luckily, Maia saw her coming, and practically had to catch the girl when she wrapped her in a hug.

"It is my birthday!" Paisley smiled widely when she pulled away from the hug. Shiloh jogged over to meet up with them, motioning for her roommates to follow.

Toby fist bumped Paisley, causing both of them to make exploding noises. Shiloh and Maia both made eye contact, and the smaller brunette rolled her eyes.

"Sometimes it's like raising a child," Maia joked, causing Shiloh to burst into laughter.

"I know what you mean," the green eyed girl reached out and fixed the beanie on Paisley's head, just as her three roommates caught up with them.

"Uh, guys, this is Maia and Toby," Shiloh turned to introduce her friends. "They're in our art class."

"And these are my roommates," she turned to Maia and gave her a soft smile. "Ryland, Leah, and Vanessa," she pointed to each girl. Paisley giggled behind her.

"Ryland is mean," Paisley whispered to Toby, earning a playful glare from the light haired girl.

"I'm hungry," Vanessa announced, nudging Paisley in the direction of the entrance. The smaller girl laughed, running back to Shiloh's side so she could grab her hand and lead her into the restaurant.

They all slid into a circular booth, with Paisley squished happily between Ryland and Shiloh. She glanced down at the menu she and Shiloh shared, running her fingers over the small type.

When their food got to the table, Shiloh had to grab Paisley to stop her from burning her hand on the hot pan. Laughing, the green eyed girl cut them both a slice and pizza and sat back down.

"Happy birthday to me," Paisley mumbled with a mouthful of food. Giggling, Shiloh kissed Paisley's cheek and nodded.

"Happy birthday to you, goofball," she crinkled her nose and took a bite of her own pizza.

"How does it feel to be 19?" Maia spoke up from the other side of the booth. Paisley furrowed her eyebrows, thinking about this for a moment.

"I feel… the same," Paisley shrugged. "Just happy."

"I think that's pretty good, then," Shiloh nudged the smaller girl. Paisley smiled and leaned against Shiloh, taking a sip of her water and sighing contently. She was surrounded by her favorite people, and she loved the feeling.

"I missed this feeling," Paisley confessed quietly. Everyone had already moved on to different conversations, and Shiloh was the only one that heard Paisley's hushed words.

"Missed what?" Shiloh whispered, reaching out to smooth out Paisley's hair. The small girl smiled up at Shiloh, realizing she had made an effort to listen to her.

"This. Love," Paisley motioned around the table. "I like these people, and I think they like me. It feels good."

Shiloh couldn't help the small smile on her lips. She was glad Paisley was slowly getting to know that feeling. The girl deserved it more than anyone in the world.

"I like the feeling too," Shiloh whispered, poking Paisley's side and making the girl giggle.

The rest of the dinner went smoothly, at least, until the end. Just as the waiter was taking away their empty plates, a different plate was placed down in front of them. Paisley furrowed her eyebrows and looked up.

"We heard it was someone's birthday," the waitress smiled, pulling a lighter out of her pocket and lighting the candle on top of the small slice of cake. Everyone pointed to Paisley, and the cake was slid in front of her. Shiloh grabbed the smaller girl's hand to let her know it was okay.

"Haaaappy Birthday to you, Happy Birthday to you,"

Paisley didn't see who started singing, because the minute the song started her entire body froze. This was too familiar. Her grip on Shiloh's arm tightened just as she was swept away.

"Happy birthday to you..."

Paisley smiled softly and looked up from the makeshift cake in front of her. When Sydney had found out Paisley would be spending her birthday home alone, the blonde girl had driven over immediately. All they had available was a leftover slice of apple pie, but the two girls had stuck a candle in it and made it work.

"You really don't have to sing," Paisley laughed, crossing her legs on the couch and looking over at her friend who sat next to her. Sydney just shrugged and continued singing.

"Happy Birthday to you..."

Paisley froze when she heard the garage door opening. Her uncle wasn't supposed to be home for another few hours. Her heart immediately dropped in her chest and she looked over at Sydney with a panicked look on her face.

"Happy Birthday, dear Pais—,"

Paisley leaped across the couch, cupping her hand over Sydney's mouth and shaking her head. Just as Sydney opened her mouth to question the girl, they both heard the echo of the door closing.

"You can't be here," Paisley whispered, grabbing Sydney's hand and practically dragging her down the hallway. "Stay here," she pushed her friend into the bathroom and gave the girl a pleading look.

"Paisley?!"

Paisley flinched, refusing to meet Sydney's eyes as she closed the door. This wasn't going to end well. She practically sprinted back into the living room, blowing out the candle and throwing it behind the couch.

"Yeah?" she called back as casually as she could, sitting down on the couch. As soon as he entered the room, though, she stood up. She could tell just by the way he was walking that he was drunk. Great. Happy Birthday to her.

"I thought I told you to clean this house?" he spat, moving towards her. Paisley flinched, and he wasted no time in grabbing her arm, causing her to stand up straighter.

"I-I did," Paisley bit her lip and glanced behind him. "I cleaned the whole kitchen and the entire downstairs... I—,"

"The garage is a fucking mess," he growled, pushing her up against the wall. Paisley internally cursed herself.

"I didn't realize the garage counted as part of the house," she half-whispered, squeezing her eyes shut when he leaned in even closer to her. She could smell the alcohol on his breath.

"Are you fucking stupid?" he whispered between gritted teeth, taking his time to fully pronounce each syllable. Paisley held her breath, bracing for what was to come.

When the smaller girl didn't respond, a beer bottle was smashed against the wall beside her head. Paisley inhaled sharply as the glass fell around her feet and she felt what was left of the liquid now dripping down her side and soiling her clothes.

"Clean it up," he growled, letting go of her and taking a step backwards. Paisley instantly bent down, looking around nervously before trying to scoop the shards of glass together with her hands. He stood above her, laughing at the brown eyed girl's flustered state.

"Hurry," he chuckled, stomping his foot and making Paisley jump. Before she could react, she was being pushed backwards. Paisley stumbled onto her bottom, her back hitting the wall.

"I can clean it tomorrow," she quickly scrambled to her feet, cursing herself when she felt the glass crunch underneath her shoes. "Or... or I can even do it tonight, I-I..."

"You will do it tonight," he took a step forwards, pressing the sharp end of the broken bottle right underneath her collarbone. Paisley whimpered, inhaling sharply and trying to remain as still as possible.

Her shirt ripped as the man drug the sharp glass across her skin, leaving a crescent shaped cut directly beneath her collarbone. Paisley bit down on her lip as hard as she could, feeling pain sear through her body.

"I hate to do this to you, Paisley, but you just never learn," he slurred, leaning forwards and letting the last piece of glass fall to the ground. Paisley could feel the blood seeping through her shirt, but she wouldn't dare look in fear that it would make her sick.

"I-I'm sorry," Paisley whispered, feeling tears forming in her eyes. She couldn't cry. Not now, not ever.

"Don't say it if you don't mean it," he hissed, shoving her backwards into the wall. Paisley squeezed her eyes shut, but sighed in relief when she heard his heavy footsteps disappear up the stairs.

The first thing that crossed her mind when she opened her eyes was the glass digging into the bottom of her shoes. She quickly grabbed the dustpan from beside the couch, wincing as pain shot up her arm each time she moved her torso.

Just as she stood up to throw the broken glass away, she saw movement out of the corner of the eye. The second Paisley saw Sydney staring at her from the hallway, she dropped the dustpan and quickly crossed the room.

"You need to go," she said between gritted teeth, refusing to meet the girl's eyes. She grabbed Sydney's hand, pulling her towards the back door.

"Oh my god... Paisley, what just happened?" Sydney whisper-yelled, grabbing Paisley's arm once they made it to the door. Paisley stared straight ahead, opening the door.

"You need to go, Sydney," Paisley's voice grew low in the back of her throat as she tried to hold back tears.

"Holy shit, you're bleeding," Sydney pointed to the gash in Paisley's shirt. The brown eyed girl reeled backwards and shook her head. "You need to call the cops or something," Sydney stared at her with wide eyes.

"You need to leave!" Paisley snapped, yelling in panic at the girl in front of her.

"Paisley, you—,"

"What was that, Paisley?!" the man's voice boomed through the house once more. Paisley's eyes went wide and her skin practically turned white.

"Go," Paisley hissed quietly, turning to Sydney. The blonde opened her mouth to protest, but hesitated when she saw the distressed look in her friend's eyes.

Her uncle turned the corner just in time to see Paisley shoving Sydney outside and slamming the door behind her. A look of panic flashed across the brown eyed girl's face when she turned around and came face to face with the drunken man.

"Who was it?" he growled, his voice practically emotionless. Paisley attempted to back up, but was only able to take a step until she hit the wall.

"I said, who was it?" he took a step forward to match her pace.

"Sydney," Paisley confessed, squeezing her eyes shut and looking down.

"She's not allowed here again," he raised his voice. "Do you hear me?" Paisley brought her hands up to wipe her eyes, unsure of what to say.

"I said, do you hear me?!" he yelled, grabbing the front of the younger girl's shirt and practically lifting her off of the ground to meet his height. His other hand was used to land a hard slap against her face, causing Paisley to yelp in pain.

"Y-yes sir!" she gasped, struggling to try and plant her feet on the ground. She was sent stumbling backwards moments later, immediately bringing her hands up to cup her stinging cheek.

"I told your mother she should've fucking killed you before you were even born," he laughed bitterly. Paisley watched as he moved to storm down the hallway, but stumbled into the coffee table, which sent a flower vase crashing to the ground.

"Clean this up," the man spat, kicking the broken pieces of the vase aside and storming upstairs. Paisley stood frozen until she heard the slam of the bedroom door, which threw her back into reality.

Paisley gasped, suddenly being whisked back into an entirely different place. She could hear muffled voices, but her ears were ringing so heavily that she couldn't understand what they were saying. There was only one thought on her mind. Get out.

Somehow the small girl managed to clamber over everyone and scramble out of the booth. The moment her feet hit the ground, she made a mad dash for the nearest door.

Shiloh didn't hear the waitress' petty comment, or the confused whispers of the other restaurant-goers. No, the only thing on her mind was getting to Paisley.

The green eyed girl ducked under the table, taking everyone by surprise when she nearly knocked over the other diners as she made a mad dash for the door. The moment she pushed through the glass doors, she looked around desperately for Paisley.

Her eyes landed on the small figure moving ahead of her, and she took off.

"Paisley!" she called after the smaller girl, practically leaping forwards. Her fingers enclosed around the brown eyed girl's wrist just before Paisley left the curb. A car whizzed by, sending Paisley stumbling backwards into Shiloh's arms.

"Paisley," Shiloh turned the small girl around to face her. Brown eyes met green and Paisley panicked, attempting to pull away. Shiloh tightened her grip.

"Paisley, look at me," Shiloh grabbed Paisley's shoulder and held her in place. The smaller girl froze, searching Shiloh's face for any possible threat.

"It's not real," Shiloh whispered, feeling Paisley's muscles relax slightly.

"Pais, breathe," the green eyed girl inhaled slowly, motioning for Paisley to do the same. The younger girl took in a deep breath, her bottom lip trembling. Moments later, her shaky knees gave in underneath her and she fell to the ground. Without hesitation, Shiloh knelt beside her and pulled her into her arms.

"It's not real," Shiloh repeated, feeling Paisley's arms wrap around her neck as the smaller girl buried her head into Shiloh's shoulder. "It's not real," she continued to whisper softly.

Rubbing circles in Paisley's back, Shiloh rested her chin on the top of her girlfriend's head and continued to whisper the same three words over and over again. She'd say them forever if it would make Paisley believe them.

Paisley continued to cry into Shiloh's shoulder for a while, and Shiloh jumped when she felt a hand on her shoulder.

"Is she okay?" Vanessa whispered, squatting down next to the green eyed girl. Shiloh took a deep breath and glanced down to Paisley before nodding softly.

"Can I….?" Shiloh glanced towards Leah's car. "Is there any way you guys can get a ride home with Maia? I need to take her somewhere," the green eyed girl nodded down to Paisley.

"Consider it done," Vanessa gave Shiloh a soft smile before standing up. "Make sure she knows she didn't ruin anything, yeah?"

Shiloh nodded, sending a thankful smile in Vanessa's direction before tapping on Paisley's shoulder.

"I need to show you something, Paisley."

CHAPTER 18

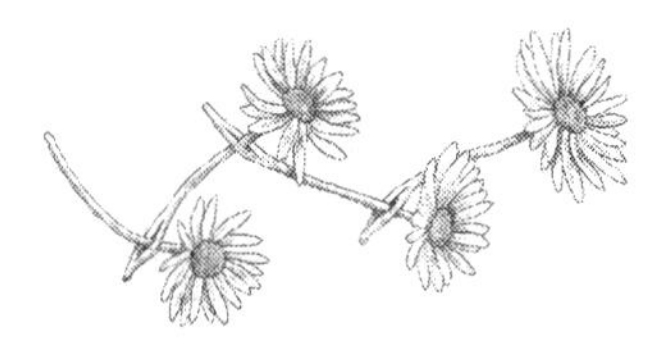

Shiloh held Paisley's hand the entire car ride, feeling her heart break each time she heard the small girl inhale shakily. She could tell Paisley was still panicking.

They only drove for a few minutes before they reached a gravel pathway. Steering as best as she could, Shiloh led them up the steep hill until them came to a stop.

"C'mere," Shiloh whispered, quickly circling the car and opening the passenger side door. Paisley looked up slowly with a confused expression on her face.

"Just trust me," Shiloh said softly, holding out her hand for Paisley. Shyly, the smaller girl took her hand and allowed Shiloh to lead her out of the car. By then, it was just beginning to get dark, giving the sky an eerie blue haze.

"Over here," Shiloh squeezed Paisley's hand and continued leading her up the gravel pathway. Paisley scooted closer to her, holding onto the sleeve of Shiloh's sweater.

"Just in time," Shiloh sighed in relief, quickly leading Paisley to the end of the pathway and in front of the clearing. Paisley furrowed her eyebrows when they came to a small cliff. Below, she could just barely make out the shape of the city.

"Come sit," the green eyed girl tugged on Paisley's hand and sat down on the grass in the middle of the clearing. Shyly, Paisley took a seat beside her girlfriend.

"There's so much more out there, Pais," Shiloh said after a few moments of silence. She noticed how badly Paisley was shaking and gave in, pulling the small girl into her lap.

"I know it seems so real," she whispered, resting her chin on the top of Paisley's head and gazing out at the dark city. "And maybe it was real at some point. But it's in the past now. And I know it's hard to understand that when it keeps coming back for you, but you just have to keep moving forwards."

She paused her small speech to check her phone, quickly tapping on Paisley's shoulder and pointing out to the city. "Watch this," she whispered, keeping an eye on the time.

Moments later, a small section of the city flickered before lighting up. Pretty soon all the streets of the city were illuminating themselves, glowing against the dark night sky. Paisley's eyes widened and she sat up slightly.

"Woah," Paisley whispered, wiping her eyes as the entire city lit up before her eyes.

"It may seem like this is the world right now," Shiloh whispered, smoothing out Paisley's hair. "But it's only a small part of you. There is *so* much more out there."

Slowly, Paisley reached up and pressed her fingers to Shiloh's cheek, tracing down her jawline. "You are real, right?" she asked quietly, studying the way Shiloh's eyes lit up in the soft light.

"Of course I am," Shiloh laughed softly. Paisley drew her hand back and nodded, lying her head on Shiloh's shoulder.

"Good," she mumbled, closing her eyes and taking a deep breath.

"Do you wanna talk about it?" Shiloh asked carefully, bringing her hand up to rub circles on her girlfriend's back.

"It was him again," Paisley mumbled. There was something else in her voice, though. Something Shiloh had never seen in her before. *Hate*.

"Your uncle?" she asked softly. Paisley nodded against Shiloh's shoulder.

"He was drunk," Paisley huffed, squeezing her eyes shut.

"Say it," Shiloh blurted out, startling Paisley. "Say it, Paisley. Just say it."

"Say what?" Paisley looked up slowly.

"You know," Shiloh whispered, reaching out and tucking a loose strand of the girl's hair behind her ear. "You're allowed to say it."

Both girls maintained eye contact for a few moments. Paisley took a deep breath and glanced out at the city, letting her eyes adjust to the light.

"I hate him," she mumbled, shaking her head and looking down.

"I hate him, too," Shiloh said quietly, lifting Paisley's chin up to meet her eyes. "And that's okay. You should hate him for what he did to you. Don't feel guilty about it."

Wiping her eyes, Paisley nodded softly. It felt like a weight was lifted off her shoulders. Just from admitting that out loud.

"He doesn't deserve to have this much control over you, Paisley," Shiloh sighed and combed her fingers through her hair. "The best revenge you can get is to just keep getting better. If you don't let him affect you, then you win."

"He hurt me," Paisley whispered, clinging onto Shiloh's shirt.

"I know, babe," Shiloh whispered. "But now he's gone. Now you're in charge," she ran her fingers up and down Paisley's back. "Now it's your turn."

"I am happy here," Paisley said after a few moments of silence. "You…" she glanced up at Shiloh before looking out over the cliffs. "You lit up the city."

"I love you," Shiloh kissed the top of Paisley's head and sighed contently. "I love you enough to fill up all the love that your uncle took away from you. I'll love you until you see that, and I'll continue to love you even after."

"Forever?" Paisley giggled softly, holding up her pinkie. Shiloh couldn't help but laugh as she brought their pinkies together, kissing Paisley's hand.

"Forever."

Both girls spent a considerable amount of time just staring out at the city, taking in all the lights and sounds of the night. Shiloh glanced down at the girl in her lap just as she started to fall asleep.

"Pais," Shiloh laughed, nudging Paisley's shoulder. The small girl looked up groggily, blinking a few times in the darkness.

"We still have to open presents," Shiloh whispered, nodding in the direction of the car. That sure woke her up.

"Presents?" Paisley sat up quickly, tilting her head to the side.

"Yes, presents," Shiloh laughed, standing up and helping Paisley to her feet. She brushed the grass off of her jeans before nudging the girl back in the direction of the car.

"For me?" Paisley asked, sliding into the passenger seat. Shiloh couldn't help but laugh.

"Whose birthday is it?" Shiloh raised an eyebrow.

"Mine…" Paisley giggled, looking away. Shiloh reached over and squeezed her hand.

"Then yes, goofball, they're for you," Shiloh laughed as she turned the car around and headed in the direction of their apartment. "Except you can't get my present today."

Paisley furrowed her eyebrows and looked over at the girl in the driver's seat. "Why not?"

"Cause we have to go get it together," Shiloh smirked. Paisley let out a long breath as she tried to figure out what Shiloh could possibly be referring to.

"Don't think too hard," Shiloh giggled. "You'll find out soon enough."

Shiloh practically had to sprint to catch up with Paisley once they got back to the apartment. When they unlocked the apartment door, they were greeted by their three other roommates watching something on the couch.

'Presents' Shiloh mouthed from behind Paisley. The girls quickly shut off the TV.

"Feeling better?" Ryland asked, raising an eyebrow at Paisley. The smaller girl nodded and padded over to the couch, sitting down and crossing her legs underneath her.

"I'm glad, Paisley," Ryland laughed, giving Paisley a playful shove. Paisley crinkled her nose before grabbing a pillow and throwing it in the girl's direction.

"Let's open presents before one of you ends up in the hospital," Leah teased, ducking behind the couch and grabbing a small silver bag. "Mine first."

Paisley smiled widely as the bag was placed in front of her. "Now?" she asked, looking over at Leah. The older girl gave her a soft nod, and seconds later Paisley was pulling the tissue paper out of the bag.

She reached in, pulling out the piece of fabric and holding it up in front of her. Her eyes widened.

"Yellow!" she laughed, turning the dress around and studying it closely. "I love it," Paisley smiled, turning to Leah and practically tackling her in a hug. Shiloh hopped forwards to grab the dress before Paisley let it fall to the floor. "Thank you."

"You're welcome," Leah laughed once they pulled away from the hug. Paisley smiled widely, sitting back down and watching as Shiloh folded the dress up neatly and put it back in the bag.

"Catch, dork," Ryland tossed a bag in Paisley's direction. Paisley quickly scrambled off the couch to catch it, sitting back down happily when she did.

She reached into the bag, furrowing her eyebrows with a curious smile when she felt something fuzzy. She tugged it out, holding it up in front of her.

"It's a blanket," Shiloh observed, grabbing one end and helping Paisley spread it out. "Oh my god," she laughed, looking at Ryland when she saw what was on it.

"Friends!" Paisley giggled, clapping her hands and running over to Ryland. "You got me a Friends blanket," she crinkled her nose before pulling Ryland into a hug. "Thank you Ry."

"And since *someone* stole my idea..." Vanessa glared at Ryland. "I just got you this, so you could have a little more control," the brown haired girl slid a small card across the table.

"For froyo?" Paisley asked, immediately recognizing the logo on the card. Before Vanessa could respond, there was a knock at the door. Shiloh raised an eyebrow in question, but jogged over to answer.

"I figured you could take Shiloh on a date or something," Vanessa whispered, which caused Paisley to giggle. The brown eyed girl moved forward to hug Vanessa.

"Thank you," Paisley laughed, smiling softly when they pulled away. Her smile instantly faded, though, when she saw Shiloh struggling to carry a large box into the room.

"What the...?" Ryland hopped to her feet to help Shiloh set the box down on the floor. "That's what was at the door?"

Shiloh nodded, wiping off her hands and standing up. "It's addressed from my parents," she said, biting her lip and kneeling down. The girls gathered around as Shiloh dug her keys from her pocket, using them to cut the tape around the edges of the box.

Paisley's eyes widened when Shiloh opened the box to reveal all different colors of tissue paper. The green eyed girl dug out a card, her lips curving into a smile when she saw the writing on the front.

"It's for you," Shiloh laughed, turning the card around so Paisley could see her name written on the front. Paisley smiled widely, sitting down next to Shiloh and looking into the box.

Dear Paisley,

We heard it was someone's birthday, and when we did, we weren't quite sure what to get. But then, we had a great idea. Shiloh will know as soon as she sees this. Hopefully this can help you out a bit with your recovery, and give you and Shiloh something to do together.

We love you,

Matthew and Colette

Shiloh grew confused at what her parents were talking about, but she watched as Paisley began to tear the tissue paper out of the box. Both girls widened their eyes when they saw the long rectangular box underneath.

"A piano?!" Paisley gasped, reaching forwards and pulling the box out. Shiloh quickly moved to help her set it down on the ground, reading over the box.

"Keyboard," Shiloh corrected her. "But same thing, really."

Ryland gave the girl an intimidating look from the couch, raising an eyebrow. "What were you parents talking about when they said you would 'know' when you saw it?" Ryland leaned forward and studied the box.

"Oh," Shiloh bit her lip. "I used to, uh, I used to play," she watched as Vanessa helped Paisley open the box, pulling out the long keyboard. Paisley tapped a key, furrowing her eyebrows when no sound came out.

"Instruments are supposed to be really good for hand eye coordination," Leah spoke up. "Maybe that's what your parents meant."

"You think they want *me* to teach *her*?" Shiloh raised an eyebrow.

"Are you good?" Ryland asked. Shiloh grew confused, shrugging her shoulders.

"I played up until my sophomore year," she admitted, looking over as Vanessa retrieved a set of batteries and let Paisley roll them into the back compartment of the keyboard.

"Then you've got to be good," Ryland laughed.

Paisley tapped a key, laughing softly when the piano actually made a sound. Shiloh couldn't help but smile when Paisley continued, pressing each individual key to see what noise they made.

"Can we keep it in the bedroom?" Paisley asked, looking over at Shiloh, who shrugged.

"If that's what you want," the green eyed girl laughed, standing up when Paisley jumped to her feet. "Here, take that end," she nodded to the smaller girl.

Slowly, the girls carried the keyboard upstairs. Vanessa followed after them with the stand, and soon enough they had the keyboard set up in the corner of the room. Paisley immediately sat down, beginning to press random keys.

"Shiloh I swear if you leave your shoes by the front door one more time!" Leah's voice rang out from downstairs. Paisley giggled to herself when Shiloh groaned.

"I'll be back," the green eyed girl laughed, jogging down the stairs and sending Leah a playful glare. The short girl crossed her arms.

"I'm a slob, I know," Shiloh held up her hands as if she were surrendering. "Fight me," she teased. Grabbing her shoes and sticking her tongue out at Leah, Shiloh was running back up the stairs before the oldest girl could respond.

Just as Shiloh reached her bedroom door, she paused. After listening for a few minutes, she realized what she was hearing. Piano. Not just Paisley's random tappings, either.

Slowly, the green eyed girl opened the door and peered in. Paisley whipped her head around, looking just as shocked as Shiloh.

"Was that you?" Shiloh asked, moving into the room and quietly closing the door behind them. Paisley looked down at her hands in disbelief.

"It was twinkle twinkle," the brown eyed girl said softly.

"Do it again," Shiloh walked over and sat on the floor next to the girl. "Play it again."

Taking her lip in-between her bottom teeth, Paisley nodded. The small girl made a pointing motion with both fingers and gently tapped one key at a time. Slowly, but sure enough, Paisley was playing the notes to twinkle twinkle.

"How did you..?" Shiloh was in shock. "Wha…?"

"I just remembered," Paisley was as confused as Shiloh was. "It came back to me."

When Shiloh didn't respond, Paisley reached out and grabbed Shiloh's hand in her own. "Can you play a song, Lo?" she asked, tugging Shiloh's hand towards the keyboard.

Biting her lip, Shiloh thought for a moment. "Uh, yeah," she ran her fingers over the keys, getting a feel for the keyboard. "I need you to help me, though."

"How?" Paisley tilted her head to the side.

"See these four keys?" Shiloh gently moved Paisley's hand to the left side of the keyboard. "You just play one at a time," she pressed each key in rhythm, showing Paisley the pattern. "And you just have to do that over and over."

"1, 2, 3, 4," Paisley counted, pressing each key just as Shiloh had done.

"Exactly," Shiloh smiled. "Now keep doing that, and I'm gonna join in, okay?" Paisley nodded. In concentration, she leaned down closer to the keyboard and began playing the notes Shiloh had given her.

Shiloh watched Paisley for a few moments before taking a deep breath and joining in. Paisley nearly lost count when Shiloh began playing, but she quickly caught up. The green eyed girl laughed softly, beginning to sing along. Paisley was able to follow Shiloh pretty quickly, and the green eyed girl found herself keeping her eyes focused on Paisley, rather than the keys.

"Good job," Shiloh laughed softly once they were done, cracking her knuckles as she took her hands off of the keys. Paisley looked up at her with wide eyes.

"You are good at that," Paisley smiled. "How did you know?"

"Piano?" Shiloh asked, Paisley nodded. "I used to take lessons. My parents signed me up when I was super little. I always used to play this song with my dad, actually."

"I like it," Paisley smiled, tapping a random key on the keyboard and giggling. "I love you. Thank you for my birthday," she looked back up at the dark haired girl.

"I love you too," Shiloh pressed a random key in return. "Thank you, you're welcome," she winked, making Paisley smile proudly.

CHAPTER 19

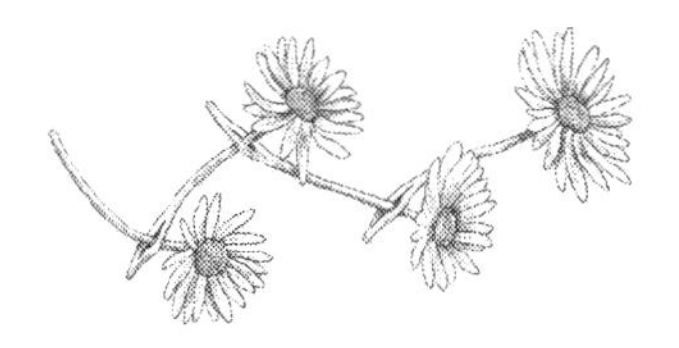

Shiloh woke up the next morning to the sound of twinkle twinkle little star on repeat. Rolling over, she rubbed her eyes and scanned the room, spotting Paisley's small figure. The green eyed girl yawned and slid out of bed, trudging over and sitting next to her girlfriend.

Paisley jumped when she realized Shiloh was awake. She quickly moved her hands away from the keys and wiped her eyes. Shiloh could immediately tell something was wrong.

"What's up?" Shiloh asked in concern, finding Paisley's hand and lacing their fingers together. The younger girl looked up nervously.

"I had a nightmare," Paisley whispered, hanging her head down. Shiloh's eyes widened.

"I thought they went away?" she asked softly, reaching up and cupping her girlfriend's cheek.

"Me too," Paisley sighed.

"Wake me up next time, okay?" Shiloh ran her thumb over Paisley's cheek. She hated the thought of Paisley waking up from one of her nightmares and being all alone. The small girl nodded softly, scooting forwards and resting her head on Shiloh's shoulder.

"If it makes you feel any better, we're going to get your present today," Shiloh whispered before kissing Paisley's forehead. The small girl gasped, scrambling to her feet.

"Right now?" Paisley asked with wide eyes. Shiloh couldn't help but smile.

"As soon as you're ready," the green eyed girl slowly rose to her feet. Paisley grabbed a change of clothes and hurried into the bathroom to get dressed. Groggily, Shiloh changed into a heavy sweater and leggings.

After the girls ate breakfast and finished getting ready, Paisley practically dragged Shiloh out to her car. As they pulled out onto the road, Paisley began interrogating the older girl.

"Where are we going?" Paisley tilted her head to the side, watching as Shiloh turned in a direction she'd never driven in before. The green eyed girl laughed, shaking her head.

"I can't tell you yet, doofus, that would ruin the surprise," Shiloh raised an eyebrow. Paisley pouted.

"Can I have a hint?" the small girl looked at Shiloh hopefully, only to groan in frustration when Shiloh shook her head.

"Patience," Shiloh laughed. Paisley rolled her eyes playfully, settling for leaning against the window and watching as they moved closer and closer to their destination.

The smaller girl grew even more confused when Shiloh pulled into a small parking lot adjacent to a brick building.

"We're here," Shiloh grinned, parking the car and sliding out of the driver's seat. The green eyed girl circled around the back of the car, grabbing a small plastic carrier. Paisley studied it in confusion.

"What is this?" Paisley asked, padding over to Shiloh's side and pointing to the carrier.

"You'll see," Shiloh laughed. Paisley groaned, but eagerly followed Shiloh inside the building.

"Close your eyes," the green eyed girl instructed. Paisley raised an eyebrow, but decided against questioning Shiloh's request. As soon as she covered her eyes with her hands, she felt a small hand on her back, leading her forwards.

Carefully, she allowed Shiloh to lead her down what she presumed to be a hallway. When they stopped walking, she bit her lip.

"Open your eyes," Shiloh whispered, sliding beside Paisley to see her reaction. The small girl let her hands fall back to her sides, studying the room in front of her.

"Kittens?!" Paisley gasped immediately shuffling forward to one of the metal cages. "Kittens?!" she repeated, turning around and looking at Shiloh with wide eyes.

"*Kitten*," Shiloh corrected her with a soft smile. "Only one. You've got so much love to give, I figured one of these little guys could use some."

"Thank you, you're welcome!" Paisley squealed, leaping forwards and pulling Shiloh into a hug. "Thank you. Thank you, thank you!"

Laughing, Shiloh pulled away from the hug and smoothed out her girlfriend's hair. "Better get to choosing," she whispered, nudging Paisley forwards. It didn't take any more prompting on Shiloh's part.

Paisley hurried towards the row of cages, peering in-between the first set of bars.

"Hi kitten," she whispered, gently bending down to get a better view. Shiloh watched, enamored by her girlfriend.

Half and hour and a lot of discussion later, Paisley still hadn't made her decision. Just as Shiloh was about to prod her to make a choice, Paisley practically disappeared behind a row of cages.

"Paisley there's no m—," Shiloh trailed off when she saw the other woman.

"This one," Paisley ran back to grab Shiloh's arm, tugging her towards the woman, who Shiloh realized was a staff member. "I want this one."

Shiloh looked down at the small kitten in the woman's arms. It was practically a bundle of pure white fluff.

"Uh, this guy isn't—," the woman shook her head. "Are you sure you don't want one of the other kittens?" She pointed to the row of cages where they had previously been. Paisley furrowed her eyebrows.

"This one," Paisley whispered in Shiloh's ear, nodding towards the tiny kitten.

"Is there a problem?" Shiloh asked softly. The woman looked down at the small animal in her arms. Paisley huffed, stepping forward and gently taking the kitten into her own arms. Shiloh bit her lip.

"He's been here for a while," the woman explained. "He's blind in both eyes. His mother rejected him, and.... Yeah," she shrugged. Nervous, Shiloh glanced back at Paisley, who was happily snuggling the small white bundle of fur in the crook of her neck.

"What do we need to do to adopt him?" Shiloh gave in, turning back to the woman. Paisley hummed happily.

"I can take you up front," the woman motioned for Shiloh to follow her. Making sure Paisley was following, Shiloh trailed behind the staff member as they walked back to the front of the building.

Paisley stood a few feet behind Shiloh as she filled out forms, snuggling the small animal in her arms. Shiloh clicked the pen shut, sliding the papers back across the counter.

"And what's his name?" the woman asked, directing the question to Paisley. The small girl thought for a moment, looking down at the kitten and then adopting a wide smile.

"Wolf," she nodded once, gently fixing the beanie on her head.

"Are you sure you want to name a cat after a w—?" the woman began, but she stopped once she saw Shiloh's warning glare.

"Wolf it is," she nodded quickly, jotting something down on the papers and stamping them. Sliding the forms back across the counter, she gave Shiloh a soft smile. "He's all yours."

Paisley hummed excitedly, padding over to Shiloh with a wide smile. The green eyed girl couldn't help the smile that tugged at her lips when she saw how happy Paisley was.

"We've gotta put him in the crate for the ride home," Shiloh explained, holding up the small plastic carrier. Paisley furrowed her eyebrows, but didn't argue. She gently placed Wolf into the carrier, smoothing out his fur.

"We are going in the car," she whispered, petting him through the cage bars. "But then we will get home. And we will play. Right?" she turned up to look at Shiloh.

"Right," Shiloh laughed, thanking the woman before nudging Paisley in the direction of their car. She placed the carrier carefully in Paisley's lap before starting the car and heading back to the apartment.

"I love this," Paisley chimed, looking over at Shiloh. "Thank you. This is the best birthday ever."

"You're welcome," Shiloh laughed, reaching over and squeezing Paisley's hand. "Why'd you pick that one?"

"His name is Wolf," Paisley corrected her, peering in the cage and humming contently. "Because he needed a friend. Like me."

"What?" Shiloh raised an eyebrow.

"You helped me when I needed a friend. And now I will help him," Paisley shrugged casually.

"That's… that's pretty smart," Shiloh stumbled over her words, surprised by her girlfriend's response. Part of her believed that Paisley was secretly a lot smarter than anyone around her.

Paisley babbled quietly to the kitten as they drove, carrying the cage carefully once they reached the apartment.

"He has to stay in the bathroom for the first few days to get used to living here," Shiloh explained, leading Paisley towards the staircase.

"He can not sleep with us?" Paisley frowned, turning around at the top of the stairs and waiting for Shiloh. The green eyed girl shook her head.

"He has to learn how to use the litterbox first," Shiloh pointed to the bathroom, where she had left a handful of cat supplies. Vanessa had agreed to set them up once they left for the shelter.

"I will sleep with him, then," Paisley shrugged and padded into the bathroom. Shiloh followed close behind and closed the door once they were both inside.

"Come on, Wolf, this is home," Paisley said softly, setting the crate down and opening the small metal door. She scooted back slightly, watching as the small kitten took a shy step forwards. Shiloh was surprised at how patient Paisley was being.

"We've gotta be careful, Pais," she reached out and twirled a piece of her girlfriend's hair around her finger. "He's blind, so he's gonna need a lot more help than a regular kitten."

"That is okay," Paisley shrugged. Carefully, she reached out and lifted the small kitten into her lap. "He has eyes like you, Lo," she gently lifted his chin in Shiloh's direction, revealing cloudy, pale blue eyes.

"Woah," Shiloh whispered, having not seen his eyes before. "They're so cool," she laughed softly and reached out to pet the kitten.

"Shit," Shiloh cursed, sighing heavily. "I have a sketch due tomorrow." Paisley giggled when the older girl rolled her eyes and slowly rose to her feet.

"I'll be back," Shiloh sighed dramatically, ruffling Paisley's hair. Paisley nodded softly, watching as Shiloh slipped out of the bathroom.

Shiloh disappeared into her bedroom, losing herself in her sketchbook as she blasted her drawing playlist into her headphones. She was so focused on her sketch that she didn't hear the door of her bedroom open slightly, and she didn't hear the soft footsteps come and go moments later.

Thirty minutes or so later, Shiloh gently removed her headphones and held her sketchbook out to examine her drawing. Something else caught her attention, though.

Shiloh's lips tugged into a smile when she heard soft laughter coming from across the hall. She raised an eyebrow after hearing the small chimes of the keyboard.

Shiloh scanned the room, realizing the keyboard was nowhere to be seen. She quietly tiptoed across the hallway, pressing her ear against the bathroom door.

"Shh, Wolf," Paisley giggled, which was followed by a small meow. "Listen, it's twinkle twinkle!"

Shiloh had to bite her lip to keep herself from laughing when seconds later Paisley began pressing the keys, slowly creating the tune of twinkle twinkle little star.

"You're getting better," Shiloh said softly, walking into the room. Paisley jumped, startled by Shiloh's sudden appearance. Her cheeks turned red and she giggled.

"Wolf likes it," Paisley noted, pointing to the small kitten who was timidly inspecting the keyboard. Shiloh laughed, sitting down next to her girlfriend and kissing her cheek.

"Can you teach me another song?" Paisley asked shyly, looking over at Shiloh hopefully. The green eyed girl smiled with a soft nod and scooted closer to her girlfriend.

"See these keys?" Shiloh asked, slowly guiding Paisley's fingers to the middle of the piano. "Just follow what I do."

Paisley nodded, watching as Shiloh began slowly pressing the keys. Paisley copied her, tilting her head to the side and trying to recognize what song Shiloh was playing.

"It's Yankee Doodle," Shiloh laughed softly when she noticed the curious look on Paisley's face. "Here, try again," she hit the first note of the song and waited for Paisley to do the same.

About an hour and a lot of giggling later, Paisley managed to play the song all the way through by herself. She smiled softly once she finished, watching as Wolf padded over to Shiloh's lap and sniffed her questioningly. Moments later, the small bundle of white fur climbed into the girl's lap and curled up in a ball, yawning softly.

"He is sleepy," Paisley laughed. "So am I," she imitated his yawn, causing Shiloh to giggle quietly. Paisley smiled, laying down and resting her head on Shiloh's knee as well.

Shiloh absentmindedly ran her fingers through Paisley's hair, humming softly to herself in the comfortable silence.

After a few minutes, Shiloh looked down at Paisley and laughed softly when she realized the small girl had fallen asleep.

"Happy Birthday," she whispered, leaning down and kissing the top of her girlfriend's head. "I love you."

CHAPTER 20

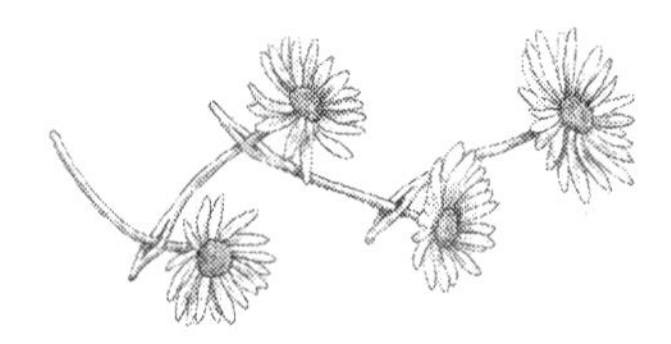

Shiloh aimlessly scrolled on her phone while both Paisley and Wolf fell asleep on her lap. Paisley had her head resting on Shiloh's thigh, and the rest of her small body curled up in a small ball atop the rug in their bathroom.

Shiloh looked down at the small girl, watching her chest rise and fall slowly. Paisley sleeping was one of the most adorable things she had ever seen. The smaller girl would crinkle her nose slightly whenever she was dreaming, and it never failed to make Shiloh smile.

The green eyed girl had almost fallen asleep herself, with her head hanging down slightly. Just as her eyelids drooped shut, she was startled when Paisley gasped and her entire body shot upwards.

Wolf awoke with a start, scrambling off of Shiloh's lap and clumsily finding a hiding spot behind his carrier. Paisley whimpered, bringing her hands up to her face. Shiloh immediately scooted closer to her shaking girlfriend.

"Hey, hey, it's me," Shiloh said softly, rubbing her hands up and down Paisley's arms and trying to get the smaller girl to look at her. "You're okay… it was just a dream."

"Lo?" Paisley whispered, moving her hands away from her face.

"I've got you," Shiloh nodded, but realized Paisley's eyes were focused on something else. Before the green eyed girl could respond, Paisley was crawling across the room and peering behind the carrier.

"I am so sorry," Paisley mumbled, squeezing her eyes shut and taking a deep breath. Wolf scooted further back into the corner, clearly still afraid from the sudden burst of noise.

Whimpering, Paisley plopped backwards against the wall and buried her head in her hands. Shiloh moved to pull the smaller girl closer to her.

"I-I scared him," Paisley mumbled, wiping at her eyes in frustration.

"Hey," Shiloh shook her head and grabbed Paisley's wrists to still her movements. "He'll be okay," she nodded. She met Paisley's eyes and wiped away the girl's tears with the pad of her thumbs. "It's you that I'm worried about right now."

"Me?" Paisley stitched her eyebrows together.

"Yes, you," Shiloh nodded and slowly stood up, helping Paisley up with her. "The nightmares are getting worse, aren't they?" Paisley simply nodded softly. For some reason, the smaller girl felt ashamed.

"Let's go lay down," Shiloh said quietly, leading Paisley out into the hallway and making sure to close the bathroom door behind them to give Wolf some privacy. The minute they set foot in her bedroom, Paisley burrowed under the blankets. Shiloh sighed.

The green eyed girl sat down on the edge of the bed, rubbing circles in her girlfriend's back to try and calm her down. Without being asked, she began singing softly.

Ryland peered her head into the room just as Shiloh finished singing. Shiloh glanced down at the now sleeping girl in her bed before looking over at Ryland, who motioned for her to come into the hallway.

The light haired girl practically dragged Shiloh into the bedroom across the hallway, making sure Paisley couldn't overhear them.

"What's going on?" Ryland asked, fed up with not being in on the situation. She crossed her arms and looked at Shiloh.

"I..." Shiloh shook her head and squeezed her eyes shut. "I just..." She just sighed, feeling the first tear break free of her waterline.

"Shy?" Ryland raised an eyebrow, taking a step forwards and placing her hands on Shiloh's shoulders.

"I just care so... so fucking much," Shiloh wiped her eyes and allowed herself to be pulled into a hug from the younger girl. "And I *hate* seeing her like this..." she whispered, her voice cracking.

"I just want her to be able to move on," Shiloh pulled away from the hug and shook her head. "I just *hate* seeing her like this."

"Have you ever considered putting her on medicine?" Ryland asked, running her hands up and down Shiloh's arms to try and calm her down. "Not for the flashbacks, cause I know she has to deal with those. But can't they give her stuff for the nightmares?"

Shiloh bit her lip and thought for a moment. "I-I don't know," she answered honestly.

"What's the harm in trying?" Ryland shrugged. Shiloh thought about this for a moment before raising her eyebrows.

"I guess we could give it a try," Shiloh looked up. She pulled her phone out of her pocket and sighed.

"I'll make us some tea and you can call the doctor, c'mon," Ryland led Shiloh downstairs. The green eyed girl obliged, sitting on the couch and finding the doctor's number in her contacts.

Ten minutes and a cup of tea later, Shiloh had scheduled an appointment for her and Paisley the following week. Just as she hung up the phone, she heard small footsteps coming down the stairs.

Paisley padded over to the couch, keeping her head hung low. Without saying anything, she crawled into Shiloh's lap and buried her head in her neck, practically collapsing into her.

Ryland headed into the living room, pausing when she saw Paisley had now joined them. Her and Shiloh met eyes, and the green eyed girl just shrugged softly.

"What's up, Paisley?" Ryland sat down on the couch beside them, nudging Paisley softly. The brown eyed girl looked up, looking from Shiloh to Ryland before shrugging.

"Pais," Shiloh whispered, smoothing out Paisley's hair and meeting her eyes. "I just talked to your doctor."

Paisley looked up, fear flickering in her eyes. She didn't like the doctor. "Why?" she bit her lip.

"We wanna try and help the nightmares to go away," Ryland spoke up. "They can put you on medicine that can help with that." Shiloh looked at Paisley hesitantly, and was surprised when the smaller girl suddenly sat up straighter.

"It can help?" Paisley asked, tilting her head to the side.

"If we find the right medicine, yeah," Ryland nodded. Paisley took a deep breath and clasped her hands together, nodding quickly.

"Yes," she smiled softly. "We can do that, right?" She turned to Shiloh. Paisley would do anything to get the nightmares to go away. She wanted to be able to sleep through the night without worrying about what she would wake up to.

Shiloh was surprised by Paisley's eagerness. She had figured Paisley would be scared. It only made Shiloh realize how desperate Paisley was to get better. It gave her hope.

"Of course we can," Shiloh smiled in relief, pulling Paisley into her side and kissing her nose. "We'll figure this out, I promise."

"Thank you," Paisley whispered, glancing over at Ryland before leaning in and pressing a quick kiss to Shiloh's lips. "I love you."

"Gross," Ryland made a gagging noise playfully. Paisley glared at her before leaning over and kissing Ryland's cheek.

"Do not be jealous just because you are lonely," Paisley teased. Shiloh burst into laughter, and Paisley turned back to watch her. Shiloh's laugh was one of her favorite things in the world. It made her feel like she was flying.

Just as Shiloh was able to catch her breath, Vanessa appeared in front of them, holding something behind her back. Paisley furrowed her eyebrows.

The dark skinned girl slowly pulled her hands out from behind her back and placed Paisley's beanie in her lap. Paisley looked at her questioningly before reaching down, realizing there was something moving inside the material.

Wolf popped his head out from the beanie and sniffed Paisley's hand, rubbing against her and yawning. Paisley giggled, looking back up at Vanessa.

"I found him curled up in there," Vanessa explained, sitting on the edge of the coffee table. Paisley smiled softly. Shiloh watched as her girlfriend gently lifted up the small animal and cradled him in her arms.

"I am sorry for scaring you," Paisley whispered, kissing Wolf's head and sighing. "I will try not to do it again. I am not a scary person."

Shiloh laid her head on Paisley's shoulder and reached out to pet the kitten. She hated knowing that Paisley was troubled by so many things, but she was also comforted by the fact that Paisley didn't seem to be giving up anytime soon.

Paisley looked up from the kitten, glancing at the girl next to her. Shiloh met her eyes and smiled softly, and then suddenly Paisley was met with a rush of familiarity.

Paisley didn't understand why high school had to be so terrifying. It was only her second day of freshman year, and she already felt like she was collapsing under all the stress. Her teachers had basically dived right into their lessons for the year, and Paisley was struggling to keep up. School never came easy to Paisley, but somehow she managed to maintain straight A's almost every year.

Shutting her locker, the small girl lugged her heavy backpack over her shoulder and glanced up and down the hallway. The school was nearly desolate. She had gotten there extra early to avoid the traffic. Paisley was considerably smaller than most of the students, and she would rather not be stampeded over this early in the morning.

After running a hand through her hair, Paisley debated where she should go. She could hide out in the bathroom until the bell rang, or she could get to her science class early and get a head start on the homework.

Paisley glanced in the direction of the bathroom before deciding against it. She quickly made her way down the hallway, jogging up the stairs and rounding the corner into her chemistry classroom. She paused when she realized she wasn't the only one who had shown up early.

In the back of the room sat a beautiful girl. Paisley knew that right away. Her hair was long, and a dark shade of brown. Paisley became even more infatuated when the girl looked up and Paisley was met with striking green eyes.

The girl gave her a warm smile before looking back down at her papers. Paisley stood frozen for a moment. Where was she supposed to sit?

Shit.

The girl was in the seat right next to Paisley's. The teacher had given them assigned seats the day before.

Apparently the girl hadn't been present in class for that. Nervously, Paisley crossed the room and set her bag down.

The two girls worked in silence for a few moments. Paisley was hit with the sudden realization that this green eyed girl would be in her lab group. Which meant partner work. Which meant an entire semester of trying to act casual around one of the most beautiful girls she had ever encountered. This should be a challenge.

"Is this right?"

Paisley nearly jumped when she heard the girl's raspy voice fill the air. Oh god, her voice. It was smooth and rough and soft and perfect. Paisley blinked a few times before realizing that the girl had addressed her.

"I think I did it wrong," the girl shook her head. Paisley quietly leaned over, looking at the problem the girl was pointing to on her paper. After scanning it for a few moments, she nodded.

"Easy mistake," Paisley shrugged. She grabbed her pencil, erasing the girl's answer and studying the question once more.

"You added 356 kilometers and 1000 meters instead of multiplying them," Paisley explained, writing out the answer as she did so. "So after you multiply across the top and bottom, and then divide it like a fraction, you get..." she pursed her lip in thought for a moment. "You get 9.8889 meters per second."

"Oh," the girl brought her palm to her face. "I'm such an idiot." She laughed softly. Paisley realized it would end up becoming one of her favorite sounds. Shit. She was in too deep.

"Once you practice a lot you'll be able to do these kind of problems in your sleep, trust me," Paisley smiled softly.

"I sure hope so," the green eyed girl laughed, studying Paisley's face. "I'm Shiloh, by the way."

Shiloh. The name fit her. Soft and beautiful. Paisley realized she had been staring and quickly shook the girl's hand.

"Paisley. Paisley Lowe."

"Pais," Shiloh shook Paisley's shoulder when she saw the dazed look in her girlfriend's eyes. Great, another flashback.

She was surprised, though, when instead of bursting into tears, Paisley met Shiloh's eyes and smiled widely. She leaned up, pressing a kiss into Shiloh's cheek and snuggling into her side.

"I love you."

CHAPTER 21

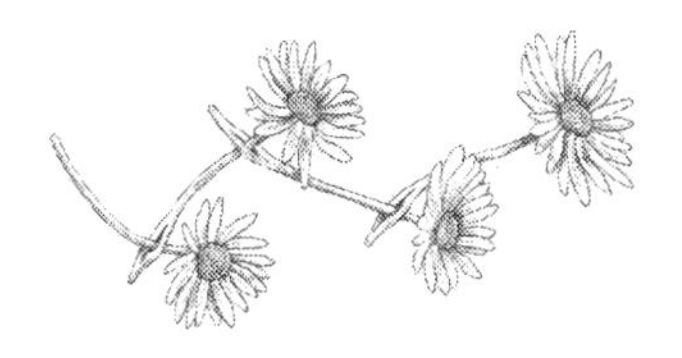

Shiloh woke up the following Monday with a pit of anxiety in her stomach. The past few days had been pretty rough for both of the girls. The nightmares seemed to have come back at full speed, and Paisley had a tendency to try and hide them when they did. Shiloh could always tell, though.

So when she woke up to an empty bed, Shiloh sighed heavily. This had become a normal occurrence between them. She cursed herself for being such a heavy sleeper.

The dark haired girl yawned, quietly shuffling across the hallway and slowly peering into the bathroom. As always, Paisley was on the floor with Wolf in her lap. Judging by the look on the smaller girl's face, she hadn't gotten much sleep that night.

Shiloh didn't even have to say anything. She simply sat down against the door and looked over at Paisley. When the girls met eyes, Paisley bit her lip and scooted closer to Shiloh. They both knew. There was no use in talking about it.

Shiloh wrapped an arm around her girlfriend and pulled her into her side. She was so tired of this. She was tired of seeing the girl she loved so much struggle to rid herself of her demons. Shiloh felt powerless.

She pressed a kiss to Paisley's temple and sighed softly. The appointment she had scheduled the week prior was today. Which meant Paisley would possibly be leaving the doctors office with a prescription that had the power to banish the nightmares.

Both girls sat in silence for a while. Wolf would look up at them occasionally, purring contently before snuggling back into Paisley's lap. The brown eyed girl felt numb. If anything, the nightmares had only been getting worse. And she didn't know what she could do to stop them. There was so much hope riding on the appointment that day. For both of them.

"Do you wanna get breakfast?" Shiloh asked after a few minutes of silence. Paisley looked down at the kitten in her lap and nodded, cradling Wolf in her arms.

Shiloh gave Paisley a soft smile, standing up and offering a hand to help Paisley to her feet. The small girl followed Shiloh down the hallway, crawling to sit on the counter once they got into the kitchen.

As Shiloh pulled a box of cereal out of the pantry, Paisley furrowed her eyebrows in thought. She spoke up when Shiloh set two bowls on the counter.

"If they are not real, why do they feel so real?"

Shiloh lifted her head and glanced at her girlfriend. She could see the conflicting emotions in Paisley's face. It pained her to know how confusing it must be for her.

"Cause our brains are pretty complicated," Shiloh laughed softly and shook her head. She poured them both two bowls of cereal and then hopped up to join Paisley on the counter. "They're good at tricking us sometimes."

"That is so stupid," Paisley huffed, crinkling her nose. She didn't like the nightmares. All she wanted was to be able to sleep without being woken up in a panic. No matter what she did, they never seemed to go away.

"I know, baby," Shiloh sighed and rested her chin on Paisley's shoulder, kissing her neck. "We just have to wait and see what the doctor tells us."

"I hope it helps," Paisley shivered.

"Me too, Pais," Shiloh gave her girlfriend a soft smile. "But if it doesn't, we'll figure something else out. We always do."

"Yeah," Paisley whispered, setting Wolf down on the counter to explore while she took a bite of her cereal. They'd only had the kitten for a week, but both girls had completely fallen in love. If they hadn't already known that he was blind, they wouldn't suspect anything. The small white kitten seemed to get along just fine without his vision.

Once they finished breakfast, Paisley gently set Wolf back in the bathroom before joining Shiloh in the bedroom. Both girls got dressed, Paisley insisting that Shiloh wear the yellow beanie to coordinate with her own. Of course, Shiloh couldn't say no.

The drive to the doctor's office was quiet. Both Shiloh and Paisley weren't sure what to expect. When the pulled into the parking lot, Paisley looked over at Shiloh worriedly.

"Don't worry," Shiloh laughed softly, leaning over the seat and cupping Paisley's cheeks. "I'm here. It's going to be fine. We're in this together."

"Together," Paisley nodded in affirmation.

They had barely gotten time to sit down in the waiting room when Paisley was called back. Her eyes widened, but Shiloh grabbed her hand and gave her a supportive smile. The brown eyed girl repeated the word *together* in her mind while they were led back to the small room.

Immediately Paisley was hit with a whirlwind of questions. She didn't even understand half of them. Why were they asking her about hallucinations? That had nothing to do with her nightmares. Shiloh held her hand the entire time.

The green eyed girl watched as Paisley shyly answered the questions. Paisley would occasionally draw a blank, not sure what she was supposed to say. Shiloh would always jump in to answer for her. They made a good team.

"We don't have a medicine that targets nightmares specifically," the doctor finally said after they had finished answering questions. He flipped through an array of colorful papers in a file folder before looking back up at the girls.

"But, anti-anxiety medicines have been proven to lessen the intensity of nightmares, or even get rid of them altogether," he nodded and wrote something down. "So I think we have a good chance at combating these nightmares."

Paisley immediately turned to Shiloh, smiling widely. The green eyed girl squeezed her girlfriend's hand.

"But we also need to have you get your blood drawn before you pick up your prescription. Just to get a baseline look at your levels before you start the medicine," he explained. Paisley glanced at Shiloh in confusion, but Shiloh just nodded.

After discussing various medicines and getting their prescription from the doctor, Shiloh took Paisley's hand and led her to the next building over, where the smaller girl would have to get her blood drawn. Surprisingly, Paisley didn't seem too scared when Shiloh explained to her what they were doing.

Shiloh stood and watched as the nurse prepared the needle. Paisley just watched absentmindedly.

"Why don't we go get froyo after this?" Shiloh offered, trying to distract Paisley while the nurse slowly slid the needle into Paisley's vein. The smaller girl winced slightly, but besides that, she didn't seem to care.

"Yes please," Paisley giggled, watching while the nurse covered up the small cut.

"It didn't hurt?" Shiloh asked in shock. Paisley furrowed her eyebrows and bent her arm a few times before shrugging.

"I have done it before," the brown eyed girl remembered. "I think I am used to it."

"Well I'm glad it wasn't that big of a deal then," Shiloh leaned down and kissed Paisley's forehead. They thanked the nurse and then headed out to the car. Paisley couldn't stop babbling about how the weather was starting to warm up.

"Hey, doofus, we're here," Shiloh laughed once she parked the car and Paisley continued to talk. The smaller girl immediately whipped her head in Shiloh's direction, smiling widely and hopping out of the car.

Paisley pulled Shiloh into the small store, happily handing her one of the small froyo cups and studying the different flavors. Shiloh just stood and watched her for a few moments, finding it funny how Paisley insisted on reading each flavor when she always ended up choosing banana.

"You are slow, Lolo," Paisley giggled, walking back over to Shiloh and pulling her over to the machines. "What are you getting?"

"Surprise me," Shiloh smiled softly and switched cups with Paisley. Satisfied with her new mission, Paisley began to study the different flavors once more.

Her eyes widened when she found the birthday cake flavor, clapping her hands together happily. She filled up Shiloh's cup, moving over to the toppings bar and adding rainbow sprinkles. The small girl skipped happily over to Shiloh and traded cups.

"Birthday cake. Because we did not get to eat the cake on my birthday," Paisley explained with a soft smile. Shiloh was so endeared by her girlfriend's attention to every small detail. She leaned down and kissed Paisley's cheek.

"Perfect," she smiled, leading Paisley over to the cashier and pulling her wallet out of her purse. Paisley's eyes widened, and she quickly shook her head.

Shiloh watched in confusion as Paisley pulled off her beanie, retrieving a small card from within the light blue material. She presented it proudly to the cashier and tugged her beanie back onto her head.

"Happy birthday to us," Paisley smiled proudly up at Shiloh, whose mouth had fallen open slightly in shock. "This is a date, right?" Paisley asked, taking her cup and starting to walk over to the tables.

"I… yeah," Shiloh smiled, slightly enamored that Paisley had stored the gift card in her beanie. "I'd like that. Thank you, by the way," she added, sliding into one of the small chairs.

"Thank you, you're welcome," Paisley smiled widely. She liked doing nice things for people, especially Shiloh. The small girl reminded herself to thank Vanessa again when they got back home.

"This is actually pretty good," Shiloh raised an eyebrow when she took a small bite of the frozen yogurt. Paisley clapped her hands together happily.

"I knew it would be," Paisley crinkled her nose.

Before Shiloh could respond, Paisley's attention was elsewhere. The green eyed girl watched as Paisley bent down, picking up the small toy car that had bounced across the floor and landed at her feet.

Paisley studied the toy for a few moments. She glanced across the room at the little boy who was watching her worriedly. A small smile spread across her face and she slowly rose to her feet.

"Vroom vroom," Paisley said softly, holding out the toy and pretending to drive it back across the room. The child wasn't sure what to think for a few moments, but when Paisley set the toy back at his feet, he laughed softly.

"Thank you, lady," he smiled, bending down to pick up his toy and giving Paisley a toothy grin.

"You are welcome, kid," Paisley nodded once, padding back over to Shiloh with a small smile on her face.

The same smile spread across Shiloh's face as she watched the interaction between Paisley and the young boy.

An image of Paisley as a mother flashed in her mind, and Shiloh sighed contently. She could easily imagine her and the smaller girl growing old and raising a family together. It just made sense.

Just because Paisley was a little… exuberant, didn't mean she wouldn't be a wonderful parent, Shiloh realized. Hell, Paisley had taught her more about love and life than anyone else she had ever met. Shiloh was sure she would do the same for a child of her own, when the time came, of course.

"Banana," Paisley whispered, holding out a spoonful of her froyo and waving it in front of Shiloh's face. "It is good. Try it, Lo."

Shiloh laughed, leaning forward and allowing Paisley to feed her the small spoonful of yellow froyo. Even though banana wasn't her favorite, she smiled softly and nodded. "It's good."

Paisley smiled widely and set her spoon back in her empty cup, around the same time that Shiloh finished. Both girls threw their trash away and headed back out to the car. Paisley skipped the entire way, dragging Shiloh along with her.

Once they got home, Paisley headed back upstairs with a new set of batteries for the keyboard, claiming she was putting on a concert for Wolf. Meanwhile, Shiloh dragged her easel downstairs and focused on painting a cityscape from in front of the window.

Dinnertime came and went as usual. Except for one small change.

"Pais," Shiloh's voice rang out from the kitchen. The other four roommates were watching *Friends* for the millionth time. Paisley lay on the couch with her head in Ryland's lap, nearly falling asleep.

"Paisley," Ryland nudged the small girl. "Shiloh's calling you."

Paisley looked up slowly, blinking a few times. She smiled widely and rolled off of the couch, padding into the kitchen.

"Look," Shiloh held up two small circular pills. "They match your beanie."

Paisley furrowed her eyebrows. "Blue," she noted.

"You've gotta take em'," Shiloh handed Paisley a small cup of water. "And wish all the nightmares away."

"Forever?" Paisley took the cup and allowed Shiloh to place the small pills in her hands.

"Let's hope so," Shiloh nodded. "Remember, he said they may not kick in for a week or so. We've gotta give it some time to do its job."

Paisley nodded softly. A few moments later, she stared down at the pills in her hand and looked up at Shiloh questioningly. "What do I do?"

"You take them with the water, like pills, yeah?" Shiloh raised an eyebrow. Paisley stared at her aimlessly.

"Okay, uh," Shiloh shook her head and took the cup from Paisley, setting it back down. "We'll do it an easier way."

Shiloh retrieved a small cup of applesauce from the refrigerator and opened the tinfoil lid. After grabbing a spoon, she popped the two pills into the plastic cup and mixed it around.

"Just don't choke," Shiloh handed the spoon to Paisley and set the applesauce down on the counter. The small girl hummed in approval, nearly devouring the entire cup within minutes. Shiloh chuckled, realizing Paisley hadn't even struggled to take the pills.

Paisley yawned, setting the spoon down and rubbing her eyes. Shiloh moved forwards, placing her hands on Paisley's hips and kissing her forehead.

"Ready for bed?" Shiloh asked softly. Paisley nodded, yawning once more and laying her head on Shiloh's shoulder.

"C'mon," Shiloh tried to lead her towards the door but Paisley just giggled and leaned more into Shiloh's shoulder.

"What? Am I supposed to carry you?" Shiloh laughed. Paisley just giggled and wrapped her arms around Shiloh's shoulders.

"You're kidding me," Shiloh rolled her eyes, but didn't hesitate to scoop Paisley into her arms. Paisley hummed happily.

"*Whipped*," Ryland sang from the living room as Shiloh carried her girlfriend over to the stairs. Shiloh flicked her off with her free hand, while Paisley giggled.

Once she laid her girlfriend down in bed, Shiloh changed into her pajamas and joined the small girl under the covers. Paisley curled up in Shiloh's side and sighed contently.

"You know what to do," Paisley giggled. Shiloh raised an eyebrow.

"Oh yeah?" she teased. Paisley nodded. "What am I supposed to do, then?"

"Sing?" Paisley hummed. Shiloh nodded, kissing Paisley's cheek.

"Only for you," Shiloh smiled, running her fingers through Paisley's hair and gazing up at the ceiling.

"I love you," Paisley whispered, nuzzling her face into Shiloh's neck and kissing the soft skin. Shiloh shivered. And as she began singing quietly, she realized that if she were to die in this very moment, she would die happily.

CHAPTER 22

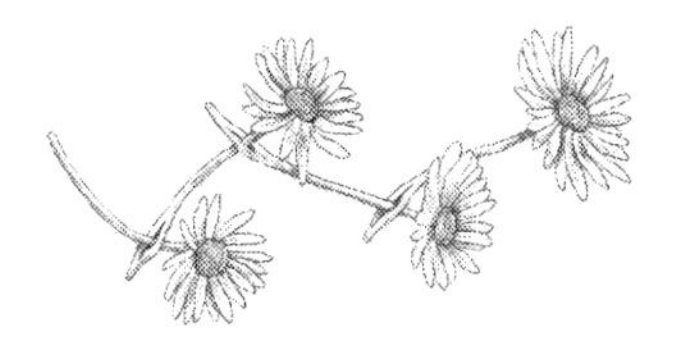

Shiloh woke up the next morning to find the blankets gone from overtop of her. This was a usual occurrence with Paisley, but when she rolled over to pull the blankets back from the smaller girl, she realized she was the only one in the bed.

She sat up quickly, becoming even more confused when she saw the blankets in the corner of the room, secured to one of her dresser drawers and draped over to the wall. They were creating some kind of fort. And the culprit had two small feet sticking out from underneath it.

Shiloh quietly rolled out of bed, which startled Paisley. The brown eyed girl sat up from within her fort, pushing one of the blankets aside and gazing up at her girlfriend.

"Why're you down there?" Shiloh asked, tilting her head to the side. Paisley bit her lip.

"Did you have another nightmare?" Shiloh knelt down next to Paisley. The small girl simply nodded, feeling somewhat guilty that she'd disturbed Shiloh.

"And you built a fort…?" Shiloh raised an eyebrow.

"To keep the bad things away," Paisley mumbled softly. Shiloh nodded.

"Well scoot over then," she smiled. Paisley grew confused, but moved aside and allowed Shiloh to crawl into the fort next to her. The green eyed girl laid her head back on one of the pillows Paisley had brought under and held out her arms.

"Remember, the medicine isn't going to work right away," Shiloh motioned for Paisley to lie down next to her. The brown eyed girl sighed softly and laid back beside Shiloh, who pulled her closer to her side.

"You sound tired," Shiloh noted, turning over slightly so she could run her fingers up and down Paisley's arm. "Try and sleep a little more. I'll be right here when you wake up."

Nodding softly, Paisley yawned and curled her hands out to find the sleeves of Shiloh's hoodie. Holding onto the older girl, she allowed sleep to overtake her once more.

About an hour or so later, Shiloh felt Paisley stir beside her. She reached out, smoothing out her girlfriend's hair as Paisley's caramel brown eyes fluttered open. At first, it took her a second to realize where she was, but she smiled softly when she saw Shiloh.

"Morning," Shiloh whispered, wiping her eyes. She'd managed to fall back asleep as well.

"Good morning," Paisley smiled widely. She yawned, sitting up and pulling Shiloh up to do the same.

"Someone's e—," Shiloh was cut off when Paisley crashed her lips against hers, pulling her into a deep and hungry kiss. Shiloh was taken aback when Paisley pushed her backwards, crawling on top of her and slipping her tongue into her mouth. A wave of euphoria rushed though Shiloh's body and she had to separate the kiss to catch her breath.

Paisley sat up, adorning the same goofy smile she always had. "Good morning," she smiled widely, crawling off of Shiloh and out of the fort before Shiloh could even process what had just happened.

As Paisley skipped contently down the hallway to go into the kitchen, Shiloh laid in the fort trying to figure out what had just happened. Paisley had never been that… eager before. This was new.

Shiloh sat up, running her hands through her hair and trying to steady her beating heart. After she calmed down, she pushed herself out of the small fort and headed downstairs.

"Tacos?"

"No, Paisley. It's breakfast. Tacos are for dinner."

"Cereal is for lunch."

"Oh my god," Ryland shook her head, taking the box away from Paisley and putting it on the top shelf of the pantry. Paisley huffed in annoyance. Shiloh watched their interaction with a small smile on her face.

"This?" Paisley dug into the back of the pantry, pulling out a box of muffin mix. Ryland eagerly took it from her, glad that Paisley had finally picked something that could actually pass as a breakfast food.

Shiloh wandered into the kitchen as Paisley clapped her hands excitedly and retrieved a bowl from the cupboard. Her lips curved into a smile when she saw Shiloh had entered the kitchen.

"We are making cupcakes!" Paisley smiled, hopping over to Shiloh so she could grab her hand and pull her over to the island. "See?" she held up the box of muffin mix.

"Those are muffins," Shiloh laughed, pointing to the writing on the box. Paisley furrowed her eyebrows and inspected the box closely.

"Oh," she nodded once. "Even better!"

Shiloh couldn't help but laugh at Paisley's sudden burst of energy. Leah and Vanessa both wandered into the kitchen, both equally as tired.

"Good morning!" Paisley greeted them, forgetting about the box of muffin mix. Ryland quickly grabbed it before Paisley dropped it, tearing it open and beginning to stir the ingredients together.

"Happy morning," Paisley hummed, hurrying over to Leah and Vanessa and giving them each a big hug. "You look grumpy," she observed, causing Shiloh and Ryland to both burst into laughter.

"*Tired*," Vanessa mumbled, giving Paisley a thumbs up before trudging over to the couch and plopping down. Leah just mumbled something inaudible before following suit.

"Grumpsters," Paisley mumbled, shaking her head and moving back over to see what Ryland was doing. The minute she heard the *Friends* theme song, though, she bolted into the living room.

"This is a good one!" Paisley smiled widely, practically falling back on the couch between Vanessa and Leah, who were still basically half asleep. Shiloh and Ryland both exchanged amused glances.

"What's up with her energy all of a sudden?" Ryland raised an eyebrow, sliding the muffin tray and cups in Shiloh's direction. The green eyed girl began putting a cup in each section of the tray, shrugging softly.

"You look flustered," Ryland observed. Shiloh's eyes widened and she quickly glanced in the living room before moving closer to Ryland so they couldn't be heard.

"Paisley practically made out with me this morning," Shiloh said softly, biting her lip. "Like as soon as she woke up."

"Damn," Ryland laughed. "Get it Paisley."

"Do you think it's the medicine?" Shiloh asked, sliding the muffin tray back over to Ryland. The light haired girl shrugged.

"It might be," Ryland began pouring small amounts of the mix into the tins. Shiloh bit her lip and leaned against the counter.

"He said it wasn't supposed to start showing any effects for a week or more," Shiloh noted. Ryland shrugged once more.

"Progress," Ryland turned back to Shiloh. "At least they aren't bad side effects." Shiloh nodded, deciding she'd accept whatever good came out of their situation.

About twenty minutes later, the sound of the timer sent Paisley scrambling back into the kitchen. "All done!" Paisley smiled, moving forwards to open the oven.

"Paisley!" Shiloh jumped forward and tugged Paisley away from the hot oven. "You're gonna burn your hands off, goofball." Paisley just furrowed her eyebrows and looked down at her hands to make sure they were still there.

"Here," Shiloh grabbed an oven mitt and carefully brought the muffin tin out of the oven. She set it on a cooling rack and turned off the oven, turning back to Paisley. "They've got to cool first. You can go let Wolf out while you wait."

Paisley nodded, clapping her hands at the idea. She padded upstairs and into the small bathroom where they'd been keeping Wolf. Because he was still young, and because of his vision problems, they kept him in the bathroom at night so he wouldn't get lost or get himself into trouble.

"Good morning, Wolf," Paisley whispered, turning on the light and kneeling down next to the small crate. Paisley had brought one of her shirts into the bathroom and used it to create a small makeshift bed. Wolf was currently curled up beside it.

"We made muffins," Paisley said softly, reaching out stroking his fur. The small cat jumped at first, but sniffed Paisley's hand and relaxed when he realized who it was. Paisley gently took the small kitten into her arms.

"Come on, sleepyhead," Paisley giggled. She cradled the small kitten in her arms and headed back down the hallway. "Rise and shine, goofball."

"He is sleepier than Vanessa," Paisley laughed, joining Shiloh back in the kitchen and nodding down at the kitten in her arms. Shiloh laughed, walking towards them and gently petting the small kitten.

"He sure loves you," Shiloh observed. Wolf yawned, nuzzling his face against Paisley's arm.

"Of course he does, who does not?" Paisley smiled. Ryland chuckled from where she stood at the sink, cleaning out the dishes. Shiloh nudged her playfully.

"Let's eat, doofus," Shiloh laughed, grabbing them each a plate and retrieving a muffin for both of them. She followed Paisley into the living room, where they each took their spot on the floor. Both Leah and Vanessa had fallen back asleep on the couch.

Paisley set Wolf down beside her and watched as he sniffed around the carpet cautiously.

"These are good," Shiloh noted after taking a bite of her muffin. Paisley glanced down at hers, unwrapping it and picking off a small piece. She studied it for a moment before popping it in her mouth.

"Mmmm," Paisley hummed, nodding in agreement. Shiloh crinkled her nose playfully.

"Rise and shine, fatass," Ryland plopped down on the couch beside Vanessa and shoved the girl's shoulder. Vanessa mumbled something inaudible and rolled over on her side.

"Oh my god," Ryland rolled her eyes, pulling the pillow Vanessa had been using away from the girl. Groaning, Vanessa tried to grab it back from her but Ryland tossed it out of their reach.

"Asshole," Vanessa muttered. Ryland just smiled in victory.

"Ryland *is* an asshole," Paisley nodded, taking another bite from her muffin. Shiloh practically snorted trying to hold back her laughter.

"You heard her," Vanessa laughed, wiping her eyes and sitting up. "How come you didn't wake up Leah?" They both glanced at the oldest girl, who was sound asleep on the other end of the couch.

"I know how to wake her up!" Paisley clapped her hands together. She cleared her throat.

"Look what I can do!" Paisley called out loudly. As if it were magic, Leah stirred awake and immediately scanned the apartment.

"Paisley, don't you dare do anything st—," she stopped when she heard all of the other girls laughing beside her. Glaring playfully at Paisley, she rolled her eyes and laid her head back.

"Can we go to the park?" Paisley asked once they finished eating. Shiloh stood up, taking both of their plates and heading into the kitchen.

"Once we get dressed," Shiloh shrugged. "We can't go to the park in our pajamas."

"Why not?" Paisley pouted, crossing her arms. Shiloh just laughed and shrugged.

"If *you* want to go in your pajamas, you can," she nodded. "But it's still a little bit cold out. Especially in the mornings."

"I have a jacket," Paisley nodded, grabbing Shiloh's hand and dragging her upstairs. Once they both were dressed, Paisley pulled her red coat on over her pajamas and followed Shiloh back downstairs. They walked outside, being hit by the brisk morning air.

"I love the sky," Paisley chimed, walking happily beside Shiloh. "It is so pretty. Like you," she turned to Shiloh and planted a kiss on the cheek. "I love you more than the sky."

"Someone's romantic," Shiloh laughed, pulling Paisley into her side and waiting for the traffic light to signal that it was okay to cross. Once the numbers began counting down,

Paisley skipped happily across the street, nearly stumbling over the curb once they reached the other side.

"Careful," Shiloh bit her lip, jogging up to her girlfriend and signaling for her to stop. She knelt down, quickly tying Paisley's signature white converse and standing back up. "Can't have you tripping any more than usual."

"Hush," Paisley giggled, nudging Shiloh's shoulder. Both girls began walking down the park pathway. Paisley kicked a pebble ahead of them, racing forwards every few seconds to kick it again. Shiloh watched her, completely enamored by her small girlfriend.

"Lolo!" Paisley squealed. Shiloh's head shot up, thinking something was wrong. Paisley came running back towards her, only to grab her hand and tug her forwards.

"What's wrong?" Shiloh asked worriedly, following Paisley. The small girl just shook her head and stopped running, pointing forwards. Shiloh raised an eyebrow and followed Paisley's eyes.

"They are growing," Paisley whispered. Shiloh felt her lips curve into a soft smile. "They did not die, Lo. They only left for the winter," Paisley knelt down beside the small flower buds and studied them carefully.

"I told you," Shiloh said softly, reaching out to fix Paisley's beanie. "In about a week's time, they'll be as good as new."

"I love you," Paisley blurted out. She stood back up, wrapping Shiloh in a hug and burying her face in her neck. "Please do not forget it."

"I won't," Shiloh shook her head, snaking her arms around Paisley's waist. "I couldn't if I tried."

"I love you," Paisley repeated, cupping Shiloh's cheeks and pressing kisses on both sides of her face. "More than everything. That is a lot, you know that?"

"I do," Shiloh whispered, realizing her face must be redder than Paisley's coat. The small girl nodded, looking into Shiloh's eyes and smiling.

"There are oceans in your eyes and I am drowning in them," Paisley said softer, running her fingertips over Shiloh's skin.

The green eyed girl's breath got caught in her throat and both girls just stared at one another in silence for a few moments.

"I don't think you realize just how amazing you are," Shiloh finally spoke, reaching out and tucking a strand of loose hair behind Paisley's ear. "If there's oceans in my eyes, then you've got the entire galaxy in your hands."

Paisley pulled her hands away, looking down at her palms and blushing.

"You are the galaxy," Paisley whispered quietly before pulling Shiloh into another hug. In moments like this, she was hit with the realization of how happy she was that she had the green eyed girl in her life.

CHAPTER 23

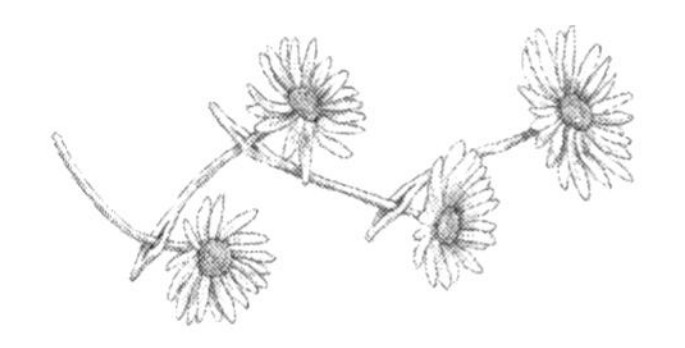

Paisley's energy only continued as the week went on. Shiloh would wake up and Paisley would already be downstairs, cooking breakfast or playing with Wolf. Her nightmares still came and went, but Paisley seemed to bounce back faster than she had before. And each night, she continued to take the two small blue pills before bed.

And then Wednesday came.

It started out as every other morning had. The blinding light streamed in from the window and caused Shiloh to roll over groggily. And that's about where the normalcy ended.

"Pais?" Shiloh furrowed her eyebrows, surprised that Paisley was still in bed. She was normally already awake and bounding all over the house by this time.

"Paisley," Shiloh rolled over completely, nudging the small girl. Paisley mumbled something inaudible and pulled the blankets over her head.

"Are you okay?" Shiloh whispered, trying to gently move the blankets away from Paisley's face. The brown eyed girl only held them tightly, scooting away from Shiloh.

"M'sleep," Paisley mumbled. Shiloh raised an eyebrow, but decided not to annoy her girlfriend.

"Well I'm going to get breakfast," Shiloh said softly, crawling over Paisley and padding over to the dresser. "Come join me if you want blueberry muffins," she smirked, raising an eyebrow and expecting Paisley to jump out of bed.

Instead, Paisley just pulled the covers further over her head. With a heavy sigh, Shiloh tugged on a t-shirt and headed downstairs.

Shiloh hoped the smell of freshly baked muffins would lead Paisley downstairs, but when she finished her breakfast and the small girl had still not appeared, she began to grow worried.

She quietly made her way back upstairs, turning on the light in the bedroom and stepping inside. Paisley groaned, covering her eyes with a pillow.

"What's wrong?" Shiloh asked softly, walking over to the bed. "Why aren't you getting out of bed?"

"Tired," Paisley yawned, allowing Shiloh to pull the pillow away from her face. "M'tired, Lo."

"Did you sleep last night?" Shiloh asked, raising an eyebrow.

Paisley nodded. "Yes. I had a nightmare, but I fell back asleep," she confessed.

"Are you okay?" the green eyed girl sat down on the edge of the bed. Paisley nodded and sat up, furrowing her eyebrows and blinking a few times.

"Yes," she nodded slowly. "I am only tired."

"I made muffins," Shiloh nodded towards the door. Paisley smiled softly, stretching out her arms and yawning quietly.

"Yum," Paisley hummed, scooting out of bed and padding softly towards the door. Wolf bounded happily after her, sticking right by her legs for guidance.

Shiloh followed her, grabbing Paisley's beanie from the dresser on the way out and tugging it onto the small girl's head once she caught up with her. Paisley giggled softly, picking up Wolf and cradling him in her arms when they went downstairs.

Shiloh raised a questioning eyebrow when Paisley paused at the bottom of the stairs and brought a hand to her forehead, blinking a few times.

"You okay?" Shiloh scooted around her and placed a hand on Paisley's shoulder. Paisley simply nodded, shaking it off and setting Wolf back down.

Shiloh sat down on the couch while Paisley got her breakfast, joining her in the living room. All three of their roommates had already left for school, leaving them home alone for the day.

"Where do we go when we die?" Paisley turned to Shiloh after she took a bite of her muffin. Shiloh's eyes widened, surprised by Paisley's sudden question.

"Why'd you ask that?" Shiloh crossed her legs underneath her and turned so she was facing Paisley. The small girl picked at her muffin and shrugged.

"No one knows for sure," Shiloh said softly. Paisley nodded.

"That is what I figured," Paisley took a small bite of the muffin and thought for a moment. "Will we be together?"

"What?" Shiloh grew confused.

"When we die," Paisley bit her lip. "Will you and me be together?"

"I'd like to hope so," Shiloh looked down at her hands and then back to Paisley, who had set her plate aside and was thinking intently.

"Me too," Paisley whispered, hanging her head down and playing with her fingers in her lap. She sighed softly before rising to her feet and bringing her plate back over to the sink.

"You didn't eat much," Shiloh observed. Paisley turned around, glancing at her plate and shrugging.

"I was not hungry," she tilted her head to the side slightly before setting her plate on the counter. Shiloh bit her lip.

"I am going to play with Wolf," Paisley decided with a soft nod, picking up the small kitten that had followed them into the kitchen. She padded into the living room and set him down, rolling one of his small toys across the floor. Hearing the jingling of the bells in the toy, Wolf hopped after it. Paisley giggled softly.

Shiloh watched them for a few moments before grabbing her backpack and falling back on the couch. She pulled out her sketchbook, tracing her fingers over the various crayon scribbles on the cover. They'd been there since the day Paisley had come to live with them. She couldn't bring herself to replace the sketchbook.

Unsure of what to draw, Shiloh began absentmindedly doodling. As always, the figure suddenly started to look very familiar. Shiloh glanced up at Paisley before turning her attention back to her drawing.

Shiloh got so lost in her sketchbook that she didn't notice Wolf wander over to the couch and curl up by her feet. When she looked back up, she was surprised to find Paisley asleep on the floor in the middle of the living room.

"What're we gonna do with her?" Shiloh said softly, bending down and cradling Wolf into her arms. "I just want her to be happy," she whispered. Wolf sniffed her hand before curling up in her lap.

Shiloh simply sat in silence for a while, watching Paisley's chest rise and fall. It was like someone had taken the Paisley she knew yesterday and swapped her out with a completely different person. She didn't understand.

Shiloh jumped slightly when Paisley shot up from the floor, looking around the room in sheer terror. The second she saw Shiloh on the couch, she hurried over to the green eyed girl and looked at her hopefully. Shiloh saw tears forming in her eyes.

"Again?" she asked softly. Paisley nodded. With a heavy sigh, Shiloh set Wolf on floor and patted the space beside her. "C'mere."

Paisley slumped down on the couch beside Shiloh, wiping her eyes. The green eyed girl wrapped an arm around her girlfriend and kissed her temple, smoothing out her hair. She hated seeing Paisley like this.

Paisley didn't say anything, instead she just laid her head on Shiloh's shoulder and exhaled deeply. Shiloh knew she was just as fed up with it as she was.

"Do you think it's the medicine?" Shiloh asked softly. Paisley didn't respond, she just closed her eyes and crinkled her nose. Shiloh began to wonder if the medicine was really going to fix the *real* problem. The root of her problem didn't seem like something a few pills could fix.

The day carried on slowly. Paisley moped around the house, occasionally finding something interesting and entertaining herself with it for a while. Shiloh spend most of her time on homework, checking on Paisley every few minutes.

Ryland and Vanessa got home from class, soon followed by Leah. Paisley followed Vanessa around for a bit, quietly observing whatever the older girl was doing. Shiloh took advantage of this and moved upstairs to finish typing out one of her essays.

She heard a group of footsteps coming upstairs, assuming that Paisley was among them. But when she heard a thud and a crash from downstairs, she immediately grew worried.

"Lolo?"

Shiloh sat up quickly, setting her laptop aside and jogging to the top of the stairs. "Pais?" she called, hearing the smaller girl moving around downstairs and quickly making her way down.

"I got hurt," Paisley's voice rang out softly from the kitchen. Shiloh ran in worriedly, finding Paisley sitting in the middle of the tile floor and clutching her ankle. Around her, a stool lay on its side and an array of glass pieces were shattered across the floor.

"Oh my god, what happened?" Shiloh gasped, grabbing Wolf just as the small kitten tried to wander over to Paisley. She set him aside, quickly maneuvering over the glass and pushing the stool aside so she could kneel next to her girlfriend.

"I could not reach it," Paisley sniffed, wincing when Shiloh moved her hands away from her ankle. "Ouch."

"Reach what?" Shiloh scanned the room, trying to find a sign of what Paisley had been up to. She sat down, gently pulling Paisley's shoe off of her foot.

"Ouch," Paisley shook her head, trying to pull her foot away.

"I need to see your ankle," Shiloh protested, tossing her shoe aside and pulling off her sock with it. Paisley's ankle was already red and bruising. The small girl squeezed her eyes shut and shook her head.

"What did you do, Paisley?" Shiloh asked.

"I was trying to reach the fancy cups," Paisley mumbled, looking down at the floor in embarrassment. Shiloh realized, glancing at the broken stool.

"I told you not to stand on that stool," Shiloh sighed, standing up and moving Paisley so she could lift her into her arms. The smaller girl winced and brought her hands around Shiloh's neck, trying to keep her ankle as still as possible.

"I-I was trying to make you dinner," Paisley confessed as Shiloh gently lay her down on the couch. "I could not reach, Lo. I could not."

"It's okay," Shiloh whispered, smoothing out Paisley's hair and moving back down to her ankle. "Tell me if this hurts, okay?" she pressed gently above where the ankle was swollen.

"Ouch," Paisley mumbled. Shiloh took that as good enough of an answer.

"Stay here," the green eyed girl held up her hand before jogging back into the kitchen. She grabbed an ice pack from their freezer, snatching an extra pillow as she ran back into the living room.

"It's gonna be cold at first," Shiloh warned her, slowly sliding the pillow under Paisley's ankle and laying the ice pack overtop of it. Paisley inhaled sharply but stayed still.

"Stupid," Paisley whispered, shaking her head and covering her face. Shiloh's eyes widened. She hadn't heard that in a while.

"Don't say that," Shiloh whispered, shaking her head. They couldn't go backwards. She wouldn't allow that to happen. "You're not stupid. Don't kill the flowers."

Paisley's eyes shot open and she stared at Shiloh for a few moments before letting her hands fall to her sides. Shaking her head, the small girl sat up slightly to look down at her ankle.

"Am I going to die?" she whispered shakily, looking at Shiloh with fear in her eyes.

"No, no way," Shiloh shook her head, laughing softly to try and lighten the mood. "You just landed on your ankle a little funky. It'll feel better tomorrow. You've just gotta keep the ice on it."

Paisley sighed, nodding and laying back so she could stare up at the ceiling. She was tired of messing things up. All she wanted to do was do something nice for Shiloh. She couldn't even do something as simple as getting a cup. The small girl squeezed her eyes shut just as the first tear rolled down her cheek.

Shiloh saw this, and immediately leaned forwards to cup Paisley's cheeks, kissing her forehead softly. "Be nice to the flowers," she said softly, wiping the tears from Paisley's cheeks.

"I am trying," Paisley whispered shakily. Shiloh bit her lip.

"Let's get you upstairs," Shiloh nodded, moving to pick the small girl up. Paisley reached out to stop her and shook her head.

"I need Wolf, first," she said quietly. Shiloh couldn't help but smile, and she retrieved the small kitten from behind the couch. After placing him in Paisley's arms, she carefully lifted her girlfriend into her own arms.

"Ouch," Paisley mumbled, wincing at the pain in her ankle. Shiloh slowly carried her up the stairs and gently placed Paisley in the middle of their bed.

Shiloh sat on the edge of the bed, gazing out the large window across the room. The sun was just beginning to disappear behind the buildings.

"It hurts," Paisley whispered, sitting up slightly and holding her ankle. Shiloh glanced back at her girlfriend, adjusting her position on the bed so she could fix Paisley's ice pack.

"It's gonna hurt for a bit," Shiloh said honestly. "You can try thinking of something to distract your mind, though."

"Can you sing?" Paisley looked up at Shiloh, searching her eyes pleadingly. As always, Shiloh couldn't say no.

"Only for you," she whispered, scooting back on the bed so she could run her fingertips up and down Paisley's arm.

CHAPTER 24

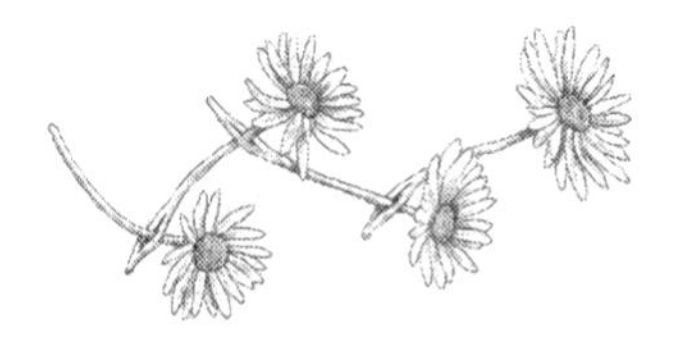

Paisley's mood continued to plummet. Two days later, Shiloh managed to drag her out of bed and make her tag along to class. They sat at their usual table with Maia and Toby, and Shiloh immediately got to work on finishing her painting. It was the Friday before spring break, and she had no time to waste.

She was so focused on her easel that she didn't pay much attention to Paisley, who was painting her own canvas. Shiloh finally finished her painting, and just in time. The teacher dismissed the class just as she set her brush down and took a step backwards.

"Whatd'ya think, Pais?" Shiloh turned around, smiling softly. Her smile quickly faded when she saw Paisley asleep with her head on the table, and a completely black canvas next to her.

"Pais… Paisley," Shiloh moved over and gently shook the girl awake. Paisley mumbled something inaudible and looked up at Shiloh with a confused expression on her face.

"What is this?" Shiloh laughed nervously, pointing to the canvas. Paisley squinted, blinked a few times, and shrugged before lying her head back down on the table.

Shiloh glanced over at Maia worriedly. The other brunette raised an eyebrow, just as confused as Shiloh was. Growing concerned, the older girl quickly cleaned up their table before tugging Paisley to her feet.

"C'mon, sleepyhead, we're gonna go get pizza," Shiloh bit her lip hopefully. Luckily, Paisley smiled and nodded her head.

"I *liiiikeeee* pizza," she yawned mid-sentence, tugging on her beanie. Shiloh looked over at Maia and Toby.

"Wanna celebrate spring break with us?" Shiloh asked, inviting them to join along. They accepted, and soon all four classmates were packed into a booth at Lorienzo's.

"Pizza," Paisley whispered, tapping Shiloh's shoulder and looking around. "Where is it?"

"It's coming, goofball," Shiloh laughed and ruffled Paisley's hair. The smaller girl scoffed playfully and reached up to fix her beanie.

Surprisingly, when the pizza did arrive at the table, Paisley didn't even finish once slice. Typically, the girl would barrel through at least two slices. Shiloh grew concerned, but when she asked Paisley if something was wrong, the smaller girl simply shook her head.

Paisley was quiet on the drive home. The only sound that could be heard was the smaller girl's steady tapping of her fingers against the window.

"We're home," Shiloh said quietly. Paisley just nodded and followed Shiloh upstairs to the apartment. Shiloh watched as her girlfriend headed towards the staircase as soon as they got inside.

"Wait, Pais," Shiloh jogged forwards and grabbed Paisley's hand. "Something's wrong. I can tell."

"I am fine," Paisley insisted, shaking her head. Shiloh didn't believe it one bit.

"Paisley, you h—,"

"I am fine!" Paisley snapped, yanking her arm out of Shiloh's grip and storming upstairs. The unexpected outburst took Shiloh by surprise, and it took her brain a few seconds to register what had just happened.

Shiloh knew better than to continue to question Paisley. It would only bother the girl more. Unsure of what to do, Shiloh ascended the stairs slowly. She heard rustling in the bathroom and realized Paisley was with Wolf. Hopefully that would help her calm down a bit.

Shiloh was just about to enter her bedroom when she heard a groan of frustration. Raising an eyebrow, she quietly moved towards the door and listened.

Paisley was playing the piano, Shiloh realized. The smaller girl would get the first few notes of twinkle twinkle little star, but then miss a key and slam her hands down on the keyboard in anger. This would result in a loud screeching noise from the piano, and another frustrated groan from Paisley.

Taking a deep breath, Shiloh forced herself to move away from the door. She had to give Paisley time to herself. With a heavy sigh, Shiloh slipped into her bedroom and left the door open a crack behind her.

If she hadn't been listening intently to Paisley's piano playing, she probably wouldn't have noticed the way her mattress made an odd crinkling noise when she sat down. But she did.

Shiloh raised an eyebrow and stood up. Confused, she pressed down on her mattress with her hand, earning a soft crackling noise. Her first instinct was to lift the mattress, and so she did.

Her eyes widened when she saw what was underneath. Dried, dead flowers were scattered under the mattress, with stray petals everywhere. Shiloh bent down, gently taking one of the flowers into her hand and turning it around.

"What the hell?" she whispered to herself, setting the mattress back down and standing up. She had a feeling Paisley would have something to say about this. Shiloh couldn't help but feel like this was some twisted form of symbolism.

Swallowing the lump in her throat, the older girl cupped the flower in her hands and hid it behind her back. With her free hand, she slowly opened the bathroom door.

"Hey Pais," she leaned against the doorway, trying to play it cool. "Wanna go for a walk and check on the flowers?"

Paisley froze. She looked up at Shiloh slowly, panic flickering in her dark brown eyes. Biting her lip, Paisley shook her head and looked back down at the kitten in her lap.

"Why not?" Shiloh tilted her head to the side. Paisley just kept her head down, fumbling with her fingers nervously.

"Does it have something to do with this?" Shiloh sighed and held out the flower she had hidden behind her back. The moment Paisley looked up, her hands started to shake. She set Wolf down and stood up, backing away from Shiloh.

"I-I..."

"What's going on Paisley?" Shiloh asked, desperation in her voice. "What does this mean?" she held up the flower between them.

Paisley looked down at her feet guiltily and shook her head. She toyed with the sleeves of her sweatshirt, trying to find a way out of this. Desperately, she tried to slip past Shiloh and out the door. The green eyed girl quickly moved to her side to block the exit. Paisley inhaled sharply.

"Paisley, please," Shiloh held up the flower once more and looked at her girlfriend pleadingly.

“I... I..." Paisley shook her head and took a step backwards. "I did... I did not... They cannot die!" She brought her hands up to her face and breathed in deeply.

"I can not lose the pretty things, I can not!" Paisley let her hands fall back to her side and she shook her head, beginning to pace back and forth in the small space between them.

"If I lose them, then I lose y-you… then… then I… I just…" Paisley groaned in frustration. "I do not feel like Paisley!"

"You don't… what?" Shiloh quickly moved forward and grabbed her girlfriend's shoulders to calm her down. "You don't feel like Paisley?"

The small girl shook her head, holding up her hands between them. "My hands shake and I am tired and I can not think," she squeezed her eyes shut. "I can not lose you…"

"Lose me? Who says you're going to lose me?" Shiloh grew even more worried, feeling her heart start to speed up. She hated seeing Paisley like this, but she needed answers.

"The… the…" Paisley stumbled over her words and she brought her hand up to knock on her own forehead softly. Shiloh understood what she meant.

"The nightmares?" Shiloh remembered the hand motion Paisley had used for a long time to describe the 'bad things.' Paisley nodded softly.

"I am scared," Paisley shook her head and drew in a deep breath. "I am scared he will take you away."

"Who?" Shiloh grew worried and ran her hands up and down Paisley's arms.

"Tommy," Paisley whispered quietly and closed her eyes. Shiloh took a deep breath and cupped Paisley's cheek in her hand.

"Pais, he's gone," she shook her head. "He's not going to hurt me. He's not going to hurt you. We're safe." Paisley's breath was shaky, and she took a long, deep breath.

"I can not lose the pretty things," Paisley whispered, reaching out and taking the flower from Shiloh's hand. The small girl studied the flower for a few moments before clutching it close to her chest. "I-I killed it."

That was the last straw for Shiloh. She shook her head, grabbing Paisley's hand and pulling her across the hallway into their bedroom. Paisley watched anxiously as Shiloh dug around in her closet and pulled out a suitcase, tossing it on the bed and throwing it open.

The green eyed girl walked over to the dresser, opening each drawer and grabbing a handful from each. The small girl's eyes widened and she quickly shook her head. Tears stung in her eyes as she backed up.

"No," Paisley shook her head and held her hands up. The tears quickly blinded her and she backed into the wall, bringing her hands up to her face. "Please, no."

Shiloh was brought out of her trance when she heard a small sob escape her girlfriend's lips. She whipped her head up and felt her heart drop in her chest when she saw Paisley slide down against the wall and bury her head in her knees.

"Please do not," Paisley whispered. "I will be good. I p-pr-promise," she whimpered. Shiloh quickly knelt beside her and tilted her head to the side.

"What are you talking about?" Shiloh asked softly, reaching out and putting a hand on the smaller girl's knee. Paisley flinched and looked up. "Paisley, I don't understand."

"Please do not make me leave," Paisley sniffed. Shiloh's breath caught in her throat and she glanced back and forth from Paisley to the suitcase on the bed.

"No," Shiloh quickly shook her head. "No, no, no, Pais," she reached out and tilted Paisley's chin up and met her eyes. "I am *not* making you leave. I promise." She reached down and locked pinkies with the small girl.

"But… but why?" Paisley pointed to the suitcase on the bed. Shiloh shook her head and squeezed Paisley's hand.

"We're going on a vacation," Shiloh stood up slowly and helped Paisley up to her feet. "This medicine isn't helping. So we're going to try something different… is that okay?"

"Vacation?" Paisley asked softly, wiping her eyes and taking a deep breath to calm herself down. Shiloh nodded, leading Paisley over to the bed and motioning for her to sit down.

"We're gonna go visit my family," she explained. This was an idea Shiloh had had in the back of her mind for a while. It had only taken this situation to make her realize what she had to do.

"Florida?" Paisley remembered. "With Maggie?" Shiloh nodded, moving back over to the dresser and resuming packing.

"Just think of this as a... a different type of medicine," Shiloh said, folding a pair of pants and lying them in the suitcase. "Is that okay?"

"Mhm," Paisley nodded. She reached up and fixed her beanie, smiling at Shiloh softly.

"Can you finish packing while I go call your doctor?" Shiloh asked, pointing to the suitcase and them nodding towards the dresser. Paisley stood up and studied Shiloh for a moment.

"Yes," she nodded softly, taking Shiloh's hand and kissing the back of her palm. "I love you. Thank you for being here."

"I'm always gonna be here," Shiloh promised, reaching up and smoothing out Paisley's hair. "I love you, too."

Shiloh headed downstairs, breathing a sigh of relief. She knew the worst was yet to come, but she was somewhat relieved that she had a backup plan. Plopping down on the couch, she pulled out her phone and dialed the doctor.

After canceling Paisley's prescription and paying way too much for a pair of plane tickets, Shiloh took a deep breath and let her phone fall to her side. She gave herself a few minutes to compose herself, but it was cut short when the front door opened and her other three roommates arrived. They immediately knew something was up.

"This medicine is bullshit," Shiloh mumbled, standing up and shaking her head. "I'm taking Paisley to Miami."

"Wait, what?" Vanessa laughed in disbelief, raising an eyebrow.

"We're going to Miami," Shiloh reaffirmed. "I'm tired of trying to beat around the bush. We're facing her past head on and there's nothing you can do to stop me."

All the three roommates exchanged glances. Ryland was the first to break the silence.

"If that's what you think is best," the light haired girl shrugged. Shiloh was surprised that they didn't tell her she was insane. Her roommates knew what needed to be done.

"I brought Chinese," Ryland spoke up, holding up a brown paper bag before bringing it into the kitchen. Leah followed her, leaving only Vanessa and Shiloh.

"It'll all work out, y'know," Vanessa said softly, walking over and pulling Shiloh into a hug. "You're the best thing that's ever happened to her."

Shiloh nodded softly when the hug pulled away. Before they could say anything else, a pair of soft footsteps could be heard coming down the stairs.

"I finished, Lo," Paisley said softly, walking over to Shiloh and leaning into her side. "It is all neat."

"Perfect," Shiloh smiled, kissing Paisley's cheek and glancing back up at Vanessa. "We're leaving in a few hours. Let's have some dinner."

Shortly afterwards, all 5 roommates sat on the floor in the living room. The TV was off for once. They wanted to savor their last night together for a week.

"Ryland," Paisley spoke up, setting her fork down. "You *have* to play with Wolf a lot. Or else he will get sad and lonely."

"I know, dork," Ryland nodded, not looking up from her plate. Paisley furrowed her eyebrows.

"His favorite toy is the jingly mouse," Paisley continued. "And you have to make sure his bed is nice and neat, or he will sleep on the floor. And the floor is cold, and I do not think he wants to be cold."

"I kn—,"

"Oh, and you have to make sure he eats his food," Paisley nodded quickly. "Sometimes he thinks it is a toy and makes a big mess. But if he does that, he will be hungry."

"I think she's got the hang of it, Pais," Shiloh laughed, giving her girlfriend a soft smile. "You can call her and see Wolf whenever you want."

"Okay," Paisley glanced back at Ryland. "I am trusting you."

"I've got this, dork," Ryland laughed, holding out her fist. Paisley giggled, bumping their fists together and making her signature exploding noise. There was a mixture of excitement and uncertainty in Paisley's stomach. But she trusted Shiloh knew what she was doing.

Once they finished dinner, Shiloh brought their bags downstairs and glanced around the apartment one last time. Paisley was on the couch, cradling Wolf in her arms and giving him a long speech, promising she would be back in a few days.

"Y'ready, goofball?" Shiloh asked, leaning against the door and smiling softly at her girlfriend. Paisley and Wolf were the cutest combination.

"Yes," Paisley nodded, looking down at Wolf and kissing him softly. "Take good care of Ryland, Wolf," she giggled before setting the kitten down on the couch and padding over to Shiloh.

They had already said their goodbyes to the other girls, who had just left for a party. Paisley tugged on her converse, looking up at Shiloh and holding out her shoelaces. With a soft laugh, Shiloh bent down and helped the small girl tie her shoes.

"All set," Shiloh nodded, extending a hand to help Paisley to her feet. "Here's to a whole new adventure," she wrapped an arm around Paisley's waist and pulled her closer, kissing her cheek. After giving the apartment one last look, the two girls made their way out into the hallway.

CHAPTER 25

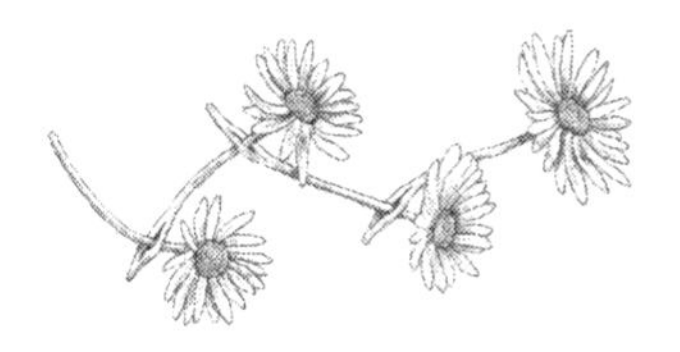

"You've gotta take off your shoes, silly," Shiloh nudged Paisley towards the security check, slipping off her own boots and tossing them into one of the plastic bins. Paisley followed suit, placing her white converse carefully beside Shiloh's shoes.

"One at a time," Shiloh whispered, gently pushing Paisley in the direction of the large metal detector. Hesitantly, Paisley walked forwards and waited for Shiloh to do the same.

"See? Not so bad," Shiloh laughed, grabbing Paisley's hand and adjusting her backpack on her shoulder. "Now all we have to do is wait until our plane gets here. We're gate…" she pulled the ticket out of her pocket. "A21. So somewhere down there," she pointed down one of the long hallways.

Smiling widely, Paisley followed Shiloh as they made their way to their gate. Something else caught Paisley's eye, though, and she let go of Shiloh's hand to check it out.

The small girl padded over to the front of the gift shop, making a beeline for the rack of hoodies. Shiloh raised an eyebrow, jogging after her to see what she had found.

"Look, Lo," Paisley help up a blue hoodie with the words *'I Love New York'* in white lettering. Shiloh nodded, acknowledging that she'd seen the sweatshirt.

"Can I get it?" Paisley tilted her head to the side slightly. "It is your favorite color," she nodded, clutching the hoodie to her chest and moving to whisper in Shiloh's ear. "And I am your favorite girl, right?"

Laughing, Shiloh took the hoodie from Paisley's hands and studied it for a moment. "You're a goofball," she laughed, nudging Paisley towards the cash register and handing her back the hoodie. "Go put it up there."

Paisley glanced up at Shiloh hesitantly but the green eyed girl gave her a supportive smile. Taking a deep breath, Paisley padded over and laid the hoodie on the counter.

"Hi," Paisley said softly. The cashier gave her a small smile and scanned the hoodie. Putting a comforting arm around Paisley's shoulder, Shiloh handed the cashier her credit card.

"Can I put it on?" Paisley asked quietly once they made their way out of the store with the bag in tow. Shiloh laughed, taking the bag from Paisley's hand and unfolding the hoodie. She helped the smaller girl tug it on over her shirt.

Paisley smiled happily in the hoodie, even though she had chosen one that was two sizes too big for her. Shiloh thought she looked adorable with the extra long sleeves. Paisley shook her arms a few times so she could wiggle her hands through the openings.

"My favorite girl in my favorite color," Shiloh teased, leaning in and kissing Paisley's nose. She didn't mind the stares she got from people. She didn't mind at all.

With Paisley, things that usually mattered to her didn't matter. Shiloh tended to get too worked up over everything. If someone looked at her the wrong way, she'd panic. But now, she had Paisley. When she was with Paisley, her only focus was Paisley. They were both in their own little world, and nothing could ruin that.

"Thank you, Lo," Paisley smiled and pulled Shiloh into a hug. "I like this better than my last plane."

"Your last plane?" Shiloh raised an eyebrow. Paisley nodded, grabbing Shiloh's hand and pulling her forwards before she could ask any more questions.

"Right here," Shiloh pointed to the sign above their gate. Paisley clapped her hands and sat down in one of the black chairs. Shiloh sat beside her, pulling out her phone and handing Paisley one of her ear buds.

The girls listened to music while they waited to board their plane. About twenty minutes later, she was being pulled down the aisle by an excited Paisley, who was eager to get a window seat.

Shiloh was worried that Paisley would be scared when the plane began to take off, but luckily she didn't have to worry. Paisley fell asleep even before the plane lifted the ground.

Keeping her fingers laced with Paisley's, just in case, Shiloh lay back in her seat with a book as they made their way to Miami.

"Pais," Shiloh giggled, nudging Paisley's shoulder. When the small girl continued to stay asleep, Shiloh unbuckled her seatbelt and moved so she was standing in front of Paisley, cupping her cheeks.

"Paisley," she laughed, kissing her girlfriend's forehead. The brunette's eyes fluttered open and she stared at Shiloh in confusion.

"Our plane landed, goofball," Shiloh whispered, smoothing out Paisley's hair and fixing her beanie. By the time she finally managed to get Paisley fully awake, they were two of the last passengers on the plane.

"Maggie's gonna be so surprised," Shiloh laughed, leading Paisley over to baggage claim. The small girl smiled and yawned, still slightly dazed from being asleep for so long.

"I didn't tell them we were even coming, so hopefully they're actually home," Shiloh added, spotting their bags and jogging over to tug them off of the conveyor belt. Paisley eagerly grabbed her bag, rolling it behind her as she followed Shiloh.

Paisley didn't quite understand the concept of a taxi. When Shiloh hailed one of the yellow cars, Paisley clutched her bag and took a step backwards.

"C'mon, goof," Shiloh laughed, grabbing Paisley's bag and loading it in the trunk. Paisley's eyes widened when Shiloh took her hand and pulled her towards the car.

Shaking her head, Paisley stood her ground. "It is a stranger," she whispered, nodding towards the car. Shiloh was confused at first, but quickly caught on.

"It's a taxi," Shiloh explained. "He's gonna drive us to my parent's house. It's like a plane… but smaller. And with wheels."

"Promise?" Paisley tilted her head to the side, causing Shiloh to laugh softly.

"Of course, goofball," she whispered, locking their pinkies together at their sides. "Now c'mon, I can't wait to see the look on Maggie's face when she sees us."

Paisley nodded, cautiously sliding into the back of the taxi next to Shiloh. As soon as they started moving, though, Paisley was quickly distracted by looking out the window.

Even though Shiloh could look out the window at the tall palm trees, she would much rather look at Paisley. The small girl viewed everything with a sense of awe and bewilderment that Shiloh had never seen on anyone else. Maybe she was impartial because she was in love, but there was just *something* about Paisley that made her so captivating.

It didn't take them long to get to their parents house. Once they pulled up in front of the small brick building, it was already dark out. Shiloh paid the driver and thanked him, jogging around the car to open Paisley's door for her.

They got their bags. Well, *Shiloh* got their bags. By the time she had set both suitcases on the sidewalk and given the taxi driver the 'all clear', Paisley was already running towards the door.

Laughing softly to herself, Shiloh quickly grabbed both suitcases and struggled to pull them up the walkway. She set them both at the bottom of the steps and jogged up to grab Paisley's hand. The small girl had already rung the doorbell more times than necessary.

Shiloh grinned when she heard tiny footsteps approaching the door. Moment's later, the door was thrown open. A small blonde with wet hair and purple pajamas stared up at them in shock.

"Shiloh? *Paisleeee?*" Maggie tilted her head to the side.

"Hi," Paisley giggled. "It is us."

Squealing excitedly, Maggie jumped forwards and wrapped them both into a huge huge. Shiloh laughed, leaning down and kissing her sister's forehead just as both of her parents appeared in the hallway.

"Shiloh?" her mother's voice was laced with shock. She hurried over to them and pulled her daughter into a hug. "What are you doing here? Is something wrong?"

"No, mom, everything's fine," Shiloh laughed, jogging back to pull the suitcases inside. "We actually… we just wanted to get away for a bit. I figured we'd pay you guys a visit." She motioned to the suitcases beside them. "I was sort of hoping we could stay here… but we could always get a hotel if y—,"

"Of course you can stay here," her father interrupted, pulling her into a hug and then holding out his fist in Paisley's direction.

"You remembered!" Paisley's face lit up and she bumped his fist, making an exploding noise. Shiloh couldn't help but laugh.

"Daxton is at practice and Tara's at her friend's," her mother explained, motioning for them to come inside. "I just wish you'd told us you were coming earlier… your father's Aunt Sylvia passed away last week and her funeral is tomorrow."

Paisley furrowed her eyebrows, glancing between Shiloh and her mother. She padded forwards, tapping on Shiloh's shoulder. "What is a funeral?" she whispered, biting her lip.

"A funeral… it's like a celebration of someone's life, when someone dies you have a funeral to say goodbye to them," Shiloh tried her best to explain. Paisley nodded.

"Yes, I remember," she smiled softly. "Can we go, Lo?"

"You want to go to a funeral?" Shiloh raised an eyebrow at her small girlfriend. Paisley nodded furiously with a soft smile on her face.

"Is it cool if we…?" Shiloh glanced back to her parents, hoping they'd heard what Paisley had asked. Her mother laughed, nodding softly.

Shiloh had never even met her Great Aunt, but for some odd reason, Paisley wanted to go to the funeral. She couldn't say no. Hell, there was no denying it. She was whipped. She didn't even care. Who wouldn't be whipped for Paisley?

"We've got to finish baking this stupid casserole for the funeral," her mother laughed, nodding towards the kitchen. Shiloh knew she had smelled something when they walked in.

"That's okay," Shiloh laughed, glancing at Paisley who was practically struggling not to fall asleep while standing up. "We've had a long day, anyway. I think we're gonna head to bed." Paisley nodded in agreement.

They said their goodnights and Shiloh followed Paisley upstairs, lugging the two heavy suitcases behind her. When she pushed the door open to her bedroom, Paisley was already burrowed under the covers.

"Brush your teeth, weirdo," Shiloh teased, unzipping one of the suitcases and tossing Paisley her bathroom bag. The small girl wasn't prepared and it only hit the lump under the covers before bouncing onto the floor.

"Meanie," Paisley mumbled playfully, crawling out from under the blankets and grabbing the yellow bag. Shiloh grabbed her own, heading into the bathroom. Paisley quickly padded over to catch up with her.

"Can you braid my hair?" Paisley asked once they were done. She ruffled her hair jokingly, sliding off her beanie and setting it on the nightstand.

Shiloh nodded mid-yawn, sitting on the bed and patting the space in front of her. Smiling widely, Paisley hopped down next to her and turned around so Shiloh could comb her fingers through her hair.

"Why'd you wanna go to the funeral?" Shiloh asked, grabbing a section of hair at the top of Paisley's head and beginning to braid it down the back.

"Celebrating life is fun," Paisley shrugged. She thought for a moment. "And I want to spend time with you."

"You always get to spend time with me, goofball," Shiloh laughed, finishing the braid and tying it off. She wrapped her arms around Paisley's stomach, pushing the braid aside and resting her chin on Paisley's shoulder.

"I love you, y'know," Shiloh whispered, kissing Paisley's neck and causing the younger girl to shiver.

"I know," Paisley giggled softly, turning her head so she could kiss Shiloh's forehead. "But I love you more."

Shiloh feigned shock, moving her head back. "That's impossible!" she gasped.

Paisley giggled and turned around. "Nuh uh."

"Yeah huh," Shiloh raised her eyebrows, reaching out and tickling Paisley's stomach. "I love you *way* more."

Paisley squealed, falling backwards on the bed and shaking her head. "No, Lolo!" she giggled, reaching up and grabbing onto Shiloh's shirt. Shiloh fell forwards, quickly moving to straddle Paisley so she would fall completely on top of her.

"I'll call it even if you kiss me," Shiloh smirked, poking Paisley's stomach and making the brown eyed girl laugh even harder.

"Okay, okay!" Paisley reached up and wrapped her arms around Shiloh's neck, pulling her closer so their foreheads were nearly touching. Shiloh's hair hung down over her shoulders, practically shielding them both so only their faces were visible.

"I love you," Shiloh whispered, lingering a moment before leaning down and closing the space between them. Paisley wasn't the most experienced kisser, but damn, the feelings she could draw out of Shiloh were a mile above anything she'd ever experienced.

Their lips moved together rhythmically until Shiloh had to pull away to catch her breath. Paisley gazed up at her, fluttering her eyelashes and breathing heavily.

"I love you too," Paisley whispered, reaching up and running her fingers over Shiloh's cheek. "You will not forget, right?"

"Right," Shiloh nodded, gently moving off of Paisley so she could lay next to her. "I'll never ever forget you, goofball."

"You and me?" Paisley smiled softly, crawling off of the bed and digging around in her suitcase until she found her stuffed yellow dog, causing Shiloh to laugh softly.

"Me and you. Always," Shiloh nodded before rolling over to turn off the light. Paisley immediately curled herself in Shiloh's side, intertwining their legs and working her hands into the sleeves of Shiloh's hoodie to keep warm.

"Sing?" Paisley whispered, finding the glint of Shiloh's eyes in the dark room.

"Only for you," Shiloh laughed softly, reaching out and stroking Paisley's cheek.

Shiloh had nearly fallen asleep by the time she was finished, and judging by the steady rise and fall of Paisley's chest, the small girl had beat her to it. Laughing softly, Shiloh kissed her girlfriend's forehead and pulled the covers over them. Sleep followed quickly after.

It wasn't long before Shiloh woke up once more, though. She blinked a few times, nearly gasping when she saw the small figure in front of her.

"Shiloh?" Maggie whispered, clutching her purple stuffed bunny close to her chest.

"Mags?" Shiloh rubbed her eyes, glancing to the other side of the bed to make sure Paisley was still asleep. "What's up?"

"I don't like the dark," Maggie shook her head, bringing one of her hands up to her mouth and toying with her bottom lip nervously. "There are monsters."

Glancing back at Paisley, Shiloh scooted over slightly and held up the blankets. "C'mere," she whispered, patting the space next to her. Maggie nodded softly, crawling onto the bed and allowing Shiloh to lay the covers back down over them.

"It's like a sleepover," Maggie giggled softly, hugging her bunny to her chest. Shiloh found it funny how both Paisley and Maggie slept with stuffed animals.

"It kinda is," Shiloh laughed, laying on her back and staring up at the ceiling. "Now go to sleep, weirdo. The monsters won't get you in here."

Maggie nodded, burrowing under the blankets and curling up into a ball. Shiloh, on the other hand, rolled over and gazed at Paisley. She looked so peaceful in her sleep.

Every once in a while her nose would crinkle slightly, which Shiloh found absolutely adorable.

"Goodnight, Shiloh," Maggie whispered from under the blankets, causing Shiloh to laugh.

"Goodnight, Maggie. Don't let the bed bugs bite."

CHAPTER 26

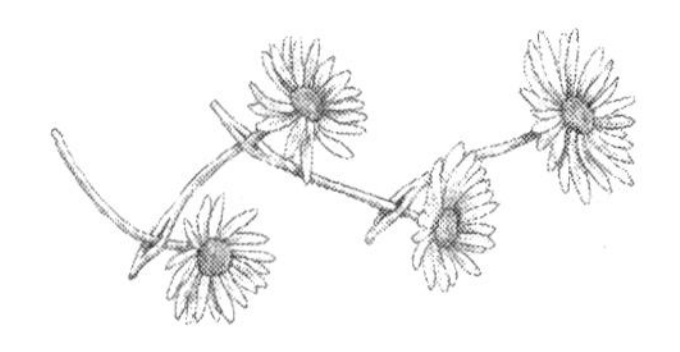

Shiloh's eyes fluttered open the next morning to come face to face with her younger sister's stuffed bunny. She crinkled her nose, rolling over and closing her eyes once more. Only moments later, though, her eyes shot back open when she realized someone was missing. Paisley.

Shiloh sat up quickly and ran a hand through her tousled hair. She scanned the room, seeing no sign of Paisley. Just as she moved to get off of the bed, she heard laughter. Raising an eyebrow, she listened quietly. She could make out Paisley's soft giggle.

Rolling her eyes, Shiloh yawned and stretched her arms out. She glanced over at Maggie, who was still sound asleep under the covers. Of course the two heaviest sleepers would be the last to wake up.

"Mags," Shiloh whispered, rolling over and nudging the small blonde's shoulder. "Maggie, time to get up," she laughed. The small girl blinked a few times and sat up.

"Is it morning?" Maggie hugged her bunny to her chest and looked around the room.

"Yep," Shiloh nodded, rolling out of bed and combing her fingers through her hair in the mirror. "Everyone else is already downstairs."

"Let's go!" Maggie smiled, scrambling out of bed and grabbing Shiloh's hand. The green eyed girl was practically dragged down the stairs, and she eventually pried her hand free from the smaller girl's grip once they made it to the living room.

She raised an eyebrow when she saw her entire family squeezed onto the couch. Paisley sat on the floor in front of the TV, watching it intently. Before Shiloh could ask what she was doing, she was tackled in a hug by Daxton and Tara.

"You were already asleep by the time I got back," Tara pouted once they pulled away from the hug. "I missed you."

"I missed you too. But I'm here now," Shiloh gave her sister a quiet smile. She raised an eyebrow when she heard Paisley and her parents laugh at something on the TV.

"What're they watching?" Shiloh asked, glancing down at her siblings. Tara and Daxton both smirked and looked at one another.

"What?" Shiloh laughed nervously, giving up on getting an answer for them and making her way into the living room. "You've got to be kidding me."

"You were cute, Lo," Paisley giggled, hopping to her feet and walking over to her girlfriend. "See? You were cute," she pointed to the screen, where a grainy video of Shiloh as a baby was playing.

"Come on guys," Shiloh glanced at her parents, motioning to the screen. "Really?"

"Paisley picked it," her father chuckled, holding his hands up as if he were surrendering. Shiloh rolled her eyes.

"Like I'm supposed to believe that," she crinkled her nose, turning back to Paisley and fixing the lopsided beanie on her head. "How'd you sleep?"

Paisley shrugged and looked down at her feet, feeling uncomfortable talking about her nightmares in front of anyone but Shiloh. The green eyed girl quickly caught on and shook her head, planting a kiss on Paisley's cheek.

"How about we eat breakfast instead?" Shiloh quickly moved over to the TV and turned it off before they could protest. Paisley pouted, but Shiloh distracted her by taking her hand and leading her into the kitchen.

After Paisley made a show of showing the rest of the family how she could crack an egg, her father made them all chocolate chip waffles. Shiloh noticed how Paisley still didn't eat as much as usual. Hopefully that would go away now that she wasn't taking the medicine.

"We leave in about two hours," her mother informed them as she finished washing the dishes. Shiloh nodded, bringing both of her plates to the sink and thanking her parents. She nudged Paisley towards the stairs, which resulted in a race between both of them to the bedroom. Paisley won.

"You are a loser," Paisley teased once Shiloh jogged into the bedroom. Shiloh stuck her tongue out at the girl, lifting their suitcases onto the bed and digging through hers until she had found the simple black dress she had brought just in case. Paisley watched her intently.

"Gotta get dressed sometime, goofball," Shiloh laughed, snapping Paisley out of her trance. The small girl padded over to her suitcase and pulled out her dress with a wide smile. Shiloh nearly choked on thin air when she turned around.

"You're wearing *that* to a funeral?" Shiloh bit her lip, watching as Paisley studied the bright yellow sundress that Leah had given her for her birthday.

"Yes," Paisley smiled proudly. "It is a happy color. Is that bad?"

Shiloh bit her lip, studying the dress once more. "No, it's fine," she laughed softly, wondering what her parents would think. "People just normally wear black to a funeral."

"Well that is a sad color," Paisley pursed her lips in thought. "Yellow is happy, right?" Shiloh nodded. "Okay then. Yellow it is," Paisley grabbed her bathroom bag from the suitcase before disappearing across the hallway.

Shiloh laughed softly to herself, closing the door before changing into her dress. She had just gotten started on her hair when she heard small footsteps behind her.

"Look, Lo," Paisley said softly. Shiloh set her curling iron down, turning around and feeling her heart flutter when she saw Paisley. The small girl spun around once in her dress before hopping forwards and kissing Shiloh's cheek.

"That sure is your color," Shiloh giggled, helping Paisley adjust the straps of her dress. Paisley paused, reaching up and twirling one of Shiloh's curls around her finger.

"Can you do my hair?" she asked, pulling off her beanie and setting it down. Shiloh nodded with a soft smile, promising Paisley she would curl her hair once she was finished with her own.

A little less than an hour later, Paisley stood in front of the mirror, running her fingers through her loose curls. She'd managed to put on a little bit of blush and mascara on her own, with a little help from Shiloh.

Shiloh stood up from the spot by the mirror where she had been doing her makeup and studied Paisley. Her eyes landed on the shelf of her old dolls in the back of her room and she gained an idea.

Holding up a finger to signal for Paisley to wait, Shiloh jogged over and grabbed a light blue bow from one of her dolls. She gently cupped Paisley's cheek and clipped the bow into her hair, spinning her back around so she could see herself in the mirror.

"I knew something was missing," Shiloh laughed softly. Paisley clapped her hands together and reached up to gently fix the bow in her hair.

"You have to say it," Paisley whispered, turning around and smiling hopefully up at Shiloh. The green eyed girl laughed and raised an eyebrow.

"Who says?" she teased. Paisley crinkled her nose, feigning disappointment and sticking out her bottom lip.

"Okay, okay," Shiloh gave in, resting her arms on Paisley's shoulder and leaning in to peck her lips. "My favorite girl in my favorite color."

Paisley smiled widely, pulling Shiloh closer and leaning into a deeper kiss. When the pulled away, Paisley smiled shyly and took a step back to study Shiloh's outfit.

"You make sad colors look happy," Paisley observed, spinning around in her dress once more and looking at herself in the mirror.

"You look like a princess," Shiloh laughed when Paisley continued to spin around.

"I feel like a princess," Paisley nodded, wandering over to her suitcase and pulling out her worn white converse. One day in class, Shiloh had doodled on them with a sharpie out of boredom, and now they had small daisies lining the edges. It only made Paisley love them even more.

"Lolo," she hummed, sitting back on the bed and shuffling her feet on the carpet. Shiloh couldn't help but laugh as she made her way over to help her girlfriend tie her shoes. Paisley could easily learn if she wanted to, but she liked having her little traditions with Shiloh. They meant something to her.

They made their way downstairs to meet the rest of Shiloh's family in the kitchen. Shiloh had to bite down on her bottom lip to keep from laughing when she saw her parent's eyes widen upon seeing Paisley's yellow dress. Surprisingly, they both shrugged it off, which Shiloh was thankful for. Who really cared if they broke a little tradition?

The drive to the funeral was mostly filled with Maggie asking questions about where they were going. Shiloh and Paisley sat in the way back of the van next to Daxton. Paisley was practically in Shiloh's lap.

Paisley padded quietly behind Shiloh once they made it to the funeral home. Shiloh noticed the small girl's nervousness and quickly took her hand.

"No need to be scared, goofball," she whispered, kissing Paisley's cheek while they stood outside the door. The small girl nodded, keeping her grip on Shiloh's hand as they made their way into the old building.

Shiloh couldn't help but laugh softly when she saw how many heads turned to observe the girl in a bright yellow dress. Paisley was literally the *only* person in the building that wasn't wearing black. Paisley didn't even notice, she only studied the room in awe of the various paintings on the walls.

Paisley had already met some of Shiloh's family when they visited for Christmas. She greeted everyone with a fist bump. In the meantime, Shiloh nervously glanced over at her Aunt Nancy. The woman was *extremely* strict, and Shiloh wasn't sure how well she would receive Paisley.

Figuring she might as well get it over with, Shiloh squeezed Paisley's hand and led her over to the older woman.

"Hi," Shiloh smiled softly, hugging her Aunt in greeting. "Aunt Nan, this is Paisley. My girlfriend," she laughed nervously, holding up their connected hands. The woman studied them both.

"That's an interesting outfit choice you've got there," she nodded, turning to Paisley. Shiloh held her breath.

The small girl simply nodded and smiled, letting go of Shiloh's hand so she could spin in a circle. "Yes it is," she smiled. "It is my favorite color."

"Just trying to bring a little happiness to a sad day," Shiloh added, glancing at Paisley adoringly. Her aunt nodded, looking back and forth between the girls for a moment before speaking once more.

"That's admirable," she nodded. Shiloh sighed in relief. "It's nice to meet you, Paisley."

"It is nice to meet you too…" Paisley glanced at Shiloh nervously.

"Nancy," the woman laughed softly. "You can call me Nancy."

"Nancy," Paisley repeated, glancing at Shiloh with a mischievous smile on her face. As they walked away, Paisley tapped Shiloh's shoulder and leaned up to whisper in her ear. "Fancy Nancy," she giggled, pulling away and covering her mouth.

"Weirdo," Shiloh laughed, nudging Paisley playfully. They took their seats at one of the rows of chairs in the back. The service dragged on, and Shiloh nearly fell asleep a few times. Paisley, on the other hand, was sitting up straight with her hands in her lap, practically hanging onto every word.

"If I start snoring, let me know," Shiloh whispered jokingly. Paisley furrowed her eyebrows and looked at Shiloh, shaking her head.

"Shh," she whispered. "You have to be re.... res.... respectful," she nodded curtly and turned her attention back to the front of the room. Shiloh had to cover her mouth to hide her laughter. Paisley's seriousness was adorable.

After what felt like hours, the service was over. Shiloh was in a daze. She'd been staring at the floor and watching a line of ants crawl back and forth. She only looked back up once she heard quiet conversation beginning to form.

"Well thank god that's o—," she paused when she looked over at Paisley, who was still looking longingly up at the front of the room. She sniffed and wiped her eyes, hanging her head down.

"Hey, what's wrong?" Shiloh asked, scooting over and grabbing Paisley's hand. "Why are you crying?"

"It is sad," Paisley whispered, sticking her neck out and nodding towards the front of the room. "It is."

"It's okay, Pais," Shiloh said softly. "You didn't even know her."

"Was she a good person?" Paisley asked, tilting her head to the side. Shiloh shrugged.

"I think I only met her a few times when I was a baby," the green eyed girl admitted. Paisley furrowed her eyebrows.

"No need to cry," Shiloh whispered. "This is a celebration of life, remember?" She pointed to Paisley's dress and ran her fingers down her arm. "It's okay, babe."

Paisley nodded slowly, wiping her eyes and turning so she could study Shiloh. "You are very pretty today," she smiled softly, running her fingers through her hair. "And always."

"Why thank you," Shiloh blushed, running her thumb over the back of Paisley's hand. "And so are you. You look like a beautiful sunflower," she giggled. Paisley crinkled her nose and stood up, pulling Shiloh up with her.

They followed everyone outside and said their goodbyes. Once Shiloh found her parents, she led Paisley over to their car.

"We're gonna walk home," she announced, earning confused glances from everyone. Even Paisley.

"We are?" Paisley tilted her head to the side. She hadn't been informed of this.

"Yes. There's a reason why we came here, remember?" Shiloh said softly, squeezing her girlfriend's hand. Paisley nodded slowly, a little uncertain.

"We'll be home in time for dinner," Shiloh added. Her mother looked at her curiously, but didn't question her. They said their goodbyes and Shiloh turned to Paisley, taking a deep breath.

“Ready?"

CHAPTER 27

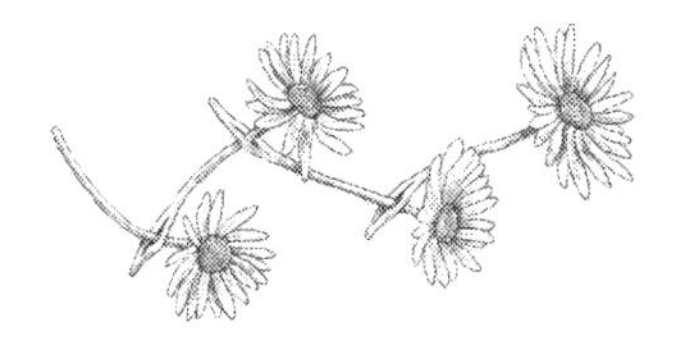

"We've got three stops to make," Shiloh explained as they walked. Paisley listened intently, curious as to what Shiloh had in store.

"We're only going to one place today," Shiloh continued, reaching over and lacing their fingers together. Paisley smiled up at her, nodding and skipping happily in front of them to inspect a dandelion poking out of the sidewalk.

Shiloh bit her lip, wondering if she was doing the right thing. She was aware that it may be somewhat frightening for Paisley, but she was also tired of trying to fix anything *but* the real problem.

They walked for a while, and eventually Paisley stole Shiloh's phone to call Ryland and check up on Wolf. She trailed behind Shiloh as she dialed Ryland's number, holding the phone up to her ear and smiling excitedly.

"Hello?" she tilted her head to the side. Shiloh glanced back at her, watching as the small girl widened her eyes and squealed excitedly. "Hi Ryland!"

Laughing to herself, Shiloh jogged back and grabbed Paisley's free hand to pull her forwards. The small girl babbled on and on to Ryland about the funeral, even explaining her entire outfit in detail.

"I would bump your fist, but I can not see you," Paisley giggled. Shiloh rolled her eyes playfully, tugging on Paisley's hand to make her turn down the sidewalk.

"Is Wolf taking good care of you?" Paisley teased. Shiloh couldn't help but laugh. Paisley's jokes were cheesy but extremely endearing.

They walked for a while longer until Shiloh made a turn onto a familiar street. She bit her lip and glanced back at Paisley, squeezing her hand and pointing to the building across the street.

Paisley's eyes widened and she nearly dropped the phone. Shiloh quickly grabbed it, telling Ryland they had to go and glancing over at her girlfriend, whose eyes were scanning the large building up and down.

"I remember," Paisley said softly, turning to Shiloh. "We had Chemisty."

"We did," Shiloh nodded, looking both ways before leading Paisley across the street. "Do you know why we're here?" Paisley tilted her head to the side, following closely behind Shiloh.

"This is all stuff that was familiar to you… before… the accident," Shiloh explained quietly. Paisley started walking towards the front door of the building but Shiloh nudged her around the side. Confused, Paisley followed.

"The best way to conquer your fears is to face them," Shiloh continued. Paisley nodded quietly, jogging forwards and holding onto Shiloh's arm as they neared the back of the building.

"So this is step one," Shiloh whispered, turning around to the back entrance of the building. Paisley stopped walking when she saw someone else leaning against the wall. She recognized the blonde hair.

"Pais," Shiloh whispered, gently leading Paisley forward. The girl smiled, greeting Shiloh. Paisley continued to study her. She knew her. She recognized her.

And then it clicked. Paisley scooted closer to Shiloh, holding onto her arm and biting her lip.

"You left," Paisley whispered, shaking her head and looking at the girl, who she remembered as Sydney. "You left."

Sydney glanced at Shiloh before shaking her head. "What do you mean?"

Paisley bit her lip. "You left. You did not come back," she looked up at Shiloh pleadingly. The green eyed girl squeezed her hand and gave her a supportive smile.

"You don't understand, Paisley," Sydney shook her head, trying to explain herself. "I did. I mean… I tried to come and see you. I swear," she held her hands up in the air as if she were surrendering. "But… your uncle… he…"

"He didn't let anyone see you," Shiloh finished Sydney's sentence, giving her a soft smile before turning to Paisley. "Sydney didn't do anything. She tried her best."

Paisley bit her lip, looking up at Shiloh to see if she was telling the truth. She looked back at Sydney, thinking for a few moments.

"Did he hurt you?" she asked quietly, taking a step forwards but still holding onto Shiloh's arm. Shiloh was surprised at Paisley's concern for the other girl.

Sydney shook her head and held her hands out in front of her as if to show Paisley that she was fine. "He just yelled a lot," she laughed nervously. "The real question is, are you okay?"

Paisley glanced up at Shiloh and then back to Sydney with a small smile on her face. "Yes. I found friends," she reached up to fix the bow in her hair and looked at Shiloh for approval. "Friends and Lolo."

"You don't know how happy that makes me," Sydney laughed softly. "I was so worried about you."

Paisley smiled widely, letting go of Shiloh and stepping forward so she could pull the girl into a hug. "Do not worry. I am happy," Paisley laughed softly once they pulled away from the hug. "Thank you for being my friend."

Sydney was surprised, as was Shiloh. The green eyed girl was proud of Paisley for being able to forgive and move on. "I've got to go before my parents ask where I was," Sydney laughed, pulling a key out of her pocket and unlocking the back door. Paisley looked at Shiloh questioningly.

"She was on the cheer team so she has the key to the gym. I asked her to help us out," Shiloh explained, giving Sydney a thankful smile.

"Hey," Sydney nudged Paisley's arm to get her attention before reaching into her bag and digging around for a moment. "After your accident we had to clean out your locker and I held onto this just in case," she pulled out a blue, while, and yellow bow that all the cheerleaders had worn. "I thought maybe you'd want this."

Paisley studied the bow for a few moments, a spark of familiarity filling her. She smiled softly, taking the bow into her hands and turning it around.

"Thank you, you're welcome," she smiled, clutching it to her chest and then turning to show it to Shiloh. Sydney laughed softly and closed up her bag.

"Thank you," Shiloh added, addressing the blonde girl.

"No problem," Sydney shrugged it off, keeping the door open with her foot. "Good luck."

"Thanks," Shiloh laughed softly, nudging Paisley into the building. "I'll message you or something just to let you know we left."

After the girls said their goodbyes, Shiloh led Paisley into the dark gym. She quickly turned on her phone flashlight to light the way until she could find the lights and turn them on. Paisley clung onto her arm, a bit concerned about what they were doing.

"Do you remember any of this?" Shiloh asked, motioning around the gym. Paisley shrugged softly. It felt familiar, but nothing stuck out to her. Shiloh simply nodded and led her through two double doors into a wide hallway.

Paisley studied the school in awe as she followed Shiloh down the hallway. It felt familiar to her. Shiloh reached out, grabbing her hand and leading her into one of the classrooms.

"We had Chemistry, remember?" Shiloh smiled softly, flicking on the lights to the classroom. Paisley's eyes widened, taking in the familiar surroundings as her memories came rushing back to her.

"Ten minutes left, ladies and gentlemen!"

Paisley looked up from her book, watching the green eyed girl across from her scramble to finish up the lab they had been working on. She glanced at the two other students in her lab group. One was asleep, and the other was doodling aimlessly on the worksheet. They wouldn't be any help.

Paisley had been done for a while now. She glanced over at Shiloh once more, wondering if she should try and help the girl out.

She knew it would end badly. She knew Shiloh would just snap at her. After what she had done to the girl less than a month ago, it was probably well deserved.

Paisley found herself staring at the girl, realizing just how beautiful she really was. Cursing herself for being so stupid, she tore her eyes off of Shiloh and rubbed her shoulder, wincing when her fingers came in contact with the sensitive skin.

She tried to focus on her book, but she found herself reading the same paragraph over and over. Meanwhile, Shiloh huffed in frustration, erasing her answer once more.

Giving in, Paisley glanced up and snuck a look at Shiloh's paper. Taking a deep breath, she took a chance.

"You're using the wrong formula, you've got to u—,"

"I've got it," Shiloh snapped, not even looking up at the other girl. Paisley sighed, slumping back in her chair and forcing herself to take her eyes off of the girl.

Paisley kept her eyes down on her book for the rest of the class. As soon as the bell rang, Shiloh shoved her paper in Paisley's direction and bolted out of the classroom.

In each lab group, one student was assigned the job of gathering everyone's papers and taking them to the folders in the back of the classroom. That just so happened to be Paisley.

As she was shuffling the papers together, Paisley heard footsteps. She glanced behind her, realizing the teacher had gone out to monitor the hallway.

On a rush decision, Paisley found Shiloh's paper and scanned it over. Every answer was wrong. Grimacing, Paisley grabbed her pencil. Making sure no one was watching, she erased Shiloh's answers and rushed to scrawl the right answers overtop of them. Giving the paper one last look over, Paisley set it on top of the pile and hurried to put them away in the back of the classroom.

She figured it was the least she could do to make up for what she had done to the other girl.

Paisley collected her things and hurried out into the hallway, anxious to get to lunch. She raised an eyebrow when she saw a few girls in cheer uniforms crowded by some of the lockers.

Paisley hurried over to see what was going on, wincing when her backpack rubbed over one of the sore spots on her shoulders.

"So you really are gay?" One of the cheerleaders laughed. Paisley's heart dropped in her chest when she realized who they were talking to. She stood on her tiptoes, spotting Shiloh and one of her friends by her locker.

Paisley quickly ducked down so Shiloh wouldn't see her. The girl didn't need another reason to hate her.

"Is there a problem with that?" one of Shiloh's friends stepped towards them.

"We were only asking," Harper laughed. Paisley could tell from the tone of her voice that she wasn't serious.

"Ryland, just ignore them," Shiloh hissed, bent down over her backpack and looking for something in the bottom of her bag. Ryland ignored her.

"Ooooh," Harper raised an eyebrow and turned to the girls beside her, holding a coffee cup in one hand. "I think they've been fucking," she teased, nodding towards Ryland and Shiloh.

Paisley's heart sped up when she saw Ryland take a step forward. At the same time Shiloh jumped up to grab the back of her friend's shirt, Paisley 'accidentally' turned quickly and let her backpack run into the coffee cup in Harper's hand, spilling the hot liquid all over the floor.

"Oh my god, I'm so sorry," Paisley shook her head, hoping she sounded believable. She felt everyone's eyes on her, even Shiloh and Ryland's piercing glares.

"Come on, Paisley," Harper scoffed, rolling her eyes. "You're such a clutz," she laughed. Everyone else took it as a joke, but Paisley knew there was a bit of truth to her words.

"I'll buy you a new one, come on," Paisley mumbled, grabbing Harper's arm and pulling her down the hallway

before they could say anything else to Shiloh. Paisley had to force herself not to look back.

As she followed the other cheerleaders into the cafeteria, Paisley took a deep breath and tugged on the sleeves of her uniform. She hated school. She hated seeing Shiloh suffer for something she had done.

Paisley had debated telling Shiloh the reasons behind what she had done multiple times. But that meant risking her friendship with the other girls, as well as telling Shiloh about her uncle. And what if Shiloh didn't even believe her? Hell, Paisley wouldn't blame her.

She'd been trying to do little things to gain back some good karma. Obviously outing Shiloh had granted her all the bad luck in the world. All she could do now was try and subtly protect Shiloh and hope that Ryland didn't pound her face into the lockers.

One thing that scared her the most, though, was seeing how unaccepting all of her closest friends seemed to be towards Shiloh's sexuality. What happened if Paisley was gay? What if she told them? Would they do the same thing?

Paisley sighed, sliding into the same chair she had sat at during every lunch. Every day. Every week. For what felt like forever. Except now it felt a lot different.

She just wanted to go home. She wanted to go home, take her shoebox full of money she had saved up, and drive off into the sunset. She wished it was that simple, really.

Paisley stole a glance behind her, finding the familiar head of dark hair a few tables back. Shiloh was laughing with her friends, covering her mouth to hide how widely she was smiling. Paisley wondered if Shiloh was truly happy. Because she knew that she wasn't.

CHAPTER 28

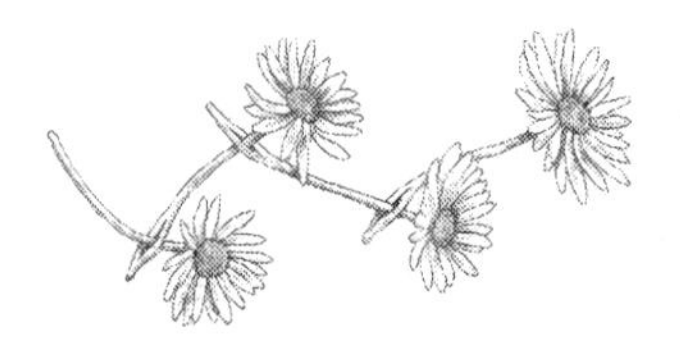

Shiloh watched as Paisley's eyes fluttered back into reality, immediately searching the room for the familiar green eyed girl. Paisley met Shiloh's gaze tentatively, looking for any sign of anger or danger. When she was only met with pure adoration, Paisley moved swiftly forwards and threw her arms around Shiloh.

"I tried," she mumbled, squeezing her eyes shut and tucking her head into the crook of her girlfriend's neck. The small girl held her breath to contain her tears.

"What?" Shiloh whispered, grabbing Paisley's shoulders and separating them. "What are you talking about?" She watched as tears clouded Paisley's eyes. Shiloh moved forwards to pull her girlfriend into another hug, but Paisley stopped her, shaking her head.

"I want to talk," Paisley sniffed, wiping her eyes. Shiloh hated to see Paisley struggling, but the green eyed girl held herself back. Paisley took a deep breath.

"I-I did a bad thing to you, didn't I?" Paisley whispered. Before Shiloh could speak, Paisley shook her head and continued talking. "I do not… I do not remember the bad thing. But… I tried, Lo," she reached up and traced Shiloh's jawline with her index finger, letting it linger on her face for a moment.

"You tried?" Shiloh said softly. She placed a hand on Paisley's arm, trying to ease her to continue. The small girl nodded furiously.

"The things they said…" she shook her head. "They were bad." Paisley didn't quite understand much of the meaning of what she remembered, but she could tell just by the tone of the girl's voices that they were *anything* but nice to Shiloh. And it infuriated her.

"I tried, Lo, I tried," Paisley bit her lip. "I did not want them to say those things to you, I did not!" She threw her hands down at her sides, becoming frustrated with her inability to express her words.

"Hey, hey," Shiloh shook her head, grabbing Paisley's wrists and forcing her to look up. "Breathe," she whispered, rubbing Paisley's arms to calm her down. "Take your time."

"I… I tried to stop them," Paisley reached up to roll her bottom lip inbetween her fingers, looking down at the ground.

"You did?" Shiloh asked, somewhat surprised with Paisley's words. The brown eyed girl nodded softly.

"Those things were not good for you," Paisley whispered. "It hurts to know that I could not help," she hung her head down, disappointed with her past self. How could she have been so cold?

"It got me here, didn't it?" Shiloh squeezed Paisley's hand. The girl looked up in confusion.

"I mean, yeah, it sorta sucked at the time. Not gonna lie," Shiloh shrugged and bit her lip. "But what if it hadn't happened? What would my life be like? Would I be here with you? Or would I be somewhere else?" She watched Paisley's eyes shine with realization. "I wouldn't go back to change it and risk never meeting you."

"You… you would not?" Paisley looked up in disbelief. Shiloh laughed softly and shook her head.

"Never in a million years," she kissed Paisley's forehead and reached up to adjust her bow. "If you can't tell, I'm pretty happy with things just the way they are. And I'll be even happier when all of this sucky stuff..." she motioned around the room. "...is behind us."

Paisley nodded softly. Her mind was all over the place. She could barely focus her eyes on one spot. None of this made sense, yet all of it did. She was confused, yet completely content. It was an unexplainable feeling.

"Y'think you can walk around a little more?" Shiloh bit her lip nervously.

Paisley studied her girlfriend's face. That was the one thing that always remained constant. Everything could change and she could be perfectly fine as long as every time she looked up, she was met with the same pair of emerald eyes. They captured her, pulling her away from everything bad and making everything okay, even if just for a moment.

And with that, Paisley gave Shiloh a soft nod, finding her hand and lacing their fingers together. She gave her girlfriend a soft smile, silently letting her know that she was going to be alright.

Shiloh, slightly surprised, squeezed Paisley's hand and led her out of the classroom, making sure to turn off the lights behind her. Sure, *technically* they were breaking and entering. But also, she was *technically* just a returning student that got a little too excited.

She paused once they made it down the stairs, leading them down a long row of lockers. Her lips spread into a smile and she pointed to one of the tall, dark blue lockers. "That one was mine."

She turned around when she felt Paisley let go of her hand. The small girl was across the hall, pressing her fingertips against a locker.

"This one was mine," Paisley whispered, turning to look at Shiloh with a shocked expression on her face. "I remember."

Shiloh raised both her eyebrows. She had never paid much attention to where Paisley's locker was in high school.

Paisley clasped her hands together, tentatively taking the lock into her hands and fiddling with it for a few moments.

Shiloh nearly choked on thin air when the locker clicked open. Hell, she had already forgotten her combination, and she'd used the same locker for all four years of high school. Somehow, Paisley remembered hers.

"My hands know," Paisley glanced at Shiloh. "Even if my head does not." She turned back to face the locker, frowning when she realized it was empty.

"There was a mirror here," she nodded softly, tapping the inside of the locker door. "I remember, because I used to look at—," she paused, cupping her hands over her mouth as her eyes widened in realization.

"What?" Shiloh grew worried, moving forwards to grab Paisley's hand. She was relieved when the small girl giggled, shaking her head and taking a step away. Paisley looked down shyly, covering her face.

"I used to look at you," she mumbled.

Paisley took a deep breath, dialing the same combination that was practically carved into her memory. 12-29-39. She flinched when someone slammed the locker beside hers, looking around nervously.

Pulling her locker open, Paisley let her door slam against the wall. When the metal stopped shaking, the small girl caught a glimpse of shiny black hair in the reflection. She bit her lip, subtly watching as the girl bent down to retrieve something from the bottom of her locker.

Nope, no, not today. Paisley shook her head, prying her eyes away and shoving her history textbooks into her backpack. When she looked back up, she couldn't help but glance in the mirror once more.

Shiloh had shut her locker now, and was leaning against it. From the way her eyes were lit up, Paisley knew she was talking about something important to her. She watched as one of Shiloh's friends – Vanessa, she believed – handed the girl her sketchbook and hugged her goodbye.

Paisley fumbled with her bag, spilling her pencils on the ground. Cursing under her breath, the small girl bent down to collect them. When she stood back up, the image of the green eyed girl was gone from the mirror.

Disappointed, Paisley turned her head and glanced down the hallway. She caught sight of Shiloh's white blouse. Ugh, she had to stop wearing that color. She looked like an angel. But hell, every color looked good on her. Paisley brought her hand up to her face and groaned. She was in way too deep.

Too late now. Paisley raised an eyebrow as Shiloh scanned the hallway to see if anyone was watching. The small girl ducked behind her locker, making sure she wasn't seen.

Paisley watched as Shiloh quickly slipped into the art room, which had been previously unoccupied. She quickly shoved the rest of her things into her bag and closed her locker.

She walked down the hallway slowly, holding her breath when the door to the art room burst open and Shiloh hurried out. She was in such a hurry to get to class that she didn't even notice Paisley.

In a burst of courage, Paisley jumped forwards and grabbed a hold of the door before it could close and lock. She quickly slipped inside the room, wondering why she had even done that in the first place.

Paisley, on the other hand, was in no rush to get to history class. She felt around on the wall until she found the light switch, blinking a few times when the light invaded her pupils.

The first thing Paisley's eyes landed on was Shiloh's sketchbook, which had been placed in one of the corner tables. She glanced at the door once more before quietly walking over to the back of the room.

Paisley knew she shouldn't be doing this. But she was just so curious. She tossed her backpack over her shoulder and traced her fingers over the cover of the sketchbook. Taking a deep breath, she flipped to the first page and studied the drawings.

Okay, she knew Shiloh was an artist. But she had no idea that Shiloh was actually amazing. Like, insanely amazing. Paisley's jaw was practically on the floor as she paged through the sketches.

Everything was in black and white, Paisley realized. It was all sketched with pencil. Where was the color? Paisley furrowed her eyebrows, closing the sketchbook and taking a step backwards.

She nearly screamed when she ran into something behind her. Paisley quickly turned around and held her hands out, catching her breath when she realized it was just a shelf. Upon further investigation, she realized each shelf had a nametag on it.

Curiosity overtook her and she began scanning the shelves for Shiloh's last name. It was one of the top rows, so the small girl grabbed a chair and scooted it over to the shelves, climbing on top of it and peering inside.

There were two canvases on Shiloh's shelf. At first, Paisley thought they were both black and white. The smaller canvas was an exquisite, detailed landscape. But what caught her attention was the larger, thicker canvas.

She carefully pulled it out further, which is when she realized it wasn't actually black and white. It looked like a city crosswalk, Paisley noted. There were people walking every which way, painted in jagged, black brushstrokes.

In the middle of the crosswalk, looking lost, was a dark red person. Somehow, just by the way the person was standing, Paisley could tell that they didn't fit in. She bit her lip, scanning over the painting once more and wondering if the red person was meant to be Shiloh.

Paisley nearly fell off of the chair when the bell rang, striking fear into her chest. Shit. She was going to be late to class. The small girl quickly slid the painting back onto the shelf and grabbed her backpack, hurrying out of the room.

As she jogged to her class, she was hit with the sudden realization that she would never, ever have a chance to know Shiloh. She would never know the meanings behind her paintings. She would never know what made the girl smile.

That realization was responsible for Paisley's quiet mood for the rest of the day.

"Pais," Shiloh reached up, cupping her girlfriend's face and expecting the small girl to burst into tears. Instead, Paisley blinked a few times before focusing on Shiloh's face. Paisley's shoulders dropped slightly and she sighed in relief.

"You are here," Paisley affirmed, nodding softly and pulling Shiloh into a hug. She didn't like the feeling of longing. She liked the feeling of knowing that Shiloh was hers.

"I'm here," Shiloh laughed softly, rubbing small circles in Paisley's back. "I'll always be here." Paisley nodded and took a deep breath, breathing in the sweet vanilla scent that she associated with the girl she loved.

"So you really used to look at me?" Shiloh smiled, raising an eyebrow. Paisley's face grew red and she quickly took a step back, an embarrassed smile on her face.

"I liked you *a lot*," Paisley nodded softly, holding out her arms to show Shiloh just how much she liked her. "It is embarrassing."

This time it was Shiloh's turn to blush. She took a step forward and moved Paisley's hair out of her face. Brushing the brown curls aside, she cupped the small girl's cheek before planting a soft kiss on her lips.

"I think it's cute," Shiloh whispered a few inches in front of Paisley's face before she pulled away. The small girl giggled shyly, hiding her face behind her hands.

"Stop," Shiloh teased, pulling Paisley into her side and ruffling her hair. "Goofball."

"Meanie," Paisley teased, tilting her head up and crinkling her nose. Shiloh led her down the hallway, her smile slowly fading when she realized what was just around the corner.

"You good?" she asked nervously, glancing over at Paisley. The brown eyed girl raised an eyebrow.

"Is there something bad?" she asked softly, pointing up ahead. Shiloh bit her lip, hesitating for a moment. Paisley sensed this and tightened her grip on her girlfriend's hand.

"It's..." Shiloh shook her head, picking up the pace as she walked. She had to stop second guessing herself. She just had to get it over with. "It's the cafeteria."

"And?" Paisley tilted her head to the side, somewhat confused. Shiloh just sighed and shook her head.

"You'll see," she said softly, giving Paisley's hand a supportive squeeze before leading her through the large double doors. She glanced at the small girl, seeing no signs of discomfort on her face.

Paisley let go of her hand, wandering into the room and studying the tables. Shiloh jogged to catch up with her and grabbed her hand once more, just in case.

"I do not understand," Paisley whispered, turning to her girlfriend. Shiloh scanned the room for a moment, thinking quietly to herself. Paisley watched her intently.

"Oh hey, look," Shiloh laughed softly, letting go of Paisley's hand and walking over to one of the tables in the corner. "They still haven't fixed the broken wheel," she laughed, pushing down on the table and making it wobble slightly. "This was my old lunch table," she added, turning back around to face her girlfriend.

It was then that Paisley froze, looking down at her feet and suddenly remembering standing in this exact same spot.

CHAPTER 29

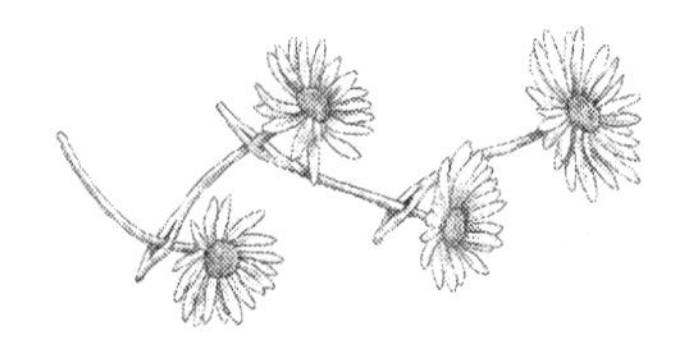

"Today, Paisley," the man snarled, his fingers curled into a fist around the front of her shirt. "It happens today, or else. Do you hear me?"

Paisley nodded frantically, subtly trying to wiggle out of her uncle's grip. When he let her go, she stumbled a few steps backwards and reached up to smooth out her shirt.

"I will," she nodded quickly, clearing her throat and looking shyly at the man in front of her.

"I know you will," he said, his voice low in the back of his throat. "Get out."

"Yes sir," Paisley whispered. The small girl fixed her backpack on her shoulders before practically sprinting out of her house. Today. Today was the day.

Okay, so practically any interaction with Shiloh already made her nervous. But now... this was different.

She remembered it clearly. Her uncle had come home the night before, slurring his words and waving his empty bottle around at her. "I am not working with that son of a bitch Everest," he had yelled, sending Paisley into a panic. What had he meant?

And then she had seen something change in him. As if he has appeared calmer. That's when he turned to Paisley, presenting her his perfect plan.

"You're going to make them hate us," he had laughed bitterly. "You're going to get that daughter of his to despise us."

Paisley had been confused at first, and somewhat panicked. Her fear only grew as he demanded that she do something... ANYTHING, to make Shiloh hate her. Enough that she would go home and tell her father.

And then he would brag about his perfect little Paisley. Enough that Matthew Everest just couldn't take it anymore. And then, her uncle would have the job all to himself.

Paisley thought it was ridiculous of him to use his own niece as a weapon. But of course, she'd learned not to underestimate him.

So now, a few hours after leaving for school, Paisley stood nervously in the front of the cafeteria. She'd planned this out as best as she could. All she would do is take Shiloh's phone and mess around for a few moments. That wouldn't do much harm, right?

But she had to make this believable. She couldn't mess up. If she didn't do this right, Paisley knew things wouldn't end well for her.

But hell, look at her. She was Shiloh Everest. And she was beautiful. And Paisley wouldn't deny herself of that fact, even if she was supposed to be in love with Scott. Which she wasn't.

After debating what to do for way to long, Paisley took in a deep breath and swiftly made her way across the cafeteria. Suck it up, Lowe. She'd been in theatre classes. She could play a character.

"I'm not into guys like that."

Paisley paused when she heard those words escape Shiloh's mouth. None of the girls at the table had caught onto her presence yet.

"Or maybe you're not into guys at all," Paisley blurted out.

She'd heard the rumors. Hell, everyone had. She wasn't sure if they were true, but she was playing a character. She had to make Shiloh hate her. She couldn't risk it.

Paisley's eyes landed on Shiloh's phone and she quickly grabbed it, just as the girl looked up. Their eyes met briefly, and Paisley felt her stomach drop into her chest. She couldn't look at Shiloh, so she quickly diverted her eyes down to the girl's unlocked phone.

It was open to Shiloh's messages, and Paisley immediately raised an eyebrow when she saw someone had been sending Shiloh pictures of female models. Clothed, of course. But still. She had to be in character.

"That's interesting," Paisley laughed, trying to rid herself of all empathy for the girl. She forced herself to focus on what would happen to her if she didn't do this. "I knew you were gay, but I didn't know you were this gay."

Okay. So that was low. But she was in character. And the adrenaline coursing through her had basically taken over at this point.

"Don't you dare, Lowe."

Paisley flinched when one of the other girls at the table, Ryland, jumped out of her seat and glared at her. When she looked away, she caught a glimpse of Shiloh once more. Her eyes were on her, pleading for her to stop. Paisley felt sick to her stomach.

"You know, too?" Paisley raised an eyebrow, holding up the phone and addressing Ryland. She might as well make them all believe that she was about to reveal Shiloh's deepest darkest secret. The whole point of this was just the scare.

It became clear to Paisley that everyone's attention was on her. She could see the other students turned around in her seats, watching the events unfold. With a deep breath, she scrolled up a bit more in the messages.

Now the easy part. Just read a few, harmless messages. Give her a scare. That's all it was. Paisley took a deep breath and brought her phone up to her face.

"I don't know, Tori," she read, picking a handful of random messages further up in the conversation. "I told him I was gay, and he seemed like he was okay with it. I don't know how I'm going to tell my mother, though."

It was only when Paisley looked up from the phone that she realized the messages hadn't exactly been harmless. She saw the look of sheer terror on Shiloh's face, and the look of shock spreading across her friend's faces.

She quickly looked down at the phone and re-read the messages, realizing what she said. Her heart dropped in her chest and the phone nearly fell out of her hands.

She had to finish this. She had to. Stay in character, Paisley.

"I knew it," was all she could manage to stutter out before she practically dropped Shiloh's phone and swiftly walked back towards her lunch table, feeling tears forming in her eyes.

All her friends were cheering her on, but the moment Paisley passed her table, she broke into a sprint, hearing Ryland yelling from behind her. She flew through the gym doors and into the bathroom, practically tripping into one of the stalls just in time to lose her breakfast.

She'd just ruined someone's life.

And not just someone. That someone was Shiloh. Shiloh Everest. The girl she really, really liked.

Paisley wiped the back of her mouth on her hand a few minutes later and slumped backwards against the side of the stall, burying her head inbetween her knees. Shiloh was going to hate her. Any possibility of forming any sort of friendship with the girl was completely destroyed.

Paisley didn't even feel bad for herself, though. She just hoped with everything in her that Shiloh was okay. This was her fault.

But hey, her uncle would be proud of her.

The moment the thought crossed Paisley's mind, she kicked the other side of the stall, jumping when the entire wall rattled.

A few minutes later, Paisley nearly screamed when the door to the bathroom burst open.

"Paisley?"

The small girl tensed, peeking under the stalls and relaxing slightly when she realized it was only the cheer team. She had been terrified that one of Shiloh's friends would come after her and make sure she never lived to see another day.

"Y-yeah?" she half-whispered, pulling herself up to her feet and quickly smoothing out her shirt.

"Are you okay?" Sydney's voice appeared from in front of her stall. Paisley slowly stepped out, wiping her eyes and nodding. Her friend immediately knew something was wrong, though, and raised a questioning eyebrow at her.

"I don't feel too good," Paisley mumbled. It technically wasn't a lie. "I think I'm gonna go to the nurse."

Luckily, her friend was understanding. Paisley denied her offer to walk with her. She needed to alone. No, she deserved to be alone.

Hell, she was alone.

It wasn't just about playing a character anymore. Paisley had been playing different characters her entire life. She didn't even know who she really was. The real Paisley was hidden behind layers and layers of fear and insecurity. The real Paisley never would have done something like that to Shiloh.

But maybe the real Paisley was gone.

Paisley inhaled sharply the moment she met Shiloh's green eyes once more.

"No," Paisley whispered, bringing her hands up to her face and pulling out of Shiloh's grip. She took a few rushed steps backwards and continued shaking her head.

"Pais," Shiloh bit her lip and moved forwards, attempting to place her hands back on Paisley's shoulders. The small girl flinched away, looking Shiloh up and down.

"No," Paisley repeated herself, feeling tears stinging her eyes as they began to spill over her cheeks. Shiloh reached out for her but the small girl panicked and swatted her hands away.

"Paisley, Paisley, it's me," Shiloh said quietly, trying to get the small girl to focus on her.

"I know," Paisley mumbled, holding out her hands to prevent Shiloh from getting any closer to. "You…" she shook her head. "You are supposed to hate me."

"What?" Shiloh whispered, running a hand through her hair and trying not to panic.

"You do not deserve me," Paisley shook her head, her hair falling in front of her face. "I hurt you. I… I hurt you," she continued, her voice cracking and becoming merely a whisper.

Shiloh felt her heart drop into her chest and she shook her head quickly. She reached out to grab Paisley's hand but the small girl flinched and stumbled backwards, as if she was scared of the girl. In reality, Paisley was only scared of herself.

"Pais…" Shiloh whispered, unsure of what to do. She let her hands fall to her side and she looked around the cafeteria. This place held such bitter memories for her, and yet the fact that she had Paisley there with her made all the difference.

"Stupid," Paisley mumbled, shaking her head and bringing her hands up to her face. She weaved her fingers into her hair and bunched it into handfuls, continuing to walk backwards until she was met with the brick wall of the cafeteria. The small girl slid down to the floor, burying her head in her knees.

Paisley struggled to breathe between sobs. When she heard footsteps leaving, she bit down on her bottom lip to keep herself quiet. This is what she deserved.

"I'm gay."

Paisley lifted her head slowly when Shiloh's voice filled the empty air. She watched as the dark haired girl jogged over to one of the tables, glancing back at her before hopping on top of it.

"I'm gay," she said louder, shrugging her shoulders and meeting Paisley's eyes. She threw her hands in the air, yelling this time. "I'm gay!"

"See? It doesn't matter, Paisley," Shiloh shook her head and hopped off of the table, sending her girlfriend a pleading look. "I don't blame you for doing what you did."

"Hell, Paisley, I would've fucking… fucking screamed it from the top of the Empire State Building if it meant keeping your asshole of an uncle from putting his hands on you!" She threw her hands down at her sides, taking a careful step towards her girlfriend.

"For the longest time I thought that all I wanted an apology from you," Shiloh sighed, walking over to the wall and sitting down a few yards away from Paisley. She wanted to give the small girl her space.

"But then I realized it wasn't *you* I wanted an apology from," Shiloh bit her lip. "I mean, in the grand scheme of things, you basically just confirmed something that was already true. Yeah, I was gay. Still am."

Paisley wiped her eyes, blinking a few times and letting Shiloh's face slowly fade into her vision. She held her breath when she saw that Shiloh had tears in her eyes, as well.

"I think what I really wanted was an apology from myself… because of who I was," Shiloh continued. "I thought an apology would somehow change who I was and make things easier for me."

"But I've realized that's not how it works," the green eyed girl shook her head and glanced down at her hands in her lap. "I don't need to apologize for who I am. I don't need to apologize for taking up space… for existing."

"And hell, why does everyone seem to want things to be easy?" Shiloh let her hands fall to her side. "I want challenge. I want a struggle. I want all of that because I want the relief that comes when you realize that you've made it. I just… I like knowing I've *done* something. Or conquered something."

"And I'm sorry, Paisley," Shiloh wiped her eyes. "I'm sorry for telling everyone I hated you and taking out all my anger on you and I'm sorry for not being there for you when I could have. I'm sorry I didn't notice you were struggling. And I know… I was a bitch to you for the rest of high school, and I said things about you that I shouldn't have. I should have been there. I'm sorry. I'm so s—,"

Shiloh was cut off by a pair of arms being thrown around her neck, nearly knocking her over. Paisley crawled into her lap, burying her head into Shiloh's neck and holding tightly to her, making sure she was real. Making sure that she couldn't be taken away.

Shiloh's breath caught in her throat. Paisley looked up at her, tears streaming down her face. "I forgive you," Paisley managed to whisper. She cupped her girlfriend's face, pressing kisses all over her tear-stained face and pulling away to wipe her eyes.

Paisley knew that trying to stop Shiloh from apologizing was worthless. Paisley didn't need an apology, nor did she want one, but she had realized that it was Shiloh's way of apologizing to herself.

"I am sorry t-too," Paisley whispered, letting her hands rest on Shiloh's shoulders and combing her fingers through the older girl's hair. Somehow, in her own apology, Paisley felt a weight lifted off her own shoulders.

Shiloh just nodded softly, knowing that was enough. She brought her hand up to cup the back of Paisley's head, gently guiding her to rest her head back on her shoulder. Shiloh laid her head against Paisley's, feeling some sort of silent agreement pass between them. They had apologized. Both to themselves and each other. And for them, that was enough.

CHAPTER 30

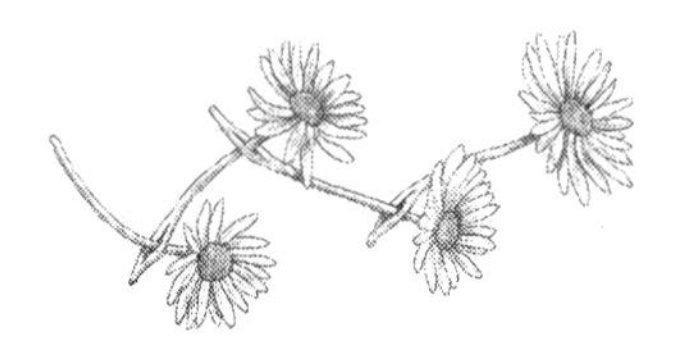

Both girls sat there in silence for a while, feeling so many different emotions at once. Paisley eventually lifted her head and squeezed Shiloh's hand. They met eyes for a few moments and Paisley gave her a soft nod, letting her know she was ready to leave.

Shiloh stood up before helping Paisley to her feet. There was a comfortable silence between them. They were both in a state of knowing. The girls were close enough that words weren't necessary. They just *knew*. Neither of them had ever experienced that with someone.

Paisley leaned her head against Shiloh's shoulder as they made their way back through the gym and around the front of the school. The drive home was silent. It was at this point that Shiloh began to wonder when Paisley would say something. She wanted to know what she was thinking.

The house was busy when they made it back home. Shiloh tugged on Paisley's hand, trying to lead her upstairs before anyone figured out they were back. Unfortunately, they were interrupted by small footsteps coming down the stairs.

Maggie tilted her head to the side when she saw the two girls. She could immediately tell something was wrong.

"Why are you sad?" the small blonde hopped down the last two steps and tugged gently on Paisley's sleeve to get her to look down. "What's wrong, *Paisleeee*?"

Shiloh opened her mouth to stop Maggie, but Paisley beat her to it.

"I hurt Lo," Paisley whispered, shaking her head. Shiloh raised an eyebrow, but before anyone could respond, Shiloh heard her father's voice echo through the house.

"Shy? Are you home? I need your help with something!"

The green eyed girl glanced at Paisley, but her girlfriend surprisingly nodded for her to go.

"Are you sure?" Shiloh whispered. Paisley just nodded. Shiloh bit her lip hesitantly, but jogged to the other side of the house to see what her father had needed.

Maggie tugged on Paisley's sleeve once more to get her attention. "I always talk to mommy when I'm sad and she helps me. Come on," Maggie pulled Paisley in the direction of the stairs.

Paisley bit her lip, allowing the smaller girl to lead her upstairs and into the master bedroom.

"Mommy, *Paisleeee* is sad," Maggie pouted, letting go of Paisley's hand and crawling onto the bed where Shiloh's mother sat with a book in her hands. The woman looked up when Maggie grabbed her hand.

"What?" Colette glanced up at Paisley, who was standing shyly in the doorway with her head hung down to the floor.

"She said she hurt Shiloh," Maggie whispered. The woman raised an eyebrow and turned to her daughter.

"Can you help Tara get dinner started? This is a big kid conversation," Colette gave Maggie a soft smile. The small girl nodded, hopping off of the bed and slipping past Paisley out of the room.

"Come sit," Colette addressed the younger brown eyed girl, patting the edge of the bed. Paisley looked up slowly. She wasn't sure if Colette was being serious or not. Hesitantly, the smaller girl padded over to the bed and sat down slowly.

"I'm not mad at you, Paisley," the woman laughed softly, urging Paisley to scoot closer.

"I hurt her," Paisley whispered. She shook her head and looked down. She didn't like knowing that she had once had a negative affect on Shiloh. She only wanted to do good things for the girl.

"You did," Colette nodded. "At one point, you did hurt her. You can't change that." Paisley swallowed hard and looked away.

"And you know… for a long time I was mad. I'm always protective over my children. Any good mother is, right?" the woman continued. Paisley nodded slowly.

"You saw. You were there during Christmas," she said, remembering how she had resented her daughter's girlfriend when they were introduced. "But you know what changed my mind?"

Paisley looked up slowly and shook her head.

"You," the woman laughed and reached out to squeeze Paisley's shoulder. "I had this whole predetermined vision of what you would be like. And then I saw the way you put a smile on my daughter's face, and I realized I was completely wrong."

"Even before what you did to her in high school, Shiloh was never anything close to as happy as she is when she's with you. I see it. Matthew sees it. Everyone sees it," Colette smiled softly. "You've brought enough joy into her life to make up for what you may have done. And it brings joy into my life seeing how happy you two are together."

"And maybe going through that in high school was some sort of blessing in disguise. Because I see how strong of a person she's become because of it," the woman gave Paisley a sympathetic smile. "You need to allow yourself the forgiveness that everyone else has already given you."

Unsure of what to say, Paisley simply nodded. There was a lump in her throat and she felt like she had done enough crying to last her a lifetime.

"You're part of this family now," Shiloh's mother pulled Paisley into a hug, squeezing her shoulder. "Don't argue with me on that one," she chuckled when they pulled away.

"Thank you," Paisley whispered softly, her voice still slightly hoarse from earlier that day. "I like this family."

"Mom, have you seen Pa—?" Shiloh froze when she entered the room and saw her girlfriend with her mother.

"I am here," Paisley nodded, quickly slipping off of the bed and walking over to Shiloh. "I am here and I love you," she added softly before wrapping her arms around Shiloh's waist and resting her head on her shoulder.

Shiloh sent her mother a questioning look from over Paisley's shoulder, but the woman only gave her daughter a smug smile before turning her attention back to her book.

"Are you okay?" Shiloh asked, glancing at her mother one last time before gently leading Paisley back out into the hallway. Paisley's caramel eyes met Shiloh's and she shook her head, answering honestly. Shiloh's shoulders dropped slightly.

"I am still sad," Paisley confessed, finding Shiloh's fingers and lacing theirs together. "But I have you. And I have a family. I am going to be okay," she nodded. "I may not be okay right now, but I am on my way there. I know." She nodded, searching Shiloh's eyes for approval.

"How did I get so lucky?" Shiloh laughed softly, feeling tears forming in her own eyes. She pulled Paisley into her side, pressing a kiss into the crown of her head. "I don't deserve you."

"You deserve the world," Paisley whispered, resting her head against Shiloh's shoulder.

"You are my world," the green eyed girl turned so she was facing Paisley. Cupping the smaller girl's cheeks in her hands, Shiloh slowly leaned in, capturing Paisley's lips in her own. Paisley's small hands made their way to rest to Shiloh's shoulders, wrapping around her neck once they pulled away.

Before either girl could say anything, they quickly had to separate when they heard tiny footsteps coming back up the stairs.

"Dinner is ready!" Maggie smiled, throwing her hands in the air. "Me and Tara made pizza all by ourselves," she giggled, running over to Shiloh and holding up her arms to be held.

Shiloh glanced over at Paisley, who was blushing softly and trying to contain her smile. With a soft laugh, Shiloh scooped Maggie up into her arms and motioned for Paisley to follow them down the stairs.

Everyone gathered around the dinner table, and Shiloh found Paisley's hand under the tablecloth, rubbing circles in the back of her palm to comfort her. Paisley gave her a shy smile and used her free hand to take a sip of her drink.

The conversation at the dinner table flowed naturally from person to person, Paisley remained quiet most of the time, happy with just listening to what everyone had to say. It was only at the end of dinner that Maggie addressed her.

"Paisley?" Maggie set her fork down and tilted her head to the side. "Can you stay here forever?"

"Forever?" Paisley raised an eyebrow, glancing at Shiloh. "Why?"

"Because I like happy Shiloh," Maggie explained, hopping off of her chair and nodding softly. "And happy Shiloh is always here when you are. So I wanted you to stay forever," she shrugged, grabbing her plate and heading into the kitchen.

Both Paisley and Shiloh turned to look at one another at the same time. Shiloh's face was bright red, but Paisley only giggled softly and leaned over to kiss her girlfriend's cheek.

"Forever sounds good to me!" she called after Maggie, making Shiloh laugh and hide her face behind her hands.

Both girls stole away into Shiloh's bedroom after helping clear the table. Shiloh plopped back on the bed, letting out a tired sigh. The day had already exhausted her, and they still had two more trips to make. Paisley giggled, crawling on top of her so her knees were on either side of her torso and planting a kiss on her girlfriend's nose.

"Goofball," Shiloh laughed. Paisley simply crinkled her nose, rolling off of the bed and wandering over to the suitcase. Shiloh sat up, wiping her eyes and watching as Paisley dug around until she found her blue hoodie.

The small girl changed, leaving her in only the hoodie and her undergarments. The hoodie was so big on her that it came down to the middle of her thighs, almost as if it were a dress. Paisley giggled and wiggled her arms to find the opening of the sleeves.

Shiloh followed suit, changing into a pair of pajama shorts and a sweatshirt. Paisley had already disappeared into the bathroom, and once Shiloh was dressed, she snuck up behind Paisley and wrapped her arms around her waist.

"Y'look beautiful," Shiloh whispered, resting her chin on Paisley's shoulder and looking at their reflection in the mirror. "Especially your eyes. They tell so many stories. That's what I love about them."

"They do?" Paisley tilted her head to the side, setting her toothbrush down and wiping her mouth. Shiloh nodded.

"They tell me things your words could never say," Shiloh pressed a kiss in the crook of Paisley's neck and met her eyes in the mirror. "I've always loved your eyes."

"You know I love your eyes," Paisley smiled shyly, turning around and meeting Shiloh's green orbs, studying them adoringly. "They hold the ocean. I like that," she nodded softly. "I always liked the sound of the ocean. It calms me down. That is what your eyes do, too."

Before Shiloh could respond, Paisley continued talking. "You know what I think, Lo?" Paisley asked, tilting her head to the side.

"What?" Shiloh smiled softly, following Paisley back into the bedroom and sitting down on the edge of the bed. Paisley crawled beside her, sitting cross legged and thinking for a moment.

"I think my eyes were meant to look into yours," Paisley said softly, planning out each word carefully. "When I look at you, it just feels right. It does, Lo," she nodded, scooting forward and taking Shiloh's hands in hers.

No matter how many times Shiloh heard Paisley's thoughts, she was always in awe. Paisley had a way of taking the most complex things and breaking them down into something so simple. It just made sense.

"God I love you," Shiloh laughed softly, nudging Paisley's shoulder.

"I *loooooove* you too," Paisley giggled, yawning mid-sentence and wiping her eyes. Shiloh couldn't help but laugh.

"Tired?" the green eyed girl raised an eyebrow, scooting back on the bed and patting the space beside her. Paisley eagerly curled up in her girlfriend's side. As always, she snaked her arms up the sleeves of Shiloh's hoodie and sighed contently.

"Sing?" Paisley whispered once Shiloh reached over and turned off the light. It was still fairly early, but both girls were more than exhausted.

"Of course," Shiloh laughed, moving slightly so she could plant a quick kiss on her girlfriend's lips. "Only for you, goofball." Paisley giggled and crinkled her nose.

"I will stay," Paisley whispered abruptly, interrupting Shiloh’s singing and meeting her eyes with a shy smile. "I always will."

CHAPTER 31

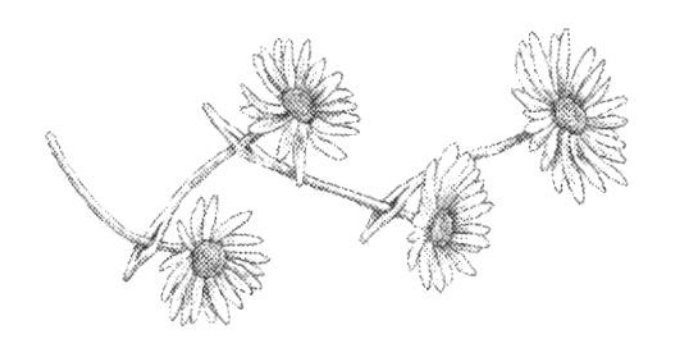

Shiloh was jolted awake the next morning when she felt something press into her side, nearly rolling her off of the bed. The green eyed girl quickly sat up to prevent herself from falling to the ground.

She immediately realized what was going on when she saw the small girl next to her mumble something inaudible and curl up into a ball.

"Pais?" Shiloh whispered, nudging Paisley's shoulder. The small girl almost immediately shot awake, sitting up and looking around the room in a panic.

"Pais, Pais, it's me," Shiloh said quickly, finding Paisley's hand and squeezing it. "I'm right here."

Paisley studied Shiloh's face for a few moments, slowly coming down from the panic. She found familiarity in the girl's eyes and quickly crawled into Shiloh's open arms.

The older girl pulled Paisley into her lap, wrapping her arms around her girlfriend and rocking back and forth slowly to comfort her. "You're okay, I've got you," she whispered, combing her fingers through Paisley's hair.

"I-It keeps h-happening," Paisley sniffed, shaking her head and wrapping her arms around Shiloh's neck. All the small girl wanted was to be able to get a good night's sleep, but the nightmares always seemed to prevent that from happening.

"I know, baby," Shiloh sighed, holding Paisley tighter. "I'm sorry I can't just take them in your place," she separated them slightly so she could wipe Paisley's tears with the pads of her thumbs. "We're gonna get rid of them, I promise."

"Promise?" Paisley whispered, holding up her pinky. Shiloh nodded, interlocking their fingers and hoping this was a promise she could keep.

They sat there for a while, simply holding each other. They were interrupted when Shiloh caught sight of two blonde pigtails watching them from a crack in the door. The green eyed girl raised an eyebrow at her younger sister. Paisley lifted her head from Shiloh's shoulder, suddenly growing embarrassed when she saw Maggie watching them from the door.

The small girl quietly slipped into the room, walking over to the bed and studying the two girls before crawling up beside them. Shiloh was surprised when Maggie leaned forward and wrapped her arms around Paisley's neck, hugging her gently.

"When I see monsters, I have to be brave and tell them to go away," Maggie nodded confidently. "You've gotta tell them that you're not scared of them."

Paisley nodded softly, wiping her eyes and giving Maggie a soft smile. The small girl simply gave Paisley another hug before hopping off of the bed and disappearing out into the hallway.

"You okay?" Shiloh asked softly, moving Paisley's hair out of her face.

"I will be," Paisley nodded, taking a deep breath and giving Shiloh a genuine smile. "I like it when you sing," she added shyly. Shiloh couldn't help but laugh.

"I can tell," the green eyed girl teased, lying back on the bed and bringing Paisley down next to her. "I'll keep on singing for you until the end of time."

"That's a long time," Paisley giggled, hiding her face in the crook of Shiloh's neck. The older girl just laughed, running her fingers up and down Paisley's arm.

They laid in silence for a while, just enjoying one another's company. Eventually, Maggie convinced them both to come downstairs where the rest of the family was having breakfast.

Shiloh was now clearing the table while Paisley fiddled aimlessly with a Rubix cube she had found in one of the drawers. Everyone else had already gone into different rooms of the house, leaving just the two girls in the kitchen. Shiloh was taken by surprise when Paisley's small voice filled the air.

"What are we doing today?" the brown eyed girl set the Rubix cube down, wandering over to Shiloh and looking at her curiously.

"I, uh," Shiloh cleared her throat, thinking for a few moments. "You'll have to see when we get there, if you remember it." She bit her lip and watch a look of confusion spread across her girlfriend's face.

"It might be a little scary," Shiloh answered honestly. "But I'm gonna be there the whole time, okay? You say the word and we can leave if it's too much for you."

"Okay," Paisley whispered, still thinking over this in her head. "I can do it, Lo," she added, giving her girlfriend a soft smile.

"I know you can," Shiloh nodded softly, hoping what she said was true. She wasn't sure how this was going to turn out, but she felt ready to get it over with.

After cleaning up the table, Shiloh led Paisley out to the car, watching her girlfriend as they drove the familiar route. Paisley didn't seen to remember anything, but Shiloh reached over and grabbed her hand just to keep her calm.

Paisley grew confused when Shiloh abruptly pulled off onto the side of the road. She didn't see any buildings around, only trees.

"It's through here," Shiloh nodded, getting out of the car and helping a hesitant Paisley out of the passenger side. Even though she was somewhat confused, Paisley allowed Shiloh to lead her through the trees and into the woods.

"Here," Shiloh whispered, pushing them through the brush and into the clearing. Paisley instantly knew where they were when her eyes fell on the back of the small brick house that she had come to know so well.

"Do you remember?" Shiloh asked, leading her over to the storm cellar. Paisley raised an eyebrow, wondering what Shiloh was doing when she began to crawl in.

"I lived here," Paisley said before shaking her head. "That is now how you get inside."

Shiloh paused, standing back up and raising an eyebrow as Paisley lifted one of the potted plants on the back porch, revealing a dull colored key. She held it up, dusting it off on her shirt before handing it to Shiloh and pointing at the sliding glass door.

"That would've been useful the first time," Shiloh laughed nervously, turning the key in the lock. Sure enough, it clicked right open, and she slowly slid the door to the side.

Shiloh carefully set foot into the house, glancing behind her as Paisley stood hesitantly on the porch. Just as she was about to ask if she was okay, Paisley hurried to join Shiloh inside, grabbing onto her girlfriend's arm.

"Do you remember any of this?" Shiloh asked, motioning around the living room. Paisley just shrugged. She knew this is where she had lived. That's about where it ended, though.

"I lived here," Paisley nodded slowly, scanning the room. "Before I found friends. Before I found you."

Shiloh nodded. She bit her lip, looking around the room one last time before leading Paisley over to the staircase. The small girl clung onto Shiloh's arm as they made their way upstairs, slowly following her down the hallway.

Paisley froze when they stopped in front of the last door, which Shiloh slowly pushed open. The green eyed girl took a step forwards, but Paisley grabbed her hand and pulled her backwards just as a rush of memories overwhelmed her.

"Help?"

The man looked up from his chair, scanning Paisley, who stood in front of him. She had half of a hairbrush in one hand, the other half was still knotted in her messy hair.

"Broken," Paisley mumbled, looking down guiltily. She limped forward, the large black boot on her foot thumping down in front of her. She grimaced, glaring down at the annoying cast-like material.

"Get out of my face," he muttered, ignoring her and taking another swig from his bottle. The girl tilted her head to the side and held out the handle of the brush.

"Help?" she inquired, wiggling the brush in front of his face hopefully. She flinched back when only moments later, he snatched the handle out of her hand and sent it flying across the room.

"Ouch," Paisley mumbled, shaking her head and limping over to retrieve the handle once more. She stumbled over her boot, running into the wall and mumbling something inaudible under her breath before waddling back over in front of her uncle.

"Dropped it," she held out the handle once more, tapping on the brush still stuck in her hair. "Help."

"Get the fuck out!" he snapped, standing up and taking a step towards her. Paisley instantly stumbled backwards and brought her hands up in front of her face.

"Please!" she whimpered, shaking her head.

"Oh, do you need help?" he laughed bitterly, feigning concern and moving forwards. Confused, Paisley slowly nodded and pointed to the brush in her hair.

"Too bad," he growled, taking a step forwards and grabbing the front of her shirt, which was on inside out. "You can't even fucking dress yourself, how do you expect to do anything with your life? You're fucking useless."

"Ouch," Paisley whimpered, shaking her head and trying to pull out of his grip. He only held on tighter.

"Here, let me help," his voice was laced with venom as he curled his fingers around the brush in her hair. Paisley paused, looking up hopefully.

"Thank yo—," she paused when he practically tore the brush out of her hair, making her wince in pain and nearly fall backwards. Tears stung at her eyes and she flinched when he threw the brush across the room.

"Ouch," she whimpered, bringing her hands up to her face to hide her tears. When she saw him moving back towards her, she panicked and tried to push him away.

His eyes immediately darkened when he stumbled backwards. Paisley whimpered when he grabbed the collar of her shirt once more, practically dragging her towards the stairs. At first she tried to break free from his grip, but she yelped in pain when her boot got caught on the edge of the couch and twisted her leg in a painful direction.

He completely ignored her, though, forcing her up the stairs and shoving her into the bedroom. Paisley whimpered when she heard the door slam shut behind her, immediately bringing her hands up to cover her ears.

She tried to hold back her tears, limping over to her closet and sliding down against the wall to bury her head in her knees. Paisley did her best to keep herself quiet, knowing what would happen if he heard her crying.

She sat there for god knows how long until she eventually fell asleep.

Paisley was only awoken hours later when the rumble of her uncle's old pickup truck stirred her from her slumber. She blinked a few times, glancing at the window and realizing it was nighttime.

Paisley immediately stumbled to her feet, limping over to the window and pressing her palms against the glass. She raised an eyebrow when she saw his truck begin to back out of the driveway. Where was he going?

She hurried over to her bedroom door, but was met with a new problem. The small girl began to panic when she couldn't pull the door open. Something was holding it shut from the other side.

"Tommy!" Paisley cried, pounding her fists against the door as she felt tears forming in her eyes once more. She didn't understand any of this.

When no one answered her cries for help, the small girl slid down to her knees and pressed her forehead against the door, tears streaming down her cheeks. She just wanted things to get better. She didn't like hurting all the time. What was she doing wrong?

"N-no," Paisley's voice trembled, tugging Shiloh away from the bedroom. "Bad… bad things," she clung onto Shiloh's arm and looked up at her slowly.

"Okay, okay, I won't," Shiloh quickly shook her head, pulling Paisley into her side. "What's wrong?"

"Tommy…" Paisley shook her head, slipping past Shiloh and opening one of the closets in the hallway. She dug around in the towels, tossing them every which way until she pulled out a long, metal chain. She held it up to show Shiloh with shaky hands.

"What…?" Shiloh grew confused. Paisley shook her head, moving over to her bedroom door and pulling it shut before frantically looping the chains around her doorknob. Shiloh watched as she moved across the hallway, trying the opposite end of the chain to the other door, so that neither door could be opened from the inside.

Shiloh nearly choked on thin air when she made the realization. Paisley looked at her shamefully, shaking her head and looking down at the floor. The small girl couldn't help but blame herself.

"We don't have to go in there," Shiloh shook her head and moved forwards, pulling Paisley into her side and kissing the crown on her head. "I'm so sorry you had to go through that."

Paisley just nodded softly, allowing Shiloh to lace their fingers together and lead her downstairs. The green eyed girl paused, glancing at Paisley and then taking a breath. Might as well jump in with both feet.

Paisley followed right behind Shiloh into the kitchen, scanning the room. The small girl quickly looked down when she felt something crunch under her feet. Tilting her head to the side, she bent down and carefully picked up the clear material. *Glass*.

Suddenly, everything hit her at once.

C H A P T E R 3 2

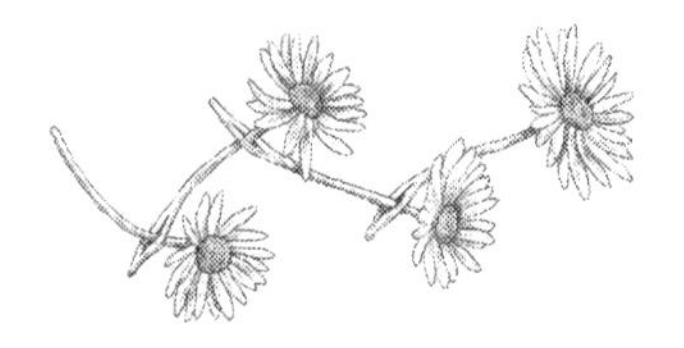

Paisley smiled widely, carefully holding the heavy vase in her hands and padding into the kitchen. She hummed happily when she saw her uncle was home, sitting at one of the stools at the island.

"I made flowers," Paisley smiled, walking over to him and holding up the vase to show him. "They are pink and white," she nodded proudly. Her smile wavered when he raised his head and she caught sight of the bottle in his hand.

"You don't 'make' flowers, dumbass," he muttered, rolling his eyes. Paisley didn't like when he drank, he always got like this. "They're going to die without water. God, do you have ANY common sense?" he laughed bitterly and took another swig of his drink.

Paisley grew concerned, looking down at the vase and shaking it slightly to make the flowers move around. Frowning, she moved forward and held the vase further in front of his face.

"I made flowers," Paisley repeated, shaking the vase slightly just to prove her point. "See? I made them."

Suddenly, the vase was whacked out of her hand, sending it crashing to the ground at her feet. Paisley whimpered, looking down at the collection of glass and flowers that now covered the floor.

"Fuck off," he slurred, before turning his attention back to his drink. Paisley stood frozen for a few seconds before her eyes landed on the remains of her flowers. Tediously, she

navigated her way around the broken glass so she could bend down and retrieve them.

"They need water?" she asked softly, remembering what he had said earlier. She looked down at the colorful flowers in her hand before shoving them in front of his face, looking at him pleadingly.

That's when everything changed.

Paisley inhaled sharply when he stood up, bringing his hand out from behind his back and pressing something cold under her chin. Paisley stumbled backwards when he took a step towards her.

She yelped, feeling the shards of glass under her bare feet. A few steps later and she was pressed up against the wall, her feet growing numb from the constant, painful throbbing.

"Ouch," she whispered, feeling tears form in her eyes as she shook her head furiously."Ouch, ouch," she repeated herself. When he removed the gun from her chin and pressed it to her chest, Paisley panicked. She knew what that was. She knew what it could do.

"N-no," Paisley whimpered, squeezing her eyes shut. "Please, no," she shook her head furiously, trying to back up even further.

"It'd be so easy just to pull the trigger," he slurred, dragging the barrel of the gun across her chest and up her collarbone. "Wouldn't it?"

"Please," Paisley whispered, trying to wiggle out of his grip.

"Please what?" he chuckled, moving the gun back up to jaw. "You want me to end this?"

"Pl-p-please," Paisley stuttered. She couldn't form any other words at the moment.

For a second, he pulled the gun away and turned it around in his hands, inspecting it. "If only someone loved you," he laughed bitterly, rolling his eyes. "Maybe there'd be someone who cared when you're gone."

Paisley's breath practically vanished when, arms outstretched, the barrel of the gun was pressed straight against her chest.

Paisley never fought back. But her adrenaline took over, and she panicked. She reached up, trying to push the gun back towards him.

"Please," Paisley shook her head, squeezing her eyes shut and tightening her grip on the gun, pushing it back towards him with everything she had. "Please put it aw—,"

A loud, piercing noise cut through the air. Paisley instinctively brought her hands up to her ears and squeezed her eyes shut.

She wasn't sure what she felt next. But something was different. When the sound dissipated from the air, Paisley cautiously lowered her hands and opened her eyes.

That's when she saw it. The moment her eyes landed on the man, now lying on the floor, Paisley panicked. His eyes were half lidded, blood pooling around his chest and staining his t-shirt.

"No!" Paisley cried, looking down at the gun on the ground and feeling the tears finally spill down her cheeks. "No!" she repeated. The small girl slid down to her knees next to the man.

"I am sorry," Paisley whimpered, begging for his forgiveness. "I am sorry. Sorry, no," she shook her head and grabbed his shoulders, trying to shake him back into consciousness.

"Wake up!" Paisley cried out, tears blinding her vision. "Do not... do not...." she whimpered, pulling back and studying the crimson substance on her hands. The small girl was suddenly hit with the reality of the situation and she reeled backwards, stumbling back up to her feet and scanning the room.

Something besides glass crinkled under her feet and she quickly stepped aside, gasping when she saw the flowers scattered on the floor. She quickly picked them up and held them tightly against her chest.

That's when she felt the petals crumble under her fists. Paisley whimpered, uncurling her fingers and watching as a few of the delicate petals fell to the floor. She had killed them.

With her shaky hands, Paisley gently bent down and placed the remains of the flowers on top of the body. Once she stood back up, the small girl was suddenly reminded of the throbbing pain in her feet. She had to get out.

Paisley limped over to the door, quickly discovering that it hurt less if she walked on her tiptoes. He shoes lay next to the door, and she remembered the rule. She always had to wear shoes outside. Otherwise, she would get hurt for tracking mud into the house.

Paisley struggled to tug her shoes onto her feet, squeezing her eyes shut as she felt the glass did even deeper into her soles. Her only concern was getting out. She wasn't sure where. But her urge to run was stronger than her urge to stay where she was.

The moment Paisley came to, she immediately looked down at her hands. Tears clouded her eyes and she didn't even realize she wasn't alone.

She needed to run. She felt the exact same urge as she had felt before.

Shiloh immediately reached forwards to grab Paisley when she saw the small girl turn towards the door. Her fingers met empty air, though, and she quickly stumbled forwards before running after Paisley, who had already disappeared out of the front of the house.

The minute Shiloh burst through the door, she felt her heart drop in her chest.

"Paisley!" she screamed, her eyes focused on the car coming down the street - heading straight towards her girlfriend. The next few seconds passed in a blur as Shiloh sprinted towards the road, hearing the screech of tires.

Shiloh grabbed onto Paisley before the smaller girl could run once more, pulling her out of the street and keeping a tight grip on her wrist. Before either of the girls could address each other, the driver's side of the car burst open.

"Paisley?"

Shiloh's eyes widened and she held onto Paisley, her heart beating against her chest. The woman in the car took a step forwards, studying the girls.

"Paisley, honey, is that you?" the older woman asked in shock. Paisley glanced at Shiloh and then nodded softly. When she looked back at the woman, something suddenly clicked.

Paisley looked up from the book she had been aimlessly flipping through when she heard the doorbell. Her face lit up and she quickly rolled off of the bed, groaning when she remembered her boot was still on. She limped down the stairs and into the foyer, excitedly pulling the door open and clapping her hands.

"I just saw your uncle leave," the woman whispered, nodding towards the driveway. "Come on, I have enough dinner to share," she smiled softly.

Mrs. Carmela had lived next to Paisley's uncle for years. When Paisley had come to live with them at first, the small girl would always wander into her yard and watch the older Italian woman work on her garden.

After Paisley's accident, Carmela made sure to occasionally check up on the family. She soon became aware that Paisley's situation wasn't ideal, and took it upon herself to help the younger girl out.

"He was mean," Paisley admitted, tugging on her shoes before following the woman out into the front yard.

"I know, honey," the woman sighed and shook her head. "Remember what I told you?"

Paisley furrowed her eyebrows before shaking her head. "I do not know."

"Just ignore him," she held the door open and guided Paisley into her small kitchen, the smell of homemade pasta sauce wafting through the house. "Nothing he says to you is true."

"It is hard," Paisley stood hesitantly in the doorway, watching as the woman scooped a spoonful of pasta into two bowls. Her own children had grown up and moved out long ago, and she enjoyed Paisley's company, even it was only for an hour or two.

"Don't listen to a word he says, Paisley," the woman motioned for Paisley to join her at the table. The small brunette padded over, sitting down slowly and grimacing at the weight of the boot on her foot.

"I do not listen, I feel," Paisley tilted her head to the side, somewhat confused. "I hurt," she added, biting her lip before pointing to her shoulder, where a new bruise was forming. Paisley grew confused when she saw the woman's eyes widen.

"Paisley... does he hurt you?" Carmela set her fork down and gave Paisley a look that told the smaller girl she didn't want to lie. Paisley nodded hesitantly.

A few seconds of silence passed between them. Paisley stabbed a noodle with her fork, taking a bite and watching as the woman pursed her lips in thought.

"Paisley, do you have any friends from high school?"

The small brunette furrowed her eyebrows in thought. Friends? Friends were good. She nodded.

"Who?" the woman prodded, completely forgetting about the food. Paisley grew confused.

"Who?" Paisley repeated her, tilting her head to the side.

Sighing, Carmela stood up and motioned for Paisley to follow her. "You have a yearbook, right?" she asked, waiting for Paisley, who quickly followed her out of the front door and back across the lawn.

"A what?" Paisley crinkled her nose, following the woman back into her own house.

"Where's your room?" the woman pointed to the staircase questioningly. Paisley raised her eyebrows, happily leading the woman upstairs into the brightly colored bedroom. She grew confused when the woman immediately inspected her bookshelf.

"Thank god," Carmela turned back around, holding out Paisley's senior yearbook. She flipped through it, finding the senior class and scanning over the faces. One page in particular caught her attention.

"Is she your friend?" the woman asked, showing Paisley the page in the yearbook that had hearts doodled all over it. Paisley narrowed her eyes, inspecting the page. There was something about the girl that was familiar. It struck something in her. She nodded eagerly.

The woman didn't say anything else, she only dog eared the page and tucked the yearbook under her arm. "Just in case," she nodded softly. Paisley nodded absentmindedly, not quite understanding what it meant.

Paisley's eyes widened and she took a step forwards. "Hi," she whispered shyly, studying the woman and wondering if she remembered her. She was still slightly shaken up from the day's earlier events.

"Oh my god," the woman breathed out a long sigh of relief and pulled Paisley into a hug. Shiloh watched in confusion. "I was so worried."

Paisley glanced at Shiloh once the pulled away from the hug, shyly scooting back to her girlfriend's side. The green eyed girl raised a questioning eyebrow at Paisley.

"She helped," Paisley whispered to Shiloh, biting her lip. "She helped me."

Knowing better than to push an explanation out of Paisley, who was already struggling to keep her composure, Shiloh instead turned to the other woman. "You helped her?"

"It's you!" the woman realized when Shiloh addressed her. Shiloh raised an eyebrow.

"Oh my god, forgive me," the woman laughed, holding out her hand. "I'm Carmela. I've lived in the house next to Paisley for years," she explained, pointed across the yard.

Shiloh tentatively shook her hand, still somewhat confused. "You helped her?" she asked, hoping not to come off as rude.

"We went on a plane," Paisley whispered, wiping her eyes and clinging onto Shiloh's arm.

"After the… accident," the woman nodded. "She told me you were one of her friends. One of the women in my book club works at the high school and I found out where you moved after college. I held onto that just in case."

"And then one day I got home from work and found…" she sighed, glancing at Paisley. "She was trying to start the car. She had… blood… all over her hands."

"Ouch," Paisley whispered, looking down at the ground. Shiloh glanced over at her girlfriend before wrapping an arm around her waist and pulling her into her side to comfort her.

"After I figured out what happened, I couldn't let her get in trouble and have no family to protect her. My husband was a frequent flyer so I got two tickets and figured I'd pay my son in New York a visit and take this one to safety at the same time," the woman shrugged.

"You did *all* that?" Shiloh asked in shock, finding answers to the questions she'd had in her head for the longest time.

"Listen, honey, he deserved to die," she shook her head. "I just couldn't let this innocent girl get taken away for doing what anyone in her situation would've done even sooner. I wouldn't have been able to live with myself if I did."

"I don't even know what to say," Shiloh admitted, holding securely onto Paisley, who had practically buried her head into Shiloh's shoulder. "Just… thank you. For looking out for her," she nodded down at Paisley. "I'd hug you but…" she laughed softly, looking down at the small girl who was holding onto her.

"No need to thank me," the woman shook her head. "Seeing her alive and okay is worth it," she shrugged and smiled at Shiloh. "Is she… okay?"

Shiloh glanced down at Paisley, slowly separating them and cupping the girl's cheeks. Paisley gave her a sad smile, still shaken up. Shiloh nodded, looking back up at the woman. "She will be," she said quietly, kissing Paisley's forehead.

"Guess what?" Paisley spoke up softly, glancing over at the woman. "I found my home. I am happy now." She stood on her tiptoes and kissed Shiloh's cheek.

Shiloh watched as the woman's eyes widened, looking back and forth between the girls. Before Shiloh could say anything, Paisley gently took Shiloh's hand and smiled. "This is my Lolo," she said softly, nodding towards the woman. "I found her."

"I *was* right," the woman laughed, shaking her head and rolling her eyes. "I always suspected it." Shiloh raised a questioning eyebrow.

"When she was just a little one, she'd come over and watch daytime television with me while her Aunt was at work," Carmela explained, laughing softly. "She was always very talkative when it came to the female characters. Not so much the males… I always had a hunch," she smiled softly.

"I'm happy if you're happy," she addressed Paisley, reaching out and squeezing her shoulder. "I'm so glad to see that you're doing well, Paisley."

A few minutes later, the girls said their goodbyes when Carmela had to head off to work. Paisley clung onto Shiloh's arm, still somewhat nervous.

"Are you okay?" Shiloh whispered, leading her around the back of the house and to the woods. They'd had enough of the house.

"I do not want to talk about it," Paisley mumbled, shaking her head and scooting closer to Shiloh. The green eyed girl bit her lip, knowing better than to push anything out of her.

"Two stops down, one to go," Shiloh laughed nervously, wondering just how things were going to turn out after today.

CHAPTER 33

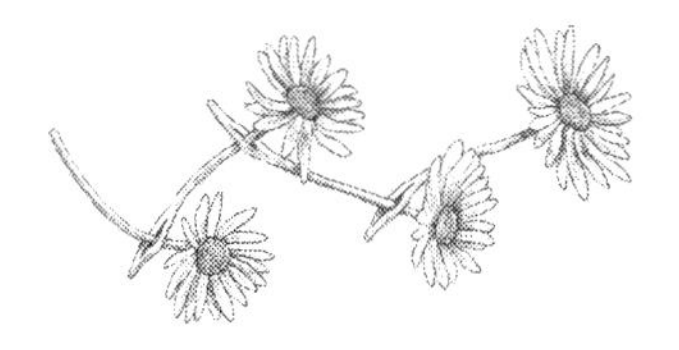

"Stop!"

Paisley's voice pierced through the empty air, nearly causing Shiloh to swerve off the road. Shiloh slowed down, and before she could ask Paisley what was wrong, the smaller girl was scrambling out of the car.

"Paisley!" Shiloh called after her in shock, quickly parking the car and chasing after her. What the hell was she doing?

"Paisley!" Shiloh yelled even louder, circling around the house that Paisley had disappeared behind. She dug her feet into the ground, looking around frantically for the smaller girl. Her eyes immediately darted towards the trees in the back of the property when she heard a rustling noise.

"Pais?" Shiloh jogged over, pushing through the brush and finding the small girl knelt down in a small patch of grass, brushing the leaves aside.

"What… why did you…?" Shiloh coughed, catching her breath. Paisley shook her head, obviously concentrating on something. Shiloh grew even more confused when Paisley gasped and began digging at a patch of dirt at the base of the tree.

"I'm so confused," Shiloh sighed, shaking her head and leaning against a tree to try and catch her breath. Moments later, Paisley was tugging some sort of metal box out of the dirt, setting it down and brushing it off. Shiloh's jaw dropped.

"How'd you… you just… what?" Shiloh stumbled over her words, crouching down next to Paisley, who was gently running her fingers overtop of the old metal lunchbox.

"Why are you bringing a shovel?" Paisley asked, skipping to keep up with her father as they descended down the hill in their backyard and into the very front of the woods.

"We have to bury it to keep it safe," he chuckled, reaching down and squeezing her shoulder.

"So then I can find it when I'm an old lady?" Paisley giggled and looked up at him, hugging the metal lunchbox to her chest, the contents rattling on the inside as she walked.

"Not too old," he laughed and shook his head. "I did the same thing when I was about your age and dug it up on my 17th birthday. I still have it, it's probably stored away somewhere in the basement," he pushed the brush aside and let Paisley slip into the woods beside him. "Someday you'll come out here as a teenager and remember burying all these things as a kid. You'll like seeing what was important to you at this time in your life."

"Pick a spot," he nodded towards the small clearing in the trees. Paisley took a careful step forwards and inspected the land intently, determined to choose the perfect place to bury her time capsule.

"Right here!" Paisley exclaimed, pointing down at the very bottom of a large tree. "That way I'll know exactly where I put it."

"That's a good idea," he laughed, tapping a spot at the base of the tree with his shoe. "Right here?" Paisley nodded happily, taking a step backwards as her father dug the shovel into the ground.

Soon enough, Paisley was able to gently lay the metal tin in the hole her father had dug. She used her hands to help him refill the hole with dirt, watching as her lunchbox was soon completely immersed in the ground.

The small girl stood up, brushing her hands off and helping her dad stomp down on the dirt to back it down. She smiled proudly once they were finished.

"To many more memories, kiddo," her dad laughed, ruffling his daughter's hair and pulling her into his side.

"Yeah, what you said!" Paisley giggled, jumping up and grabbing his hat off of his head. Squealing excitedly, she ran back towards the house, laughing when he caught up to her and tossed her into the air.

"I never wanna grow up," she giggled, tugging the hat onto her head and making a funny face at him.

"It's a time capsule," Paisley said softly, brushing off the front of the lunchbox and glancing at Shiloh with a nervous look on her face. Shiloh suddenly realized where they were, glancing at the house behind them. Luckily, she hadn't seen any cars in the driveway.

"You grew up here?" she asked softly. Paisley nodded, following Shiloh's gaze to the house behind them.

"It feels different," Paisley whispered. "It feels empty."

"It is just a house now," the smaller girl sighed. She looked down when she felt Shiloh's fingers slide between hers, giving her hand a gentle squeeze.

"It's not the same as it used to be, isn't it?" Shiloh asked. Paisley nodded softly. "I know the feeling," Shiloh laughed, scooting closer to Paisley and pointing to the lunchbox. "What is this?"

"A time capsule," Paisley gently undid the small clasp, glancing at Shiloh tentatively. "I do not remember what is inside."

"You don't have to if you don't..." Shiloh slowly trailed off when Paisley opened the lunchbox, studying the contents inside. She reached down, holding up a macaroni necklace and giggling softly.

"Oooooh," Paisley whispered, grabbing a small bottle of yellow nail polish and turning it around in her hands. She held it up to show it to Shiloh, who laughed quietly.

"Haven't changed as much as you thought?" she smiled softly. Paisley blushed, shrugging and turning her attention back to the small lunchbox.

"Oh..." the small girl's tone suddenly changed when she pulled what Shiloh believed to be a crumpled up ball of paper from the lunchbox. Upon further inspection, Shiloh realized it was a small origami bird.

"A bird?" Shiloh asked softly. Paisley quickly shook her head.

"Crane," Paisley corrected her, gently turning the figure around in her hands. "My dad used to make these. I remember." She carefully let Shiloh hold the bird, watching as the darker haired girl studied it quietly.

"They must've been important to you if you kept one in there," Shiloh nodded, handing it back to Paisley. The small girl bit her lip and set it down.

"He used to throw away a lot of scrap papers. But I would save them and rip them into squares, I remember," Paisley nodded. "And then I would make him make cranes out of them. I had a lot," she smiled softly at the memory.

Before Shiloh could say anything else, Paisley pulled one last item out of the lunchbox. It was a piece of paper, which she slowly began unfolding. Shiloh watched as the small girl revealed a colorful drawing, holding it with shaky hands as the first tear spilled over her cheek.

"I..." Paisley shook her head, reaching out and running her fingers over the family portrait she had drawn. "This was important to me," she whispered, retracting her hand and looking over the drawing. "I lost it."

"I-I lost it, Lo," Paisley shook her head, looking up at Shiloh and squeezing her eyes shut to try and stop the tears from falling. Shiloh put an arm around her girlfriend, pulling her close and allowing her to lay her head on her shoulder.

"Life can be like that sometimes," Shiloh sighed softly. "You win some, you lose some." She reached up and ran her fingertips up Paisley's arm. "Things change and people leave when you least expect them to. That's why you've got to be your own constant."

"My what?" Paisley asked softly, lifting her head slightly and looking at her girlfriend.

"Your own constant," Shiloh nodded. "You have to make sure you stay true to yourself even though everything around you is changing."

"And leave little parts of yourself wherever you go," Shiloh continued. "Make an impact. That way when your body is gone, your memories will still live on."

"I remember them," Paisley whispered, looking at the drawing in her hands. She held it closer to her face, studying the small crayon signature in the corner.

"That was me," she pointed to her name scrawled in orange crayon. "I do not feel like her anymore," she took a deep breath and failed to fight back her tears.

"You just grew up, Pais," Shiloh whispered, reaching out and running her thumb across her girlfriend's cheek to catch her tears. "I think she's still in there," she reached out and knocked on Paisley's heart, imitating an action the smaller girl used to do. "She's just got a little more wear and tear than she used to. Doesn't make her any less valuable," the smiled softly, bringing Paisley's hand up and pressing a kiss to the back of her palm.

"Here," Shiloh said quietly, the yellow nail polish catching her eye. "Tell me everything you remember about them. I wanna know all about the people who raised this wonderful girl sitting right in front of me," she smiled softly at her girlfriend.

Paisley looked up shyly, somewhat in shock by Shiloh's patience with her. Not that she had anything against it, it was just that she was still constantly surprised that people like Shiloh actually existed.

"My dad liked to paint," Paisley began shyly. She thought for a moment while Shiloh took her hand, beginning to run the small brush over her nails. Paisley looked up quietly and gave her a soft smile.

"He used to paint everything," Paisley added, laughing at the memory. "If he got bored at his desk, he would paint it. His art desk had colors *all* over it," she used her free hand to gesture.

"He taught me how to paint the sun," the small girl nodded. "Did you know it is not just yellow? There is orange too. And sometimes white."

Paisley looked up at Shiloh to see if she was still listening. The green eyed girl met her eyes and gave her a comforting smile, urging her to go on.

"My mom always read to me," Paisley remembered. "She never said no if I asked her to help me with something. Even if she was busy."

"They're drying," Shiloh whispered, moving Paisley's finished hand over and taking the other. "Keep going," she added, genuinely interested in what Paisley had to say.

"We... we used to have pizza nights," Paisley remembered with a fond smile. "We would eat pizza and watch a movie. And sometimes we would go outside and catch fireflies past my bedtime."

"I-I remember when they left," Paisley whispered, her mind suddenly traveling to a darker place. "It was normal," she nodded softly and stole a glance at Shiloh, who was listening closely while keeping her eyes on the small girl's nails.

"I was excited. For Christmas," Paisley whispered. "But it did not feel like Christmas in a hospital," she sniffed and hung her head down.

"Hey," Shiloh whispered, reaching up and cupping Paisley's cheek. "Happy memories. What kind of music did they like?" she asked, trying to draw Paisley's attention to a lighter subject.

Surprisingly, Paisley let out a small giggle amidst her tears. "Dad liked records. He had a big collection," she remembered, thinking about the large shelves in their living room that had been drowning in old vinyl. "We listened to Elvis together, I remember," she smiled sadly, wiping her eyes with the back of her hand.

"My mom liked music that was calm," Paisley laughed softly. "Not Elvis," she shook her head and watched as Shiloh continued carefully painting her nails. "They always argued over music in the car. Mom always won," she giggled.

Paisley paused for a moment, somewhat distracted by watching Shiloh. With a heavy sigh, she scooted over and laid her head on her girlfriend's shoulder. "I miss them," she whispered softly, closing her eyes. Shiloh set the nail polish aside and wrapped an arm around Paisley, humming softly.

Shiloh stayed humming quietly for a while, filling the quiet air between them. Paisley's eyes were fixed on the house in front of them, faint memories playing through her mind.

"It is not a home," Paisley whispered, lifting her head and glancing back at the things in front of them. She began setting everything back into the lunchbox, closing it up tightly. "This is not a home," she repeated, standing up and bending down to bury the box back in the ground.

"What are you doing?" Shiloh asked in confusion as Paisley began piling the dirt back into the hole, covering up the lunchbox once more.

"I have them in here," Paisley stood back up, knocking on her own heart and looking at Shiloh shyly. "I do not need anything else," the small girl nodded and bit her lip nervously.

"I'm proud of you," Shiloh whispered, closing the gap between them and wrapping Paisley in a tight hug. "I'm so, so proud of you Paisley," she shook her head and pulled away. "Your parents would be, too. I know that for a fact."

Paisley smiled softly and tugged on her beanie, fixing it on her head. "Promise?" she whispered, tilting her head to the side.

"Promise," Shiloh nodded softly and locked their pinkies together. Both girls leaned in and kissed their hand, causing Paisley to laugh softly.

Shiloh swung an arm around Paisley's shoulders, pulling her into her side and kissing the crown of her head. "Let's get outta' here before the neighbors start to wonder," she laughed, leading her girlfriend back to the car.

CHAPTER 34

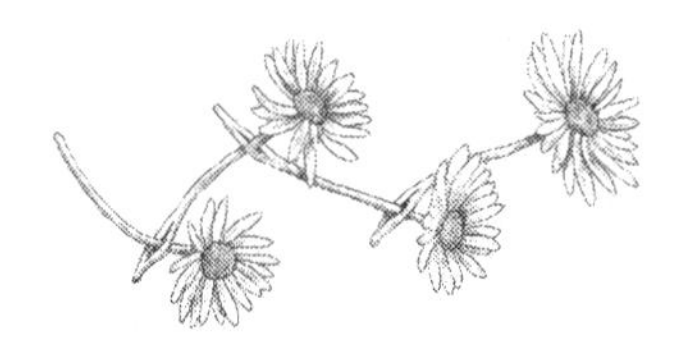

The car ride home was silent. Shiloh glanced over at Paisley, knowing by the expression on the girl's face that she was thinking over everything in her head. Paisley needed time to process everything, Shiloh understood that.

Quietly, Shiloh reached over and took Paisley's hand in her own. The small girl looked up at Shiloh before looking back down at their hands, feeling her girlfriend trace small circles on the back of her palm. It surprised her how just one simple touch could bring her so much comfort.

Once they pulled into her driveway, Shiloh gave Paisley's hand a light squeeze to let her know they had arrived home. The small girl looked up, glancing back and forth from Shiloh to the house and smiling nervously when she saw multiple cars parked in the driveway.

"Shit," Shiloh cursed under her breath. "My dad must have people over…" she bit her lip and studied her girlfriend's expression. Surprisingly, Paisley put on a brave smile and squeezed Shiloh's hand before slipping out of the car.

"We can just go upstairs," Shiloh shook her head, catching up to Paisley and following her up the path to the front door. "We don't have to—,"

"Paisleeee!" Maggie smiled widely, pushing open the front door and running out to grab the older girl's hand. "Daddy's making hot dogs! Come on!"

Shiloh was about to say something, but Paisley glanced back at her and gave her an apologetic smile before following Maggie into the backyard. Shiloh stood confused for a few seconds, quickly recomposing herself and jogging after Paisley.

Shiloh was quickly swept off to greet the family members that had come for dinner, but she continued to keep a watchful eye on Paisley, who had been pulled into a game of keep-away with the younger kids.

Once Shiloh was able to peel herself away from her relatives, she jogged over to the group of kids and gave Paisley a small smile, motioning for her to come over. "Mind if I borrow her for a little bit?" she laughed, turning to Maggie, who nodded happily before returning to her game.

"Figured you could use a break," Shiloh laughed softly when Paisley looked at her in confusion. The small girl nodded in agreement. Sometimes Shiloh knew her better than she knew herself.

Shiloh grabbed Paisley's hand, glancing behind them before leading her over to the treehouse in their backyard. She'd spent many days in there as a kid when she needed to get away and clear her head. Maybe it would do the same for Paisley.

After climbing up into the treehouse, Shiloh offered a hand to Paisley, who took it tediously. Shiloh laid back on the wooden floor and stared up at the roof, turning to look at Paisley who sat quietly next to her. She realized the girl hadn't spoken a word since they got in the car.

"What're you thinking about?" Shiloh asked quietly, reaching out and lacing their fingers together. Paisley glanced down at her girlfriend, biting her lip and looking down at their hands.

"Was it my fault?" the small girl finally spoke, filling the empty air. Shiloh instantly sat up, tilting her head to the side.

"What?" the green eyed girl asked. Paisley shrugged and shook her head, trying to dismiss her question. Of course, Shiloh wouldn't allow that to happen.

"No, what?" Shiloh asked quietly, tugging on Paisley's hand. "I wanna know what's on your mind."

The brown eyed girl sighed heavily and looked back at Shiloh, pausing for a moment. "Why?" Paisley whispered. Shiloh opened her mouth to speak, but Paisley shook her head, causing Shiloh to quickly clamp her jaw shut.

"Why did her hate me?" Paisley spoke up, furrowing her eyebrows. "Why did he hurt me? What did I do wrong?" her voice cracked slightly and Shiloh immediately shook her head, scooting forwards so she was facing Paisley.

"It's not a matter of *you*, Paisley," she whispered, reaching out to tilt Paisley's head forwards. "Look at me, I want you to really hear this," she said quietly. Paisley's eyes flickered up to meet hers and the girl offered her a small nod.

"You had no control over him. What he did? That was all him. You didn't ask for it. You didn't do anything that deserved what he did to you," Shiloh took Paisley's hands in both of hers, meeting her eyes. "What he did is only a reflection of himself. I guess that was his way of expressing his anger. A fucked up way, at that."

"People who aren't happy with themselves think it's their duty to drag everyone else down with them, too," Shiloh explained, watching Paisley's dark eyes flicker down to their hands.

"He was not happy?" Paisley asked after a few moments of silence. She looked up at Shiloh, who nodded softly. The small girl furrowed her eyebrows, unsure about how she felt about that. "Why?"

"There's no excuse for what he did," Shiloh reinforced the fact. "From what I've heard from you, he seemed like a very unhappy person from the start. Maybe losing his sister and his wife just pushed him over the edge," she shrugged softly, making sure to watch Paisley's expression closely.

"I feel bad…" Paisley whispered, looking down at the ground and remaining silent for a few moments. "Maybe… maybe it was okay," she shrugged, glancing up at Shiloh. She instantly regretted what she said when she saw her girlfriend's expression quickly change.

"He has *no* excuse for what he did," Shiloh shook her head. "You were going through the exact same thing as he was at an even younger age, and you *never* resorted to violence like he did."

"But…" Paisley whispered. She saw how serious Shiloh grew, though, and quickly sighed in defeat. "It is just hard," she confessed, absentmindedly playing with Shiloh's fingers.

"I know, babe," Shiloh sighed, reaching up with her free hand to smooth out Paisley's hair. "It doesn't go away overnight," she continued. "But one day, you're gonna wake up and realize that it's over. All those chains that were holding you down are going to be gone. And trust me, it's going to be the most refreshing feeling for you."

"And he may have had a bad past, but that's no excuse for him to throw those burdens on someone else," Shiloh studied Paisley's face. The small girl simply nodded, keeping her head hung down to the ground. A sudden realization hit Shiloh.

"He blamed you for it… didn't he?" Shiloh whispered. Paisley froze, and Shiloh immediately knew when the small girl's hand tensed in hers. Hesitantly, Paisley looked up, giving Shiloh a soft nod.

Seeing tears forming in her girlfriend's eyes, Shiloh scooted next to her girlfriend and pulled her into her arms, allowing Paisley to rest her head on her shoulder.

"It wasn't your fault," Shiloh whispered, kissing the crown of Paisley's head. "They loved you, Paisley. They loved you *so* much. It's impossible not to," Shiloh kept her arms wrapped tightly around her girlfriend. "They would *never* blame you for what happened and you shouldn't either."

Paisley didn't respond, but Shiloh knew she had already planted that seed of knowledge in the girl's brain. She just held her, being there for her in silence. They sat like that for a while, in quiet comfort.

"Why did you stay?"

Shiloh tilted her head to the side when Paisley's quiet question broke the silence. Paisley shook her head, taking a second to reword her question.

"You just… you have not left me. Ever," Paisley mumbled softly, to which Shiloh nodded quietly in acknowledgement. "Why?" Paisley whispered, lifting her head and meeting Shiloh's eyes.

"Why not?" Shiloh laughed softly, watching as Paisley's eyes fluttered back down to the ground. "I'm not just gonna give up on someone when things get hard. That's not like me."

"I'm in love with you. I love the Paisley I know now and I love the girl you were in high school that I've gotten to know through you," Shiloh said softly, running her fingers through the small brunette's hair.

"I like listening to you talk," Paisley laughed quietly, feeling her cheeks tinge pink. Shiloh just gave her a soft smile and kissed her nose, pulling back and admiring her girlfriend's eyes. "Can you sing?" Paisley whispered hopefully.

"Only for you," Shiloh giggled, planting a soft kiss on her girlfriend's lips.

Moments later they were interrupted by someone else scrambling up the ladder into the treehouse. "I found you!" Maggie giggled, clapping her hands together. "It's bedtime for me," she pouted, crossing her arms.

"We should head inside too," Shiloh laughed, helping Paisley to her feet. "While we can still see our way back."

Soon enough, Maggie was in bed and the two girlfriends were in Shiloh's bedroom. The green eyed girl was sprawled out on her bed with her nose stuck in a book, waiting for Paisley to finish in the bathroom.

She was so distracted by her book that she didn't notice the passing time. She was only pulled out of her trance when she heard a small sniff coming from the corner of her room. Shiloh set her book down, looking over her shoulder and growing confused when she saw Paisley sitting by their suitcases.

"Hey, I didn't even notice you were—," Shiloh quickly cut herself off when she saw that the smaller girl was crying. Moments later, she realized what the small girl was holding in her hands.

"So much has changed, Lo," Paisley whispered shakily, holding up the small leather journal and turning it around in her hands. Shiloh immediately pushed her book aside, scooting off of the bed and moving to sit next to her girlfriend.

"It's a lot to take in, yeah?" Shiloh laughed nervously, reaching out and moving Paisley's hair out of her face. The small girl simply nodded, already distracted by another journal entry. Instead of trying to talk to her about it, Shiloh simply laid her head on Paisley's shoulder and watched her while she read, offering her quiet support.

Shiloh grew confused when Paisley began paging through the blank pages absentmindedly, pausing suddenly. The green eyed girl watched as Paisley furrowed her eyebrows, peeling apart two pages that had been previously stuck together. Both girls exchanged glances, realizing this was an entry neither of them had seen.

Sensing Paisley's hesitation, Shiloh gently took the journal from her hands before taking a deep breath and beginning to read aloud.

Hey.

I can't sleep. It's the night before my senior year and I'm slightly terrified. Everyone says that high school is the best years of your life, but if it is... then I don't know what sort of hell is waiting out there for me. High school sucks.

Senior year is even worse. That means thinking about the future even more than usual because time is running out. What am I going to do? I don't know if there's anything out there for me. What if I'm not good at anything?

There's so much going through my head at once. What's going to become of me? What if I become just like my uncle? The thought makes me sick.

I want to do something. I want to be happy. I want to somehow break free of this box I've put myself in. There's so much out there and I feel like I've barely seen any of it.

I just feel so trapped. And I feel like I'm never going to break free of this. I'm sad. I'm sad and I'm scared. I just feel incompetent. And I can't shake it.

I just wish I had a promise that things will be alright.

- *Paisley*

Shiloh glanced over at Paisley when she was done reading. The small girl was looking down at her hands in her lap, biting her lip nervously. Without saying a word, Shiloh reached over and locked their pinkies together.

"C'mon," Shiloh whispered, setting the journal down and standing up. She helped Paisley to her feet, leading them both over to the bed.

They lay in silence for a while, Paisley staring up at the ceiling and Shiloh with her eyes closed in thought. Shiloh opened her eyes when she felt Paisley roll over and start tracing the flower tattoo on her shoulder.

"What'cha thinking about?" Shiloh whispered, causing Paisley's eyes to flutter up to her.

"I am thinking that I love you," Paisley said softly, looking back down at the tattoo. "I think I always have."

Shiloh's heart skipped in her chest and she couldn't form a coherent response. Instead, she leaned over and pressed a soft kiss to Paisley's forehead, lacing their fingers together.

They laid there for a while. Shiloh didn't even realize she was singing until Paisley sighed happily and nuzzled into her side. The green eyed girl felt sleep beginning to take over. Paisley, also, had relaxed slightly into her side. Which is why she was surprised when she heard the small girl's voice make a reappearance.

Paisley sang softly, continuing the song Shiloh had started. She sat up, reaching out to pull the blankets over them. Shiloh couldn't help the smile that spread across her face.

Paisley continued singing, leaning over and turning off the light before curling back up in Shiloh's side. By then, the green eyed girl had already allowed sleep to wash over her.

"I love you," Paisley whispered, kissing Shiloh's cheek and taking a moment to admire her girlfriend. *Her* girlfriend. "I always will."

CHAPTER 35

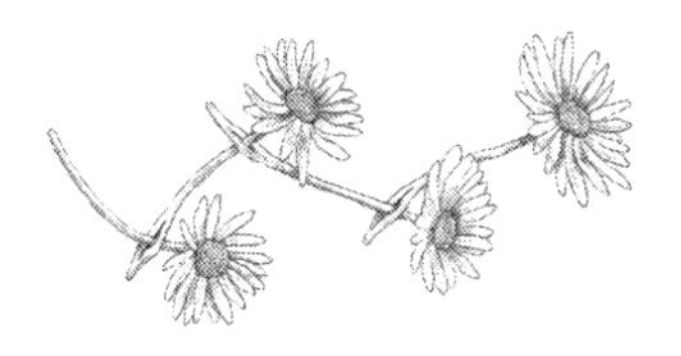

Shiloh woke up the next morning slightly confused when she didn't feel the warmth of her girlfriend pressed into her side. Her eyes fluttered open and she immediately saw the small figure across the room, slumped down against the wall.

She slowly sat up, wiping her eyes and furrowing her eyebrows in confusion. Paisley was fast asleep, the journal sprawled out open beside her. Her head hung down, causing her dark hair to cascade over her face. She looked adorable, but Shiloh was distracted by the fact that Paisley wasn't asleep in the bed.

"Pais?" Shiloh whispered, rolling off of the bed and kneeling next to the girl. "Paisleyyy," she hummed softly, cupping the girl's cheeks and brushing her hair out of her face. Soft brown eyes fluttered open and met hers, confusion flickering across her features.

"I fell asleep?" Paisley's voice was raspy. Shiloh raised an eyebrow, nodding softly. Paisley instantly frowned, sitting up and searching the floor for the journal.

"Why were you over here?" Shiloh asked, watching as Paisley retrieved the journal and held onto it tightly. The small girl's face froze upon hearing Shiloh's question, and she bit her lip nervously.

"I..." Paisley paused, cupping her hands over her mouth and yawning. "I did not want to sleep. I am tired of the nightmares."

Shiloh bit her lip and sighed, giving her girlfriend a sympathetic nod. "You need sleep, goofball," she laughed nervously, standing up and bending down. Paisley giggled softly when Shiloh picked her up, carrying her over to the bed.

"Just get some rest, yeah? I have some stuff to do and then we're gonna go out," Shiloh explained, handing Paisley a blanket. The small girl looked at her curiously, but managed to give her a soft nod.

"I love you," Shiloh whispered, bending down and kissing Paisley's forehead. "I'll be right downstairs."

Paisley curled up under the blankets, listening as Shiloh's footsteps disappeared out of the room. Meanwhile, the green eyed girl made her way downstairs and into the kitchen.

About an hour later, Shiloh wiped her hands off and set the last of the food into her picnic basket. Just as she did so, small footsteps could be heard coming down the stairs. Paisley tugged on her beanie, peering into the kitchen and smiling when she saw Shiloh.

"What is this?" Paisley asked softly, padding over to Shiloh's side and peering into the basket. She furrowed her eyebrows and looked up at her girlfriend. "What is this for?"

"I figured we'd pack a lunch," Shiloh shrugged. "Is that okay?"

Paisley nodded quickly. "I like food," she giggled. "Where are we going?"

Shiloh pursed her lips and thought for a moment, wanting to explain it as best as she could. "We're going to… visit… some people that you should know pretty well," Shiloh nodded softly. Paisley raised an eyebrow, but didn't question her further.

"C'mon, goofball," Shiloh laughed, pointing out Paisley's shoes to the smaller girl. Paisley tugged them on, looking up at Shiloh and laughing softly when the girl bent down to help her tie her laces.

Paisley had plenty of questions as they drove. Shiloh tried her best to avoid them, attempting to distract Paisley with the radio. Eventually, they arrived at the small park. Paisley raised an eyebrow in confusion, but followed Shiloh as the girl retrieved their food and led her over to a sunny patch of grass.

"This isn't it," Shiloh laughed softly, noting Paisley's confusion. "We're just gonna eat here, and then walk the rest of the way."

Shiloh laid out the blanket they had brought with them and set the basket down, to which Paisley eagerly sat down and dug into the basket. By the time Shiloh had sat down, Paisley already had taken a bite out of her sandwich. Shiloh couldn't help but laugh when the small girl's face contorted in disgust.

"If you would have waited I would've given you the right sandwich," Shiloh teased, switching bags with Paisley. "I like spicy mustard."

"Bleh," Paisley mumbled, giggling quietly. She took a bite of the right sandwich, looking up at Shiloh and giving her a thumbs up. "That is better," she whispered bashfully, making Shiloh laugh even harder.

The girls laughed and talked all throughout their lunch, just enjoying the simple time together. The minute Paisley finished, though, her mood changed. She was nervous about what was to come. The other two places Shiloh had taken her hadn't exactly been a walk in the park.

"Ready?" Shiloh took a deep breath, bringing Paisley out of her thoughts. The small girl looked up and nodded nervously, tossing her trash back into the basket and allowing Shiloh to help her to her feet.

"I am nervous," Paisley admitted, biting her lip. She followed Shiloh as they walked back to the car to put the basket away.

"Don't be," Shiloh shook her head, locking the car once more and turning around to take Paisley's hands in her own. "It's not bad, I promise," she said softly, leaning in and planting a soft kiss on her girlfriend's lips. "C'mon."

Paisley nodded, trusting Shiloh enough to quickly follow the girl. They walked for a while through the small park, existing in comfortable silence. The small brunette became curious when a large iron gate appeared in the distance along the path, and she glanced at Shiloh when the girl tugged her hand in that direction. Something felt familiar about this place, but she couldn't quite put a finger on it.

Shiloh glanced at Paisley softly before gently pushing open the gate. The small girl took a nervous step forward, holding onto Shiloh's arm as they walked down a smaller path. When the graves began appearing, the familiarity became even stronger.

And then, when Shiloh paused in front of two graves, Paisley remembered exactly where they were.

"I remember," Paisley whispered, looking up at Shiloh, who was already looking down at her nervously. "This is Aunt Susie," she nodded, pointing to one of the graves in front of them. "I used to bring her flowers. Until…" Paisley's voice trailed off as she remembered the painful memory.

"Do you know who this is?" Shiloh asked tediously, pointing to the grave beside hers. Paisley tilted her head to the side, leaning in slightly to read the writing on the tombstone. Her hand tightened around Shiloh's and she nodded quickly.

"Tommy," she whispered, biting her lip and standing closer to her girlfriend.

"Hey," Shiloh shook her head. "He can't hurt you, look," she motioned to the grass in front of them. "There's nothing to be afraid of anymore."

Paisley took a deep breath, nodding softly. She repeated Shiloh's words over and over in her head, kneeling down in front of the graves. Shiloh watched quietly, taking a few steps back to give the girl some privacy.

"I am sorry," Paisley whispered, turning her attention to her uncle's grave. "I am sorry you were sad. I am sorry I was not good enough for you." She took a shaky breath. "But I am good enough for myself now. I am not going to let you hurt me anymore. You *will* not hurt me anymore," she shook her head, taking a deep breath and turning away from his grave.

Paisley stared in silence at her aunt's grave for a moment, fighting back tears. When she couldn't find any words, she simply kissed her hand and pressed it against the tombstone.

Shiloh was surprised when Paisley stood back up and took her hand, looking up at her hopefully. "Can I…?" she shook her head. "I want to go somewhere else," Paisley nodded softly. Confused but curious, Shiloh allowed Paisley to take her hand and lead her further down the pathway.

The green eyed girl tilted her head to the side when Paisley pulled her off of the path, leading her to a small patch of grass underneath a tree. She watched as Paisley knelt down, brushing the overgrown grass aside and revealing two small plaques in the ground. The small girl bit her lip and stood back up, looking over at Shiloh shyly.

"Mom… Dad… this is Paisley," the brown eyed girl said quietly, turning back to the small graves. "Your daughter." She glanced back at Shiloh shyly before continuing.

"I am sorry I have not visited in a long time," she bit her lip. "A lot has happened. But I found someone," she slowly looked back at Shiloh and took her hand gently. "Someone I love very much."

"This is Shiloh," Paisley smiled over at the green eyed girl shyly. Shiloh squeezed her hand gently, pulling Paisley into her side and resting her head on her shoulder. Paisley couldn't help but breathe a sigh of relief.

"She is my girlfriend," Paisley continued. "I like to think that you will be happy when I am happy. And I think I am," she nodded softly.

"Things have changed... since I last talked to you," Paisley knelt down, crossing her legs underneath her. Shiloh lowered herself into a sitting position beside her, pressing a soft kiss to Paisley's cheek.

"There is lots of bad. But lots of good, too," Paisley nodded, reaching out and pressing her fingers against the cold marble. "I lost you for a little bit. But Shiloh helped me. And I found you again." She felt her girlfriend rubbing small circles on the back of her hand and blushed.

"I made lots of friends," Paisley smiled, closing her eyes and allowing her words to flow freely. "I had to do a lot of scary things. But I think they helped me," she nodded. "Yes, they did. They helped me a lot."

"I am the same Paisley," she whispered, retracting her hand and tugging on her beanie. "I hope you see that." She felt Shiloh squeeze her hand in assurance.

Time passed in a blur as Paisley continued to talk, filling her parents in on everything that they missed. She mentioned every small detail, explaining her past as best as she could. Shiloh sat patiently; hanging onto her girlfriend's every word.

Paisley didn't even notice when it started raining lightly. Shiloh glanced up at the sky, the shade of the tree protecting them slightly. Shrugging, she laid her head on Paisley's shoulder. She wasn't about to stop Paisley just because of a little rain. Hearing the girl talk to her parents like this was endearing.

"I miss you," Paisley whispered after a minute or two of silence. "I miss you and I am sorry I have not visited." She felt the tears that she had been holding back begin to spill over, and she quickly brought her hands up to wipe her eyes.

"It's okay," Shiloh whispered, reaching out and replacing Paisley's hands with her own to gently wipe her tears. "It's okay to miss them."

"Can you sing?" Paisley sniffed, looking up at Shiloh hopefully. "I want them to hear you," she bit her lip.

"Only for you," Shiloh gave Paisley a soft smile and kissed her forehead, puling her into her side and letting her rest her head on her shoulder.

It was calm while Shiloh filled the empty air. Paisley watched Shiloh quietly, reaching out to run her finger's through the girl's hair gently.

Once Shiloh was finished singing, Paisley gave her a soft smile. The small girl took a deep breath, calming herself down before turning back to the graves.

"And… and now I am here," Paisley nodded softly, squeezing Shiloh's hand. "I am here and I am happy… I am here and I am in love. It is a good feeling. Like someone balled up the entire sun and put it in my chest." Shiloh couldn't help but laugh softly.

"I love you," Paisley whispered, kissing her hand and pressing her fingertips to both of the graves. She paused for a moment before she retracted her hand, remembering something.

"You got your wish, mom," Paisley whispered, a bittersweet tone in her voice.

Tiny footsteps made their way down the hallway, clutching her small stuffed dog to her chest. The small child was wary of every shadow, which is why she eventually ended up running all the way down the hallway and knocking nervously on door.

When she didn't get an answer, she pushed the door open slightly and poked her head into the room. "Mommy?" the small girl whispered, hugging her stuffed animal nervously.

"Sweetie?"

Paisley sighed in relief when she heard her mother's voice and quickly slipped into the room, crawling onto the bed and practically throwing herself into her mother's arms. "There's monsters in my room," she whispered, squeezing her eyes shut.

"Monsters?" her mother raised her eyebrows, smoothing out her daughter's hair and hugging her to her chest. "Do we need to stop giving you sugar before you go to bed?"

"No!" Paisley shook her head quickly. "We need to get rid of the monsters."

"And how would we do that?" her mother laughed softly.

"Uh... I dunno," Paisley shrugged, bringing her hand up and toying with her bottom lip. "I could sleep in here, where there is no monsters?" she offered with a hopeful smile, causing her mother to laugh.

"I guess it does get a little lonely in here when your father's away on business," she laughed when Paisley squealed happily, practically leaping under the blankets and curling up into a ball.

"Mommy look!" Paisley whisper yelled, pointing to the window. "It's a shooting star!" She sat up, crawling over to the edge of the bed and gazing out the window longingly. "You have to make a wish!"

"Mommy quick!" Paisley grabbed her mother's arm and pointed at the star. "You have to make a wish and it'll come true!"

"A wish?" her mother sat up, looking out the window and pulling Paisley into her lap. "Hmmm, let me think," she whispered, resting her chin on the top of her daughter's head and rocking them back and forth.

"I wish...." she started, Paisley looking up at her in awe. "I wish for you to find happiness in someone who looks at you like you put the stars in their sky," she whispered, kissing her daughter's hand.

"That's a good wish," Paisley whispered, yawning and leaning her head against her mother's shoulder. "Do you think it's gonna come true?"

"I hope so," her mother laughed softly, picking up her daughter and lying her back in the space beside her.

"I know so," Paisley nodded, yawning once more and hugging her stuffed dog to her chest. "It's a wish on a shooting star. It has to come true."

"You let me know when it does then, yeah?" her mother laughed, pulling the blankets over both of them. Paisley nodded eagerly, leaning over and kissing the bridge of her mother's nose with a soft giggle.

"What wish?" Shiloh asked softly, squeezing Paisley's hand and bringing her out of her thoughts. The small girl looked over at her girlfriend with a nostalgic smile. That's when she saw something in Shiloh's eyes that she hadn't noticed before. Love. True, pure love.

The small brunette leaned over, cupping Shiloh's cheeks and closing the gap between them into a soft kiss. When she pulled away, she met Shiloh's eyes and glanced over at the graves one last time.

"I found you."

EPILOGUE

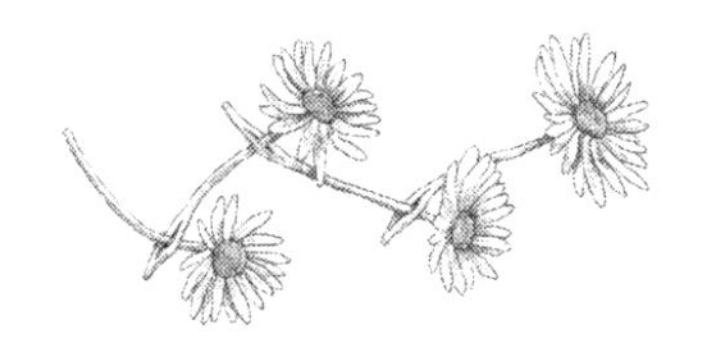

Hi.

This is Paisley. I am a lot different now. But I like to think that I am still the same person I was before. That is what Shiloh says, too. I have just been through a little more. Or a lot more.

I used to think it was a bad thing. I used to want to change everything about myself and the things that happened to me, because I thought maybe things would turn out better. But I met someone who I do not think I would have met if things had been different. And I do not want to risk never knowing her. Because I think she is a lot better than anything I could have found on my own.

Her name is Shiloh. But I call her Lolo. She has eyes like the ocean and a heart like the sky. I think that is why I love her so much.

I did not know people like her existed. I thought they were impossible to find. But I found her, even though I had to see a lot of bad things first. I think she was worth it, though. No, I know she was worth it.

I hear people talk about finding their other halves a lot. But I do not like that. I do not need my other half because I am not a half. Lolo is definitely not a half. I need her because she makes me a better whole. And I hope I do the same for her.

I need her because she makes me smile. She makes me feel things I have never felt before. I did not know what it was like to laugh so hard that your stomach hurt until I met her. I do not think I really knew how to love until I met her.

Love is weird. I do not know how to put it into words. It fills you up and leaves no space for fear. I am safe when I am with her. Because I love her. And in that moment, that is all that matters to me. It is a weird feeling.

I am lucky. I am lucky because I found somewhere better. I do not know what I would have done if I did not end up here. It scares me just to think about it.

It is weird to read my old words in here. It is hard to remember feeling the way I did. I wish I could have shown myself the good things I would discover here.

The bad things are going away. And I am happy.

- *Paisley*

The small girl quickly scrambled to shut the leather journal and hide it back under the bed when she heard footsteps approaching down the hallway. The door opened and a wide smile spread across Paisley's face when she saw Shiloh. She quickly lifted Wolf from her lap and hopped to her feet, making her way across the room to greet the girl.

Paisley was confused when Shiloh held out a hand to stop her. Tilting her head to the side, Paisley watched as her girlfriend pulled something out of her sweatshirt pocket and handed it to her.

"Read it," Shiloh said softly, nodding towards the bed. Confused but curious, Paisley padded over to sit down, turning around the folded paper in her hands.

"Don't be scared," Shiloh laughed, shoving her hands back in her pockets. "It's nothing bad."

Paisley pursed her lips, tilting her head to the side as she slowly unfolded the paper. Her eyes widened when she saw the page was covered in Shiloh's small print, crammed onto the sheet from top to bottom. She gave her girlfriend a questioning look.

"Go on," Shiloh laughed, leaning over and kissing Paisley's shoulder. "You'll like it."

With a soft nod, Paisley scanned over the page a few times, letting her eyes adjust to the darkness in the room before she slowly read aloud.

Dear Paisley,

I love you. You probably already know that but I just wanted to make that clear from the start. You deserve to hear it all the time.

I remember the first day I saw you. You walked into my science class and I remember thinking how pretty you were. I thought we had the chance to be good friends.

Although situation changed that for us, I had always looked up to you. You were always so calm and serene, and I used to wonder if you ever actually had a bad mood. I've come to find out that you were just really good at covering it up, but I think it takes a strong person to put on a smile when they're really hurting on the inside.

I'll be honest when I say that when I left Miami, I never really expected to see you again. I had so much pent up anger against you. I was mostly focused on getting out of the box I was trapped in and exploring a whole new part of the world. I was excited to start a whole new chapter in my life.

Which is why I was confused when you showed up at our door. It's funny, because I had always thought you would just be a chapter in my book, but you ended up becoming the entire novel. I didn't realize that at first, though.

Somehow you ended up staying with us. And I admit, I was mad. I didn't want anything to do with you. I've apologized a thousand times for how I treated you. You were vulnerable and I was scared of letting anyone in.

I think I knew something between us was inevitable the first night you wandered into my room. You were clutching my shirt to your chest and I remember feeling so affected by someone else's sadness for the first time in forever. That feeling terrified me.

The day I realized what I felt for you was turning into love was when you got taken away. Things had happened between us before that, yeah. But I didn't really know what to call it. But the day I lost you was the day that I realized what I really could lose. And that's why I thought that maybe, just maybe, the universe wanted me to fall in love.

And in a way. I think I loved you from the start. It was like I just knew from the moment I saw you that there was something between us. I think something in us knew... and something in us will always know.

When I got you back... it was the best feeling in the world. I made a promise to myself in that moment that I would do whatever it took to keep you safe. I hope I've managed to keep that promise.

We've been through a lot together, goofball. You've helped me in ways I can't even put into words. You've brought out this person in me that I never knew existed. You've taught me how to see the beauty in the smallest of things, even a flower. There's something so innocent about the way you love and I'm forever grateful that you've shared your spirit with me.

So thank you. Thank you for finding me. Thank you for helping me find parts of myself that I didn't know existed. Thank you for loving me and thank you for giving me the pleasure of loving you.

I remember when we were in Miami and you found the hidden journal entry, the very last line really struck me. You said you wished you had a promise that things will be alright. I'd like to give you that promise, Paisley. Forever and always.

Paisley looked up at Shiloh quietly when the letter ended, thinking over everything she had just read aloud. She was so busy going over the words in her head that she didn't notice Shiloh slowly removing her hand from her sweatshirt pocket.

"Pais," Shiloh whispered with a soft laugh. The small girl snapped out of her trance, only to find Shiloh holding up her pinkie between them.

Paisley's eyes widened and she immediately stood up, moving in front of Shiloh and gently cupping her hand. She examined the delicate writing that was now inked into Shiloh's finger.

"*Things will be alright*," Paisley whispered, reading the cursive font. She looked up at Shiloh, her mouth slightly agape.

"I promise," the green eyed girl said softly, a shy smile on her face. Paisley couldn't help but smile, and she slowly brought her hand up to lock pinkies with Shiloh's, watching as the inked words wrapped around her finger.

Both girls leaned in to kiss their hands at the same time, resulting their heads bumped together. Paisley inhaled sharply, bringing her hand up to rub her forehead.

"Oh my god, I'm so sorry," Shiloh shook her head, moving to cup Paisley's face. The small girl quickly stopped her, giggling softly before leaning in and capturing Shiloh's lips in her own.

Shiloh's breath was taken away the minute Paisley's lips met hers. She eventually caught up and laughed softly into the kiss, wrapping her arm's around Paisley's waist and pulling her into her lap.

When the kiss broke, Paisley just continued to giggle, leaning her forehead against Shiloh's and biting her lip to hide how widely she was smiling. Shiloh couldn't help but laugh as she pulled her into another kiss, feeling Paisley wrap her arms around her neck.

The kiss ended abruptly when Paisley sat up, hopping off of the bed with wide eyes. Shiloh immediately grew concerned, but the small girl held up a finger, signaling for her to wait.

"I have something for you, too," Paisley nodded happily, reaching up and tugging her beanie off of her head. Shiloh laughed softly when Paisley turned the beanie inside out, retrieving a folded up piece of paper and presenting it proudly to the girl on the bed.

"Open it," Paisley smiled, sitting down next to Shiloh and clasping her hands together. The green eyed girl turned the square around in her hands, looking at Paisley for approval before slowly unfolding the paper.

Shiloh couldn't hold back her smile when she saw the drawing and she immediately pulled Paisley into her side. "I love it," she said softly, looking down at the colored pencil sketch.

"It's us," Paisley smiled proudly, scooting closer to Shiloh and laying the paper between them. "That is me," she pointed to the wavy haired figure in a yellow dress, complete with a blue beanie. "And that is Wolf," she giggled, moving her finger over to the blue eyed cat in her arms.

"I'm guessing this one is me?" Shiloh asked, pointing the figure in a black jacket next to Paisley, complete with bright green eyes. Paisley nodded happily.

"I could not get your eyes right," she frowned slightly. "They change color all the time."

"I think it's perfect," Shiloh whispered, leaning over and planting a kiss on the crown of Paisley's head. "You've gotten a lot better at drawing, too," she added, making Paisley smile shyly.

"Here," Shiloh started, pushing herself off the bed and rummaging through her doors. Shiloh watched as she grabbed a roll of tape, moving over to the mirror and hanging her drawing right beside it. "That way we can see it every morning," she said softly.

The small girl sighed happily, falling back onto the bed and staring up at the ceiling.

"I love this," Paisley whispered, tugging on her beanie. "You and me… It is everything I could have ever wished for."

"You know what?" Shiloh laughed softly, walking back to the bed and moving to lie on her side. Paisley raised an eyebrow, turning to face her. "I think you're the answer to a wish I never even knew I had."

"I love you," Paisley murmured after a few moments of silence. She yawned quietly, cupping her hands over her mouth and letting her eyes flutter shut. This caused Shiloh to laugh, completely endeared by her girlfriend.

"Tired?" Shiloh asked, moving back on the bed and pulling the blankets over their legs. Paisley nodded softly, a content smile on her face and she crawled across the bed to curl up in Shiloh's side.

"Sing?" Paisley whispered, wiping her eyes and looking up at her girlfriend. Shiloh couldn't help but laugh softly.

"Only for you," she smiled, pressing a soft kiss to Paisley's cheek.

As Shiloh sang, she felt Paisley slowly relax into her side, snaking one of her hands up the sleeves of her hoodie like the small girl always did.

Her other arm, however, made its way across Shiloh's stomach and found her hand. Shiloh smiled softly when she felt Paisley's pinky finger lock with her own.

Once the song was over, Shiloh could tell just by the rhythmic pattern of Paisley's breathing that she was fast asleep. She adjusted her position slightly to get a better view of her girlfriend, watching as Paisley's chest rose and fell.

"I love you," Shiloh whispered, leaning in and kissing the girl's forehead. "I always will." She laid her head back down, allowing sleep to overtake them both.

Shiloh couldn't help but be disappointed when she was shaken awake the next morning. It had been a week since they returned from Miami, and the nightmares had still been relentlessly haunting the smaller girl.

So when Shiloh's eyes fluttered open to face the brown eyed girl with tears in her eyes, she immediately sat up and reached out to pull Paisley into her arms. She was surprised when the smaller girl shook her head and pulled away, reaching out and grabbing Shiloh's shoulders.

"I did not!" Paisley whisper-yelled, looking into Shiloh's eyes hopefully. "They did not… I did not…" she shook her head, trying to form her words in the moment of excitement. "The nightmares did not come, Lo!"

Shiloh immediately sat up straighter, looking Paisley dead in the eye. "Wait… what…?" she asked in disbelief, watching as Paisley slid off the bed and wiped her eyes.

"It did not happen," Paisley sniffed, disbelief in her own voice. "Lo, I swear," she shook her head.

"You're serious?" Shiloh asked, her mouth practically falling open when Paisley nodded furiously with tears in her eyes. The green eyed girl hopped off the bed, reaching out and grabbing Paisley's shoulders.

"Paisley, you're serious?" Shiloh half-whispered, meeting the smaller girl's eyes. Paisley nodded frantically.

"I promise, Lo, I pr—," she began, but was cut off when the green eyed girl practically tackled her into a hug, picking her up and spinning her around.

"We did it!" Paisley giggled, throwing her arms around Shiloh's neck and burying her head in her shoulders. "We did it, Lo, we did it," her voice grew softer as tears clouded her eyes.

"*You* did it, baby," Shiloh whispered, setting Paisley down and bringing her hands up to wipe her own eyes. "That was all you," she smiled widely, pulling Paisley into another hug and laughing when she saw Wolf sitting up questioningly from his bed on the other side of the room.

"I love you," Paisley smiled widely, jumping into the hug and causing them both to trip backwards onto the bed. Paisley couldn't control her laugher and she rolled to the side, covering her face with her hands and giggling as she felt a rush of emotions wash over her.

Once both girls calmed down and caught their breath, Paisley sat up and wiped her eyes. She blinked a few times, finding Shiloh's electric green eyed through her tears. With a soft smile, she leaned in and gently connected their lips, pulling Shiloh into a soft but passionate kiss.

"I love you," Paisley mumbled once they pulled away, feeling her body ignite from the kiss. "I love you more than I ever thought I could love someone."

Shiloh couldn't help the blush that spread across her cheeks once the kiss broke. Paisley had some way of drawing the most intense feelings out of her, and she was left breathless each time.

"And *you*..." Shiloh whispered, reaching out and cupping Paisley's cheek. "You're constantly giving me more reasons to fall in love with you. Every single day."

"Can you sing?" Paisley whispered, meeting Shiloh's eyes hopefully. The green eyed girl leaned in, planting a soft kiss on Paisley's lips before she pulled away.

"Only for you."

acknowledgements

➻

We meet again.

I don't think I'll ever get used to this, to be honest. Writing was just a casual hobby for me but being able to hold a physical copy of my own book...? That was a dream. And now it's a dream come true. I'm still processing it all, haha.

But thank you. Out of the entire trilogy, Blue has probably been my favorite to write. Even though it may be a bit raw and emotional at points, I love the insight you get into Shiloh and Paisley's characters. I think it adds a lot more to their relationship.

Thank you for always supporting me and making me laugh and connecting with the characters, just as I have. This is for you.

I love you endlessly. Be nice to yourselves.

lena nottingham

my social media

wattpad - txrches

tumblr - txrches

twitter -@lenajfc

Coming Soon

Green

By now, Paisley and Shiloh both know to expect the unexpected. But you can never be prepared, especially when their lives take a turn in a completely different direction. The couple finds themselves faced with challenges they never thought they'd encounter.

Growing up is hard to do.

Made in the USA
San Bernardino, CA
24 January 2016